WW2 Wo[...]
B[...]

CW01496291

Your Name
is
Jane

By

Pearl A. Gardner

Your Name is Jane

eBook edition

ASIN: B06W5JR9RR

Print edition

ISBN-13: 978-1543260434

ISBN-10: 1543260438

Printed by CreateSpace, an Amazon.com Company
Available from Amazon.com and other online stores.

<u>Get your FREE eBook here</u>
http://www.pearlagardner.co.uk/html/free_book.html

Exclusive to new subscribers.
Be the first to hear about my new releases,
offers and occasional
FREE GIFTS.

More WW2 Novels by Pearl A. Gardner
Each book in the series' listed below can be read as a stand alone novel,
but might be better enjoyed if read in sequence

Women of Verdun
A Three Book Series following three generations of Women from
Verdun in the late 19th century to the end of WW2
Belle
Belle's Girls
Nicolette

Women of Wakefield
A Two Book Series showing how women lived and loved during the
war years in Wakefield
Evelyn's Fight
Peace for Gladys

WW2 Women of Courage
A series devoted to the oppressed women in Europe during the most
horrific of times.
Your Name is Jane
Hannah's Conflict
Ingrid's Mission
Freedom for Cassie (Coming soon)

More WW2 stories of love and drama
These stand alone romantic novels follow the lives of ordinary British
women in times of war
Scent of Bluebells
Lost in the memories
Snowdrop's Promise

Table of Contents

Your Name is Jane

Foreword

Sheffield suffered two terrible nights of bombing in December of nineteen-forty. This fictional account begins on the first of those two nights of hell.

The total destruction of The Marples Hotel on the night of December twelfth is well documented. More than seventy people were killed in that building. Only seven men walked away from the devastation, so it was not beyond reason for me to imagine a young woman might also have survived that terrible night and slipped through the net in the chaos.

I wove her story around researched facts adding large doses of fiction to increase the drama and interest to an already dramatic backdrop of a world in turmoil.

I read as much as I could about Sheffield and the situation in Europe in World War Two, and am grateful to the people who left accounts of their histories in books and in various places on the internet. Those many moving stories gave me an authentic taste of the times and a great insight into what those people endured.

For those who lived through that conflict, in the places mentioned here, may I apologise in advance if you find discrepancies in street names, buildings and institutions. Where possible, I've used the documented facts, but much of the detail here is fictionalised where facts could not be corroborated, or just didn't work for the story.

The people mentioned are no more than figments of my imagination. Any resemblance to actual persons, either living or dead, is purely coincidental.

I hope I have created a novel that will bring you a flavour of those times and one that will hold your attention long after you have read the final words.

Chapter One – Awakening

She came to her senses, feeling pain in hundreds of places along her body, and in her head. When she opened her eyes, she couldn't see anything. She seemed to be surrounded by a thick, dense darkness. Was it night-time? She wasn't in bed. The ground beneath her was hard and lumpy. Something pointed was poking sharply into the back of her ribcage each time she took a breath. She was shivering. The dusty air around her face was bitterly cold.

As she slowly became aware of her situation, she fought to resist her rising fear. Panic would not help her. She would need a clear head to escape her unfathomable confinement. She needed to think. She took a deep breath to calm her mind and instantly wished she hadn't when the spiky prong poked her painfully in the back.

A cloying powder coated the inside of her mouth and clogged her nose. She tasted acrid soot on her tongue and gagged. She coughed and instantly winced from the flash of pain as the sharp thing dug deeper into the back of her chest. Where was she? What had happened?

Gauging her position, she was lying on her left side, with her head slightly higher than her feet. Her right hand was the only part of her that she could move. Her right elbow was stuck fast against her body, but the hand was close to her head. She tentatively touched her face and then moved the hand forward. Her fingers travelled less than a foot into open space, but she couldn't stretch more.

The silence was unnerving. She strained to listen but could hear nothing above the sound of her own shallow breathing. Her heartbeat thrummed painfully in her head, confirming she was alive. The soreness in the back of her chest was another clue to her continued existence. Would she feel pain, if she were dead? Would she feel this awful, numbing cold? She didn't think so.

She tried to ease her chest away from the sharp object, but something heavy was pressing down on her from above and obstructed her movement. She wriggled, and the throbbing in her head exploded. Fortunately, she suffered the excruciating pain for only a moment before she blacked out.

The next time she opened her eyes; she remembered the pain and stayed as still as she could, waiting for her thoughts to clear. She tried to take stock of her situation. Hesitantly, she wriggled her freezing toes. They seemed to move, as far as she could tell. She used her mind to mentally work her way from her feet to her head, assessing the damage. She knew she was hurt. Soreness throbbed in many small places but didn't seem too severe in any of them, except her head, and the back of her chest. The pain was worse in her head. She didn't think anything was broken.

After a few minutes, she concluded that she was thoroughly trapped. Something heavy was pressing down on her, pinning her to the uneven surface below. The only part of her that had freedom to move was her right hand, and even that had a limited range. She would not be able to free herself.

Why didn't she know where she was? She felt she should know. She tried to concentrate on her surroundings, but her mind felt fogged and unclear.

Her skull felt tight, and she realised her head was being held in a vice-like grip. Panic welled again, and her temple began to throb alarmingly.

"Dies nicht tun," (*don't do this*), she whispered into the silence, her voice steadying the rising tide of fear. She coughed, tensing her chest, bracing it against the sharp object digging into her ribs from behind.

She let out a slow, shaking breath and tried again to remember what had happened. She found nothing in her mind. She searched the foggy blankness, worrying more with each passing minute. Why couldn't she remember anything?

She lifted her hand to touch her head and felt a dried, crusty substance on the skin of her forehead. Was it blood? She scraped the crust gently, with a fingernail, and brought it to her mouth to taste. The coppery tang verified her suspicion. She'd suffered a head injury, but the bleeding seemed to have stopped. She felt no stickiness.

How long had she been here, she wondered? Where was, here? What had happened? How was she going to get out? She had to get out. She couldn't stay here. She'd die for sure. Was anyone looking for her? Would anyone know where she was? Did she know anyone who might look for her? Why couldn't she remember anything?

Her head throbbed alarmingly with each beat of her heart. The rhythmic pulse filled her skull with a ringing pain. She did her best to ignore the regular, slicing thrum of agony and tried to concentrate on something else she thought she'd heard. There it was again. A faint scraping sound broke through the surrounding silence.

"Hallo!" she called hoarsely and her throat burned. She coughed, choked and tried again. "Ich bin da." (*I'm here*).

The sound stopped.

"Hilf mir!" (*Help me*), she cried again, her throat feeling raw with the effort.

"Hold on, love. We're coming."

She felt a trickle of wetness from her eyes. Relief flooded her mind for a second but was instantly replaced by fear. The deep, male voice had spoken in English. She understood the communication perfectly, but the words didn't feel like her native language. Her thoughts were in German. She was German. Why did she hear English voices? Was she in England?

She was no longer alone. Someone was moving closer. She heard slow, hesitant footfalls on gritty surfaces. Scraping and rasping sounds accompanied by the occasional trickling of gravel. Something heavy shifted to her left. She heard the noise and felt the vibration, but nothing changed in her small, cramped space.

"Go carefully, lads. This rubble is treacherous. She's down here somewhere. Can you shout again, love?"

"Here!" she called in English. "I'm here!" The walls of her throat seemed to stick together. She was choking. She coughed to clear the sticky tar and felt another stab in her back.

She tried not to panic. This nightmare will end in a little while, she told herself.

The man was inching closer. She would get out of this living tomb. Soon, she would know the answers to her questions. Her rescuers would tell her where she was and what had happened. They would lift the heavy object and take her from this dark place. They would tend her injuries, and she'd recover.

Something moved, and a shaft of light pierced the darkness, blinding her. She squeezed her eyes to shut out the painful intrusion, wincing as her head throbbed. She lifted her hand in front of her face, further shielding her eyes.

The noise of more boots scrambling on rubble filled her ears. Deep voices called urgently.

"Move that beam!"

"Get those bricks shifted!"

"Careful!"

Warm fingers touched her hand. "How are you doing?"

She opened her eyes. The man was shining a torch under his chin to illuminate his face. The strange lighting angle made him look like a grinning gargoyle.

"What happened?" she asked.

"Bloody Jerries. They bombed the whole city. There's not much of this place left standing. It's taken us hours to dig this deep into the rubble. We thought there'd be nobody else left alive. It's a miracle we found you. You're lucky, lass."

"Lucky?" She didn't agree with his assessment of her fortune but didn't have the breath or strength to argue the point.

"We were going to pack up and go home. We've only found, well, err..." he hesitated. "Let's just say the others we found down here weren't as fortunate as you." He turned to the men working feverishly around her. "That masonry will need to be supported before we can dig her out. It could collapse and make matters worse for us all."

"We're on it, Sarge."

"Would you like some water?" he asked.

She tried to nod, but her head was stuck fast. "Yes, please."

He took out a water flask and held it to her lips. The angle was awkward and most ran down her cheek, but she managed to get some in her mouth. She rinsed the liquid around with her tongue and spat the sooty dust from her lips. "Sorry, but I couldn't swallow that filth."

"Here, have some more." The man tipped the flask to her lips again.

She swallowed a small mouthful, feeling the coolness descend all the way into her stomach, making her shiver violently.

"Are you in any pain?"

"Yes, but my head feels the worst. I don't think I've broken anything."

"We'll soon sort you out."

"I'm glad you didn't leave me."

"What's your name, love? I can let the others know we've found you."

She opened her mouth to reply but couldn't bring her name to mind. She was confused and felt embarrassed. Why couldn't she remember her name? How silly. She concentrated, trying to dig into the fog that filled her head. Who was she?

"Take your time, love. No rush."

"I don't know." Tears trickled from her eyes, and she felt a moment of anger at her display of weakness. "I feel stupid, but I can't tell you who I am. I can't remember anything." She stifled a sob, and the sharp thing dug into her ribcage again. "Please get me out of here. I can't stand this any longer." Fear was taking hold, sending her mind into a spin of terror. She'd been brave and calm for so long. She couldn't hold it together a second more. Something snapped in her mind. "I can't bear this. I can't breathe. Please get me out," she pleaded pathetically, hating herself for being so feeble.

The man took her hand in his and held it gently. "Won't be long, love. Try to stay still. I'm here. I'll stay with you."

She closed her eyes and made an enormous effort to slow her breathing. Losing control now would not help her. She should stay calm.

"What's the last thing you remember?"

She tried to think. If her head had been free, she would have shaken it. The first thing she could remember was the blackness. She knew nothing before opening her eyes in this place. She looked into the man's face, her eyes filled with confusion. He was no longer illuminated by the flashlight. Daylight was streaming down through holes in the broken structure above her. The rescuers were making progress.

"I'm sorry, I can't remember anything."

"Try not to worry about it. From what I can see, you've had a nasty knock on the head. You've probably got a concussion."

"Yes."

"Your memory will come back in a few days."

"Do you think so?" She croaked and took comfort from the glimmer of hope he offered her.

"Perhaps some of the other survivors might know who you are."

She felt an inexplicable spark of fear at the notion that others might know who she was. What reason did she have to be afraid? What did she have to hide? Something was niggling at the edges of her consciousness. Something was warning her to be wary of her neighbours. She didn't understand the feeling, but she trusted her instincts. "Are there many survivors?"

Her rescuer shook his head. "It's carnage out there. We've been searching for hours but haven't found anyone alive since dawn. I don't think we'll be able to account for everyone in this building. We can't reach the cellars where most would have been taking shelter."

"Were there more people here with me?" She thought she'd been alone in this horror.

"Most have perished, love. I'm sorry, but only six or seven walked away from this building, and they couldn't tell us much about anyone else who might be here."

"No one has missed me?" She tried to think clearly, but her thought process was muddled and confused. The niggling sensation of the need to be cautious squirmed through her mind again, and she knew it was important. "If no one missed me, perhaps I was alone."

"Well, you could be right. Even if you hadn't been alone, with so many dead, your companions might be among them. I'm sorry, love."

"Where is this place?" She thought she might be able to remember something if she knew where she was.

"The Marples Hotel. It was open to anyone. People came in to shelter here. As it turned out, they'd have been better staying in the open."

"The Marples?"

"Did that shake a memory? Do you remember being here?"

"No, but I can't think why I would be in a hotel."

"Perhaps you came in to shelter from the air-raid? Like I said, lots of people did, thinking they'd be safe in the cellars."

"Am I in the cellar?"

"No. You didn't make it that far. It's difficult to tell what part of the building we're in here."

"You said there was an air-raid." Her brain had now worked out she was the victim of a bombing raid. "Where am I?"

"In the Marples, I told you."

"I'm sorry. I wasn't clear." She knew her question might sound odd to her rescuer. "What town are we in?"

"Sheffield!" He wrinkled his brow. "Goodness, lass. Where did you think you were?"

She was amazed. How could she be in Sheffield? She didn't remember anything, but somehow everything seemed wrong. "Sheffield is in England, isn't it?"

"Oh, dear. You do have a bad case of concussion, love."

"Give us a hand, Sarge," one of the men called from above them.

"What do you want me to do?" he asked his companions.

"Give a shove to that big plank when I say."

The man let go of her hand. "Not long now, love. Hold tight."

Chapter Two – Changed Identity

The nurse was busy changing the dressing on her chest. Her wound felt sore, and she flinched, despite the nurse's gentle touch.

"Sorry, love. I know it hurts. Soon be done, and I can leave you to rest."

She concentrated on a neat crease in the girl's crisply starched uniform while inhaling the clinical disinfectant-laden air. Focusing on small details, and breathing slowly, helped to calm her. Panic was never far from her mind. She felt disoriented and afraid. She knew she was in a hospital. She was injured. She'd been trapped in a building that was flattened by an enormous German bomb. England was at war with Germany and had been for the last year or so. Why did she not remember that important fact? What was she doing in England? Why was she here?

The nurse was keeping up a constant flow of chatter. "This wound is healing nicely, just like your head. Are you in any pain?"

"A little." She touched her head. Her temple throbbed with a deep ache, but she didn't want to make a fuss. The ward was full of people much worse off than she was.

"I'll get you something to take the edge off when I'm done here."

"Thank you."

"You were lucky your lung wasn't pierced. The wound is deep, but it could have been a lot worse. I expect you'll be able to go home in time for Christmas."

"Home?" She didn't know where home might be and felt a slight surge of alarm. Where would she go?

"Oh, sorry, forgive me. You're our Jane Smith, aren't you?"

"Jane Smith?" The name sounded unfamiliar.

"That's what the doctors decided to call you until your memory comes back."

"I see."

"Well, we can't keep saying, *hey miss*, now can we? It wouldn't be polite." The nurse gave a quiet giggle and began to wrap a bandage over the clean dressing, passing the roll around Jane's chest. "So, for the time being, your name is Jane."

"What if my memory doesn't return?" The possibility had occurred to her that she might be locked in this no-man's land with no identity and no past and it scared her.

"Give yourself time, love. Concussion isn't a permanent condition." The nurse fastened the bandage and patted Jane's hand.

"You've had ten stitches in that head-wound and the discolouration is gruesome, but most people start to remember things after a couple of days as the bruising fades. I know you're not a pretty sight right now, but I'd say you're quite a stunner under all that swelling."

"That's not what the mirror in the patient's bathroom tells me. My face is lopsided with all the swelling, and I'm so sore I can't get a brush through my hair. It hurts so much."

"Nonsense. You have cheekbones like Ava Gardner and hair like Dorothy Lamour. I'd love to have curls like yours. We washed your hair before we shaved and stitched you. We had to; it was full of plaster dust and soot. I expect it would benefit from another shampoo."

"I don't think I could manage to wash my hair. I feel too weak, and my head hurts too much."

"I'll help you, later. You'll feel better when you look more like yourself."

"Even with the bald patch?" Jane had been mortified to see how much hair had been shaved back from her temple. She'd always been proud of her hair.

"Oh, that will grow back in no time. It had to be done so the doctor could clean the wound and stitch it."

"How long have I been here?"

"You were brought in on Friday afternoon. Now it's Sunday. It's still early days, so try not to worry."

"What's *your* name?" Jane asked. "Did you tell me? I can't remember."

"I'm Nurse Wallace. I did tell you yesterday, but it's normal for you to keep forgetting things at this stage. Like I said, don't worry. You'll improve with time."

"I hope so. It feels strange, not knowing who I am."

"Well, you didn't have any belongings with you to give us a clue. No identity card. Not even a purse. You didn't have a coat on, so the police think you were probably a resident of the hotel but the papers and records in the reception were destroyed, and there's no way to tell who you are."

Jane's intuition alerted her to a sense of danger at the mention of the police. She didn't know why she felt anxious but knew enough to rely on her gut-feeling. "Why are the police interested in me?" she asked cautiously.

"Oh, they're just doing their job. Though, I wouldn't like to be in their shoes. Hundreds of people were killed or injured in Thursday's raid. Trying to identify all those bodies must be a nightmare for the authorities. The hospitals that weren't destroyed are overflowing and short of beds. The wards are crawling with people trying to find missing relatives. It's mayhem!"

"It must have been a big raid." Jane only knew about her own situation. She'd had no idea of the scale of the destruction but was beginning to understand the city had suffered terrible losses and damage.

"I'll say!" The nurse looked sad. "I've only had a few hours of sleep since it happened. The Royal is full to bursting."

"I mustn't keep you, then. I'm sure you have many patients to attend to."

"I do, but you're one patient that needs more help than I can give you. There's a lady from social services coming to see you soon. She'll be able to sort you out with somewhere to stay until you get your bearings again."

"I don't need social services!" Jane began to protest. She didn't like the idea of getting involved with strangers.

"Listen, my love." The nurse offered a sympathetic smile. "A young woman in your predicament needs all the help she can get, wouldn't you say?"

Jane closed her eyes and pressed her lips together. She hated feeling helpless and dependant on others, but the nurse was right. How could she survive when she had nothing but the clothes she was found in and didn't even know her own name?

"It'll be Christmas in ten days. You'll need somewhere to stay. The social services can help with that and might also help you find your relations. You must have someone somewhere who cares about you. I bet they're going out of their minds with worry."

"I don't know whether I have relatives in... err, in Sheffield." She'd almost said, '*in England*.' She would have to be careful.

In her heart, she felt she was German. She thought in German. Although, she considered it strange that her spoken English didn't have a German accent. Instead, her voice had a slight South Yorkshire dialect, like the nurse. Perhaps she'd lived in Sheffield for some years, or maybe she'd had a good language teacher. She simply had no idea why she spoke English so well.

"If you have relatives, they'll be sure to be looking for you."

"Not if they are dead or injured."

The nurse's eyes grew wide. "Have you remembered something? Was someone with you at the Marples?"

Jane shrugged. "I have no idea."

"I have to leave you and see to the lady over there. Poor thing lost her whole family in the raid. She's still in shock."

"Go, I'll be fine. Thank you for your consideration." Jane glanced at the older patient in the bed opposite. "She looks desolate."

Nurse Wallace turned to Jane with a frown. "I just realised something about you."

"Oh?" Jane held her breath, waiting warily for the nurse to speak.

"You talk posh. I mean, you don't talk like a factory girl."

"Don't I?"

"I'd say you probably come from a wealthy family. I know some nurses who use big words like you do."

"Do you?" Jane's mind began to spin. Could the nurse be right about her background?

"Or perhaps you've been to college and had an education. That can make a difference in how you talk."

Jane had a fleeting glimpse of memory. She was staring at a chalkboard full of writing and she was taking notes. The memory disappeared as quickly as it had appeared.

The nurse continued speaking, apparently unaware of the shocked expression on her patient's face. "That small detail might make it easier to find your folks. At least it could help to narrow down the search for who you are. You're from a posh area of town, I'm willing to bet on it."

"Do you think so?"

"I'll mention my thoughts to the social services lady. You never know."

Jane watched the nurse cross the ward to check the pale-looking woman in the bed opposite. Was Nurse Wallace right about her background? Jane didn't think so. She'd been born in Germany, she was sure of it. She couldn't tell anyone what she felt, though. Germany was responsible for the destruction of the city. The people of Sheffield would not take kindly to having a German in their midst. She could not afford to admit the one small detail she knew for certain about herself.

She closed her eyes to shut out the confusion and fear. She didn't like the feeling of being out of control. She had no ability to organise her life or plan what to do. She felt she had no future without knowing her past. How could she move forward until she knew who she was and why she was here? Why was she in England in the middle of a war with her home country?

She slipped down the bed and pulled the thin blanket high around her shoulders. She wanted to hide away from the scary reality of not knowing anything about who she was. Perplexing ideas ran through her mind as she searched for explanations. She desperately needed to bring back her memories. The sense of impending danger was strong, but she had nowhere to run and nowhere to hide from the unknown threat. She felt exposed and vulnerable.

She had to know more about her predicament. She reached for the fleeting image of the classroom she'd seen in her mind, but the memory eluded her. She thought about the writing on the chalkboard, feeling it might be important, but when she pictured the board, it was blank. She sighed with frustration.

Her body ached all over, and the nurse hadn't been back with the pain relief she'd promised. The throb in her head was less severe when she tried to relax, so she steadied her breathing and allowed the stress to flow out with each exhalation. She somehow knew how to force her body to unwind. Fleetingly, she wondered where she might have learned the technique, but as with everything else, the memory wasn't there. Eventually, she gave in to her weariness, and as her puzzling thoughts dwindled to nothing more than dark shadows, she fell into a deep sleep.

She slept soundly for a few hours until her rest was interrupted by dreams full of darkness and crushing pain. She was buried alive and choking on black dust. She heard voices and called out, shocking herself awake.

When she opened her eyes a slim woman in a tweed suit with softly waved, grey-streaked hair was looking at her with interest. "Hello, Jane."

Jane stared at her visitor but stayed silent. She had a feeling the woman had heard what she'd yelled in her dream. She called out a name. A German name. It meant nothing to Jane. She didn't recognise the name, but someone called Gottfried was important to her. He must be. Why else would she be calling for him?

"You missed your tea. I can call the nurse to bring you something. Are you hungry?"

"No, thank you." Jane was too nervous to eat.

"Who is Godfrey?"

Jane shook her head slowly as her thoughts whirled quickly. She'd called out the German name, Gottfried, not the English version of Godfrey. Perhaps this woman misheard, or misinterpreted the sound into what her English mind expected to hear?

She shrugged. "I don't know." She stared at her tightly clenched hands resting on her stomach.

"Don't distress yourself, my dear. I can't imagine how you must be feeling."

Jane lifted her gaze to meet the woman's kind eyes. "It's difficult. I have these flashes of recognition. I can almost touch them. I feel I'm on the verge of seeing the memories, but they vanish and leave me feeling worse than before."

"Did you have a dream about your memories, just now?"

"I don't know. Perhaps." She tried to recall the visions of her sleep. She was in the bombed building. She was trapped, and she was reaching out to someone. Gottfried. The man had no face, but she felt a bond with him. Was he a friend, a relative? Did she love him?

"Tell me about it. Perhaps it will help."

"There is nothing to tell." She eased herself to a sitting position, giving herself time to think and clear her head from the fog of sleep. "My dream was no more than a few fragments. Brief pictures. Fleeting thoughts. It had no substance."

"How awful for you." The woman smiled briefly. "But I'm here to help if I can. I'm Miss Rosalind Humphrey, from social services." She held out her hand.

Jane smiled and shook her hand briefly. "Can you tell me anything about who I am?"

"Not yet, but we do have something to go on."

"Oh?" Jane didn't know whether to feel relieved or afraid.

"The name Godfrey obviously means something to you. It's not much, but it's a start."

"I see. Yes." Jane let out the breath she'd been holding.

"And Nurse Wallace was right about your way of speaking. You do have a distinctively posh accent for these parts."

"Do I?" Jane's defences flared again.

"It's more in the way you use big words. You seem to have a wider vocabulary than most young women from hereabouts."

"Do I?" Jane realised she was repeating herself inanely. "Sorry. I'm finding this all rather strange."

"I quite understand, my dear. Try not to worry. I'm here to offer you a lifeline or two until you can get back on your feet, as it were."

Jane felt a rush of relief. She had no reason to be afraid of Miss Humphrey. The social worker was simply doing her job. "What can you do to help me?"

"Well now, I can organise some clothes for you and some temporary identification papers. You'll need an emergency allowance to give you some money, and you'll need somewhere to live."

"Can you do all that for me?" Jane was impressed.

"Not without help from some very thoughtful and kind individuals, but the German bombing has brought out the best in the people of Sheffield. Adversity makes us stronger. Hitler doesn't seem to understand that about us. If he did, he wouldn't try so hard to defeat us. But I don't need to lecture you about our stiff upper lip, do I, dear?"

Jane smiled but had nothing to say. She knew who Hitler was. She instinctively understood all kinds of things about the world in general. She knew that Britain was at war with Germany. She'd recently witnessed the death and destruction first-hand. How was it possible to know so much about the events around her, yet still not see what her place was in all of it?

Miss Humphreys continued to praise the brave people of the city and didn't seem to expect a response. Jane ignored the monologue and concentrated on her inner turmoil, struggling to find explanations and answers to the many questions she couldn't ask the English woman.

Was she a spy? Is that why she was in England? Was she a supporter of Hitler's regime? She didn't think she could be. He was a cruel dictator. She didn't understand how she could remember a man like Hitler, but couldn't remember her own name. She trusted her deep-felt sentiments for the arrogant and evil German leader. How could she possibly be a spy for someone like him? The idea of such a thing was preposterous. What other explanation could there be, though? Why would a German woman like her be here in England in the middle of war? Why did she feel the need for caution? Her instincts were warning her to be careful and wary of everyone. Was that simply a natural response to her memory loss, or was there something more to the feeling?

Miss Humphrey lifted a bag to her lap, the movements alerting Jane back to her dialogue. She watched the woman take some papers from her bag.

"Well, let's get down to business, shall we?"

"What business are you referring to?" Jane stared at the official looking forms with suspicion

"Nothing too formal, my dear. I'd normally fill some forms in about you first, but as we have no official name or previous address for you, we can dispense with the formalities."

"I see."

Miss Humphreys handed her a sheet of paper. "Here is the address of one of our lodging houses. You'll have your own room, but the facilities will be shared with the family. Mrs Woodcock has four children and will be grateful of the rent we'll give her on your behalf. Her husband is away in the army."

"I see." Jane hid the disappointment of shared accommodation. She was a private person. She liked space to herself but realised that beggars could not be choosers. She wasn't happy that she would be throwing herself on the mercy of a stranger, but she had no choice.

"We'll arrange for you to have a subsistence allowance until you are well enough to find work to support yourself, or until someone comes forward to claim you."

"To claim me!" Jane felt a rush of anxiety.

"I meant someone who knows you, my dear. We can't rule out the possibility that you have a husband, a mother, or someone who could take care of you."

"I'm not wearing a wedding ring."

"No, but your ring finger looks as if you recently *did* have one." Miss Humphrey pointed to the third finger of Jane's left hand.

Jane glanced at her hands. She could see why the social worker had thought she might have been married. Her left ring finger was slightly narrower and paler at the base than the other fingers. She'd worn her late mother's ring there. She gasped. "Oh, my!" Her eyes flew wide. "I remember my mother."

"Do you?"

"She's dead." Jane felt a rush of emotion at the images and feelings that suddenly filled her mind. "It happened seven years ago. I was eighteen." She remembered her age clearly, and she knew exactly how many years had passed since she'd lost her mother, but the rest came as mere fragments of a terrible event. Strong arms held her tightly, keeping her safe inside the doorway of an apartment building. She sensed the aroma of baking bread and heard the soft hiss of falling rain. The strangled sound of her own ragged, suppressed scream overlaid everything as she struggled ineffectually to escape her protector.

She saw and felt the splintered memory in her mind's eye. The raw emotion felt as fresh as the day it happened. She struggled to hold herself together.

"I'm so sorry to hear that, Jane. How awful for you. What happened?"

Jane took a shuddering breath and shook her head. She didn't understand the awful images and sensations of the memory. What *did* happen? "I don't know. I can't recall the details. I only know that I wore her wedding ring." She lifted her hand. "I don't know why I'm not wearing it now."

"Well, at least you remembered her. That's a good thing, surely? And we now know how old you are. Your mother died seven years ago when you were eighteen, so that makes you twenty-five. We'll soon have all the pieces of your jigsaw at this rate."

Jane realised that Miss Humphrey was right about her age. She was twenty-five. She also knew she was single. If she'd been married, the wedding ring would have been on her right hand. German brides wore the wedding band on the right. Her right ring finger was unblemished. She'd never been married.

The wail of an air-raid siren brought a sickening silence to all conversation on the ward, and fear-filled eyes turned to the heavy blackout drapes at the windows. A group of nurses hurried through the doors, directing visitors and able-bodied patients.

"Make your way downstairs. Quickly now. Fast as you can."

Nurse Wallace ran to the pale woman opposite to assist her from the bed. She called over, "Miss Humphrey, would you help Miss Smith to the shelter?"

"Can you walk?" Miss Humphrey asked Jane, reaching to help her from the bed.

"Where can we go?" Jane felt an overwhelming fear envelop her. "I can't go through that again. Please help me! I can't do this! I don't want to die!"

"Now, Jane, calm yourself." Nurse Wallace's voice was stern as she hurried to her side. "Go with Miss Humphrey; she'll take you to the shelter. You'll be as safe as we can make you."

Jane shuddered but allowed the neatly dressed woman to guide her. She had no choice. She didn't know where she was, or who she was. Her life was in the hands of strangers.

Chapter Three – Trusting Strangers

Jane stood cowering with the social worker in the hospital shelter, shivering with fear. The hands she held over her ears did nothing to muffle the agonising drone of approaching heavy aircraft, the screaming of bombs, the deafening explosions and the rat-a-tat-tat of anti-aircraft guns.

The ground shook and vibrated beneath her feet with each earth-shuddering boom. She'd never been more afraid in her life. Then she suddenly thought of the awful memory she'd recently recalled, and understood that perhaps she once had reason to be much more afraid. The realisation startled her. What happened when she was eighteen? How did her mother die? Who had been holding her so tightly? Had she been in danger too? She wished she could remember more.

The whistling howl of a falling bomb screeched close to the shelter, and the resounding boom of the explosion rocked the floor beneath her feet. Miss Humphreys threw her arms around Jane, and the two women clung to each other, listening to the sobs, curses and terrified cries around them. The social worker's lips were close to Jane's ear, and she could hear the woman praying.

"Please, God, keep us safe. Please keep us all safe this night."

"Amen to that," Jane whispered.

More explosions shook the ground, but the wave of bombers seemed to be moving away. As the raid went on, the noise diminished, and the frequency of distant detonations grew less. Jane began to relax, and Miss Humphreys guided her to sit on a long bench against a wall. Nurse Wallace sat close by with her arm around the sobbing bereaved patient.

"How is she?" Jane mouthed the question silently.

"Not good." The nurse held the woman's hand, her fingers covering the pulse point. She glanced at Jane and shook her head. "I'm afraid all this is too much for her."

"What's her name?" Jane asked.

"Ethel Rowbottom."

The distraught woman glanced up, on hearing her name.

"Hello, Ethel." Jane gently touched the woman's shoulder. "I'm Jane. I heard what happened to your family. Would you tell me about them?"

"What do you think you are doing?" Nurse Wallace glared at Jane and spoke through clenched teeth, "The last thing this poor woman needs is to rake over her heartbreak. Have you no thought or consideration for her feelings?"

"Of course, I have!" Jane kept her voice low and smiled at Ethel. "Perhaps if you told me about them, it would help to keep them close to you." She pointed to the woman's chest. "In there."

Ethel's lips trembled with a wan smile, but she stayed quiet.

A rattle of anti-aircraft fire broke the silence, making Ethel jump. A distant whoosh of a bigger gun joined the cacophony of noise, and the older woman began to shake uncontrollably.

"Our men are seeing them off. I hope they get a few of the buggers!" An old man shook his fist at the ceiling.

"I lost my memory in the last raid, Ethel." Jane tried again with the older lady, hoping to calm her violent trembling. "Imagine that! I don't know who I am."

Ethel looked vaguely interested, but her shivers continued.

"This bump on the head is to blame, I'm told." Jane pointed to the bandage around her head. "I don't know whether I have a family. I can't remember."

"I'll never forget my lass and my grandkids," the woman spluttered through chattering teeth. Her sobs increased, and she buried her head in her hands. "Why didn't He take me?"

"Would you like to tell me what happened?" Jane pressed, taking the woman's hand; somehow understanding how important is was to talk about the traumatic event.

The nurse pursed her lips and glared at Jane.

"Perhaps if I tell you what happened to me first, eh?" Jane began. "We've all got sad and sorry tales to tell, but perhaps the weight of pain will grow less if we share our stories. Pain festers if we hold it in. It's good to let it out."

"You speak like a therapist, Miss Smith," Miss Humphreys looked surprised. "Your suggestion will at least help pass the time and take our mind off this racket until they sound the all-clear."

"Well, my story won't take long." Jane winced as another explosion rocked the ground and looked at the distraught woman cowering in Nurse Wallace's arms. "Apparently, I was in the Marples Hotel when a bomb dropped on it."

People close by began to take interest and one man exclaimed, "That place was flattened!"

"Along with the C and A building opposite," another man added. "Both buildings took direct hits."

"I don't remember," Jane concentrated on the pale woman, who appeared to be listening. "When I came to my senses I was trapped under something heavy. I couldn't move and could barely breathe."

Ethel hiccupped and took a shuddering breath. "You must have been scared to death," the older woman said, haltingly, and lifted her red-rimmed eyes. She pressed Jane's hand with her frail, thin fingers.

"I was. It was dark, and my head hurt." She touched her bandaged temple. "I don't know how long I was there, but I was relieved when I heard someone coming."

"I can imagine." The older woman's shakes were subsiding as she took an interest in Jane's account.

"The man was very kind. He reassured me and kept me calm while the others worked to free me."

"Bloody heroes, the lot of 'em," a man exclaimed.

"I'm certainly very grateful to my rescuers. I could have died down there if they hadn't decided to continue searching. He told me they almost gave up."

"Oh, lass. You poor thing."

"What about you, Ethel? Do you think you can tell me your story?"

"I don't know." Ethel shook her head and stared at the floor. "I keep going over it in my mind. If I'd stayed in the shelter with them, I would have been killed too. If I could go back and change things, I would never have gone back to the house. I wish I'd been with them. I feel so guilty."

"Why do you feel guilty, Ethel?" Jane asked.

"Because I'm still here, and they're gone."

Jane looked into the woman's tear-filled eyes. "What happened?"

Ethel took a deep breath and let it out in a long sigh. "Lucy, my daughter, she was upstairs putting the children to bed when the sirens went off." She hesitated and glanced at Jane.

"Go on," Jane encouraged her.

"We were going to put the Christmas decorations up when the little ones were settled. We planned to give them a surprise when they woke up the next morning. It would have been our Tommy's first Christmas."

"How many grandchildren, Ethel?" Jane asked gently.

"Three." Ethel's lips trembled as she smiled briefly. "Danny's the eldest. He's four. Then, Shirley, she's almost three, and Tommy's the baby. My Lucy didn't waste time having them. I'm sure she'd have had another on the way by now if Albert hadn't joined up when he did."

"Did you get them to the shelter in time?" Jane asked.

"Yes," Ethel nodded. "We set out to the shelters at the end of the street, and the skies were still clear when we were settling them on the floor in their blankets. Our Shirley was upset, though. We'd forgotten her teddy, and she can't sleep without her bear. I knew it wouldn't take more than a few minutes to go back for it, so I promised my little angel I'd get it for her. I left Lucy to comfort the little ones and told her I wouldn't be long."

"What happened next?" one of the other sheltering patients asked.

"I ran back to the house and dashed upstairs to get the teddy. I could hear the bombers getting closer, but I thought they'd be heading for the steelworks. I hoped I'd be able to get back to the shelter before they started dropping their bombs."

Another man interrupted. "Bloody bastards didn't wait to get to the factories, did they? Sorry for swearing, ladies," he apologised quickly. "They dropped the first wave of bombs on the houses."

Another voice added, "It wasn't as if they couldn't see where they were. There was a full moon, and it was a clear night. They knew what they were doing all right."

The shelter resounded with heartfelt agreement and condemnation of the German bombers.

Ethel took up her story again as the murmurs grew quiet. "When I heard the first bomb screaming close by, I dived under the kitchen table. I was scared witless, but when I felt the explosion shake the floor under my knees, I realised I was safe. My house was still standing. I didn't dare move, though. The planes were overhead, and I could hear more bombs whistling down all over the place. I don't know how long I stayed under that table, but it went on for hours. The ground kept shaking, and the noise was awful. When the kitchen window blew in, I thought that was it. If it hadn't been for the white tape holding the bits together, I would have been cut to ribbons by flying glass."

Jane realised the woman's tears had stopped as she concentrated on telling her story.

"I decided to wait for the all-clear. I'd have been daft to try to get back to the shelter in that commotion. I thought my lass was safe and I knew I wouldn't be doing her any favours if I tried to get the teddy back to Shirley and got myself killed in the process." She paused to stifle a sob, but a fresh wave of tears trickled down her cheeks.

Nurse Wallace tightened her arm around Ethel's shoulders. "That's enough, love. You don't have to go on."

"No, I want to." Ethel lifted her head. "Like this young woman said, it feels good to get it out."

"What happened next, love?" another sheltering patient asked.

"The all-clear sounded around four in the morning, and I picked up the teddy and hurried into the street. I couldn't believe what I was looking at. I could see the sky where houses should have been and fires burned up and down the street. I didn't worry about my neighbours. I'd seen most of them at the shelter and thought they'd be safe. I knew they'd be upset when they saw what had happened to their houses, though. I hurried along, making plans to let old Mrs Bradshaw and her husband stay in our parlour. Their house had gone, you see."

Another woman patient called out, "You could be describing my street, love."

Ethel looked up. "I know. It was awful, wasn't it?"

"What happened at the shelter, Ethel?" Jane prompted.

"That's just it." Ethel turned to Jane with a blank expression. "There was no shelter. All I saw was a massive hole in the ground where it had been. I didn't understand it."

"It must have taken a direct hit," someone commented.

"I wandered around the edge of the crater, poking at the rubble. I was looking for them, you see. I couldn't take it in that they'd gone. How could they be gone? I still can't understand how there was nothing left of all those people."

"What did you do?" Jane prompted.

"I picked up scraps of clothing and saw what looked like bits of bone and torn up meat but I couldn't understand what I was looking at." Her face crumpled, and a fresh wave of sobs tore her throat. After a few seconds, she cleared her throat and made an effort to continue. "I know now what it was, but my mind couldn't put it together at the time."

"It must have been horrific." Miss Humphreys looked as if she might be ill.

"It's all I can see when I close my eyes. Those bits of gore are seared into my brain. They should have been safe!" Ethel squeezed her eyes closed. "They were in the shelter."

"Even shelters don't guarantee safety if they get a direct hit," a man said quietly.

"Did anyone come to help you?" Jane asked.

Ethel shook her head. "I don't really remember much more until I got to the hospital. They said I was in shock. I just felt numb. I still do."

"Try to keep them alive in your mind, Ethel. Don't dwell on the end," Jane suggested. "Tell me about your daughter. What was she like?"

"My Lucy?" Ethel smiled briefly, and her eyes stared into the distance. "Always bright as a button, she was. Could have gone to university, you know." Ethel focused on Jane's face. "She made me proud. Her teachers always said she'd go far if she applied herself. Always had her nose in a book."

"What did she do?" Jane asked, noticing that conversations had started in the shelter and Ethel was no longer the centre of attention.

"She got married young and gave me three grandchildren. You're about her age. You know what it's like. Girls grow up to be mothers and books grow dusty. Our Tommy wasn't even a year old." Tears fell slowly down the woman's cheek. "Why didn't that bomb take me? I've had my life. Them children had all their lives in front of them."

"God works in mysterious ways." Jane took the woman's hand again. "Your daughter and grandchildren will not grow old, but you were blessed in knowing them. Will you tell me more about them?"

"Our Danny was the mischief maker." A small smile creased the corners of Ethel's mouth. "Always into something he shouldn't be. Lucy baked some tarts that morning, and he'd scoffed half of them before she found him under the table with the few that were left."

"Danny was the oldest, wasn't he?" Jane encouraged the older woman to tell more about her lost family.

As Ethel spoke, her face became animated, and a little colour returned to her pale cheeks. Jane glanced at Nurse Wallace, who she noticed had placed two fingers on the lady's pulse. The nurse raised her eyebrows, pressed her lips together and gave a nod of approval.

As the sounds of destruction from beyond the shelter quieted, the hospital patients and staff began to relax. Someone began to play a harmonica and voices joined to sing the popular songs of the day.

Jane continued to ask questions to keep Ethel talking. The older woman seemed brighter, and less inclined to weep as she talked more about her memories of her grandchildren. When the harmonica began the introduction to a familiar tune, Jane felt the older woman begin to sway beside her and was surprised when Ethel began to sing in a high-pitched, reedy voice.

"We'll meet again, don't know where, don't know when...

But I know we'll meet again some sunny day..." Ethel smiled bravely and continued singing as many other voices fell silent around her.

"Keep smiling through, just like you always do,"

By the time Ethel reached the end of the song, the all-clear siren was wailing, and many faces in the shelter were wet with tears.

Jane took the older woman's hand. "You survived, Ethel. There must be a reason that God chose you to live."

"Aye, well, I'm blowed if I can understand His reasoning." Ethel's face crumpled. "What good is an old lass like me to anyone?"

"Don't underestimate yourself, love." Nurse Wallace smiled at her patient. "You're not so old, and you certainly lifted the spirits of a few people in here tonight."

"What did I do?" Ethel looked surprised.

"You have the voice of an angel, and you touched my heart." Jane squeezed her hand. "You made me forget my troubles for a few minutes."

"Oh, lass. Whatever are you going to do? Where will you start to find out who you are?"

"I'm hoping to help her." Miss Humphreys leant over to explain. "I'm from the social services."

"Oh, you're one of those nosey parkers, are you?" Ethel sniffed disdainfully and turned to Jane. "You want to watch her sort," she warned, but grinned and winked impishly.

Jane chuckled. "Why?" she asked.

"She'll have a file on your affairs as thick as King James' Bible before you know it. No stone will go unturned until she knows everything about you. She'll find out what you owe the tally-man, where you get your stockings from, and woe betides you have owt to do with the under-the-counter stuff at the butcher!"

"Well, I never!" Miss Humphrey squared her shoulders.

Ethel grinned mischievously. "I'm only saying what I've heard. I'm sure you've a good heart, really, miss."

Jane couldn't help giggling at the old woman's playfulness. "Well, she's promised to find me somewhere to live in time for Christmas. She can't be as bad as you've heard."

"Have you no home to go to?" Ethel asked.

"I don't know. Perhaps I have, but I wouldn't know where it might be." Jane realised that she might have a home and family who were looking for her, but until they found her, she was alone.

"Well, aren't we a couple of lost causes?" Ethel smiled sadly. "Here I am with no family and an empty house I don't want to go back to, and here you are with no home and nobody to care for you." The woman had a twinkle in her eye. "I think I just worked out one of His mysteries." She pointed to the ceiling and frowned. "Maybe there is some rhyme and reason to this suffering."

"Are you saying what I think you're saying?" Nurse Wallace asked.

"I've a couple of spare rooms and a need for some company if she wants it." Ethel sighed. "I don't think I'd do too well on my own just now." She looked into Jane's eyes. "I won't be good company. We'll have a miserable Christmas."

Jane glanced at the social worker.

Miss Humphreys shrugged. "It's highly irregular, but as far I know, you're a free agent, Jane. You can live where you like."

"I think it's a perfect plan." Nurse Wallace took the older woman's arm. "Now let's get everyone back to the wards. We can discuss the details of your release in good time."

Chapter Four – Scary Prognosis

Jane was settling to sleep. She had endured a long night, and she wasn't the only patient in the ward who had taken to her bed after lunch for an afternoon nap.

She'd just begun to relax when a male voice disrupted her rest. "Do you mind if I ask you some questions before you drift off, Miss Smith?"

Jane opened her eyes and eased onto her back. The young man needed a shave and had dark circles under his hazel eyes. He looked as weary as she felt. He wore a white coat and had a stethoscope around his neck.

"Are you my doctor?" she asked.

"Guilty as charged, I'm afraid." He perched at the end of her bed. "I'm Dr Fisher, and I'm responsible for the very unflattering haircut you'll discover when that dressing is removed." He nodded to the bandaged area of her head. "Sorry about that."

Jane felt a flicker of alarm. She didn't recognise the doctor. Could she be sure he was who he said he was? Her eyes darted around the ward, searching for reassurance that the man was known to the staff. "I'm sorry, but I don't remember you."

"No reason why you should. If I recall, you were in and out of consciousness while we worked on your injuries. You mumbled something when I touched your chest, though."

"Did I?" Jane flinched with fear and wondered what language she'd used. "What did I say?"

The doctor smiled and shook his head. "You didn't make much sense."

Nurse Wallace hurried past, glancing at Jane and raising her eyebrows. "I thought you were going to get some sleep, Miss Smith." She looked accusingly at the doctor. "Don't tire her out, Dr Fisher. My patients need rest after the awful night we spent in the shelter."

Jane felt her shoulders relax a little. The doctor was no threat, and she hadn't betrayed her secret by speaking German while in his care.

"What do you want to know?" she asked, reluctantly easing to a sitting position, holding her head against the throb of pain that came each time she moved. She hoped his questions wouldn't take long. She was tired.

"You know how things are out there." He gestured to the blackout curtains at the windows. "Our casualty department is overflowing, and

I've been asked to assess which of my patients can be safely allowed home."

"But I have no home to go to. At least, I have no memory of one."

"That's what I wanted to talk to you about."

"My loss of memory?"

The doctor nodded. "Brain injuries can be tricky things, as I'm sure you will have noticed." His warm smile seemed genuine. "I understand you still can't remember very much. Has there been any improvement?"

Jane decided to cooperate and shook her head. "I don't know my name or where I live, though I did remember my mother is dead and I know I'm twenty-five."

"Mm." The doctor scratched his chin thoughtfully. "How do you feel in general?"

"What do you mean?"

"Well, apart from the obvious injuries that I know will be giving you some discomfort, how do you think you are dealing with your lack of identity?"

"Oh, I see." She thought she was coping well enough and didn't know what to say.

"I know you'll be apprehensive about the state of your mind. You'll probably feel vulnerable and perhaps have the idea that you can't trust anyone."

Jane flinched. The doctor had summed up her feelings exactly. How would he know that she felt so disconnected and wary of everyone around her?

"Please try not to worry. I've known a few patients who suffered a temporary loss of memory. Apparently, the condition gives you the feeling that you can't be certain about anything, and I'm told that is quite disconcerting. Feelings of paranoia and distrust are common. I wanted to give you some reassurance that these feelings are typical for some brain-injured patients."

"Are they?" Jane wasn't convinced. Her deep suspicion of people was connected to what she *did* know about herself, rather than any uncertainty she had. No matter what the well-meaning doctor thought, she couldn't afford to trust anyone completely. She was a German woman, deep inside enemy territory. Until she remembered who she was and why she was in England, trust was a luxury she could not afford.

"I can see you're not persuaded. You have every reason to doubt me, but I hope you'll let me help you."

"What can you do to help me?"

"Nothing at all without your trust."

"When will my memories return?" she asked.

"How long is a piece of string?" The doctor smiled. "I wish I could tell you, but the brain is a fickle organ. You could wake tomorrow, and everything will be back in place, or it could be that some memories might never return."

She felt dismayed by his prognosis. "Are you saying I may never know who I am?"

The doctor shook his head but smiled. "The signs are promising. You're already starting to recall some of your history. As time goes on, you'll remember more. Unfortunately, there may be gaps, but I'm hopeful that you'll make a full recovery, given the type of injury you sustained."

"What kind of gaps can I expect?"

"I don't know." He shrugged and sighed, giving her a sympathetic smile. "Let me put it this way." He scratched his chin again. "I like to think of memory as a million microscopic octopuses all linking tentacles in an infinite number of combinations. Their bodies hold the core memories, and the tentacles are the many pathways our minds use to get to those memories. It's an extremely simplified explanation, but it might help you to understand what's happened to you."

"You give me a very odd picture to contemplate." She couldn't help smiling at the strange image of a head full of tentacles.

"That's better." The doctor's grin widened. "You have a pretty smile."

"Pretty?" She huffed. "I think you must be more tired than you look. I've seen the mirror in the patient's bathroom, and my face is definitely not pretty."

"Mm," Dr Fisher nodded sagely. "Fortunately, I can see beyond the bad haircut and the bruising. In a few weeks, your hair will grow, and the swelling will go down. Perhaps when that happens, you might recognise yourself."

"I hope so."

"You seem to be coping with things better than I'd have expected."

"I don't have much choice, do I?"

"You seem a resourceful young woman. I'm sure you'll do fine. What about your short-term memory? Any problems there?"

"I don't understand."

"Do you have problems with remembering instructions from the nurses, for instance?"

"I don't think so."

"What did you have for breakfast this morning?"

"A poached egg on toast. Why?"

"Just asking if you remembered. Some people have problems with short term memory. Yours seem fine."

"You said you could help me to remember things. How?"

"Hypnosis."

Jane tried to keep the alarm from her face. She'd heard of hypnosis. She knew enough about the technique to understand she would be at the mercy of whoever hypnotised her. She would have no control and would be compelled to answer any question truthfully, no matter what the implications might be for her safety. "How would hypnosis help me remember who I am?"

"I can't guarantee that it will, and in any case, it would be much too early to attempt the treatment. Perhaps we could try in a few weeks when you're stronger?"

"I'm not sure I want to go down that road." Jane knew she could never allow herself to be put in such a vulnerable position. "I'd prefer to wait for my little octopus friends to recover all by themselves."

"And if they don't?"

"What's the worst I might expect?"

"I'd rather think in terms of the best prognosis. Try to stay positive."

Jane's tiredness was getting the better of her, and she stifled a yawn. "Sorry, but I really am weary."

"I'll let you get some rest, but think about what I suggested. Hypnosis might help in your case."

"What makes you so sure?"

"I can never be sure, but I have had good results in the past with patients like you." He lifted from the bed and moved closer to her. "You see, I think the knock on your head shocked some of your octopuses, stunning them for a while. They will recover. The memory of your mother and the fact that you know how old you are proves that some of your memories will come back."

"Only some? Why not all of them?" Jane couldn't help feeling worried

"I don't know whether the blow to your head might have shaken some of the tentacles apart, leaving them waving around inside your head, trying to reconnect. They may not link back in the same way.

Your memory pathways may be repaired, but might not be exactly as they were before."

"Do you think hypnosis might help to realign the connections?"

The doctor looked impressed. "I was told you're an intelligent girl. Well done. Not many people would make the leap of understanding that you just made."

Jane didn't feel conceited by the doctor's praise. She didn't think she'd done anything special. Dr Fisher's theory seemed feasible, and the next step was obvious to her. "I think I had a good education," she explained. "I have vague recollections of attending lectures."

"A university education? I wonder what you studied."

Jane wondered the same thing but was not prepared to be hypnotised to find out.

Nurse Wallace returned to the ward and marched to Jane's bed. "Are you still here, Doctor Fisher?" She folded her arms and lifted her chin.

"I'm just about to leave, Nurse Wallace." He put his hands up to the nurse in a gesture of surrender. "There's not much more we can do for Miss Smith, and as we are desperately in need of beds, I'm going to discharge her. She can leave tomorrow as soon as arrangements can be made for her." He turned to Jane. "I hope you understand, Miss Smith."

Jane was shocked. She couldn't wait to escape the confines of the hospital, but was afraid of whom or what she might find waiting on the outside.

"Don't look so alarmed." The doctor smiled reassurance. "I know Miss Humphries from social services has been to see you. You won't be cut adrift without a lifeline. You'll come back to have the stitches taken out in about a week, but I want to see you back here in the New Year. I'll make you an appointment to see me and leave the details with Nurse Wallace."

"Thank you." Jane gave the automatic response but felt her insides quaking. She watched the doctor walking away with the nurse and wondered whether she would have a say in his choice of treatment. She couldn't allow him to hypnotise her.

She shuffled down the bed and hid her head under the blanket. Perhaps she wouldn't need to keep the appointment. Maybe her memories would return, and she wouldn't need further medical help.

As tired as she was, sleep refused to come. Her fuzzy mind conjured up all kinds of nightmare scenarios to keep her awake. She questioned her reasons for being in England, and couldn't think of anything that seemed reasonable or lawful. She was a German woman of intelligence. She had been educated well enough to speak English like a native. She'd been found in the most well-known hotel in Sheffield on the night it was blown to bits by the Luftwaffe. The story added up to one of espionage no matter how she looked at it.

"I'm sorry, Jane." Nurse Wallace seemed jumpy. "I know you're not well enough to leave. That chest wound still needs care, but you can see how things are."

Jane was folding her newly acquired clothes and getting ready to leave with Ethel. The ward had already taken in more patients than it had room for. Injured women sat two to a bed and some hunched on the floor holding bandaged limbs.

"This last raid has put us under more pressure than ever but sending some of you home before you're ready to go really goes against the grain."

"I'm sure I'll be fine, Nurse Wallace. Ethel will take care of me." Jane gave the older woman a smile as she watched her put some possessions into a hospital pillowcase.

"I'm sure you'll take care of each other as best you can."

Jane smiled again. "She needs me as much as I need her. I can't replace her daughter, but I can give her a reason to go on. A small one, but it will be a start for her."

The nurse gave Jane a quizzical look. "I think Miss Humphreys was right about you."

"What do you mean?" Jane was curious and wondered what had been said about her.

"You do sound as if you know what you're talking about. You might have worked in social services or psychiatry. Do those occupations sound as if they might be familiar to you?"

Jane shrugged and shook her head. "I'm still open to suggestions. Nothing seems to fit yet. I'm still adrift up here." She touched her head.

She was becoming accustomed to feeling like a fish out of water. Nothing seemed natural or normal. She'd been given a few items of clothing but felt she would not have worn the styles from choice. Even her hair had been shaved at the front to allow for the stitches in her scalp. Now the bandages had been removed; she looked like a freak. She wore a coloured headscarf over the smaller dressing to hide her disfigurement.

The face that looked back at her, from the mirror in the patient's bathroom, was not one she recognised. She knew the bruising and swelling could account for her odd appearance, but it still felt weird to be looking at herself and seeing a stranger.

"Well, you'll have to come back to the ward on the twenty-third for the stitches removing, but meanwhile, if you have problems with that chest wound, come back anytime."

"You've told us to keep it clean, and I know it will heal in time."

"I've given Ethel some clean dressings. Let her look after you."

"Don't worry about us, Nurse Wallace. You have more patients to see to." Jane inclined her head to the waiting line of unhappy, injured women in the corridor outside the ward. "We're already yesterday's news."

The nurse sighed. "Take care, Jane Smith, or whoever you are."

"I will." Jane sighed too. Would she ever know her true identity? It had already been four days since they dug her from the ruined building and all she could remember were snippets of her past that meant nothing to her. The only meaningful thing she recalled was about her mother, and even that was not a whole memory. The only thing she knew for certain was her nationality, but given her circumstances, that fact would condemn her as a spy if it became known.

Chapter Five – A Walk Through Hell

The journey through Sheffield was more arduous than either woman had expected. Trams and buses ran intermittently and stopped where collapsed buildings blocked the road ahead. They rode as far as Queen Street but had to walk from there.

As they made their way through the centre of the ravaged city, Jane became aware of an eerie silence punctuated by urgent calls, scraping shovels and the trickle of running water. The normal sounds of a bustling city were absent. Buildings they passed had been reduced to twisted metal and roads were pockmarked with enormous craters.

They saw men and women toiling together to move the piles of rubble into waiting trucks. It looked to be back breaking work. Another team of women were struggling to tether a barrage balloon with long ropes to a twisted lamppost. Jane stopped to ask if they needed help.

"Thanks, love." One of the young girls handed her a length of rope. "Could you hang on to that while we secure the other ones?"

Jane obliged and watched the girls complete the task, handing back the rope when asked. When the young women seemed satisfied, they stood back to watch the grey balloon drift on the tether above the city.

"What are the balloons for?" Ethel asked.

"We're going to be putting more of these around Sheffield. The bigwigs think they'll help to discourage enemy planes from flying too low."

"Let's hope they know what they're talking about." Ethel watched the large shape floating above them.

"Which way now?" Jane asked her new friend.

"Where are you trying to get to?" one of the girls asked.

"Valley Road. It's up towards Meersbrook Park. I thought we'd try getting to the outskirts and hoped the roads might be easier once we get out of the centre."

"Meersbrook is the other side of the railway line, isn't it?" another girl asked.

Ethel nodded. "Aye, it is."

"You'll have a job crossing the railway from here." Another young woman was packing some tools into a bag. "I heard they're not letting anyone near the station and there's some commotion at the end of Granville Road. You might be better going around the other side of The Moor, and head for Bramall Lane. I think the bridge at Myrtle Road is still standing."

"That's taking us miles out of our way." Ethel's face crumpled. "I'm parched. I'll never make it without a drink of something."

"There's a soup wagon set up in St Paul's Gardens," another girl suggested. "You might get something there, love."

Jane thanked the girls for their advice and took Ethel's arm. "Which way to the gardens?"

"It's not far from here." Ethel began to walk. "Down here, I think."

They avoided the blazing torches where ruptured gas mains burned from cracks in the road. They splashed through streams caused by spouts of water gushing from broken pipes.

They passed other people wandering the streets. Some looked lost and confused; others were frantically hurrying along, and calling out names, searching for loved ones in the chaos of the damaged, smoking ruins.

After almost an hour of trying to find a way through the unrecognisable streets, both women were exhausted. They were already in a weakened state. Jane felt the pain of her injuries with each step she took, and Ethel was hindered by her fragile state of mind. Her grief affected her deeply. She stared at the ground and dragged her feet as they walked. Jane tried to lift her new friend out of the doldrums by keeping her chatting, but Ethel found the devastation of the city a terrible reminder of her very recent loss. They trudged on through streets of rubble, turning back and retracing steps many times when the roads became impassable.

Jane was feeling worn out. Her head ached, and she knew Ethel would be in desperate need of a rest. When she saw a vehicle emblazoned with the initials, WVS, she took Ethel's arm and steered her towards it.

"I think we've found St Paul's Gardens. That van is serving meals to survivors and workers."

Ethel managed a small smile. "I'm not hungry, but I could murder a brew, love."

Jane approached the back of the truck where two women were ladling a steaming liquid from a large tureen. She stood in line behind waiting firemen and people in unrecognisable, filthy uniforms who reached for the bowls in turn. Exhausted workers were resting on piles of bricks and broken paving to drink the soup.

"Can you spare some for us?" Jane asked when she reached the head of the line. "We're trying to get home, but it's taking us hours."

"Where's home, love?" one of the women asked.

Ethel took a mug from the woman. "Ta, love. I live on Valley Road. We've just been discharged from the Royal and can't seem to find a clear road through."

"You're just out of the hospital?" The other woman wrinkled her brow. "What you doing walking the streets?"

"We tried the trams, but they can't get through," Jane explained.

"It's hell everywhere, love," a young fireman sympathised. "Steer clear of Granville Road it's like a ploughed field, and last I heard there was an unexploded bomb near the railway line there. You'd be better heading for Bramall Lane. You should be able to cross the rail line farther down on London Road."

"Thanks, love. We'll try that way." Ethel dropped her pillowcase of belongings and sat beside the dishevelled men and women. "Come and take the weight off, Jane." She patted the hard ground beside her. "We have a long walk ahead of us. Better rest while we can, eh?"

The weary fireman nodded a greeting at Jane. "That looks nasty, love." He pointed to the bruising on her temple. "What happened?"

Jane didn't like to be in the spotlight. She shrugged and dropped to the ground next to her friend.

Ethel answered for her. "She was dug out of the Marples on Friday morning."

A few heads turned to stare at Jane, making her feel more uncomfortable.

The fireman's eyes widened. "You were in the Marples?"

Jane nodded. "So I'm told."

"I was working down there the night it got flattened. I didn't think anyone could have got out of there alive. You're very lucky, lass."

Jane tried to smile, but her lips trembled.

"She's still a bit shaky." Ethel put her arm around Jane and gave her a gentle squeeze.

"Is she your daughter?" the fireman asked.

Ethel froze, and Jane shook her head quickly, feeling the need to protect the older woman. "We're not related. Ethel lost her family that same night. We met at the hospital, and now we are helping each other."

The man frowned sadly. "I'm sorry for your loss, Mrs."

"I still can't believe I'll never see them again." Ethel wiped the sleeve of her coat over her face and sniffed. "Why did they bomb houses and shops? It doesn't make sense. Why did my lass and her little bairns have to die?"

"That's the way of war, love." The fireman stared at his dirty boots. "One minute I was standing next to me best pal, both of us holding the hose to fight the fire under the Wicker Arches, and the next I was blown off me feet. Couldn't see Will anywhere. Then I saw his body hanging from the top of a tram at the other side of the road."

"Oh, lad. You poor thing." Ethel reached out to the man. "You should be at home resting. You're in shock like I was."

"No, Mrs, I can't afford to rest. Got to keep working. Only way to keep from thinking about it."

"Aye, well, I know what you mean." Ethel glanced at all the other weary workers taking a short break.

A young ARP girl wiped her forehead with the back of her hand. "I heard the planes got the wrong targets. The bombs must have been meant for the steelworks."

An older man sneered. "Well, if that was the case, I don't see how they could have missed them. It was a clear night, and the moon was lighting up the foundries like it was daylight."

"They can't have meant to bomb civilians, though," the young girl insisted.

"Who knows what their orders were?" The older man snorted angrily. "Bloody Hitler could have told them to kill every last man, woman and child in Sheffield. Feels to me like they tried to."

The girl fell silent; her face pale between the streaks of mud and soot.

"Are you ready to head back, Sally?" another young woman asked the pale-faced girl. "We've had our half hour."

The two young women linked arms and began to trudge back into the ruins of the city.

"Them lasses deserve a medal." The fireman gazed after the girls. "Been working all through the night, they have. They've been clearing rubble from the roads with their bare hands so the trucks can get through to pick up the last of the bodies."

"You're all heroes in my book," Ethel told him.

"Just doing what needs to be done." The fireman got to his feet. "Like you two ladies are doing. Look after yourselves."

"You too, son."

Jane watched the young man stride away after the ARP girls and couldn't help feeling a shiver of guilt. What if she were somehow responsible for the devastation in Sheffield? Had she given information about the steelworks to the Germans? Did the Luftwaffe try to bomb the targets she'd told them of, or did they deliberately target civilians? She shook herself. No! It was impossible. Even if she were a spy, she wasn't heartless. She could never work for such an evil man as Hitler. She hated him!

Jane felt a shuddering chill trickle down her spine as her mind filled with a clear image. A group of youths in brown shirts were marching towards her. She was cowering against a wall, and they were chanting something. She could see their hate-filled faces glaring at her, and she was scared for her life. Part of her mind wanted to shut out the image, but the rational part tried to understand what she was recalling. What were they chanting? Why were they targeting her? The image vanished as quickly as it had appeared. What did it mean?

"Are you all right, love?" Ethel asked. "You were miles away."

"I think I just had a memory of something."

"That's good news. Dr Fisher will be pleased your memory is coming back. What did you remember?"

Jane shrugged. "Nothing of importance." She couldn't have tried to explain what she'd remembered. She didn't understand the mind pictures or the fear that accompanied them.

"Well, I expect most memories are about something and nothing, but when you have them, they all add up to something special."

Ethel had a faraway look in her eyes, and Jane guessed she was thinking about her family.

"And when you don't have any, the world can seem a scary place." She didn't like to admit her fear but felt she could trust Ethel with her feelings. The older woman was a kindly person. Even though she was grieving for her recently lost daughter and grandchildren; she could spare a thought for others and reach a helping hand to a stranger.

Jane had a fleeting sense of her mother. The emotion was of immense pride and admiration for the woman she felt in her heart, rather than remembered with her mind. "I have a feeling my mother was a tough woman like you, Ethel."

"I'm not tough, lass."

"You are," Jane insisted. "Look at you! I don't think many women would have lived through what you have in the last few days and still been standing, let alone have the strength left to help someone like me."

"Aye, well. As that young man just said, we're all doing what needs to be done to get by."

"And I need to get you home, Ethel. You look worn out. What way should we go?"

After more hours of walking and backtracking, the two women eventually reached Valley Road. Ethel clutched Jane's hand tightly as they skirted the huge crater where the air-raid shelter had stood.

Jane glanced into the large hole and was grateful to see that someone had cleared the grisly remains. The crater looked to have been swept clean.

Ethel put a hand to her mouth to stifle a sob. Her voice shook as she choked, "How can I have a funeral for them without their bodies?"

"Oh, Ethel." Jane put a hand on the older woman's shoulders. "Don't think about that now. I'm sure your neighbours will help you organise something."

"I don't have many neighbours left. They were all in the shelter, as far as I know."

"Which one is your house?" Jane asked as they walked along the bomb-damaged street.

"You see the three houses still standing in that row?" She pointed to some houses at the far end of the long street, with all the windows covered in sheets of cardboard. "Mine is the middle one."

"Looks as if someone came to cover the broken windows for you."

"It'll take more than a few sheets of cardboard to fix what the Jerries did that night." Ethel's face was wet with tears.

Jane linked her arm through Ethel's. "Let's go see what we can do, shall we?"

Ethel seemed reluctant to approach her home. "Give me a minute, will you, lass?" She leant against a lamppost. "I'm not ready to face that empty house yet."

"Are you all right, Ethel?" Jane was concerned about her friend. They'd already endured an arduous morning, and now Ethel was being painfully confronted by the reality of her lost family and damaged neighbourhood.

The older woman nodded and sighed. "Our Lucy came to live with me when her Albert joined up." Ethel dropped her chin. "If she hadn't, they might still be alive."

"You don't know that, Ethel."

"She asked if I'd help look after the children so she could do her bit for the war effort. She took a job at Vickers Works. My Lucy made parts for Spitfires, you know."

Jane nodded, letting the woman speak.

"Perhaps if she'd stayed in the house she rented with Albert, things would be different."

"Don't think like that, Ethel." Jane didn't know what else to say to comfort her friend. "You heard what people in the city were saying. It seems homes all over Sheffield have been bombed. Nowhere was safe."

Ethel's lips trembled. "Not even the shelters."

The older woman looked as if she might start crying again, so Jane urged her to walk. Valley Road was long, and she could see that before the raids, it would have had rows of terraced houses on either side. Now, there were large piles of rubble and solitary walls where houses had been. They walked past a water tanker on the other side of the road, where a small line of people were waiting to take a turn at filling various containers.

"Mrs Rowbottom! Is that you?" A woman of about Jane's age dropped her bucket with a clang and raced over the road. She flung her arms around Ethel and began to cry. "Oh, I thought you were dead!" She drew back to look into Ethel's face. "Where's Lucy and the bairns?"

Ethel shook her head and tears slipped from her eyes.

"Oh, no! Were they in the shelter?"

Ethel nodded. "I left them there when I went back home to get Shirley's teddy."

"Oh, love!"

"What did they do with..?" Ethel turned to stare at the crater. "Where did they take them, Edna?"

"Some soldiers from the barracks came to clear the remains. I'm not sure what's going to happen. They said something about a mass grave at the City Road Cemetery."

"No!" Ethel's eyes flew wide. "They can't do that to my Lucy and the children."

"Now, Ethel. Don't upset yourself." Jane put an arm around the woman's shoulders.

Edna looked at Jane with a frown. "Who are you?"

"She's my friend," Ethel explained. "This is Jane. We met at the hospital."

"I see."

"And you are?" Jane prompted, making an effort to lift her mouth into a friendly-looking smile.

"Edna Ellis. I work with Lucy at Vickers. That's my house over there." She pointed to a house with a hole in the roof at the other side of the street.

"I don't want my Lucy and the children in a mass grave. It's not right!" Ethel's voice began to shake. "I won't have it! Who do I have to talk to?" Her eyes darted around, searching for someone to answer her. "What do I have to do, Edna? I won't stand for it, do you hear me?"

Jane could see her friend was getting more upset and tried to calm her. She took the panicking woman by the shoulders and held her steady. "Look at me, Ethel. Listen to me." She waited for Ethel to focus on her face. "We'll find out who we need to see about this, but first we need to get you home. You need to rest."

"You won't be able to change their minds about that mass grave, you know," Edna aimed her warning at Jane.

"What makes you so sure?" Jane challenged her.

"They couldn't identify anyone from the shelter because all that was left was bits of them."

"We don't need to know the gory details, thank you." Jane knew Ethel had witnessed first-hand what remained of her family. The poor woman didn't need a reminder.

"They had to question all the neighbours to work out who might have been in there once they knew who was left."

"I could tell them some names," Ethel said, sadly. "I was only there a few minutes, but the shelter was full of folks I know, well, I mean... folks I knew." She sucked in a shuddering breath.

"Oh, you'd better let them know you're alive. I gave them your name, along with Lucy's and the bairns. When you didn't come back to the house, well, you know what we thought."

"I know." Ethel took another shaky breath. "Where were you that night, Edna?"

"Over at Mam's house in Norton Lees. It was her birthday, so we gave her a party. She's sixty, you know."

"Did the bombs drop around your mam's house?" Ethel asked.

"I'll say! We spent most of the night in Mam's cellar. The house came down above us, but we were safe in the cellar. By the time the wardens had dug us out, it was Friday teatime. I had to bring Mam back to stay with us. It's a good job our house was still standing, or we'd all be homeless. The soldiers helped patch up the roof so we can still live there."

"Your mam's birthday might well have saved your life, Edna." Ethel seemed to be regaining some control of her unstable emotions. "You'd have been in the shelter if you'd been at home, wouldn't you?"

"It don't bear thinking about. I'm so sorry, Mrs Rowbottom. You poor thing. Where have you been since that night?"

"They took me to the Royal. I was in shock. I didn't know what I was doing. I can't remember much about it."

"I can't imagine what you went through, love." Edna's voice was full of sympathy. "If there's anything I can do, just let me know."

Ethel sniffed and shook her shoulders back. "Who put the cardboard at my windows?" she asked, changing the subject abruptly.

"My Eddie. When the soldiers finished making the houses safe, our Eddie and his pals took it on themselves to clean up the empty houses that were left standing." Edna crossed her arms under her bosom. "I told him it was pointless if the owners weren't coming back, but he said someone else might be grateful for a tidy house. He said there'd be hundreds of homeless folks looking for a roof over their heads, and he was right. Social services have been sniffing around already." She looked pointedly at Jane. "My Eddie's got a lot of sense for a sixteen-year-old."

"What did social services want?" Jane asked.

Edna lifted her chin. "Don't you know?"

"Why should I?" Jane was beginning to understand that Edna thought she might be from the social services and smiled. It seemed people didn't trust the well-meaning organisation.

Edna shrugged. "Well, they wanted to know which houses were empty. I told 'em yours was vacant, but you'll have to let 'em know you're back, else they'll be after moving some homeless family in."

Jane could see Ethel's face was growing paler. "Perhaps we'd better get settled first, Ethel," Jane suggested. "We've had a long and tiring morning."

"I can see you've been injured yourself, love." Edna nodded, indicating Jane's bruised face. "Where did you get your war wounds?"

Jane didn't want to make herself the centre of attention again by mentioning The Marples. It seemed the whole of Sheffield knew about the fate of that building. "A bomb flattened the place I was sheltering in. It's the same story as many other people."

"Except, she can't remember who she is," Ethel added. "Poor lass lost her memory."

"But she knows her name, doesn't she?" Edna glanced at Jane suspiciously.

Jane shook her head and pressed her lips together in frustration. She didn't like strangers knowing her private business and had a feeling that if Edna had anything to do with it, she would soon be the talk of the neighbourhood.

"The doctors gave her the name of Jane Smith until she remembers who she really is. Until then, she's staying with me."

"You always did have a generous nature, Mrs Rowbottom. Too soft-hearted for your own good is what my mam says about you."

"Does she, now?" Ethel shook her head slowly. "Well, I haven't gone soft in the head. I know enough about this lass to understand that I need her as much as she needs me." She reached for Jane's hand. "Come on, love. Let's get home."

Chapter Six – In the Dead of Night

Jane found it difficult to sleep. The cold wind rattled through the flimsy window coverings, and she felt uncomfortable to be occupying the bed of her friend's dead daughter. Each time she drifted off, her dreams were populated by shadowy figures of her past and wispy ghosts of Ethel's family.

Eventually, she gave up on sleep and tiptoed downstairs. She stirred the smouldering embers of the fire and lit the Tilley Lamp. There was no electricity along the whole street, and water had to be collected from the tank on the road. Fortunately, she had brought some into the house earlier that evening. She put a pot of water to boil on the hot embers in the fire-grate.

Pulling the woollen dressing gown more tightly around her she realised Lucy must have been around the same size. Ethel had generously told her she could take whatever she needed from Lucy's wardrobe, and though she'd felt she was robbing the dead, she was grateful.

"She won't be needing clothes where she's gone." Ethel had sadly acknowledged.

The kitchen was full of flickering shadows caused by the low flames, but Jane found the gloomy room comforting. She felt safe and realised the feeling was not one she'd enjoyed much in her recent past. Fragments of her memory were tantalisingly close, but each time she felt she could capture them, they evaporated. She could sense she'd been in danger but couldn't pinpoint the threat.

The image of brown-shirted boys came back to her and in a flash of recognition; she suddenly knew who they were. She also remembered, beyond any shadow of a doubt, they meant to harm her. They were The Hitler Youth. Did they hurt her? What happened? Why did they hate her so venomously? She could see the hate-filled faces bearing down on her, but that's where the memory ended.

She huffed with frustration and went to pour the boiling water into a mug. She added a few tealeaves and put it aside to brew. There was no milk in the house, but she preferred to take her tea with lemon. She smiled in the darkness. Lemons were an unheard of luxury. When did she last enjoy a slice of lemon with her tea? How did she know she liked her tea that way? How could it be that her mind could recall a simple thing like that, but couldn't fill the blanks of more important facts of her life? Who was she? What was her name? Who was Gottfried? What was he, to her?

She picked up the mug and swirled the liquid before taking a sip. She picked a tealeaf from her lips and sat in the chair by the fire. Closing her eyes, she tried to think about the memories she *could* recall. The one involving the Hitler Youth was strongest, so she concentrated on the details she could bring to mind.

How many young men were in the group, she asked herself. Perhaps twenty or so? She thought about their faces. They were all shiny-faced youths with pale hair. Some didn't look old enough to shave. Their eyes held a rage of hatred, and they directed that fury at her. What were they chanting? She tried to think about their mouths, the shape of their lips, the rhythm of the words and the chorus jumped into her head.

"Schmutziges Mädchen Jude. Ihr eine Lektion erteilen." *(Dirty Jew girl. Teach her a lesson!)*

"I'm a Jew," she whispered and gasped. "I'm a German Jew."

Relief flooded through her. She couldn't be a German spy as she'd feared. A Jew would never work for Hitler and his henchmen. Hitler had persecuted Jews mercilessly since he came to power.

Snippets of memory jumped haphazardly into her mind. Waiting in line at the baker's shop, where people kept stepping in front of her. She didn't protest. The queue jumpers were Gentiles and more entitled to bread than she was.

She saw her Aunt Rebecca and Uncle Ezra climbing into a box car at the railway station with many other families. Each person carried a small suitcase. She clung to her father, who was crying and calling from the road. The crowd gathered outside the station were held back by soldiers with guns and dogs. She remembered trying to pull her father away. Danger permeated the scene in her head. She felt it in the sweat oozing from her pores. She was desperate to get away from the soldiers. How old would she be in that memory? When did Hitler come to power? When did he start sending people to labour camps? Where was her mother in that memory?

Another fragment of the past flew into her head, explaining the absence of her mother at the railway station.

Her father was holding her tightly in the doorway of an apartment building. The soft hiss of light rain accompanied her stifled sobs. She was listening to the dull thuds of boots on flesh as her mother was being kicked and beaten beyond the closed door.

"Why, Mamma?" Jane shuddered as the whole horrible memory clarified.

Her mother was being attacked for defying the young, brown shirted boys. They were enforcing the new law against Jews working in public offices, but her mother had been determined to go to work as usual.

Why didn't her father go to help? She remembered the heated argument earlier that morning. Her father had warned his wife not to leave their home. Her mother was not convinced that Hitler would get away with his irrational treatment of Jews. She firmly believed that their German Gentile friends would see sense and stand up to the bully. She was confident that her boss would allow her through the doors of the office across the street, and everything would continue as usual.

Hitler had been in power less than four months, but his law was all encompassing, and his followers were loyal to the extreme.

The memory of the brown shirts circled in her head. The memory rewound a few moments. The young men were taunting her mother as Jane cowered against the wall. She was calling out to her mother, pleading with her to turn around and come home.

"Don't go, Mamma!" she cried. "Please come back!"

The group of boys, not quite out of childhood, laughed at her and watched her mother stride across the road. They sneered at the stylishly dressed woman in high heels and began to mock her. One boy put his hand on his hip and sashayed mockingly behind her as she walked.

Her mother didn't flinch. She didn't respond to the taunts. She simply kept on walking to the office where she had worked as a clerk for the last five years. When she reached the door, she found it was locked. She knocked politely and waited.

Jane called out and pleaded once again for her mother to come back. She could sense the tension increasing in the street. The brown shirted boys turned to her, attracted by her pleading. One began to move toward her, chanting. "Dirty Jew girl. Let's teach her a lesson!" In seconds the group was marching beside him, like a swarm of starlings, they turned and headed in her direction.

In the next moment, her mother began to scream at the boys. "Leave her alone!"

At the same time, Jane felt hands reach out to snatch her from behind. Her father dragged her into the hallway and slammed the door, locking it against the baying crowd.

Jane shuddered. She remembered the whole incident now. The futility of her mother's defiance. The inhumane cruelty of the brainwashed boys. Her father's impotence as they sobbed together, listening to the vicious blows and accompanying shouts of abuse.

"Mein liebe," *(My love,)* her father breathed into her hair as he covered her ears with his hands. They clung together in the hallway. "Close your ears. Don't listen."

"Help her, father!" Jane had cried. "They're killing her!"

"No, my love. They would hurt us too. Your mother is strong, she will survive this. Her pride will be ruffled, but they won't kill her. They are boys. They will not have the heart to murder."

"Why don't you help her, Father?" Jane asked, repeatedly.

"I need to keep you safe. She would want me to protect you."

She struggled to escape his embrace, but he wouldn't let her go.

"They will turn on us if we go out there, my love. They would beat us too. You are too young to suffer such abuse, and I am too old. Your mother knew the risk she took. She will survive this, you'll see."

But Jane's mother did not survive. As her father reassured her in the hallway, her mother was dying in the street. By the time the young boys got bored with the sport and left, Jane's mother was beyond help. She paid the price of her defiance with her life.

Jane tried to remember more, forcing her mind to focus, but a kaleidoscope of unconnected scenes confused her and made her head spin. She slowed her breathing and stared at the embers in the fireplace. Perhaps if she could relax, the memories would be easier to see and feel. As much as she was reluctant to revisit her mother's death, she knew it was the only thing she remembered with any degree of clarity and thought she could use the memory as a starting point.

Jane's tea grew cold as she concentrated and more memories crystallised from fragments of images. The picture of her mother lying on the cobbled street, with her blood being washed away by the rain, was powerfully moving. Her grief felt fresh and raw, even though she knew the event happened years ago. She tried not to dwell on her sorrow and anger because she wanted to remember what her father did next. Did he lift her mother's body from the wet road? No, he knelt with her, weeping, holding her mother's limp hand. Other families emerged from apartment buildings. Some came to help, others to sneer.

Jane could not remember the mechanics of what happened next. She tried to imagine her mother being carried away but knew she was picturing what she wanted to happen rather than seeing what actually occurred.

When she relaxed again, hoping to bring the memory back, her mind hit a blank screen which instantly showed a different picture of a crowded railway station. Another image replaced the crowd with an unconnected image of her father weeping. The next scene to flash into her head showed a young woman screaming as she was being dragged away by two men with rifles hanging across their shoulders. She knew the woman, but couldn't remember her name. She felt she was a friend and the accompanying emotions were ones of fear and anger. The men each wore the brown shirts of the Hitler Youth, with red armbands emblazoned with a swastika.

Jane shook herself. The fragmented mind pictures were beginning to scare her. She knew about Hitler's persecution of the Jews. Anti-Semitism was rife in Europe, but nowhere was it as blatant and vicious as it was in Germany under Hitler's influence. The general knowledge of her home country and the recent history of world events were in her head very clearly. She wished her intimate memories could be as sharp.

Her personal memories seemed to be confirming that she was a German Jew, but she didn't feel Jewish. She felt sure she would remember being part of a Jewish family. She knew her mother had been killed because she was a Jew, but Jane didn't remember anything about being religious. Had she attended a synagogue? Was her father Jewish?

The memory of her aunt and uncle at the railway station returned to her mind. They were Jews. They must have been. She wondered what year it had been when they were forced to board that train. How long ago was that memory made? Why was her father not taken? Why was she an observer and not a victim? Why were the soldiers not pushing her to board that box car with her aunt and uncle? How did she escape the attention of Hitler's henchmen?

She still had so many questions. She wondered whether she would ever know the answers. Who was Gottfried? She sensed she had a deep affinity for the man behind the name. Or was it a boy? Could the name be that of a brother or a lover? The feeling of a close bond with the person was strong, but she couldn't bring the connection closer, no matter how she tried.

She saw her father in her mind's eye. He was sitting in an old rocking chair, in a room that felt familiar, but the emotion attached to the memory was not warm and cosy. She felt cold and afraid. A suitcase was by the door, and an old chenille table cover was pinned to the window frame. A cool breeze was blowing from the broken window. She felt fear and sadness, mixed with anger and resentment, but she couldn't remember what was happening in the memory. It felt important that she should know what this particular memory meant, but although she had a sense of urgency about the scene, she couldn't piece the whole memory together.

She took a sip from her tea and grimaced. The cold brew made her shiver. She pulled the dressing gown around her and made her way back up the stairs to her bed. Tiredness overwhelmed her and made her feet drag on the stairs, but she knew that sleep would not come easily. Now that her memory was beginning to return, she felt more adrift than she had before. Who was she? Why was she here? The memories that had surfaced didn't answer the most important questions she had. Those memories made her afraid of her past and more so because she couldn't share them with anyone in her present.

Chapter Seven – An Unexpected Revelation

"I brought you some tea, sleepyhead." Ethel pushed open the bedroom door and placed a steaming cup on the small bedside table. "It's getting late, and we need to get down to the social services offices to get your emergency allowance and then we have to go to the information services they set up in the library to get your ration books and replacement identity papers. We have a lot to do today."

Jane blinked a few times and pushed the eiderdown back. "Sorry, Ethel. I didn't mean to sleep so long."

"Don't you worry about it, lass. I heard you moving around downstairs in the night." Ethel gave her a small smile of sympathy. "That's why I let you sleep. Take your time. I'll make us some toast and dripping. Edna dropped some bread and a few bits in for us earlier. She knew we'd have nothing in the pantry but a few tea-leaves and some stale cheese."

"How thoughtful of your neighbour." Jane took a sip of the tea and grimaced. The brew much stronger than she liked it, but she didn't say anything.

"Edna is a good lass, but she's a bit of a busy-body. Don't you tell her anything that you don't want the whole neighbourhood to know in a matter of hours."

Jane laughed. "That's the impression I formed about her."

"Eeh, that nurse was right about you, Jane. You do talk posh for a Sheffield lass."

"Do I?" Jane felt her defences rising but then relaxed. She knew she was safe with Ethel. "I'll have to try to fit in more, won't I?"

"Don't be daft. You can't help your background, and anyway, talking posh might help us find your family."

"I wouldn't know where to start looking."

"Well, it's a good job for you that I have an idea where to start."

"You do?" Jane was surprised.

"Edna told me the Central Library has a list of missing people and another list of names of the folks looking for lost family members. We have to call there to collect your ration book and identity papers. They say the ration is going to come in after Christmas."

"You don't have to go into the city again." Jane worried about her new friend. Ethel might not be strong enough for another stressful trip into the bombed city. "If you give me directions, I could go alone."

"No, lass. I want to call at the City Road Cemetery and try to find out what's going on with my family's remains."

"Oh, I see." Jane sipped her tea, trying not to pull a face at the strong brew. She didn't want to offend Ethel.

"We can try to get some supplies in for Christmas. It's only a few days away, and I've nothing in the cupboards. Me and Lucy were going to take a trip into town to get some presents for the children when Albert's pay came in," Ethel faltered, blinked rapidly and tried to go on. "But, well... Now I'll have to write to tell him what happened. I don't know where to start with that one."

Jane knew Ethel was struggling to hold her emotions in check. She thought it best to distract her and threw back her bed coverings. "Well, give me a few minutes, and I'll be ready to enjoy the breakfast your friend was kind enough to give us. I can help you work on that letter when we get back from town."

Ethel pulled her shoulders back and lifted her chin. "Right you are, lass. I'll get breakfast ready, and we can be on our way in no time."

Jane watched the older woman stride from the room and felt a wave of sympathy for her. Ethel was enduring the worst pain a woman could experience, but she was very brave about it. A woman should not have to bear the loss of a child, and Ethel had lost her grandchildren and her daughter. How could she be so strong? Jane felt a jolt of emotional pain in her chest, and knew instinctively, that she had also known such pain. Did she have a child? Had she lost a child?

Jane touched her stomach tentatively. Had she once carried a child in there? Quickly, she lifted her nightdress to inspect her flat stomach. Were those silvery lines traces of stretch marks on her white skin? Had she been pregnant? What happened to her child?

Her eyes filled with tears. She had no memory of a traumatic event involving a child she might have had, but felt a deep and hollow ache of something missing. She felt she'd been a mother but had no memory of her child. She placed a hand on her belly, pressing lightly, trying to sense the presence of the memory of being pregnant. Nothing came to her, and she felt the frustration welling in angry waves. When would she remember who she was?

She sighed and opened the wardrobe. The cotton dresses hanging there would not offer much warmth against the bitter chill she felt blowing through the gaps between the cardboard and the window frame. She reached for a heavier woollen skirt, teaming it with a knitted twin-set for extra protection against the cold. She found no stockings in the drawers of the dresser, but she found ankle socks and some underwear.

She tried to work a brush through her hair, avoiding the bald and bruised area around the stitches on her temple. Her curls were now a matted bunch of frizz, and she found it too painful to work the tangles free. She replaced the dressing carefully. The headscarf she'd been given at the hospital would help to cover the unruly mess and the dressing. She would have to change her hairstyle to cover the scar eventually.

Ethel had breakfast ready when she went downstairs. The unappetising spread did nothing to entice her hunger, but she swallowed the bread with pork fat spread thinly and smiled her gratitude.

"Thank you, Ethel. This is just what I needed."

"There's more tea on the hearth keeping warm." Ethel pointed to the rich black brew in the mug. "There's no milk, but it's hot and wet."

Jane picked up the mug and saw the kettle nearby. "Is there more hot water in that?" She pointed. "I like mine a little less strong."

"Oh, that's good to hear." Ethel chuckled. "I thought all you posh toffs liked strong tea. I wanted to make you feel at home, but I couldn't have kept it up for long if they decide to ration tea as they threatened they might."

Jane laughed. "Oh, Ethel. You are an inspiration."

"Am I?" Ethel was still giggling. "Is that a good thing to be?"

Jane nodded. "It certainly is. You're so brave and kind and thoughtful. I think you and I are going to get along just fine."

Ethel's eyes glossed over and she blinked quickly. "If I half close my eyes, I can imagine you're my Lucy sitting there in them clothes."

"Oh, I'm sorry, Ethel. I didn't think. I'll go change." Jane jumped up. "I don't want to upset you. You must find it difficult to see me wearing her clothes. I'll wear what Miss Humphrey gave me. I'm so sorry."

"Don't talk daft, lass. That skirt fits you like a glove. You need clothes, and Lucy doesn't. You can dig out some of her shoes from the cupboard under the stairs. If you're lucky, they might fit."

"Are you sure?" Jane glanced to the small cupboard door.

"Go on, I'll clear these plates while you try some on."

Jane went to open the cupboard. She saw a basket filled with shoes and toys, and some coats were hanging on pegs at the back of the door. She reached into the basket and took out a tiny black shoe with a strap and button fastening. It fitted into the palm of her hand, and she knew it had belonged to Ethel's granddaughter, Shirley. Her heart missed a beat as she remembered holding a tiny foot in her hand. She'd been fastening a similar shoe to that foot in another life. She had a daughter. She felt it in her bones that she had a child. Where was she? Did she die? Is that why she felt such overwhelming sadness?

"Jane, whatever is the matter?"

Ethel was crouching close at her side. Jane hadn't noticed her approaching. She dashed the tears from her face quickly with the back of her hand. "I'm sorry, I saw this and thought of your loss. I couldn't help feeling your grief. I know I shouldn't have touched it."

"Give it here, lass." Ethel took the small shoe in her hand. "I don't mind seeing the reminders. I don't want you tiptoeing around me. I need to cry, and I need to talk about them. I can't let them go, you see." Ethel's face was wet, but her voice was strong.

Jane got to her feet and put her arms around the older woman. "You cry as much as you need to, Ethel. You don't have to be strong for me."

Jane added her tears, and the women sobbed together as they held each other close. Jane cried for the daughter she had but couldn't remember. She couldn't confess her recently reclaimed memory. She couldn't add to her friend's pain, and Ethel couldn't help with the confusion she felt. Nothing would be gained by admitting her own loss. She wouldn't be able to explain what had happened to her child because she didn't know.

"Eeh, aren't we a right pair of cry babies?" Ethel pulled away and wiped her face on a dish towel. She handed the towel to Jane with a weak smile. "Did you find some of our Lucy's shoes?"

Jane shook her head as she wiped her tears. "I'll take another look." She quickly pulled out a stout pair of women's ankle boots and bent to put them on. "They're a little tight, but I'll get used to them."

"We have a fair bit of walking to do," Ethel reminded her. "Perhaps you'd be better wearing those shoes the social services lady gave you. They were comfy, weren't they?"

Jane realised Ethel was right. "I'll go get them." She took off the ankle boots and ran upstairs. Her heart was still pounding from the shock of realising she had a child. Now she was desperate to know more about her past. Was the child dead? What happened to her daughter?

Chapter Eight – Unsettling Encounter

They walked for more than an hour around the city outskirts to get to the City Road Cemetery, only to find disappointment. Nobody was there to answer Ethel's questions about the fate of her family's remains. The site warden directed them to the coroner's office in the city centre.

The walk into the city was less eventful than Jane expected. Most roads were now passable, and some shops had opened for business. The people of Sheffield were getting on with things as best they could.

The queue outside the coroner's office surprised them, but they stood patiently, waiting to be seen. Eventually, they reached the door to the building where Ethel gave her name and the reason for her visit. She was then given an appointment for later that afternoon.

"Well, I suppose that will have to do for now." Ethel had grumpily agreed to keep the appointment. "At this rate, we'll be spending the whole day walking from pillar to post trying to get things done."

"We don't have anything better planned, Ethel," Jane had pointed out. "We're both in limbo, aren't we?"

Ethel nodded and sighed. "Let's cut through here." The older woman guided her down a side street, and Jane began to recognise some places, from the route they'd taken the previous day. "I don't know about you, but I'm hungry," Ethel patted her stomach.

Jane smiled as the WVS truck came into sight. They took advantage of the mobile soup kitchen in Saint Paul's Gardens again. Ethel offered a few pennies to the serving volunteers, but they declined her offer. "We're all in need, love," the young woman told her. "Save your brass."

The soup kitchen was not as busy as when they'd previously passed through the gardens, but a few unhappy souls were sitting around in the cold, sipping from steaming bowls and mugs. After a short rest, they set out to the Central Library, a few streets away.

The inside of the library entrance was busy with people lining up at desks or wandering around staring at sheets of names pinned to walls.

A few boarded-up windows and a large crack on the marble floor were evidence of the recent bombing. They found the queue of people applying for replacement ration books.

Jane handed over the forms that Miss Humphrey had given her and soon had a temporary identification card and ration book in the name of Jane Smith.

"I don't think I'll ever get used to my new name." Jane stared at her identity card and realised that she'd experienced the same feeling before. Had she been given a different name in the past? Had she changed her identity, once before?

"What is it, love?" Ethel touched her arm.

"Nothing," Jane put the cards in her coat pocket. "It's strange to see the odd name in black and white."

"Well, try not to let it get you down, eh? We're in the right place to start searching for your family."

"I can't believe there are so many people here. There must be hundreds missing and unaccounted for." Jane stared at all the people milling around, peering at lists of names on the walls.

After reading a few names on a list of missing people from the Attercliffe area, Jane sighed heavily.

"We'll never find anything at this rate." Ethel tugged at Jane's sleeve. "Without a name to go on, we'll need a bit more help, don't you think?"

"It would help if there were descriptions with the names." Jane shrugged. "I mean, surely, if you understood the logistics of this mess, you'd know enough to give a short description of the missing person, wouldn't you?"

"Well, I think I know the meaning of what you just said, lass, but not everyone has lost their memory, so why should they think to add more than a name?"

"I suppose you're right." Jane felt she wouldn't get anywhere in her search. She didn't even know whether anyone knew her in Sheffield. Anyone who *did* know her would be looking for her real name on a list. As she didn't know her name, she couldn't add it to any list.

"Perhaps you could look at the lists of people searching for their families," Ethel advised with a tight-lipped smile of encouragement. "You never know, you might see a name that jumps out at you."

Jane sighed with frustration. "Needles and haystacks come to mind, Ethel. I can see hundreds of names on these walls."

"Can I help you, ladies?" An elderly man carrying a clipboard asked. "Are you looking for someone?"

"We're hoping someone is looking for this young woman." Ethel nodded at Jane. "But she lost her memory and doesn't know her name, so we're in a proper pickle, aren't we?" The older woman gave the man a friendly smile.

The man raised his brows and nodded. "That does pose a problem, but we have some people here who like a challenge." He grinned. "Come with me." He beckoned them to follow him.

The round-faced man took them to a desk by a window where a smartly dressed elderly gentleman and a colourful young woman were reading some papers. "Mind if I interrupt you two for a minute?" he asked.

The young woman took off her wire-rimmed spectacles and smiled at the man. "What can we do for you, Charles?"

"This young lady has lost her memory, and wondered whether anyone might be looking for her."

The elderly gentleman at the desk pushed his chair back and got to his feet. He held out his hand. "Hello," he said. "I'm Bernard Crossland, and this is Hannah Rosenberg."

Jane took his hand and felt a small thrill of recognition on hearing the name of the young woman. Hannah and Rosenberg were Hebrew names. "Hello," she said, trying to keep her voice steady. "I can't tell you my name, I'm afraid, but I've been given the temporary identity of Jane Smith for now." She turned to Ethel. "This is my friend, Ethel Rowbottom."

Ethel quickly shook the man's hand. "Can you help her?"

"Take a seat, ladies." He indicated two chairs by the desk. "Thank you, Charles."

The round-faced man gave a jaunty salute to the man behind the desk and winked at Jane. "You're in good hands, love."

"Thank you." Jane watched him walk toward an elderly couple who were staring around aimlessly and looked confused.

Ethel sat on one of the chairs and took Jane's hand. Jane smiled nervously and sat beside her.

"No need to be afraid, Miss Smith." Mr Crossland took his seat. "Though, I expect it can't be pleasant to have lost your memory. You must feel a little unsettled."

Jane nodded and tried to relax. These people seemed kind, and she hoped they could help her.

"Let me take a few details, first." The young woman pulled a sheet of paper from a pile on the desk. "Formalities, I'm afraid. Let's get them out of the way quickly. We'll call you Jane Smith for now. Where are you living at present?"

Jane answered the questions and Ethel helped when Jane didn't know the answers. When the official form had been completed, the young woman turned the sheet over and smiled brightly.

"Now, what can you tell us about yourself?" Miss Rosenberg adjusted the brightly coloured shawl around her shoulders. "We know you don't have a name, but is there anything you *do* remember? She held a pencil poised over the blank reverse of the form. "Anything at all?"

Jane shook her head. "I'm sorry. The few memories I have are jumbled and don't make much sense to me."

"You'd be surprised, Miss Smith," the man said. "Even the smallest detail might be important."

"You remembered about your mother, didn't you?" Ethel reminded her and turned to the young woman. "She knows her mother died a few years ago, and she knows she's twenty-five."

"Well, that's a good start." Miss Rosenberg tucked a strand of her tightly curled red hair behind her ear and wrote something on the paper. "We know we're looking for a twenty-five-year-old woman with dark-brown hair and brown eyes. She's around five feet six?" She looked at Jane for confirmation.

Jane shrugged. "I think so."

"Good." She continued writing. "Slim build," she glanced at Jane's hands. "Possibly unmarried, probably did an office job and comes from a well-to-do family."

"How can you get all that from just looking at her?" Ethel looked impressed.

"It's not difficult, Mrs Rowbottom." The young woman pulled her spectacles to the edge of her nose and peered over the rims. "Her ring finger is bare, but has the signs of a ring being worn there at some time in the past." She turned to Jane, "Perhaps you have been married but aren't married now?"

Jane shrugged. "I know I wore my mother's ring. I don't know where it is now?"

"Well, your hands are scratched and bruised, and some of your nails are broken, but your skin is smooth, and you have no calluses. That tells me you didn't work in heavy industry."

"My Lucy had sore hands all the time," Ethel explained. "She worked at Vickers."

Hannah smiled and nodded. "You'll have noticed that Jane's speech patterns are different from yours, too."

"Yes, we worked out she was more posh than me while we were in the hospital."

Hannah scribbled something else. "Well, I'll have to listen to her speaking a little longer to be certain." The woman stopped writing and lifted her eyes to Jane. "But I'd say you're probably from one of the wealthier areas of town, and from what I've heard so far, I'd put my money on Totley."

"Eeh, that's clever of you." Ethel turned to Jane. "Fancy! We've been here only two minutes, and this young lass already thinks she knows where you come from."

Jane swallowed nervously. She knew she didn't come from anywhere near Sheffield and began to feel if she spoke much more, the woman might pick up her real origins.

The elderly gentleman got to his feet. "Does Totley mean anything to you?" he asked Jane.

She shook her head.

"Well, I'll see what we have listed from the Totley area. You never know. You might recognise the name of someone who registered a missing person from there."

She watched him cross the room and felt apprehensive. What if someone *was* looking for her? Would they know of her past? Would they know she was German? Would they be friend or foe? Would they mean her harm? How would she know? Who could she trust?

The young woman interrupted her scary thoughts. "Is there anything more you can tell us?" She adjusted the gaudily patterned shawl on her shoulders.

Jane shook her head again. She was afraid to speak. If Miss Rosenberg could pick out a particular dialect of Sheffield, it would be only a matter of time before she would detect her very slight German accent.

"How did you get to be so clever, lass?" Ethel asked the young woman. "You're good at this sort of thing."

Miss Rosenberg smiled. "I've had a mixed upbringing. I lived in many places as a child, and I got an ear for languages and speech idioms. I've lived in Sheffield for the last eight years, so I'm in tune with the locality. The rest is simple observation."

Jane felt compelled to ask where the woman was from, but stayed silent. She didn't want to give anything away. She was surprised when Ethel asked the question that was on the tip of her own tongue.

"Where are *you* from, then?"

The girl didn't hesitate to answer, but Jane heard a defensive tone in her voice.

"It might surprise you to know I was born in Russia but lived in Austria for some years before coming to England."

Ethel looked startled. "Hitler comes from there!" she blurted.

"I know." Miss Rosenberg tossed her curls over her shoulder. "But please don't think less of me for that. I have more reason than most to despise that man."

Jane detected a flash of anger and pain in the woman's eyes. She wanted to reach out a hand of comfort. She felt a kinship of sorts with the stranger, but fear held her hand and her tongue.

"Here we have it!" The man came back with a few sheets of paper in his hand. "I got the Totley list, and ones from a few other areas that might be relevant." He gave the papers to Jane.

"What should I do?" Jane asked quietly and carefully, conscious of betraying her foreign accent.

"Simply read the names on the list and see whether any have meaning for you." The man resumed his seat. "These names are people looking for family members who didn't come home to Totley on the nights of the bombings. Then we can go through the ones from Sharrow and work our way through the rest after that."

Jane began to scan the first list of names. She thought she was wasting her time, but went along with it because she couldn't think of anything else to suggest, and she didn't want to talk, from fear of her true nationality being discovered.

After a few minutes, she glanced at the flamboyant young woman and shook her head. She spoke quietly and slowly, concentrating on pronouncing her words as correctly as she could. "I can't see how this will help. I don't see any names I recognise."

"Try the Sharrow list," the man encouraged. "Take your time. There's no rush."

Ethel smiled and nodded. "My appointment at the coroner's office isn't for another hour or so."

Mr Crossland wrinkled his brow. "That sounds ominous."

"My family were killed on the night of the twelfth." Ethel took a deep breath and went on, "I heard they were going to put them in a mass grave and I want to stop them from doing that."

Jane reached to take her hand. She knew her friend would be upset. From the little she knew of the woman, she could see Ethel was bracing herself on the inside, even though her outward appearance was calm.

"I'm sorry for your loss." Mr Crossland gave Ethel a sympathetic frown. "You ladies are having quite a traumatic time of it, aren't you?"

Ethel nodded stoically and lifted her chin high. "We'll get by." She turned to Jane. "Carry on looking, lass. It's not much, but it's all you've got. Make it count."

Jane took heart from the older woman's brave attitude and turned her attention back to the list of names. She dropped the first page on the desk and began to read the next one. She read a name and moved on to the next, but quickly looked back at the previous one. 'Godfrey Robinson' seemed familiar, but she couldn't be sure. Her heart was singing Gottfried Rubinstein, and the similarity was ringing bells in her head.

Common sense told her that this couldn't be the same man, but her mind exploded with recollections of the man she had such a strong connection with. Wave after wave of fragmented memories made her dizzy with their intensity.

She was in his arms, and they were both weeping. She felt his warmth as they embraced, and the feeling in her heart was one of intense affection and longing. Another shard of memory showed him striding away from her as she begged him to stay. She couldn't see his face. He was tall. He was strong. He left her! Why did he leave her? Why did he change his name? She knew the man had changed his name to Godfrey Robinson. She'd changed her name too, but her own names were out of reach. Who was she? What was the meaning of these memories? Why could she only see frustrating scraps of her past?

Who was this man? Was he a lover? Perhaps he was a brother? Could she be recalling the name of her father?

She put a trembling hand to her aching temple. When she glanced at the man sitting opposite her, he was looking concerned.

"You recognised a name, didn't you?" he asked.

She nodded, not trusting herself to speak.

"Did you remember something, love?" Ethel asked.

She nodded again and looked at the name. This was a man she was close to; she felt sure. The man in her head was named Gottfried Rubenstein, but she knew the name had been changed to protect his identity. Pre-war Britain was not only anti-Semitic, but Germans were also distrusted. Her name had been changed too, but even though so much was tumbling into her mind, she still couldn't remember who she was.

"Are you all right, Miss Smith?" The young woman asked. "You look as if you've had a shock. Would you like some water?"

Jane nodded.

"What did you remember?" Ethel asked. "Which name did you recognise?"

Jane realised she had to be careful. She couldn't trust her memories. She was still so unsure of everything. What if this man was not who she thought he was? She could be reading too much into a simple name. If the man left her, why was he looking for her now? *Was* he looking for her? Had he given her name? She looked at the sheet and read Godfrey Robinson again, resting her finger on the name, she read the name of the missing person beside the entry. Grace Robinson. Was she Grace Robinson? She didn't recognise the name. Grace meant nothing to her.

Perhaps this person was not the Gottfried she held in her memories and in her heart. How would she ever know the truth?

She decided to be brave, like Ethel. The road to self-discovery was scaring her, but she realised she wouldn't get anywhere until she took the first step.

She pointed to the name as she passed the sheet of paper to Mr Crossland. "I'm not certain I remember everything correctly. I can't trust my mind. This man might not know me. He could be a stranger. My memories aren't clear." She was talking too quickly, trying to explain her uncertainty. She closed her mouth, realising that the young woman had returned with the glass of water and was listening intently.

"I'll cross-check the interview notes." The man pushed back his chair and stood.

"You interviewed this man?" Jane began to understand how thorough these people were being. "What did he look like?" She felt, if she could picture the man, she might have a better understanding of whom he might be. "What does he look like? How old is he?"

Mr Crossland shook his head. "Sorry, but there are lots of people working here, and we all help each other. That's why we take notes. Give me a minute to find them, and I'll soon have some answers for you."

Miss Rosenberg handed her the glass of water.

"Thank you." Jane took the glass with a shaking hand.

"Isn't this exciting?" Ethel patted Jane's hand. "You might be back with your family sooner than we expected."

Jane detected a note of disappointment in the older woman's voice. She didn't want to leave Ethel alone with her grief. "Don't worry, Ethel. I'm sure it will take some time to let this man know I've been found."

Jane glanced at Miss Rosenberg for reassurance, but the young woman had a strange expression on her face.

"Is something wrong?" Jane asked quickly, without thinking.

"No!" the young woman responded just as rapidly. She seemed to take a second to gather her composure and then spoke more softly. "You are quite right, though. We planned to send letters out to people who are searching when we find a match, but that could take weeks with how things are at the moment. We decided yesterday that we should treat each case as we see fit and perhaps give what information we have, as and when we can."

"Will you give my details to this man?" Jane asked, beginning to fear what might happen if her memories were guiding her in a dangerous direction.

"No, he probably won't return here. He'll be waiting for a letter of confirmation that you are among the injured at one of the hospitals, or that your remains have been discovered."

"Oh, my goodness!" Ethel gasped. "That's awful!"

"We'll probably give you the address he left with us, and you can take it from there."

"Thank you." Jane was beginning to notice the woman seemed on edge. She was twisting the pencil between her fingers, fussing with her shawl, and her eyes kept glancing at Jane.

"I'm sorry, but I have to ask," Miss Rosenberg blurted. "Were you born in this country?"

Jane felt her whole body stiffen with fear. "Why do you ask?" She tried not to sound too defensive.

"I thought I detected a slight throaty tone to some of your words. In my experience, it could be the accent of a European language." She paused, looking for some response, and when Jane stayed silent, she shrugged and went on, "But it might just as easily be the remnants of a childhood speech impediment."

Jane relaxed a little and tried a tremulous smile. "I wish I could answer your question, but I really have no idea."

The elderly Mr Crossland returned, carrying some papers. His smile looked promising, and Jane's heart skipped a beat. She watched him take his seat, willing him to speak.

Ethel seemed just as impatient and blurted, "Spit it out! What have you found? You look like the cat who found the cream."

"Does the name Grace Robinson mean anything to you, Jane?" he asked.

"I read the name on that list." Jane inclined her head to the papers in his hand. "It was written next to the name of Godfrey Robinson." She didn't want to talk too much. She couldn't afford to give Miss Rosenberg any more evidence of her German origins.

"Is Grace his wife?" Ethel asked. "Or perhaps it was your dad who came looking for you, love."

"Apparently, Mr Robinson was looking for Grace Robinson. She worked at The Marples."

Ethel gasped. "Oh, my goodness! That's where they found you!"

Jane flinched. Could she really be Grace Robinson?

"Is that correct, Miss Smith?" Miss Rosenberg prompted.

Jane nodded but couldn't speak. She was trembling all over, remembering her experience. Waking up in a tomb of rubble and spending hours drifting in and out of consciousness had been the most frightening experience of her life. She had since recalled more scary and dangerous events and was beginning to understand that whoever she might be, her life had not been easy.

"Well, well." The elderly gentleman smiled warmly. "From what we know of that place, there were few survivors, and they are still recovering bodies from the cellars. Unfortunately, most can't be identified, so I think your relative will be in for a welcome surprise to know you are indeed, alive and well."

"That's if I am his relation." Jane was still unsure. The name had leapt out at her and triggered a random set of memories, but she couldn't be certain the fragile connections were proof that she knew the man.

"I wonder why you weren't reported among the casualties." Miss Rosenberg asked. "How very remiss of your rescuers."

"I believe one entry might be referring to you, Miss Smith, or should I call you, Miss Robinson?" Mr Crossland flipped through the papers in his hand. "Here it is." He pulled out some dirty and crumpled sheets of paper. "Unfortunately, all we have are these scraps of notes. One of our team is working on putting these hastily scribbled records in some kind of order, but until then, this is all we have." He smoothed the crumpled paper on the desk and ran his finger down a list of entries. "Here we are. Unidentified person. Removed alive. Taken to the Royal Infirmary." He lifted his head. "There are no more details. Not even the sex or approximate age of the person." He glanced at Jane. "I'm sorry, but it looks as if they didn't expect you to live, from the scant information given here."

"I don't remember much about getting out of there." Jane felt a shiver run down her spine. She knew she'd had a lucky escape. "I couldn't tell them my name. I didn't know where I was or who I was." She could feel her fear beginning to get the better of her and Ethel took her hand.

"You're safe, love. It's all over." Ethel squeezed her fingers gently. "You're here with me. You're safe."

Jane took a deep breath and gave her friend a grateful smile.

"What happens now?" Ethel asked.

"We can put you in touch with this man, and you can take it from there." Mr Crossland passed a sheet of paper to the young woman at his side. "Would you write down the address, Hannah?" He turned back to Jane. "If he *is* your relation, the story will have a happy ending, and our job will be done."

"And if he isn't?" Jane asked. "What if I'm wrong? My memory can't be relied upon."

"The interview notes state that Mr Robinson was looking for a relation. She worked at The Marples Hotel, behind the bar. The description he gave matches you, from what I can see. His relative is tall and slim with dark hair and eyes."

"He's right, lass. It has to be you." Ethel turned to the elderly gentleman. "What do we do next?"

"Well, if I were you, I'd go to this address as soon as I could. Your relation must be very concerned about you." He took the paper from Miss Rosenberg and gave it to Jane.

She glanced at the address but didn't recognise it. "Thank you."

"You've been very helpful." Ethel got to her feet. "Come on, Jane. We still have a lot to do if we want to get to that address before dark."

"I hope things work out for you." Mr Crossland watched them as Ethel gathered her bag and gloves.

Jane moved without enthusiasm. She wasn't sure she was ready to see this man. She didn't know him. Not really. The emotional connection felt strong, but she'd remembered him leaving her. He'd walked away from her, leaving her weeping and afraid. What had happened? Why did she feel so afraid?

The young woman came around the desk and took Jane's arm. "I'll walk you to the door."

Jane felt the firm grip of Miss Rosenberg's hand on her arm. She caught a trace of the woman's perfume as she guided her from the building. Ethel walked ahead, making a path through the milling crowd in the large hall.

The young woman leant close. "I know you are from Germany," she whispered. "Losing your memory is a very convenient cover."

"I don't know what you are talking about!" Jane tried to pull her arm away.

"Miss Smith, or Miss Robinson, or whoever you are, I could have you arrested right now, so calm yourself and listen to what I have to say."

Jane stopped quickly and yanked her arm from the woman's grip, turning to face her. "I'm listening."

"Being a German is difficult in this country," Miss Rosenberg whispered. "Being a Jew is difficult in any country. Being both is impossible, especially in Germany."

Jane felt her knees might give way they were shaking so much. "How could you know I'm either of those things?"

"We are alike, you and I, Jane. You are fortunate that I am possibly the only person in Sheffield who could recognise your Jewish features and connect them to your particular accent. You must have had a good language teacher. You hide your true nationality well."

"What will you do?" Jane felt her chest flood with adrenaline. She wanted to run. She didn't want to be arrested. She knew she wasn't a spy. She was no threat to Britain.

"Meet me later. You could be of use to me."

"And if I refuse?" Jane's voice sounded much braver than she felt inside.

"I have your address, and that of your relative, if he *is* a relation of yours."

Ethel was standing outside the open doors of the building, waiting and staring at Jane with a puzzled expression.

"I have to go." Jane began to walk to the door.

"Be at the Crown Inn on Chesterfield Road at eight tomorrow night. It's around the corner from where you are staying on Valley Road."

Jane nodded and continued walking. Her legs were shaking so much she was in danger of falling over. What was happening? Who was Hannah Rosenberg? She glanced back in time to see the woman's voluminous skirts swirl out of sight. Was she a possible friend or a dangerous enemy? Could the young woman be a spy? She said she'd been born in Russia and lived in Austria. Jane shook her head. Was she a Jew? No Jew would become a German spy. It was impossible.

Chapter Nine – Surprising Proposition

Jane didn't like to leave Ethel alone, especially after the time they'd had. The poor woman had been told the day before that her family would have to be put in the mass grave as planned. When the tactful clerk explained why a personal burial would be impossible, Jane had supported Ethel while the woman sobbed in her arms. Her friend already knew the harsh facts but that didn't make hearing the gruesome clarifications any easy to bear. The bodies in the shelter had been so badly disintegrated that one could not be separated from the rest. Ethel had been inconsolable.

Jane had helped her walk back from the city, and then made some soup from a bag of vegetables they'd bought on the way home. It wasn't much, but neither woman was hungry. They'd retired early, exhausted from the long walk.

Today, Ethel seemed morose. Jane had tried to get her to talk, but the older woman was keeping her sorrow inside. She couldn't be encouraged to do anything, and Jane began to worry about her. She had to meet the girl from the library but didn't want to leave Ethel alone. Jane waited until Ethel seemed more settled before telling her she would be going out.

"Are you going to see your relative?" Ethel asked.

Jane shook her head. "I'm not ready to face a man I don't remember. I'm hoping some more memories might come back to me first."

"Don't wait too long, love. He'll be worried about you. Poor man must be out of his mind."

"He might not be related to me, Ethel. He could be a complete stranger, for all I know. Having me arrive on his doorstep would not be pleasant for him if that is the truth of it."

"But if you *are* his relative," Ethel's eyes glowed brightly in the firelight. "Just think how happy he'll be to see you."

"Perhaps I'll go tomorrow, in the daylight." She reached for the flimsy coat the social services had given her. "Are you sure you'll be all right for a few hours this evening?"

"But where are you going? You don't know your way around, and you don't know a soul in these parts."

"I don't know a soul anywhere, Ethel," Jane pointed out. She smiled and touched the older woman's shoulder. "I need some space to think, that's all."

"Aye, well, I know that feeling. Take our Lucy's red wool coat. It'll be warmer than that thin thing the social services lady gave you."

"Are you sure?"

"Be a shame to leave it in the cupboard for the moths to get. My Lucy won't be needing it."

"Thank you." Jane went to take the coat from the cupboard under the stairs. "It's almost too beautiful to wear."

"Nonsense. Albert bought it for her last birthday. It's a lovely coat. It's a bit bright for my tastes, but it's only a coat."

Jane put her arms in the sleeves and drew the coat around her shoulders. It fit perfectly. She fastened the buttons, cinching it close to her waist, and couldn't resist turning on her heel to see the wide hem lift and swirl around her calves. "I don't think I've ever worn anything as lovely as this." Even as she said it, she realised she was lying. She had owned some beautiful clothes when she lived in Germany. The chips of images faded as quickly as they had appeared in her head.

"I'll leave the door on the latch for you. Don't get lost."

"I think I'll remember my way back here, Ethel." She tied the headscarf over her head, tucking the ends under the fabric at her chin. "Don't worry about me. I'm a big girl."

Jane felt vulnerable to be leaving the security of her friend's house alone. Her insides were in knots, but she was determined to take charge of the parts of her life she was sure about. She couldn't allow her fear of the unknown to control her. Until she could learn more about whom she was and why she was here in England, she would trust nobody.

Jane had the address of a man in her pocket. That man might, or might not be her relative. She had decided not to meet him until she could remember more about her relationship with him. Her memories were coming back slowly. She felt this man was important, and believed she would soon remember more about him. If she could remember his face, she would know immediately if the man at the address was who she thought he was. Without a face, he could be anybody.

She was on her way to meet a woman who she believed was a Jew but had nothing more than Hannah's name to base that conclusion on. Hannah Rosenberg had seemed pleasant enough until she threatened her with arrest if she didn't agree to meet her. What did she want? She couldn't afford to ignore the young woman's threats. She didn't want to be arrested. She didn't think she'd done anything wrong, but without her memories, she couldn't be absolutely sure of that.

Her curiosity was aroused. Who was Miss Rosenberg? Why was she here, in Britain? If she were a Russian Jew, why was she working for the English civil authorities? Was she a volunteer, or did she have paid employment? She seemed bright and well educated. Miss Rosenberg certainly had powerful observational skills. How did she end up working for the local authority in Sheffield?

Jane slowed her steps as she remembered what her own occupation had been. The earlier conversation with Mr Crossland at the Central Library had thrown some light on what she did for a living. The elderly gentleman had said Mr Robinson gave information about her place of work and occupation. A barmaid? She couldn't picture herself as a barmaid. Why would she be employed to serve drinks when she knew she was capable of much more?

She saw the familiar image of a lecture theatre again in her mind. She knew she had studied at a university. Languages. She studied languages. She remembered she spoke French fluently and tried the sound of the language on her tongue. "Parlez-Vous Français?" she giggled. Another phrase slipped into her head. "Sai parlare Italiano?" Apparently, she knew Italian equally well.

'Why would I work in a bar?' she thought to herself as she walked.

She saw the outline of the large public house on the corner of Chesterfield Road. Heartened by the recollection of her linguistic skills, she pushed open the door and strode confidently to the bar.

"A small glass of stout, please," she asked the barmaid, instinctively remembering that she liked the taste of dark ale.

"Been in a fight, have you, lass?" The young woman tipped her head and pointed to Jane's temple.

"With a German bomb," Jane quipped, and pulled her headscarf down to cover the dressing.

"There's a few more like you around here, more is the pity." The barmaid gave her the glass of stout she'd poured. "Bloody Jerries have a lot to answer for. My Stevie will give 'em what for, you mark my words. We're getting married on his next leave."

"What does your Stevie do?" Jane asked to be polite, and handed over some coins.

"He's a navigator on a Wellington. We're all proud of him! Fancy! He was only a milkman afore he joined up."

Jane smelled a familiar perfume from the young woman who came to stand next to her at the bar.

"He was always a clever man, your Stevie," the fragrant woman said.

The barmaid grinned at the newcomer. "Hello, Hannah. What can I get you?"

"I'll have the same as my friend, please."

Jane didn't know what to make of the young woman. Hannah Rosenberg was obviously known to the barmaid. If she knew the barmaid's sweetheart, she must have lived in these parts for some time.

"Take that table in the corner." Miss Rosenberg indicated a small, empty table away from the bar. "We won't be overheard there." She turned to the barmaid to take her drink and hand over some money. "Thanks, Emma. Tell your dad those cabbages were very tasty."

"Ta, I will."

Jane was bemused. The woman had threatened to have her arrested earlier, but in here, she was everybody's friend. Her earlier decision to trust nobody came to mind. She couldn't afford to let her guard down, no matter what happened. She watched Hannah carry her glass to the table. The young woman was not wearing spectacles, and Jane realised she was strikingly beautiful. Her flame-red hair cascaded in tight curls from beneath a floppy blue-velvet beret, embroidered with red roses. She wore the multi-coloured shawl around her shoulders that Jane had seen her wear at the library. Her navy coat swirled and swayed as she walked across the room to set her glass on the table. Hannah unfastened her coat and pushed her hair back from her face with the grace of a film star. Jane realised she was staring rudely and dropped her gaze.

"Relax, Jane. I'm not an ogre."

Jane was nervous and snapped. "I'll relax when I've got proof of your true nature."

"Listen, I'm sorry I had to come over all heavy handed, but be honest," Hannah's tone sounded playful. "Would you have agreed to meet me if I'd acted all sweetness and light?"

Jane jumped to answer. "I might have."

"You were like a rabbit in the beam of a flashlight, Jane. When you weren't frozen with fear, you were jumping at shadows. I can't blame you. I think I'd be the same in your shoes."

"You know nothing about me!" Jane was beginning to feel uncomfortable and a little afraid of what this woman might know.

"It's my job to know things. You'd be surprised how much I can tell about you. You saw my party tricks at the library. That was child's play."

"Who are you?" Jane decided to get to the point. "And what do you want of me?"

Hannah shrugged. "No need to get prickly. I want to be your friend. I have a feeling you can help me."

"How?"

"Well, I'd need to get to know you more before I tell you that."

"What do you want to know? I lost my memory, so there's not much I can tell you."

"Speak to me in German."

Jane huffed. "Not possible! Do you think I have a death wish?" She glanced around the pub. It wasn't busy, but there were a few customers around that were close enough to overhear.

"Just whisper a few words. Pretty please!" She clasped her hands and pleaded childishly.

Jane leant close to Hannah's ear and whispered, "Zur Hölle fahren und lass mich in Ruhe." *(Go to hell and leave me alone).*

"Hamburg!"

"What?"

"You're from Hamburg. Strange choice of words, though. They were not very friendly."

Jane quickly glanced around to make sure no other customers had heard.

"How can you tell where I'm from in those few words?"

"What can I say? I'm a clever girl. Am I right?"

"I don't know. I speak French and Italian, would you like to hear me speak in those languages? Perhaps you'll think I'm from Paris or Rome."

"I'm not that good." The young woman giggled. "I'm not as familiar with those places as I am with Germany and Austria."

"That's good to know." Jane was relieved to hear the woman was not perfect.

"I know what will settle your nationality for certain."

"Oh?" Jane waited.

"What language do you dream in?"

Jane sighed. The girl was good. "All right, you've got me there," Jane admitted. "I know I'm German, but that's the only thing I know for sure."

"So it's true, you *have* lost your memory?" Hannah looked surprised. "I thought you were using that as a cover."

"A cover for what?" Jane didn't know what to make of the young woman, but she kept her guard up.

"You aren't from around here; that much was clear to me from the moment I saw you. Even the way you wear your clothes makes you foreign in my eyes."

"What's wrong with the way I wear my clothes?" Jane was beginning to get worried.

"Oh, don't get cross. Nobody else would notice."

"Notice what?"

"The way you tie your headscarf and tuck the ends under the knot."

"Lots of women do that." Jane wasn't convinced.

"Not the exact way you do. I bet your mother taught you to do it that way."

"Leave my mother out of this." Jane was beginning to get angry. Hannah was mocking her.

"I'm sorry. I've obviously hit a raw nerve. How did your mother die?"

Jane's mouth dropped open. "How did you know she was dead?"

"Your body language. The shadow in your eyes when you spoke of her. Your defensive stance. What happened?"

"She was murdered."

"By the Nazis?"

Jane nodded. She couldn't bring herself to speak of it.

"I'm sorry. I won't tease you again." Hannah leant back against her seat and sipped her drink. "You'll do."

Jane felt she'd passed some kind of test. "What do you want of me?"

"You have the classical looks of a Jewish girl. Am I right? Are you a Jew?"

Jane shook her head. "I don't know. I think my family might be Jewish."

"If you are Jewish, you'll know in your heart. I don't think it's something you could forget."

"I forgot my name!" Jane felt confused and angry. This woman clearly didn't understand her problem. "I don't know who I am and I didn't know where I came from until you just told me and even now I can't be sure you're right because I have no memory of being there." Jane stopped to take a breath. The woman was infuriating. "How can you expect me to know how I worship or what God I pray to?"

"I'm sorry. I have no idea how it must feel to lose your memory, but I can see you are frustrated as hell."

Jane smiled tightly. "You can say that again."

"I'm going to be honest with you, Jane." Miss Rosenberg put her elbows on the small table and leant across the table. "I'm putting my trust in you, and I hope by doing so, that you will also begin to trust me."

Jane waited, wondering what the woman was going to say.

"All right, here goes."

Hannah Rosenberg's eyes made contact with Jane's as she began to speak, making her feel uncomfortable but at the same time, she felt an honest earnestness in the quietly spoken words.

"I am a Jew and all my family were Jews. I was born in Russia when Jews were being blamed for everything in that country. See, some things never change, do they?" She paused and took a sip from her glass.

Jane waited.

Hannah put her glass down and continued. "The last war was declared when I was a few months old. My father was drafted into the Russian army and left us for the duration. Jews were good cannon fodder." The young woman closed her eyes and reached to take another a sip of her ale.

"Was he killed?" Jane asked.

Miss Rosenberg shook her head. "No, he came back to us when the war ended. Life was not easy. He'd fought alongside Russian soldiers, but he was never their equal. His time in the army taught my father that Russia was not the place for our family to thrive."

"Where did you go?"

"When I was five, we fled to Poland. A year later, Papa tried to settle us in Romania. By the time I was seventeen, I had lived in six European countries and been forced to flee from all of them because of anti-Semitic attitudes and bullying. My father made a bad choice in turning to Austria for refuge in thirty-one. I was hoping to attend the University in Salzburg." She glanced quickly at Jane before returning her gaze to the glass in her hand.

"Why Salzburg?" Jane asked.

"Papa knew some people there. Apparently, life was good for the Jews of Salzburg. As it turned out, it was! For a time. I enjoyed the freedom to think, as I had never done before. I joined debating societies, attended the festivals and took the entrance examination for the academy. I hoped to study languages and philosophy."

Jane felt a shiver of recognition. Those were subjects close to her heart. "What happened?"

"Hitler came to power and swept my dreams away. He hypnotised his followers. He brainwashed them to uphold his inhumane laws and crushed us like beetles. You must remember how such treatment made us feel!"

Jane nodded. "My strongest recollections are of the Hitler Youths beating my mother when she defied them and tried to go to work."

Hannah Rosenberg reached to take Jane's hand. "We are the lucky ones, Jane. You and I escaped."

Jane blinked back her tears. She didn't want to draw attention to herself. "When did you come to England?" she asked.

"I arrived in thirty-three with a group of young Jews. My father stayed to help others who couldn't get away."

"What about your mother?"

"My mother died when I was fifteen. See, we have a lot in common."

"I'm sorry."

"Don't be. It was a long time ago. What is happening now is more relevant, don't you agree? Some of my friends have been in hiding since Austria was declared part of the German Reich. Some were discovered and taken to the labour camps. We get scant news about them, so can't be sure whether they are alive or dead."

"I have an aunt and uncle who were sent to a labour camp."

"Which one, do you know?"

"Sorry, if I did know, I don't remember."

"It must be terrible to have no memory."

Jane nodded and sipped from her glass.

"Would you mind telling me what you *can* remember?"

Hannah Rosenberg's story had made Jane feel sympathetic to the young Jewish woman, but she couldn't forget how she'd threatened to have her arrested. "Why would I do that? You could use it against me and have me arrested."

Hannah shook her head. "I'm sorry, I'm sorry, I'm sorry." She held her hands up in surrender. "How many times do you want me to apologise. I would not betray you. You have my word."

"Your word means nothing without my trust."

"And you still don't trust me after I told you my story?"

"It's not personal. I don't trust anyone." Jane tried to smile confidently, but her lips felt stiff. "Try being in my shoes. You wouldn't trust anyone either."

"You trust your friend, Ethel."

"That's different. She's a good woman."

"I'm a good woman!"

"Prove it, and I'll begin to trust you." Jane suppressed a smile. She was beginning to like the unconventional woman. They had a common history and similar experiences, but she still wouldn't allow herself to trust her.

"How can I prove my good intentions?"

Jane shrugged. "Tell me why you wanted to meet me. You must have something in mind."

Hannah sighed and took a few seconds to respond. Eventually, she looked into Jane's eyes and said, "I want you to come back to Germany with me."

Jane shook her head. "No! It would be suicide."

"Not for two intelligent girls such as we are."

"Why would you want to go back to that hell? You just spoke about how lucky we are to have escaped. You know how they treat Jews in Germany!" She quickly glanced around to make sure she'd not been overheard.

"That's why I want to go there. I want to help bring Jewish families to safety. My father is still in Salzburg and doing his best to get false papers and travel documents for as many as he can."

"He's a brave man. Doesn't he know the authorities would have him shot if they discovered what he is doing?"

"He does, but he's not the only person risking everything to stand up for what is right."

Jane felt a flicker of unease. Hannah's words were striking chords in her heart. Something important was tickling the edges of her brain but stayed frustratingly out of reach.

Hannah was still talking, and Jane gave up chasing vague memories and focused on her words.

"So far, I've only given money to the cause when I can, but I want to do more. We could easily work undercover in Germany. With the right papers and cover story, I think we could be very useful."

"What could we do?" Jane asked. "We have no training, no skills in espionage. You're asking me to become a spy."

"Not a spy, Jane. We won't be acting against Germany, or for Britain. We'll be helping our fellow human beings to escape the tyranny of oppression, enforced labour and worse."

"You're serious about this, aren't you?"

"We don't need specialised training." Hannah was talking faster, urging Jane to understand what she was proposing. "Don't you see? With our language skills, my intuition and observation, we would make an excellent team. We are bright young women. I've asked to be more involved before, but with you at my side, I don't see how they could refuse another request."

"Who are 'they'?"

"The organisation I belong to. I told them about you, and they are keen to meet you."

Chapter Ten – Nightmares

Jane let herself into Ethel's home much later than she'd planned to. Hannah had talked for hours about her idea to help the Jews in Germany and Austria. Jane felt like a fish out of water, and because she still couldn't trust her own judgment, she declined the offer to meet the woman's friends.

"Perhaps when I'm recovered a little," she'd told Hannah. "My physical wounds are still healing. I wouldn't go unnoticed in Germany, looking as I do now, would I?" She'd pointed to the dressing on her head. "This wound would instantly raise questions from border guards and Storm Troopers. We wouldn't be safe."

"I didn't mean that we would go to Germany immediately." Hannah had looked hopeful. "We will need time to prepare. It could take months before we can be put in place. Please say you'll consider helping us."

Jane had left with a promise to think about Hannah's idea and made arrangements to meet her the Thursday after the New Year to discuss it further. She climbed the narrow staircase to her bedroom and listened for sounds from Ethel's room. A soft snore reassured her that the older woman was asleep and probably hadn't suffered too much from being left alone for a few hours. She quickly changed into her nightdress and jumped into bed, pulling the blankets up high to get warm.

As she lay shivering, waiting for the bed to warm from her body heat, she went over the conversation she'd had with Hannah Rosenberg. The young woman was persuasive and ardent about her cause. Throughout the evening, Jane couldn't shake the feeling that she was, or had been, involved in a similar organisation. That niggling itch at the edge of her mind couldn't be ignored any longer. Something from her hidden past was trying to break through. The shadowy man she had an emotional connection with, had something to do with the evasive memory, she was sure of it. If she could remember him clearly, perhaps the rest would come.

She slowed her breathing as she began to feel warmer and concentrated on the name of the man she had recalled. Gottfried Rubenstein. She pictured a tall young man. He was older than she was, with fair hair and blue eyes, but she quickly realised he was a figment of her imagination. He had no substance. Her mind was bringing him to life, to fill the void. He wasn't real. She shook her head to clear the image.

"Who are you, Gottfried Rubenstein?" she whispered to the darkness.

She drifted to sleep thinking about the man, and wondering why she could feel the essence of him deep in her heart but couldn't picture him.

Sleep shrouded her thoughts, giving her blissful respite from her worries. Close to dawn, she began to dream.

Cobbled streets and dark alleys filled her head. Someone was chasing her. Danger was fuelling her fear. The narrow streets gave way to open countryside. With nowhere to hide, she was exposed. They could see her. She began racing to a forest on the horizon. Bullets whistled past her ear, but she continued to run. The trees would be her refuge.

She couldn't stop. She couldn't allow them to catch her. If they caught her, she would die. Her heart and legs were pumping; her terror was so intense in her mind that she was startled into wakefulness, but the dream continued to play in her head.

The sun was still below the horizon and she couldn't see clearly, but she tried to focus on her surroundings. The open countryside of her dream became faded wallpaper, and the sound of whizzing bullets became the milkman's tuneless whistle as he made his doorstep deliveries.

"Eeh, lass. What happened?" Ethel hurried into her bedroom.

"Sorry, did I wake you?" Jane realised she must have been making some noise in her dream.

"Don't feel bad, lass. You've been through the mill good and proper. It's no wonder you're having bad dreams."

"How do you know about the dreams?" Jane asked.

"You woke me with your yelling."

"Sorry."

"No need to be sorry, love. I was glad to wake from my own dreams. Seems we both had nightmares, eh?"

"You too?"

"Yes, me too. How about we go downstairs for a brew?"

"I'd like that, Ethel."

Jane was still trying to shake off the lingering remnants of the nightmare and was glad to get out of bed. Movement reinforced her reality and helped to push the bad dream away. She followed her friend into the kitchen and began to set the table for breakfast.

"I never had such scary dreams before."

"I'm sure you did when you were little." Ethel put the kettle to boil.

"But I'm no longer a child. I..." Jane suddenly remembered another bad dream she'd had in her past. She was an adult. She was eighteen, and her mother had been murdered the day before. She'd dreamed someone was knocking on the door of the apartment building. Boots were running up the stairs. She called out to her father. She gasped and put a fist to her mouth.

"What is it, love? Have you remembered something else?" Ethel turned from the fire.

"I remembered another nightmare I had some years ago."

"Did you yell out?"

Jane nodded. "Why can I recall a dream so clearly and not remember the real events of my past?"

"Sounds as if you've had a few frightening things happen to you. From the way you were shouting, I think your dreams must be very bad, love. Want to talk about them? It might help."

Jane shook her head. She couldn't explain her deepest fears to Ethel. She was only just beginning to understand them herself.

"What about you, Ethel? What were your dreams about?"

"Oh, you know." She sighed. "The bombing and the crater. I keep seeing those bits of meat and I know I shouldn't dwell on what I saw, but I can't get it out of my head. In my dreams, I try to put the bits together. It's horrible, but I'm trying to make my Lucy and the children whole again." Ethel lifted her apron to dab her face.

"Oh, Ethel." Jane went to hug her. "That sounds worse than anything I could imagine. Your dreams are horrific."

"Aye, it's a wonder we both don't have sore throats with all the yelling and screaming we do in our sleep at night." The older woman tried a watery smile. "Come on, this porridge is ready. Let's eat while it's still warm."

Jane ate the tasteless oats, planning in her mind what she intended to do with her day. She'd begun to realise that cowardice and fear were her enemies. If she were going to discover anything about herself, she would have to take action. Her first step should be to visit the address of Godfrey Robinson.

"I thought I'd try to organise a glazier to fix the windows today." Ethel looked at the curtains swaying in the chill breeze. "We can't live like this for much longer. We'll die of frostbite in our beds if the weather turns icy again."

"I want to help pay for the repairs, but the allowance from social services won't go far, Ethel." Jane didn't like to live on charity, but for the moment, she had no choice.

"Well, perhaps you could look for a job when you feel up to it. Vickers is always hiring, and I know they'll have one job going."

"Lucy's job?" Jane sighed. "I'll think about it, Ethel, but I don't think I'm up to hard, manual labour yet." She stretched to ease the stiffness in her back.

"Oh, yes, that reminds me." Ethel jumped to her feet. "I need to look at that dressing on your chest."

"Finish your breakfast first, Ethel. My war wounds can wait."

"You don't complain much, lass. That head must still be aching and you've done all that walking without so much as a moan."

"What good is moaning? I won't heal any faster by complaining, will I?"

"That's the spirit." Ethel collected their empty bowls and took them to the sink. She reached for the paper bag of dressings she'd been given at the hospital. "Lift up your nightdress, let's have a look."

Ethel worked gently, inspecting the wound and applying a fresh dressing. When she was happy with her handiwork, she pulled down Jane's clothing. "There, you'll soon be good as new. The scab looks dry, and the swelling is gone. Just like your head."

"I still look a sight, though, Ethel. I think I need to do something about my hair to cover the scar. What do you think?"

"Mm." The older woman put a hand on her hip and turned her head one way and then the other, looking at Jane's face. "Perhaps you could comb that side over the bald bit and clip it near your ear. That would work for now, but goodness knows what you'll do when the hair grows back."

"Did Lucy have any clips?"

"I have some hairpins somewhere."

"Will you look for some whilst I wash the dishes?"

When the chores were done, Ethel helped Jane tidy her matted hair.

"Are you sure you don't want me to come with you? It's a long way. I don't want you to get lost."

"I'll find my way, Ethel. I have a tongue in my head and I'll ask directions if I need to."

"Sorry to fuss, lass. I know you're a grown woman."

"I'm glad I have someone to care about me." Jane patted the woman's shoulder. "I don't know how long I'll be, but I'll see you later today."

"What if he turns out to be your relation? You'll want to stay, won't you? You'll have found where you belong."

"I'll still come back to let you know, Ethel. We're friends. No matter what happens today, that won't change."

"Thanks, lass. I'm glad to hear that. You've been a godsend to me."

"And you to me." Jane hugged her briefly. "I'll see you later, good luck with finding someone for the windows."

Chapter Eleven – Truth Revealed

Ethel had given her directions to Sharrow, but her friend didn't know that area well and couldn't tell her how to get to Priory Road. Jane set out along Valley Road, heading for the public house where she'd spent the previous evening.

The doors at The Crown Inn were closed, and as she passed, she wondered what she might say to Hannah the next time they met. She wanted to help. She had a strong feeling about the young woman's proposal, but her fear and uncertainty held her back. Until she knew more about herself, she didn't dare agree to such a dangerous exploit. She understood she'd escaped Germany once. Why would she want to endanger herself by going back there?

As she walked, she began to imagine what kind of reception she might get at the address she clutched in her fingers. Was this man a relation of hers? Was her scant memory serving her well when she thought Gottfried had changed their names? If he were now living as Godfrey Robinson, had she been using the identity of Grace Robinson? She concentrated on the surname that meant most to her. Rubinstein. Was she a Rubinstein?

No matter how hard she tried, the memories wouldn't come. She seemed to have a blockage in her head. Small fragments leaked through, giving her tantalising glimpses of her past, but she couldn't build a whole picture from them.

After half-an-hour, she reached Sharrow and asked the first person she saw for directions.

"What number did you want, love?" the old man asked. "It's the long road that crosses the end of this one we're on."

"Thanks, I'll find it." Jane didn't want to let anyone know exactly where she was going. She didn't know what she might find when she got there. She might be heading for a big disappointment, or she might find the truth about who she was. She didn't know whether she was prepared for either eventuality.

Glancing at the paper to check which number she was looking for, she walked to the end of the road. It didn't take her long to find the house. It stood surrounded by gardens, set back from the road behind a low brick wall with a small wooden gate. She took a breath and pushed the gate open.

Staring at the windows, criss-crossed with white tape, she hoped to see someone looking back at her, but nobody came to see who was walking up the path. She reached the brown painted door and rapped her knuckles on the wood. The house sounded hollow and empty. She waited a few seconds and knocked again.

"There's nobody in, love!" A woman called from the street. "Are you looking for Mr Robinson?"

Jane turned and nodded at the woman holding the handle of a pram. "Yes," she called. "Do you know where I can find him?"

"Oh, it's you, Grace!" The woman looked startled. "We thought you were dead."

Jane felt her knees go weak, but she forced her legs to move and walked back down the path. This woman knew her. She'd called her Grace. She tried to smile but found it impossible. "I'm sorry, do I know you?"

"I live next door with my grandmother. You remember my Patricia, don't you?" The young woman looked into the pram. "We've been so worried about your Godfrey. Poor man was beside himself. We all thought you were dead."

"Oh, I see." Jane didn't know what to make of the information she was getting from the young woman. "Do you know where I might find him?"

"Sorry, love. He left after the second night of bombing a few days ago. He told my grandma he had no reason to stay after you'd gone."

"He thought I was dead?"

"You worked in the Marples, didn't you? He talked with my grandma after he came back from looking for you. The people at the library said only seven men walked away from that building. When he knew there was no chance you'd survived, he was really upset."

"But I did survive! Why would he leave?" Jane felt desolate. She'd been so close, and now the man had gone. She might never know who she was. Her insides cramped with a cold, icy dread.

"Eeh, Grace. You poor thing. Would you like to come home with me? I'll get Grandma to make us some tea. You've had a bit of a shock, haven't you?"

The baby in the pram began to cry. Jane felt a strange sensation in her breasts, and an overwhelming urge of curiosity made her peer at the infant. "How old is she?" she asked.

"Three weeks." The woman frowned. "Patricia was born at the end of last month, don't you remember? You gave me a cardigan you'd made for her."

"Did I?" Jane's head was reeling. This woman seemed to know so much about her. "I'm sorry, I had a bump on the head, and my mind isn't working properly yet."

"Oh, Grace! What a time you must have had. Come with me. You need to sit down. Here, hold the pram for support."

Jane took the pram handle, grateful to hold onto something solid, but a flash of memory caught her off guard, and she let go quickly, feeling she'd been stung. "Oh, my!" She knew she had pushed a similar pram before.

"What is it, Grace?" The woman took her arm. "You look terrible. Let's get you inside."

Jane allowed the young woman to guide her down the path to the house next door. They left the crying baby in the pram, and the woman pushed Jane into the large hallway. "Gran! Come quickly!" she yelled. "Grace has come back!" She turned to Jane. "Sit there. Gran will come in a minute. I have to get Patricia."

"Thank you." Jane gratefully sat in a chair next to the large front door. She didn't think her legs would support her for much longer. Memories were flooding through her mind so quickly that she felt dizzy.

Touching the pram had startled her. She'd once pushed a similar pram on the street outside of her apartment building in Germany. The sound of the baby crying had made her breasts tingle and ache. She knew she had fed a baby. Her baby. She knew beyond any shadow of a doubt that she was a mother.

She had a vision of pushing a baby into the world. She remembered holding the infant to her breast. Was it still alive? Where was her daughter? The child had been a girl, she was sure. The feeling of sorrow was overwhelming, but she didn't think the child had died. She would remember the death of a child, surely! Why couldn't she recall the whole memory? Why was her mind teasing her with snippets?

"Grace?" An elderly woman came into the hall, peering at her quizzically. "Is it you?"

Jane turned her face to the old woman.

"Oh, Grace!" She held out her hand to Jane. "What happened? Where did you disappear to? Godfrey thinks you died in the Marples."

"Where is he?" Jane asked, hoping the old woman might know.

"Sorry, my dear, he didn't say much. You know what he's like. Always a man of few words."

"Will he return? Do you know where he went?"

The front door opened and the young woman came through holding the crying baby in her arms. "Put the kettle on, Grandma. I think Grace is in shock. She went white as a sheet, and I thought she was going to fall over."

"Of course, come through, Grace. Where are my manners?"

Jane rose on shaking legs and followed the old lady through to a parlour. The room was over-warm with a blazing fire in the hearth.

"Take off your coat," the younger woman advised. "She always has it red-hot in here."

"If you had old bones like mine, you'd be grateful we can afford the extra coal." The old woman pursed her lips. "I'll go make the tea so you can get on and feed that mite. She's bawling so much I can't hear myself think."

"Thanks, Grandma."

Jane watched the younger woman settle into a chair and lift her blouse. The baby stopped crying as soon as she found the nipple. Jane was mesmerised. Her breasts tingled with the memory of feeding her child. How old would her baby be? Where did she go? What happened to her child? She instinctively clutched a hand to her stomach and held the moan of anguish deep inside.

"What happened, Grace? Were you in the Marples? How did you get out? Where have you been since that night?" The young woman adjusted her clothing as the baby continued to suckle. "Sorry, I shouldn't pry, but it's just, well, you can understand how we feel, surely? We thought you were one of the bodies they couldn't identify. Godfrey thought so too."

"Did you talk to him?" Jane asked hopefully.

"No, he spoke to Grandma. Like I said, he was a quiet sort, wasn't he?"

Jane had no idea what sort of man he might be, but she nodded. She didn't know what to say. She had so many questions, but asking them would raise more questions in the young woman's mind that Jane wasn't ready to answer.

"Here we are." The elderly woman brought a tray of tea things into the room and placed them on a side table. "I opened that bottle of port you bought, Sandra. I know you were saving it for Christmas, but this poor lass looks as if she needs something a bit stronger than tea."

"You're very kind." Jane took the small glass and sipped the syrupy liquid, feeling warmth flood her icy insides.

"Feeling better?" the old lady asked.

Jane nodded. "Yes, thanks."

"You'll want the key, I expect." She reached behind the clock on the mantelpiece and handed Jane a large key. "Godfrey left this with me to give back to the landlord, but it's your home too, so now you're back, you might as well continue to live there. Godfrey said the rent is paid up to the beginning of January, so you don't have to worry about that for now. You'll have to look for another job, won't you? What with the Marples gone, like that."

Jane wondered why Godfrey would leave a key, and then the truth hit her. "He didn't intend to come back, did he?"

"Well, he thought you were dead, love." The old woman began to pour tea into some china cups. "He said he didn't have a reason to stay here. They won't be having separate funerals for the unidentified bodies. There's going to be a mass burial. He didn't want to hang around waiting for that to be organised."

"He didn't stay long enough to make sure I was dead!" Jane's voice broke on a sob, but she took a breath and kept her frustration inside. "Why would he leave his address at the library if he didn't expect me to be found?"

"Lots of people are searching for missing family, Grace." Sandra looked up from the baby at her breast. "The raids took so many lives and some of them won't ever be found. They told the same thing to Godfrey, didn't they, Gran?" She glanced at her grandmother for confirmation.

The old woman nodded. "I think they convinced him that there was no chance you could have survived. You worked in the bar at the Marples, and that was enough evidence, as far as the authorities were concerned. If you didn't walk away from that building, you must have been dead, in their eyes."

"I was pulled out of the rubble the day after the bombing. I lost my memory. I didn't know who I was, so my name wouldn't have been on any list. I was classed as an unidentified person. They didn't even record that I was a woman. People at the library said my rescuers probably didn't expect me to survive." Jane took the cup of tea from the old lady. "Thank you."

"Perhaps you were discovered after Godfrey had been told you were dead." The old woman shrugged. "We're at war and these things happen in war."

"So you couldn't remember your name or anything?" Sandra asked. "How awful for you. You must be able to remember now, though. You came home, after all."

Jane knew this was the opportunity to confess her lack of memory, but she didn't want these kindly women to pity her more than they already did. "I remember some things more clearly than others," she began and then decided to be honest. She had nothing left to lose. "I don't remember living here, and I still don't recognise the name you're using when referring to me. 'Grace' sounds strange to my ears."

"Well, that's who you are, lass." The grandmother sipped her tea. "That's the name I've known you by, and I've known you the last two years."

"Two years?" Jane was surprised. "Are you telling me I've lived here two years?"

"That's right. You came over from Holland at the end of thirty-eight. Your dad wanted to get you out of Europe. After what happened in Germany in that November, well! It's a crime what's happening over there to the Jews."

"My father was here?"

"Oh, goodness, Grace!" The old woman looked anxious. "You can't tell me you don't remember about your father?"

Jane shook her head, but even as she denied the memory, it cascaded into her head. Her father was dead. He died in her arms of a heart attack shortly after arriving in Sheffield. She could see his grey face staring up at her while she cradled him in her arms. His struggle for breath was agonising to watch, and help didn't come soon enough. "He died in my arms." She felt the pain as keenly as if her father had died in the last few minutes. He was gone, and she would never see the elderly man again.

"Have some more, love." The old woman poured another measure and held out the glass.

"No, thank you." Jane knew she had to keep a clear head. She had more questions teaming into her mind. Did she bring her child here? "Who else lived in the house with me?"

"There was just the two of you after your father died."

"We rented the house?"

Sandra nodded. "From Mr Goldsmith. He owns lots of houses around Sheffield."

"What did Godfrey do? I mean, where did he work?" Her mind was racing. Perhaps he still worked in the same place, and she could find him there.

"He worked at Hadfield's steel works." Sandra fussed with the baby, moving her to the other breast. "Did long hours, too. He was never home."

"Not that you complained, love. You worked long hours as well, didn't you?"

"Will Godfrey be at work now? I should go to Hadfield's and find him." Jane made to get up.

"Wait, love." The grandmother raised her hand. "He won't be there."

"How do you know?"

"He told me he couldn't stay in Sheffield. He was moving on. He doesn't work at Hadfield's any longer."

"Where did he go?"

The old woman shook her head. "He didn't say. Poor man was heartbroken. He thought the world of you, you know."

Jane couldn't believe what she was hearing. She felt she was listening to the details of a stranger's life. She had to know more. "I know this will sound an odd request, but I'm feeling a little out of my depth here. You're talking as if I should know the things you are saying, but I don't. My memory is far from complete, and I wondered whether I could ask you something."

"How terrible for you, my dear." The old woman frowned sympathetically. "Ask away. We'll help all we can, won't we, Sandra?"

Sandra nodded.

Jane closed her eyes for a second and then asked her question. "What do you know about my family?"

"Well now," Sandra lifted her chin. "I have to say, we don't know very much. You two mostly kept yourselves to yourselves."

"You liked your privacy." The old woman gave her granddaughter a look of disapproval. "Nothing wrong with that."

Jane turned to the grandmother. "But Sandra said Godfrey spoke to you."

"Now and then, he did, but he wasn't known for his conversational skills. He spoke English well enough, but not as good as you, my dear. We know you much better than we knew Godfrey."

"You say we came from Holland. Would you say I was Dutch?"

"That's what your father said." The old woman nodded emphatically. "You lived in Rotterdam, but your father was afraid that you wouldn't be safe there. After Hitler had come to power, he said Jews all over Europe were afraid for the future. When Germany sent troops into Austria, your father said that would only be the beginning. He was a wise man. He was right, wasn't he?"

Jane remembered what Hannah had said to her the previous evening. She'd been in Austria but had left long before Hitler took control of that country.

"My father died soon after we arrived, didn't he? How long did you know him?"

"Perhaps a month or two." The old woman looked thoughtful. "He seemed a sad man. I believe your mother was much younger than he was, but she died some years ago, didn't she?"

Jane nodded. She felt sure these women would not know the full horror of her mother's death. More memories of her mother and father crept softly into her head. The romance of a Gentile in his late thirties falling for a younger Jewish girl melted hearts when it was spoken of in family circles when she was growing up. Her mother's parents had been against the union, but her father had made promises and charmed them into submission. He had loved her mother very much.

Why did he stand by, while she was being beaten to death, she asked herself? Because he loved me too, was the answer she knew in her heart. She experienced intense feelings of guilt with the memory. She felt it was her fault that her father didn't try to save her mother. He was afraid for his daughter's safety. The fanatical boys had already threatened her before turning on her mother.

"Grace, are you all right, love?" The old woman's concerned face loomed in front of her. "You seemed miles away."

"I was thinking about my parents."

"He seemed like a good man, your father."

"Yes, he was." Jane felt a wave of grief but swallowed it down. She had to know more, and these two women were the only ones who could tell her anything. "So, as far as you know, there was only myself and Godfrey living here?"

"People came and went. You had lots of friends passing through."

"Did we?"

"Foreigners, like you." Sandra pulled the sleeping baby from her breast and fastened her blouse. "Not that we thought anything of it, well, not until last year when we went to war. Some neighbours thought you were German spies, but Grandma put them right, didn't you, Gran?"

"I knew you were from Holland, and I told anyone who wanted to know that we had nothing to fear from you. Holland is on our side! The authorities knew all about you, so I couldn't understand what they were afraid of."

"What did you say about the authorities?" Jane's inner warning bell began to ring. "What did they know about us?"

"Well, just after you arrived, your father reported to the local police and offered his services to the country. That's what he told me, and I've no reason to doubt his word. He seemed a man of honour, from what I could tell."

"What about Godfrey and me? Did we offer our services too?"

"I presume so. Godfrey took a job working in munitions. I think he wanted to join the army, but the paperwork got held up or something."

"You wanted to join up too, but you had the same problem."

"Something amiss with the paperwork?" Jane asked, suddenly realising that their papers would not be in order. Their true identity papers would be German documents. Any Dutch identities her father might have procured would be false and couldn't be submitted for fear of discovery.

Sandra rocked her baby against her shoulder, patting the little one's back. Jane felt a rush of longing and knew she had to ask what was uppermost in her mind.

"Were there any children with us when we arrived?"

Sandra shook her head sadly. "No, you weren't blessed, love."

"What do you mean?"

"You didn't have any children. I think you would have liked a baby. You really doted on little Patricia when she came along. I felt sorry for you while I was pregnant."

Jane felt a sharp pain in her chest. She knew she would have been longing for her own child. She *did* have a baby. Where was she?

The old woman sipped her tea. "Godfrey was very understanding."

"Was he?" Jane felt confused and a little disoriented.

"You did have children to stay with you from time to time, but they were children of friends, you told us," Sandra explained.

"You always seemed happier to have the little ones around." The old woman smiled.

"You were lucky to have your husband at your side." Sandra kissed her baby's head. "Godfrey doted on you, Grace."

"Did he?" Jane's head was spinning. What had Sandra said? Had she heard her correctly?

"I wish I had my husband close. My Vernon left soon after we found out I was expecting. Goodness knows when I'll see him again."

"My husband!" Jane's mind whirled again, and she thought she might be ill. Was she was married? Was Gottfried her husband? She stared at her right hand. The ring finger was not marked. She'd never worn a ring there. How could she be married?

Chapter Twelve – Discovering Ghosts

The house sounded hollow, and echoes of her footsteps bounced back from the bare walls as she walked through the rooms. Jane found it difficult to imagine this had been her home for the last two years. She had no memory of the place.

She walked around, staring at the unfamiliar furniture and trying to remember being there. She couldn't imagine living in the house.

She climbed the stairs and went to look in the bedrooms. She found four good sized rooms. Two rooms held three single beds in each of them. A smaller room had one single bed. Why would she and Godfrey need so many rooms and so many beds? Why did they rent such a large house?

In the fourth room she came to, she found a double bed taking up most of the space. Was that the bed she had shared with her husband? She couldn't remember what he looked like, but his name was engraved on her heart. How could she not have realised? How could she not know she was married? She could feel the deep emotion she had for him. The love she felt for her husband was now creating a heavy ache in her chest. Where was he? How could she begin to find him?

She crossed to the small wardrobe and opened the door. Her clothes were still hanging there. Two cotton dresses, one woollen suit, three skirts, four blouses and a jacket. She recognised the styles and colours. She knew they were hers. She had packed and unpacked these clothes many times on the journey from Germany. Flashes of images and sensations crowded her mind. Darkened rooms in stranger's houses, wayside shacks and caves had been her sleeping places. She recalled urgent warnings to stay hidden; to stay silent, in whispered voices trembling with fear. Always fear.

She shuddered and took a small suitcase from the top of the wardrobe and began to lift the clothes from their hangers. As she folded them and placed them in the suitcase, she thought of Ethel. She would now be able to wear her own clothes and save Ethel the misery of seeing her wearing her daughter's things. She'd already decided to stay with the older woman for now. They needed each other.

Jane felt safe with the older woman who knew nothing about her past and Ethel still needed company. She didn't want to let her down. The house where she'd lived with her husband meant nothing to her. She had no memories or emotional attachments to the place. She glanced at the bed. It was just a bed. Had she made love in that bed?

Had Gottfried held her close and whispered words of endearment to her? Try as she might, those memories would not come.

She shook her head and went to open the drawers of the small dresser. She lifted out underwear, two silk scarves and a nightdress. A toiletry bag rested on the dresser. It held a lipstick, a powder compact and a hairbrush. She put it on top of the other things in the case.

Jane found nothing of Gottfried in the room. No trousers or shirts hung in the wardrobe. Two empty drawers indicated that's where he might have kept his underwear. She found no books, no shaving accoutrements, no hats or scarves that might have belonged to her husband. He had taken everything of his and nothing of hers. He had left her behind.

Sitting on the bed, she put her head in her hands. Why could she feel such intense emotion when she thought of the man, but still couldn't picture his face? She felt her heart was being torn to shreds. What would she do? Where could she start her search for him? He was a German refugee, with an English name, posing as a Dutch Jew. It would be hopeless.

A thought struck her like a bolt of lightning. Might there be some photographs in the house? All families had photographs. Her father had a camera. She remembered smiling as he framed the picture. She held her baby. Her husband stood behind, holding her shoulder. The proud parents, posing for posterity.

"Heben sie das baby ein wenig." (*Lift the baby a little*). She could hear her father's voice. "Senken sie ihre schulter, liebling." (*Lower your shoulder, darling*).

She remembered every detail of the photograph being taken. Where was that photograph? Such an image would be precious. She would have kept it close, surely. Would she have it framed and displayed, or hidden from sight here in England?

Turning to the smaller chest next to the bed, she yanked open the drawers. They were empty. Undeterred, she hurried through the house, pulling drawers, opening cupboard doors, frantically searching for something, anything that could give her evidence of her previous life.

In a kitchen drawer, she found a rent-book; a crumpled small envelope addressed to Harry Brown, and a small photograph of her mother and father.

She opened the rent book. The rent was more than she expected, but then, the house was quite large. How did she and Godfrey afford to live there?

She gazed at the photograph; the black-and-white faces gave depth to her fragile memories of the parents she'd loved. Smoothing the photograph, she put it in her coat pocket. The envelope looked promising. Even though she didn't recognise the name; it was addressed to the house. She wondered who Harry Brown might be, and why she would have kept his letter. She picked it up and opened the envelope.

The letter was written in German, and her heart did a flip. Who would be writing to this address from Germany? When was this sent? She peered at the date stamp. It had been sent in the first months of nineteen-thirty-nine before war was declared.

Dear Herman,

Jane recognised her father's name and looked again at the name and address on the envelope. The letter was addressed to someone called Harry. Her father must have changed all their names to English names to keep them safe from suspicion. How did he do that? She read on.

Forgive me for writing. I know we agreed to leave no trail, to your whereabouts, but this matter is of the utmost importance. Our network has been interrupted, and no further consignments can be sent to England. It would be suicide to try, as Herr Hitler's henchmen are everywhere, and are watching our every move. We dare not breathe for fear of antagonising the vigilant Nazis. Jews cannot move freely. They are stopped and harassed every time they leave the house.

One couple you know, the Liebermans, defied the authorities and went out without displaying the yellow star, hoping to shop for food without waiting all day behind the Gentiles. They were recognised, denounced by their neighbours and taken away there and then.

We managed to remove their children before the guards came searching for them. They are now in hiding, and we pray they remain safe.

Our precious owl is still being cared for by my friend at the farm I told you of. Unfortunately, it is not safe to set her free, and so she must remain in captivity. I will keep a close watch and visit her as often as is safe to do so.

I know this news is not what you'd hoped to hear, but it had to be told. Tell Gerda I will protect our little owl with my life.

I remain your faithful friend,
Jacob.

Jane's legs were shaking. She knew the man was referring to her daughter when he wrote of the owl. Her daughter had large brown eyes. She could see them. Her baby's face appeared from the fog in her head. The infant was looking at her. Dimples appeared in her little cheeks when her rosebud mouth curled into a smile. Her thickly fringed eyes were brown and wide and beautiful. Her hair was a blonde fuzzy halo. Jane's eyes filled with tears as she remembered her baby's face. Her father had called this grandchild his little owl.

Why didn't the baby come with them? Why had she left her baby behind? Was her child in Germany? Did she take her to Holland? Who was Jacob? There was no surname. She flicked the letter over and then inspected the envelope. She could see no return address and there was no clue about where the letter had been sent from. The letter was nearly two years old. How was she going to find her baby?

Tears trickled down her cheeks, but she dashed them away with her coat sleeve. Crying would not solve her problems. She had to take action. Gottfried was her husband, and she had to find him. He didn't even know she was alive. Where would he have gone? Could he have gone back to find their child? No! It would be too dangerous. He couldn't travel back to Holland or Germany. He couldn't risk travelling on false papers. Not while there was a war on.

Then she remembered Hannah Rosenberg. The young woman had told her she was planning to travel back to Germany. She'd asked her to go with her. It could be done. Perhaps she could go. Perhaps if she said she would help Hannah, she might be able to find her child.

After checking every last place she could think of with no more luck, Jane finally left the house with her suitcase. She took the key back to the neighbours and set out for Ethel's home.

She had intended to go to the steel works and ask whether Gottfried had left a forwarding address or if they might know of anything that she could use to start her search for him. When she'd asked Sandra how to get there, she discovered it was too far to walk. Hadfield's was on the other side of the city. She would need to get the bus and had no idea about bus routes or timetables.

Sandra offered to explain them, but Jane wanted to get going. Her nerves were frazzled, her head ached, and she felt exhausted. She thanked her neighbours, reassured them she would be fine and hurried away. She knew Ethel would help her find her way to the steelworks, and she could go the next day.

"Have you eaten, love?" Ethel asked when she arrived home.

"No, I haven't been hungry."

"Well, I got some neck of lamb, so I put a stew on." Ethel stared at the suitcase. "What you got there?"

"My things."

"Did you find Godfrey? Was he your relation?"

Jane dropped the suitcase by the door and sank into a fireside chair. "He's my husband, Ethel."

"What?" The older woman dropped the ladle into the pot of stew. "But I thought you weren't married."

"Well, I'm not wearing a ring, and I can't remember what happened to it, but the man looking for me was my husband."

"What did he say when he saw you? I mean, err… don't get me wrong, love, but why are you here? I wasn't expecting you to come back if you found your relatives."

"He wasn't there." Jane sighed and stretched her cold hands to the fire. "I spoke to the neighbours. I didn't remember them, but they seemed to know me. They called me Grace."

"So you *are* Grace Robinson." Ethel sat on the arm of the chair.

"It would seem so, but Jane will do. I can't get used to being called Grace." Jane didn't admit that Grace was probably not her real name anyway.

"Your man was probably at work, was he?"

Jane shook her head. "Those people at the library had convinced him I couldn't have survived. They had no record of a woman being pulled from the ruins of the Marples. He waited a couple of days and then packed up and left."

"Where did he go?"

"I wish I knew." She felt close to tears but shook herself. "I have to find him, Ethel. He thinks I'm dead."

"Poor man. Where would he go?"

"I have no idea, but he worked at Hadfield's. They might have a forwarding address for him, or perhaps some of his work friends might know where he went."

"What else did you find out? Were your neighbours able to tell you anything more about who you are?"

"Yes, they told me quite a lot, and I remembered more as they reminded me. I come from Holland." Jane knew she was lying, but felt it might help if she was as honest as she could be. Ethel deserved to know that she was a foreigner.

"Eeh, lass." Ethel went to stir the stew pot. "I didn't expect that, did you?"

"I thought I couldn't be from Sheffield," Jane paused; she didn't want to admit her thoughts and dreams were in a foreign language. That would be too much information to divulge. "But, yes, Holland was a surprise to me."

"And you're a married woman. Do you remember your husband?"

Jane shook her head. "I wish I could bring his face to mind, but all I know of him is what I feel." She put a hand on her heart. "I have an aching void in here. Something is missing from my life. I didn't know what it was. Not completely." Jane had assumed the emotion was connected with her missing child but now knew her absent husband was contributing to the cause of the pain in her heart.

"Oh, dear." Ethel clattered around taking dishes and cutlery to the table. "I know what that feels like, love. I miss my Lucy and the children every day."

"Your pain must be so much worse, Ethel." Jane felt a wave of sympathy for the older woman. "At least I know my husband is alive and I have a good chance of seeing him again."

Ethel smiled bravely. "I found out that they're going to hold a service at the cemetery after Christmas for all the families of people who can't be identified."

"How do you feel about that?"

Ethel shrugged. "I don't like it, but it will be better than nothing. My Lucy and her children deserve a proper grave but they can't have one, and I have to get used to the idea."

"Did you write that letter to Lucy's husband yet?" Jane knew her friend had been struggling with the onerous task. "I know I said I would help you, we can do it after dinner if you're up to it."

"I sent it this morning. I tried to break it gently to Albert, by waffling on about the raid and telling him about fetching the teddy, but I ended up throwing that letter in the fire."

"I'm sorry I wasn't here to help."

"Nay, lass. It were my job to tell the lad."

"How did you put it?"

"As simply as I could. It won't be easy for him to read his wife and children have gone. No need to give him the gory details, or try to flower it up. I just said they'd been killed by a bomb." The older woman's voice cracked, and she lifted her apron to her face.

Jane reached for Ethel's hand, and then stood to hug her. The two women held each other a few seconds before Ethel pulled away.

"Better serve this stew before it starts sticking to the pan. Hope you're hungry. I made enough to feed an army."

Jane took her cue from the older woman. Ethel had made it clear that she didn't want to wallow in her misery. "Good, because I think I could eat a horse."

While they ate, Ethel told her about the bus service into the city centre. "They don't always run on time, but you'll never walk all the way to Hadfield's and back in a day. My Lucy took the bus and then a tram to get to Vickers, and that's not far from Hadfield's."

"It sounds complicated, but I'm sure I'll find my way there."

"I hope you find what you're looking for when you get there, love."

"Well, I know I won't find Godfrey. The neighbours said he was intent on leaving Sheffield, but I hope someone might know where he's gone. If I talk to his boss, perhaps he'll be able to give me something to go on."

"Take my advice, love, and talk with the lads he worked with. He's more likely to have told them his plans than confide in his boss."

"Do you think so?" Jane didn't know who her husband would have been close to. She couldn't remember him, so had no chance of remembering any friends he might have made at his place of work.

"Don't forget to ask the cleaning ladies and the canteen staff. You never know, he could have told them something too."

"Ethel, you are an inspiration."

"You called me that once before. What does it mean?"

"It means you are full of brilliant ideas and encouragement."

Ethel lifted her chin and smiled. "I've been called worse things. Glad to help, lass."

"Would you like me to get anything from the shops on my way back tomorrow?"

"We could do with some meat or fish if you can get some, and some butter and eggs would be good, but I won't hold my breath. We can't seem to get owt in the shops these days and if your face doesn't fit you'll be fobbed off with yesterday's offal."

"I'll see what I can get in the city. I want to pay my way. I can't depend on your charity forever, Ethel."

"Well, if you find your man, you won't have to, will you."

Jane smiled. Would she find her man? Would she be able to discover where he'd gone?

Chapter Thirteen – Finding a Friend.

Jane found Hadfield's easily enough after she'd been pointed in the right direction. The massive foundry was difficult to miss. The large, imposing building fronted the road, and numerous chimneys stood behind belching orange smoke.

She entered the large doorway and walked a little way down a corridor to find someone to speak with. A half-glassed door had the words 'Hadfield's Offices,' etched into the glass, so she took off her glove and tapped on the door.

A young woman answered her knock. "Can I help you?"

"I'm looking for my husband." The journey from Ethel's house had given her plenty of time to rehearse what she would say when she got here. "He worked here until a few days ago. He gave his notice, and I was hoping he might have left a forwarding address."

"Come through." She gave Jane a friendly smile. "I'm Miss Nolan. I'm the office supervisor." The young woman lifted her chin haughtily. "I'll see what I can find." Miss Nolan left the door open, and Jane stepped into the office.

The room was long and filled with desks. Around twenty or so women sat at typewriters, their fingers tapping the keys. More young women were scurrying around with files or clip-boards, looking busy.

"What's his name?" Miss Nolan turned to Jane. "We keep records on everyone who worked here. I'll pull out his file and see whether there is anything written down about his resignation."

"Thank you. His name is, Godfrey Robinson."

"Date of birth?"

Jane shook her head. "Sorry, I don't know."

The young woman gave her a quizzical glance, and then pulled her shoulders back. "I thought you said he was your husband?" Her tone changed to one of suspicion. "We can't give out information to anyone who walks in here, you know."

"Oh, I understand." Jane was thrown.

"Do you have any identification?"

"Yes, but…" Jane sighed. Her identification was in the name of Jane Smith. She would have to tell the efficient Miss Nolan her story or she might refuse to tell her anything. "It's a long story, but I'll cut it short. I was in the Marples when it was bombed." She lifted her hair and took out the hairclip to expose her head wound. "This bump on the head made me lose my memory. I didn't know who I was, so they gave me the name of Jane Smith until my memory returns."

"So how come you remember your husband?"

"As I said, it's a long story, and it's taken me days to remember as much as I have." Jane could see the girl was not sympathetic. She began to feel her chance of finding Gottfried was slipping away. "Please, you have to believe me. I have to find him. He thinks I'm dead and has left Sheffield. You have to help me."

"Is there anyone in authority who can vouch for you and confirm your story?"

Jane tried to think. "There's a Doctor Fisher at the Royal Infirmary. He treated me. Then there's Hannah Rosenberg at the Central Library. She knows my true identity. She's the one who knows that Godfrey was looking for me."

"Wait here. I'll go make some telephone calls."

Jane stood by the wall, watching the other women working. After a few seconds, one of them caught her eye. A pale-faced blonde girl was looking at her with a wide-eyed stare of amazement. Their eyes met, and the girl smiled nervously. Her mouth formed a question, and Jane read her lips. "Is it you?" she said.

She thought she recognised something about the girl. Did she know her? Jane returned the girl's smile but got no response apart from a look of astonishment. Then the young woman looked over her shoulder and quickly turned her attention back to the typewriter, steadfastly ignoring Jane.

Who was she? The girl obviously recognised Jane or Grace, or whomever she was. She was wasting time. Every minute she spent here, Gottfried could be moving farther away from her. She decided to take control and moved to the girl's desk. "Excuse me, but do you know me?"

"Grace! I thought it was you, but it couldn't be." The girl's fingers stopped typing, and her face lost all trace of colour. "You're dead!"

"No, I'm not dead. It *is* me." Jane was slightly amused by the girl's response at seeing her.

The girl looked over her shoulder again. "Not here, Grace. Meet me at dinner time, will you?"

"Where?" Jane's heart began to beat faster. This girl knew who she was.

"There's a café down the end of Vulcan Road. Meet me there at twelve. It's so good to see you. We all thought we'd lost you."

"Mrs Robinson." Miss Nolan returned from her telephone calls and was carrying a red folder. She gave the girl at the desk a stern look and turned to smile stiffly at Jane. "I have some information for you. Please leave my staff to get on with their work."

Jane left the girl at the desk, wondering why she was reluctant to speak to her in the office.

She followed the woman to a desk near the rear of the office and watched her pull two sheets of paper from the file.

"As you can see, we don't have much information about your husband. He started work here in March of thirty-nine. He had an unblemished record of timekeeping and conduct and left three days ago. He was paid up to his final working day, but we don't have any forwarding address, other than his home address, and I believe you already have that."

"So you can't tell me anything I don't already know." Jane felt her heart sink.

The woman shook her head. "I'm sorry, Mrs Robinson. Yours is a very sad tale. I hope you find him."

"Could I talk to the people he worked with? Perhaps he discussed his plans with them?"

"I suppose I could arrange that for you."

"Would you?" Jane felt a spark of hope rekindle.

The woman consulted the file. "Your husband worked with Stanley Morrison's gang. Wait there. I'll see what shift they're on today."

"Thank you."

Jane waited again and watched the young woman consult a large sheet of paper pinned to the back wall. Within a second or two, she was back.

"They knock off at two. I'll call Mr Morrison to the office. Be back here at two, and you can question him yourself."

"Thank you." Jane remembered what Ethel had advised. "Could you ask whether any of his pals might stay to talk with me?"

"I can ask, Mrs Robinson, but after a twelve-hour shift, most of our men are keen to get home."

"All the same, I'd be very grateful if you would ask them."

"Very well." The woman gave a tight-lipped smile. "Now if you'll excuse me, I have work to do."

Jane glanced at the woman who seemed to know her. The young woman glanced at Jane quickly before continuing, very conscientiously, with her work.

She made her way from the large building and soon found the café at the end of the road. She ordered a cup of tea and sat to wait for the young woman.

"Been for an interview, have you?" the waitress asked when she brought the tea. "No need to be nervous. I don't know anyone they turned down. Desperate for workers, they are."

"Oh?" Jane could understand the woman's assumption.

"Well, there's a war on, isn't there? Hadfield's makes the best steel around, and our boys are safer in tanks made from Hadfield's steel. It's well known."

"Is it?" Jane didn't know much about the foundry where her husband had worked. She didn't know much about anything, and she was finding it more and more frustrating.

"Looks like you've been in the wars yourself, love. What happened?" The waitress pointed to the exposed wound on her head.

"Oh, I got a bump on the head from a bomb the other night." She carefully replaced the hairclip and adjusted her headscarf.

"Them Jerries gave us a right beating, didn't they? Where were you, love?"

"Valley Road." Jane didn't want to explain she was in the Marples. It seemed everyone knew about the hotel in the centre of the city. Valley Road seemed more anonymous in comparison.

"Well, our lads will be showing 'em we don't give in so easily. I heard we sent hundreds of bombers over Germany the other night."

"Did you?" Jane wondered how the waitress would know such information.

"My Billy fixes the bombers at Binbrook. He got a forty-eight-hour leave on account of his dad being killed in the raids. He said we're getting our own back on the buggers, good and proper. Not that I'm supposed to know any of that, so keep it closed. Know what I mean, love." She placed a finger to her lips.

"I won't tell a soul." Jane shuddered. Her daughter might still be in Germany. Was her little girl in danger from the British bombers?

She'd already begun to think of her baby as a little girl. Jane had lived in England for the last two years, so that would mean her child would be at least two-years-old and perhaps older if she'd been more than an infant, when she left her. Why would she leave her child? It was unthinkable.

Her mind teased her with a glimpse of her daughter. She was in the arms of a young man. She was waving and smiling and looked quite unconcerned. She appeared to be around two years old. Jane realised that image could be from the last time she'd seen her child. Why had she walked away from her? Who was the strange man? She recalled the letter she'd found in the house. Jacob's friend was looking after the little owl. Had she left her with Jacob's friend? Did she know who the man was? She couldn't imagine she would entrust her daughter to a stranger and simply walk away. What kind of circumstances would make her do a thing like that?

The door of the café opened, and the young woman from the office breezed in and quickly closed the door. "Two rounds of cheese on toast, Betty, please," she called to the waitress.

"Will you want tea with that, love?"

"Please." She dropped some coins on the serving counter and came to sit at Jane's table. "Sorry about earlier, Grace, but Miss Nolan is a cow. If she thought I was wasting time chatting, she'd have my wages docked. I can't tell you how glad I am to see you." The girl bent to hug Jane's shoulders tightly.

Jane held herself stiffly until she was released. "You know me?"

"Of course, I know you, silly! You gave us all a proper scare. Where have you been? We were all waiting for you, and when you didn't come home, well, you can imagine how we felt. Your Godfrey was a mess when he came back after looking for you."

"Do you know where he is?"

"Sorry, love. He took off a few days ago. Said he had important business to attend to and it couldn't wait. He wouldn't listen to anyone."

Jane was tired of going over her story and explaining her loss of memory, but she wanted to know more about the girl who seemed to know Gottfried so well.

"How well do you know me?" Jane asked. "I know it sounds strange, but I lost my memory, and I don't know who you are."

"Oh, Grace! I did wonder why you looked so glum in the office. You looked right through me until I smiled at you, and then old bossy knickers had her beady eye on me, and I had to ignore you. I'm sorry."

"You haven't answered my question." Jane insisted. "How do you know me?"

The girl leant closer. "We work in the same organisation. You and Godfrey held the meetings at your house, but then, after what happened to you, last week we changed the meeting place out of respect for Godfrey's feelings. Then he decided to go away since you, err, well, we all thought you were dead, and poor Godfrey said he had no reason to stay, and he left."

"What kind of organisation?"

"The Coalition for Liberation."

"What is the Coalition for Liberation, and what are the aims of this organisation you say I belong to?" Jane was beginning to feel a shiver of recognition, and it made her nervous.

"You really don't remember, do you? Oh dear!" Susan's concern was obvious and seemed genuine.

Jane shook her head. "I'm waiting."

"All right. I'll pretend you and I just met, and you know nothing about what we do."

"That's a good place to start. That's exactly how it feels to me."

"Goodness, I can't begin to imagine how that must feel. Poor you, Grace."

Jane winced on hearing the strange name but decided to let it go. She was more interested in hearing what this girl had to say.

"Well, I'll keep it simple. We are a multi-faith group, started by my dad. He was in the last war. Then he worked in the foreign office for a time. He knows people, and with his links and the help they give us, he contacted the Movement for the Care of Children from Germany."

Jane felt a flicker of recognition. "The kinder transports."

Susan nodded. "You remember?"

"Go on, please." Jane didn't remember as much as she wanted to.

"Well, dad and his friends offered to give funding for the children from the kinder transport and find them foster homes, but when war was declared, the kinder transports were more difficult to arrange and then they stopped altogether."

"Did I look after some of these children?" Jane remembered the neighbours had mentioned she and Gottfried had children to stay with them from time to time.

"You acted as a staging post for them." Susan grinned. "You *do* remember!"

"Not really." Jane shook her head. "What has the organisation been doing since the kinder transport stopped?"

"Our aim is to rescue as many Jews from the Nazis as possible."

Jane knew immediately that this was something she had been a part of. That's why she'd felt such a kinship with Hannah. She remembered the conversation in the Crown Inn and realised she'd felt a strong link to what the girl had spoken about. Now she was hearing similar words from this girl, and suddenly she knew her place. She knew how she had fitted into Sheffield after arriving so suddenly from Germany via Holland.

The flashes of memory came as images and feelings and passed through her mind so quickly that she felt bewildered. She only recalled parts of her story but knew enough to understand that she'd been forced to flee her home town. She knew why she would be involved in such an organisation but couldn't see why a young English girl would want to be part of such an undertaking.

"I'm sorry, but I don't understand," Jane began. "How did *you* become involved? You're not German and you don't look Jewish."

The young woman looked affronted. "I'm a Sheffield lass, born and bred, but that doesn't mean I don't have a heart."

"I'm sorry, I didn't mean to offend."

"It's all right. You must be feeling odd, with not being able to remember who I am." Susan took Jane's hand. "We're good friends, Grace. We're as close as sisters. I can't tell you how shocked I was to see you in the office this morning. I thought you were gone, and suddenly, now you're here."

"Here's your dinner, my loves." The waitress placed two small plates on the table. "I'll bring your tea over in a minute." She turned to Jane. "Can I get you a top-up, love?"

Jane nodded. "Yes, thanks."

Her companion pouted at Jane. "You really don't remember me, do you?"

Jane shook her head. "Sorry."

"All right. Let me try to shake some of those brain cells up a little." She took a bite of her toast, chewed slowly and swallowed. "Here goes. I'm Susan Gosney. Does that name strike any bells?"

Jane shook her head.

"My dad is Reverend Thomas Gosney. Everyone calls him Tom outside the church. He knew your dad quite well. My dad travelled a lot in the early thirties. When he was with the foreign office, he was never home."

"How could my father have met such a man?" Jane knew her father was not in politics. She remembered enough to know he'd been a businessman.

"I believe they met when my dad was visiting Hamburg with a delegation. They were trying to negotiate a trade deal. Your father was one of the businessmen who were keen to open more trade-links with Britain, but he took the opportunity to approach my dad about the Jewish situation in Germany. He explained how your mother had just been killed, and he made a big impression on dad."

Jane nodded. She could imagine her father doing such a thing.

"Well, my dad decided to help. He used his contacts in the foreign office to have false papers made for the Jewish families, and soon there was a small trickle of refugees arriving in England."

"Was my father involved?" Jane realised that her father would have been in great danger.

"Right from the start, so I'm told. I was seventeen when my dad left the foreign office, so I wasn't really interested in what he was doing back then. He was just my dad; you know what I mean?"

"Why did he leave the foreign office?"

"He returned to the church. It had always been his first love, but after the last war, he thought he could do more good working inside the government. He was a minor official, but he felt he was helping to keep peace in Europe by working with people to solve cross-border problems with trade deals and such."

"He must have been disheartened when Hitler came to power. There can be no reasoning with men like him."

"I think it took a few years, but you're right. When Hitler's harsh regime began to bite, he was beginning to get disillusioned, but your father's story was the turning point for my dad."

Jane glanced up from eating her toast. "I feel I should know all this, but it still sounds an amazing story. Your father must be an extraordinary man."

"He is, and he loves you like a daughter, that's why we are more sisters than friends. He took you and Godfrey under his wing after Harry died so suddenly. He'll be so glad to see you, Grace. I can't wait to go home and tell him the good news."

"Harry?" Jane didn't recognise the name.

The girl glanced around before whispering, "Oh, that was the name your father took on the false papers. His real name was Herman Bauder. Do you recognise *that* name?"

Jane began to shake her head, but then remembered the photograph she'd found. In her mind, she saw her parents as they appeared in the picture. She knew who they were and now she remembered their names. Sarah and Herman Bauder. She sighed with satisfaction as another piece of her jigsaw fell into place.

"Yes, thank you. I remember now."

"Eat your toast, Grace. You were always finicky about food, but I'm guessing you need to keep your strength up. Whatever happened to you, I'm betting it wasn't pleasant."

"No, it wasn't." Jane didn't want to go into details about her own misfortunes. She was more interested in hearing what the girl had to say. "Tell me more about your father."

"Well, as I said, he works for the organisation that helped with the kinder transport. He wanted to help the adults too, but that was more difficult. Germany was only allowing children to leave. Eventually, he persuaded his contacts to provide your family with new papers and then organised your travel arrangements to get you out of Germany. I became involved when our family were chosen to help you settle in. My mum volunteered because you were close in age to me, I think. That's how I got to know you."

"How many did you help to escape? Are there many Jewish families living here?"

The girl shook her head. "We helped about thirty children in the early days before the transport was stopped. Not many have made it out recently, but we do what we can. The routes through Europe are kept secret and are more dangerous now, and we have to make sure our travellers are safe, or else, what's the point? Rescuing people from fire to throw them into the frying pan isn't what we are about at all." Susan hesitated. "Are you remembering anything more?"

Jane was amazed to hear this girl speak of her escape so flippantly. Hannah Rosenberg had spoken of helping to resettle German Jews fleeing Hitler's regime. Did they work for the same organisation?

"How does it work?"

"My dad works closely with people he knows in the foreign office, and they print the necessary paperwork, but now it's harder to get the papers to the people who are waiting to escape."

"Does the name Hannah Rosenberg mean anything to you?"

Susan shook her head. "Should it?" The girl's eyes widened, and she seemed excited. "Just a minute! Is she the girl who is always pestering my dad about going to Germany?"

"Probably." Jane sighed. "She is a little intense."

Susan seemed interested. "Is she a friend of yours?"

Jane shook her head, wondering why this girl was being so insistent. "She's just someone I met recently."

"Do you know her well?"

"No, she works at the Central Library."

"Oh, I thought she helped out with our sister organisation." Susan looked deflated. "She must be happy with her own identity. Most Germans change their names when they get here. It makes life easier when they apply for jobs or school places."

"I think she's Russian."

"Oh, my! You know some interesting people."

"How much do you know about me?" Jane was eager to learn more about who she was.

"I know you arrived here with your father and Godfrey just before Christmas of thirty-eight. Dad said he had to do something for your family after reading about the night of violence that everybody came to know as Crystal Night."

"Kristal-Nacht!" Jane felt a cold shiver run through her body. Screams and chanting filled her ears. The sound of smashing glass was loudest as the cruel crowds broke windows of Jewish owned shops and businesses.

"I'm sorry, did that bring some bad memories back to you?"

Jane nodded and swallowed the bile that had risen to her throat. That night of horror was clear in her head, and she wished it wasn't. Their apartment was ransacked while they were still inside it. She cowered with her father in a blockaded bedroom, listening to the mob breaking furniture and windows in their home. They were holding each other, trying to stay silent while trembling with fear. Where was Gottfried? Why wasn't her husband with her? Where was her child?

"Are you all right?"

Jane nodded. "What else can you tell me?"

"I know your mother was murdered by the Nazis and your little girl is still hiding in Bavaria."

"Bavaria!" Jane was astonished to hear that this girl knew the full story. "You know about my child?"

"You remember her?"

"I do, but I still can't understand why I would leave her behind." She felt tears in her eyes, and blinked quickly.

"Here you go, girls. Hot and strong." The waitress came to the table. "I brought you a teapot to share. Hope that's all right."

"Thanks, Betty."

Susan poured the tea and watched the waitress go to serve another customer. The café was filling up with workers from the factory.

"You had no choice, Grace," Susan whispered. "You were desperate. You and your husband had been summoned. They were going to send you to a labour camp, and you'd been instructed to take the baby with you. You and your father watched your mother's sister and her husband being packed off on the transports. You told me how horrible it had been for you, to witness that. Your father couldn't risk losing you to the labour camps too. He already had the false papers for the three of you, but there was a problem with Sasha's papers. They'd gone missing or something, or weren't ready in time."

"Sasha!" Jane felt a flush of heat in her chest on hearing the name. She knew the name of her child. "Do you know anything about her? Is she safe?"

"As far as we know, she is still with the family you left her with. They moved to Bavaria where it was easier for them to pretend Sasha was theirs."

"Where in Bavaria?"

Susan shook her head. "I don't know the details."

"Is she safe?" Jane was desperate to know her child was alive and well.

Susan smiled. "I'm sure she is. Drink your tea while it's hot."

"Do you know how old she is?"

"Don't you?" Susan choked on her toast but recovered quickly. "Sorry, you lost your memory, didn't you? It must be awful not to remember the most basic of things."

"It hasn't been easy. Being a German woman in a city full of people who hate Germans, well, I don't know who to trust. My memory is starting to come back, but I can't rely on it yet. I still have large gaps and so many questions."

"Well, I can answer one question for you. Sasha will be four on the third of January."

"She is four-years-old!" Jane was stunned. "She has lived half her life without me. She won't remember me." Jane had thought of her child as a baby or a toddler but was coming to realise that her child was growing up without me and the pain was like a knife through her heart. "She won't know her own mother!"

"It's safer that way, Grace."

"Please don't call me Grace. I'm not comfortable with that name."

"Then, what should I call you?" Susan lowered her voice to a whisper. "I can't very well use your real name, can I?"

"Do you know my real name?"

Susan nodded. Leaning close, she whispered, "Gerda Rubenstein."

Jane knew Susan was speaking the truth. The name sounded right. She was Gerda.

"If you don't like Grace, what shall I call you?"

"The people at the hospital gave me the identification of Jane Smith. I have temporary papers in that name and I'm getting used to it."

"That's going to confuse a few people."

"Do I know many people?" Jane knew she wasn't a naturally gregarious person. She'd only had a few friends in Germany. She did have more, but as Hitler's strength grew, it became unfashionable to have Jew friends if you were a Gentile. She wasn't a practising Jew, but her mother had been. She was the daughter of a Jew, and even though her father was a Gentile, it made no difference. Her mother's background tainted the thoughts and opinions of her so-called friends.

"Lots of people know you. Grace, I mean, Jane. You get things done! We all look to you for guidance. You and Godfrey give shelter to the refugees when they first arrive."

"In the house on Priory Road?"

"The organisation pay the rent in return for your services. It worked well until, well, until last week."

"What else do I do for the organisation?" Jane was intrigued to be learning so much about her life.

"You organise housing and schooling for the new arrivals and help them with job applications. If we receive news of a family in need, you're the first to help arrange what has to be done."

"Am I?" Jane was surprised. "How, I don't understand. What do I do?"

"There are many foreign families here in Sheffield and some thirty or so unaccompanied children that are being cared for by English families. You hold English lessons in your home for these families and children. You help them settle into the English way of life. If they have problems with neighbours, you visit them and explain why they have foreign people living in their street. You are our diplomat."

"Then, I expect you will need me to return to work as soon as possible, but what about my husband?"

"Try not to worry. Lessons have been suspended. We were hoping we could replace you after Christmas, but now you're back. When do you think you could start?"

"I don't know." Jane touched her head. "I still have bad headaches, and my mind is not as clear as I feel it should be. I can't concentrate on anything until I find Godfrey. That's my priority. I have to find him. Where would he go?"

Susan shook her head and popped the last piece of her toast into her mouth.

"This organisation we belong to, when is the next meeting?" Jane asked.

"Sunday afternoon. Can I tell everyone that you're back? We could come to the house as usual. My dad will be eager to see you and talk with you."

"No!" Jane answered quickly. Things were moving too fast. She wasn't ready to become the person she had once been without knowing more. The large holes in her memory still made her feel vulnerable. She didn't like feeling out of control. "Where have you been meeting since I disappeared?"

"Last week we used the church. My dad is the vicar of St Mary's in Sharrow."

"You're not a Jew?"

"No, I'm a Christian, but it makes no difference what God we pray to. We're all human."

"I'll drink to that." Jane sipped her tea and began to understand why she would have been friends with this intelligent and optimistic girl. Susan had probably never known a day's worry in her life before the war started. "You say we are friends?"

"Good friends, Grace, I mean, Jane." Susan smiled. "Sorry. That's going to take some getting used to."

"Will you take me to the meeting on Sunday? I'd like to try to ease myself back into my life."

"Perfect. My dad will be so happy to hear you're still around. We were all devastated when Godfrey told us what happened."

"Godfrey. I have to find him. Will your father know where he might be?"

"It's possible, but you'd have to ask him."

"I'm hoping to see some of his work pals this afternoon. They might know something."

"Godfrey didn't have many friends, Gra.., sorry, Jane. He doesn't speak English well and folks around here don't like foreigners, even when they say they come from Holland."

"It's still worth a try."

"You're right. Look, I have to go." Susan stood and pulled on her coat. "Miss bossy knickers will have my guts for garters if I'm late back."

"Where will I see you on Sunday?"

"Come to St Mary's Church around three. I'll meet you there. Think you can find it?"

Jane smiled. "I'll find it."

"It's so good to see you." Susan's smile was wide and filled with genuine warmth. "See you Sunday." She bent to give Jane a hug before hurrying away.

Jane watched her leave with a pang of envy. Susan Gosney was a fortunate young woman. She had the poise and confidence of a girl who had never known heartbreak or sorrow. She didn't have a child that was being raised by strangers. She didn't have a missing husband who was heartbroken.

Jane shook herself. It wouldn't do to get maudlin. She had a job to do. She had to find Godfrey.

An hour later, when Jane pushed through the doors into the large building of Hadfield's steel foundry once again, she knew where to go, and marched confidently down the corridor toward the office door.

"Mrs Robinson."

Jane turned at the sound of the name.

"I'm Stanley Morrison."

She walked toward the older man dressed in work clothes, holding out her hand. "Pleased to meet you, Mr Morrison."

He shook her hand briefly. "So you survived the Marples, did you?"

"It would seem so." She gave him a small smile. She sensed an edge of caution to his voice. "Though the authorities didn't make a record of finding me in the ruins, and now my husband thinks I'm dead. Can you tell me where he might have gone?"

"He was never a big talker. He didn't tell me owt about his plans. He was beside himself with grief, though. We told him not to make any big decisions while he was feeling like that."

"We?" Jane was quick to note that Godfrey had talked with others. "Who else advised him? Perhaps Godfrey told someone else what his plans were."

"Well, if he did, they weren't too eager to stick around and tell you. We work long hours, love, and have to be back at two in the morning."

"I know. Godfrey worked those shifts. Did he say anything about where he might be going? Anything at all! I have to know!"

"I know, love. I understand, but he was a quiet man. You'll know that. He didn't talk much, but he's a good sort. A hard worker, you know? We all liked him."

"But you can't help me?"

"Look, Mrs Robinson, he was hurting something bad after he saw what happened at the Marples. Men don't talk about feelings much, but it tore the heart right out of me to hear him crying like a baby in the men's toilets."

Jane put her fist to her mouth. "Oh, poor Godfrey."

"He thought he was alone, you see, but I was in a toilet stall. I stayed there until he'd gone. I didn't want to embarrass the lad. He'd obviously gone there for some peace and quiet to let go, you know?"

"That's why I have to find him, Mr Morrison. I can't let him go on believing I'm dead."

"I can see that, love. I wish I could help you."

"Will you ask around? Will you ask the people on his shift if they know anything?" She fished in her bag for a scrap of paper and hastily wrote down her new address. "You can get a message to me here."

The man glanced at the paper. "Well, there's not many will go out of their way on a day off to travel to Meersbrook." He scratched his head.

"Well," Jane tried to think, but her headache was beginning to throb.

"Hang on, he was close to a young lass in the office." He blushed and went on quickly, "All above-board, I'm sure. She's a decent lass. You might know her."

"Susan Gosney?"

"That's the one. I can give her a message if there's owt to tell, she lives up Sharrow way. That's not far from you."

"Thank you. That's perfect. I'll be seeing her at Church on Sunday."

Chapter Fourteen – Facing Old Friends

Ethel was busy making the traditional pies and bread for the Christmas festivities. Jane felt comfortable to leave her alone after explaining that she had some things to do and some old friends to see.

"It's good to hear you're getting your memories back, love. Your friends will be happy to see you, I expect. Especially after thinking you were dead. I wish my Lucy could walk back through that door like you're going to do today with your friends."

"I wish she could too, Ethel." Jane felt the older woman's pain. "Are you sure you'll be all right? I'll only be a few hours."

"I can't hold you back, love. I've plenty to keep me busy here." She folded the bread dough and kneaded it down. Straightening, she pushed a strand of hair from her face with the back of a floury hand. "Listen, love. I can't change what happened that night. I have to get on with things the best way I can, but I'm glad you decided to stay and keep me company."

"It was kind of you to take me in, Ethel."

"Well, I don't know that I'd have done so well on me own. It keeps me going, thinking about you and making sure you're getting better."

"Well, you're doing a great job. I'm improving daily."

"Glad to hear it." Ethel smiled. "Go on with you, lass. My Lucy doesn't have a life to live, but you do. Go meet your friends. I'll be fine."

Jane set out to Sharrow, pulling her headscarf down and her collar up. The wind was bitingly cold and flapped her red coat around her legs, making it difficult to walk.

She was in two minds about what she would find at the church. She looked forward to seeing Susan again. The girl had told her of the sisterly relationship they shared, and she anticipated rekindling the closeness between them. She didn't know what to expect from the others who she knew would all be curious about what happened to her.

She didn't want to go over her story again. She found it too painful to think about the close brush with death. She could now remember much more about that night, and the fear in those memories was strong enough to reduce her to tears. She didn't want to appear weak in front of strangers even though Susan had assured her they were friends.

She could stay strong with Ethel. She was grateful that her friend was a strong woman. Ethel was grieving but didn't let her sorrow dominate her life. They each had much to be unhappy about, but apart from the occasional spell of weeping, when they supported each other through the tears and talked about their experiences and feelings, they didn't dwell long on the fear or their sadness.

As she got closer to the area, she saw the square church tower standing tall, miraculously unscathed, above the destruction she walked through. She'd already walked this road when searching for Godfrey a few days ago. Now she was less intent on her destination and more aware of her surroundings.

She passed through the damaged district and shuddered. Houses were reduced to mere piles of rubble. Whole businesses were annihilated. A pile of twisted metal emerging from a mountain of rock was all that was left of what appeared to have been a timber merchants. The football ground was like a ploughed field, and the stands were in ruins. She realised it would be quite some time before a football match could be played there again.

The church was surrounded by bare-branched trees and seemed an island of peace in a sea of devastation. She walked to the door and listened. The church was quiet. She began to walk around the building but heard the door opening behind her. She turned around.

"Grace!" The balding man almost tripped on his robes as he hurried to gather her into his arms.

"Ouch!" She winced as he squeezed her tightly in his arms.

"Oh, Grace. I'm sorry. Are you hurt?"

"My chest is sore," she wheezed.

"Is it really you?" He drew back and held her at arm's length. "Let me look at you."

Jane looked into the older man's eyes and recognised the warmth of love reflected back at her. "Reverend Gosney?"

"Ah, not so formal." The portly man's smile was wide and welcoming. "You usually call me Tom, but of course, Susan told us of your memory problems." He pouted. "Don't you recognise me?"

Jane smiled. Her mind wasn't familiar with the face, but somewhere deep inside; she recognised the essence of the man. She felt safe with him. She knew she could trust him. She nodded. "How could I forget *you*, Tom?"

"Come and let the others see you."

She allowed him to guide her into the church and was surprised to see a couple of dozen people waiting to meet her. They all turned as she reached the end of the aisle and she had a fleeting memory of a different church. She'd been dressed in white, and a tall blond man had been waiting at the altar. Her hand held as tightly to her father's arm then, as it was holding to Tom's right now. She had been excited in the church of her memory, but the excitement was replaced by anxiety in the present.

"These people are your friends, Grace. You have nothing to fear," Tom whispered encouragement.

The kindly Reverend seemed to have read her thoughts. She gave him a grateful smile and tried to relax. He was right. She was among friends. She could trust her instincts with these people. She spotted Susan among them and gave her a smile of recognition.

"Here she is. Our Grace is raised from the dead for all to see." Reverend Gosney lifted her arm, and the small group cheered, making Jane feel embarrassed by the fuss.

"I wasn't dead," she insisted. "Just a little knocked around."

The group of people moved closer, some smiled, others reached to touch her, but Jane kept smiling. She knew these people wouldn't hurt her.

One woman stepped forward and put her hands on Jane's shoulders. She kissed both cheeks. "Oh, Grace, you don't know what this means. We thought we'd lost you."

"I don't think she remembers you, Millie." Thomas Gosney took the woman's arm. "This is Mrs Millie Gosney. My wife."

Susan hurried to stand next to Jane, taking her hand. "And she's also my mum. She'll fuss you and try to feed you anything she has to hand, but there's no harm in her."

The gathered friends laughed at Mrs Gosney's expense.

"Cheeky madam."

"Sorry, Mrs Gosney." Jane could see the woman was a little put out by her lack of enthusiasm for her welcome. "I hope to remember everyone soon, but things aren't coming back to me as quickly as I'd like."

"No need to worry, Grace. Oh, and it's Millie. We don't stand on ceremony here."

Jane smiled but felt uncomfortable with all the people staring at her. She wanted to ask about Gottfried. He was always uppermost in her mind, but she felt these people were expecting something from her.

"Did you get it?" one woman asked.

"Sorry?" Jane didn't understand.

"Now, Harriet, Susan told you Grace has lost her memory. She barely remembers us, so how can we expect her to know what happened earlier that night of the bombing?"

"Did something happen?" Jane could feel the now familiar itch in her head that alerted her to a missing memory. "I mean, before the bombing? Something was meant to happen, wasn't it?"

"Don't worry about it now, Grace." Millie took her arm. "Come and have some tea and scones. You look frozen through."

"I told you she'd fuss, didn't I?" Susan smirked. "I also told everyone you prefer to be called Jane, but they didn't listen."

"Pah!" Tom walked along behind them as they made their way to a trestle table at the rear of the church. "How can we call you Jane when we've known you as Grace for the last two years?"

"Don't be concerned. I'll answer to anything," she told them and meant it. Her name was not important.

Jane gave up trying to put any sense of order to what was happening to her. She decided to go with the flow of things for now. She was being led to a table laid with cakes, cups and saucers. These people were being kind, yet they felt like strangers.

Susan's mother began pouring tea, and then she pushed a plate of cake into Jane's hands. All the while, she was being jostled by the group of friends, and her mind was busy forcing connections.

Memories began to burst through the fog in her head. A rapid and haphazard set of images and sensations poured into her mind. She was serving in the bar at the Marples. Laughter was part of the memory. She saw an image of people dancing. The smoky atmosphere made her eyes sting. She was in the back room dabbing her eyes with water.

Sebastian. The name barrelled into her brain. She saw a small piece of paper in her hand. Sirens blared, people drifted away. She was alone. No, someone was with her. Sebastian. Someone shouted. The cellars. She had to get to the cellars. The deafening explosion sounded from somewhere above her, and when she looked up, the ceiling was rushing down at her. She felt dizzy and sick. The world tilted, and her knees gave way.

"Grace!"

Strong arms caught her and carried her to a pew. She felt a pillow pushed under her head as Mr Gosney placed her down gently.

"Are you all right?" he asked. "What happened?" He turned to the crowd of friends hovering close behind him. "Give her some space, will you?"

"Sorry, I was dizzy." She tried to sit up.

"Don't get up, stay there a minute," Tom warned. "Should you be out of the hospital yet?"

"They needed the beds."

"But you're not well. That much is clear."

"I'm fine. I've done a lot of walking the last few days, and my head is still a mess. I've probably done too much."

"You said your chest hurt. What happened, Grace?" The man's kind eyes were glossy. "Were you badly injured?"

"Cuts and bruises, that's all."

"Seems like more than that to me, love."

"I'm fine, Tom. Really!" She tried to sit up again, and this time he didn't try to stop her. "Nothing a cup of tea and a slice of cake won't put right."

As she sipped the sweet tea and ate the cake, Tom ushered the group of friends away. Only Susan remained beside her, keeping a watchful eye for any sign of dizziness.

"Feeling better, love?" Susan asked.

Jane nodded. "This cake is lovely."

"Mum is a good baker. She makes awful dinners, but we can't fault her cakes."

Jane smiled. "Are you always making jokes at your mother's expense? She doesn't like it you know."

"So you keep telling me, but she knows I love her."

"*Do* I keep telling you?" Jane was amused to realise she'd slipped into herself without even thinking about it. She was talking and responding as Grace would have done, or perhaps Gerda might have. She was back. Her mind might not yet be whole, but she felt more normal.

"You are always telling me to respect my elders more. I know I'm a tease, but I can't help it. That's just the way I am. Do you have many dizzy spells?"

"Oh, not so many. It seems worse when I get a burst of memory, and I think I had one just then."

"What did you remember?"

"Some odd things that don't make sense. I think I need to talk with your father."

"I'll get him."

Jane put a hand on Susan's arm. "Wait, I want to know who Sebastian is. Does that name mean anything to you?"

Susan gasped. "You saw him?"

"I think so."

"He's the Secret Service man you were meant to meet that night."

"Secret Service?" Jane felt a shiver of fear. "Why would I be meeting a spy?"

"Sebastian is not a spy, Grace," Tom explained. "He works for the Secret Service, granted, but real spies are in a different league."

"Then, what does he do?" Jane asked.

"He helps with our travel arrangements across the channel. He delivers papers and helps to smooth the progress of the whole operation over there."

"So, what was he doing in Sheffield?"

"He had some information for us that could only be delivered in person. He couldn't trust it to the usual wireless operators. The communication was too sensitive for the pianists he used."

"Pianists?" Jane thought the word had been used out of context and didn't understand what Tom meant.

"A pianist is what they call the undercover wireless operators."

"I see." Jane was beginning to realise how important the message might be. "He gave me the information, didn't he?"

"That was the plan." Tom turned to his daughter. "Bring us another cuppa, love, will you?"

"More cake?"

Jane shook her head.

"I have news of Godfrey. Tell her, dad. I'll get the tea."

Jane watched Susan leave and looked at Tom. "What have you heard?"

"Godfrey told me that he had something to do. He called it unfinished business. I feared he might want to return to Germany, but thought he would have more sense."

"What business would he have in Germany?" He couldn't go back there. Why would he?"

"His supervisor at Hadfield's told Susan that Godfrey mentioned to one of his work pals that he planned to go home."

"But he left the house keys with a neighbour."

"Not to that home. I think he was referring to your previous home. I think he's planning to cross the channel."

"But he can't! He can't go back there. Why would he want to? If they find him, he'll be sent to the labour camps." Jane felt the panic rising in her chest and clamped her mouth closed. When she felt calmer, she grasped Tom's hand. "He can't go back there, Tom!"

"We don't know that he has. He's not stupid. Perhaps he'll come to his senses when he realises what danger he'll be in."

"But where would he go? We gave up our home. We have no friends in Hamburg. At least, none that would be willing to shelter him."

"He thought he'd lost you, Grace. He was in shock and grief can do terrible things to a person's state of mind. Without you, what else did he have to live for?"

Jane knew in an instant. "Sasha."

Tom nodded. "We think he's making his way to Bavaria."

"Does he know where she is in Bavaria? It's a big area to search."

Tom shrugged. "I don't know what he knows. *I* don't know where she is. The whole point of keeping people in hiding is to make sure they stay hidden. The only way to ensure secrecy is to tell as few people as possible where the hiding places are."

"But we're her parents! Surely we would know!"

"Perhaps you do."

"But I can't remember!" She clenched her fists in frustration. "He'll be in as much danger in Bavaria as in our home town. Hitler's army is everywhere." Jane could imagine her husband scouring the forests and farmland looking for their daughter. "What is he thinking?"

"I don't know what might be going through his head, love. But we know that German soldiers now have orders to shoot any Jew who runs away from them. They also have orders to take any Jew sympathisers caught with Jews hiding on their property and send them to the labour camps."

"No!" Jane began to feel a cold knot of terror in her tummy.

"Your husband believes he has only one thing left to live for. Sasha is his daughter. He wants to bring her to safety. That's what I'd be thinking in his position, no matter what the danger. If that were my Susan! Well…"

"You'd go to save her, wouldn't you?"

The bald man nodded.

"Oh, Tom! What are we going to do?"

"More tea, anyone?" Susan came back with a teapot. "There's no milk, but it's like witch water anyway." She looked at Jane's face and asked her father, "Did you tell her?"

"He did."

"I'm sorry, I wanted to tell you when you arrived, but dad said there was nothing we could do. Godfrey could already be out of the country."

"Your dad is probably right."

"Tell the others to go home, Susan. There's no point in them hanging around. We've had no news about the expected consignment."

"What are you expecting?" Jane asked.

"Five people were supposed to be arriving by boat at Dungeness this week. We strongly suspect they won't be coming. Too much time has passed since we expected them."

"What could have happened to them?"

Tom grimaced. "I'd rather not think about that."

"Is it my fault?" Jane had an overwhelming pang of guilt. "Could that message from Sebastian have saved them?"

"We don't know, Grace. Not without knowing what that message contained."

"I'm sorry, Tom. I can't remember. That night is a blur. I can see fragments if I try really hard, but all I see when I think about the message is a blank piece of paper, and I can't say whether that's a real memory when my imagination could be filling the gap."

"I understand, love. Really I do. Don't torture yourself. This is war, and you're a casualty as much as anyone else. I don't want to put you under any pressure. You've suffered enough." He touched her temple gently. "Your poor head."

"I'll survive." Jane shrugged off his sympathy. She felt wretched to know she might have been able to prevent the deaths of five people. If only she could remember. "I wish I knew what happened to those people you were expecting. I travelled that path myself. If any part of their journey was exposed! If the Nazis find out about the safe houses…" She put her head in her hands. "Oh, Tom. All those people. All those brave people who helped us. They're all in danger as well, aren't they? The Gestapo will shoot anyone caught helping a Jew to escape."

"It can't be helped, Grace. Don't blame yourself. You can't help the fact that you lost your memory."

"What happened to Sebastian?" As soon as she asked the question, her common sense answered. "He's dead, isn't he?"

"His wallet was found in the cellars. He was one of the bodies that couldn't be identified. He didn't survive."

"If he had, we wouldn't be having this conversation, would we?"

Tom shook his head. "We wouldn't need you to remember anything if he was still around to tell us in person."

Jane closed her eyes and tried to force her memories to open. So much was depending on her remembering the information she had locked away in her head.

"Don't torture yourself, Grace. It's already too late to save the ones we hoped were on their way."

"They're probably dead aren't they?" she asked.

"Yes. I'd say so." Tom stared at the floor despondently.

"What about the safe houses? The people who helped them? Do you know whether they will be in danger?"

"Without that information you have in your head, we'll never know what happened, and until we can confirm the route is safe, we can't risk bringing anyone else out."

"No pressure, you said!" Jane gave a small smile. "Lives depend on my memories, Tom. I have to find a way to get to them."

Chapter Fifteen – Meaningful Memories

Jane's head wound was itchy, and she couldn't wait to get the stitches removed. She knew her scalp would feel more comfortable without them. She remembered her way back to the ward and reported to a young woman sitting at a desk by the door.

"I was asked to come here to have the stitches taken out." She lifted her fringe to show the dressing on her temple.

"Oh, yes. I'll get Nurse Wallace. Wait there a second, will you?"

Jane waited, remembering her time in the ward. It seemed months ago that she was last here, yet it was only a week since she'd left.

"Jane, you're looking well. I barely recognised you." Nurse Wallace smiled brightly, as she came to greet her. "That bruising is almost gone, but what have you done to your lovely hair?"

Jane touched the matted mess of curls. "I can't manage to keep it tidy with this." She pointed to the dressing on her temple. "It hurts too much to brush the tangles out each morning."

"Oh, your beautiful hair. What a shame."

"Perhaps I'll try to wash it once these stitches are removed."

"Come with me."

Jane followed the nurse into a side room and took the opportunity to ask what was uppermost in her mind. "Is Doctor Fisher around today?"

"I think he has a clinic in outpatients. We don't expect to see him on the ward until later this afternoon. Take off your coat and sit here, will you, love?"

Jane did as instructed. "I was hoping the doctor might agree to see me. It's rather important."

"Is your chest wound bothering you?"

"No, that seems to be healing well. It's my lack of memories that are causing me distress."

"I'll take a look at your chest while you're here. Will you lift your cardigan and blouse?"

Jane did as she was asked and let the nurse inspect her chest wound. "I have an appointment to see him on the third of January, but something has happened, and I really need his help." Jane knew she would be taking a risk. The doctor would discover she was German, but she hoped he would understand when he knew the full story of why she was in England.

"Well, I can ask him, but don't hold your breath, love. Dr Fisher is a busy man."

"Thank you." Jane breathed a sigh of relief. If the doctor could help her remember what happened that night of the bombing, and access the information she held in her head, she could possibly prevent many more deaths.

"Well, your back looks in good shape. Tell Ethel she's done a marvellous job on that chest wound. You don't need the dressings now. Nature and fresh air will do the rest." The nurse tugged her clothing down. "Now let me see your head."

Jane stayed as still as she could while the nurse cut the stitches and jerked them out. The pain was minimal, and with each tug, she felt a release of tension on the wound.

"The stitch wounds are bleeding a little, so I'll put a small dressing on for now. You can remove it when you get home. The bleeding will have stopped by then."

"Thank you."

"You're welcome, Jane." Nurse Wallace placed a small dressing on the scar and wrapped a bandage around her head. "Don't try to wash your hair until tomorrow, will you? Let the scabs form first."

Jane nodded. She was desperate to wash her hair, but it could wait a day longer.

"Now what shall I tell the doctor? Did you say you were still having memory problems?"

"Yes." Jane stood to put her coat back on. "He said he might be able to hypnotise me to help me remember."

"Did he?" Nurse Wallace looked sceptical. "Well, he knows best, I expect, but his newfangled methods are frowned on by some of his colleagues, you know."

"Are they?" Jane suppressed a smile. She could imagine hypnosis might be considered unconventional by some in the medical profession.

The nurse hesitated. "Would you still like me to ask if he'll see you today?"

"Yes, please."

"Come and wait by the desk. I'll see what I can do."

Jane followed her back to the desk and waited while Nurse Wallace left the ward in search of the doctor. Ten minutes later, she returned with unwelcome news.

"Sorry, Jane. He's too busy. He said to tell you that he would need a longer appointment for what you have in mind." The nurse gave a wary glance to the girl at the desk. "He's asked me to schedule you in for the afternoon of the third. If you come for about one, he'll be able to give you an hour."

"Oh, I see." Jane felt deflated. She was hoping to get some answers today, but now realised she would have to wait. "Thank you for trying."

"No problem, my dear. Take care of that head, and remember, no washing that hair until tomorrow at the earliest."

Jane was reluctant to get out of bed. Christmas day meant little to her, but she knew it was important to Ethel. She'd promised to go with her friend to the church service. She couldn't let her down. She pushed the blankets back and went to the washstand.

She'd struggled to wash her hair there the previous day, but it proved more difficult than she'd expected. Ethel came to help, but even with the two of them, they couldn't work the tangles from her matted muddle of curls. With more pressing matters to attend to, they didn't have the luxury to take their time, so Jane wrapped her hair in a scarf to hide the mess.

This morning, she hurried to dress and began to try to brush her hair. The curls were tangled beyond all hope of recovery, and she didn't dare tug too hard because the scar at her temple was tender. She'd always been proud of her long curly hair. Gottfried liked to brush it for her. The memory of him standing behind her was bittersweet. She closed her eyes to savour the feeling; imagining it was his hand holding the brush as he gently pulled it through a mass of tangles. The brush stuck fast and the moment was gone. She pulled the brush from her hair and made a decision.

Ethel was stirring a pan of porridge when she went downstairs.

"Do you have some sharp scissors, Ethel?"

"In that drawer, love." She pointed with the spoon. "What do you need them for?"

"To cut my hair."

"Oh, you can't do that." Ethel dropped the spoon and lifted the pan from the fire. "Why would you want to cut that beautiful hair?"

"Because it's impractical, and it hurts when I brush it." She found the scissors and began to hack at the tangles.

"Stop!" Ethel came to take the scissors from her. "I used to cut my Lucy's hair. If you're determined to do this, will you at least let me do it for you?"

Jane sighed and nodded. "You'll probably make a better job of it than I could. Here." She handed the scissors to her friend.

"Sit down and sit still."

The older woman began to snip Jane's hair at shoulder length. The long, discarded strands soon coated the linoleum floor around their feet.

"What do you think to a fringe?" Ethel asked. "If I cut it at a slant, it should cover the bald patch quite well."

"Do what you think best. I just want to brush my hair without pain."

"Here we go." Ethel snipped some more, teased the brush through the remaining curls and stood back to admire her handiwork. "Not bad, if I say so myself."

"Can I see?"

Ethel lifted her handbag from a peg on the back door. "Here, it's the only mirror I have in the house that isn't broken." She took out a powder compact from her handbag and flipped it open.

Jane peered into the small mirror, turning her face this way and that to see the full effect of her new hairstyle. "Thanks, Ethel. I'm sure it will be much easier for me to brush now."

"More modern, too. All the girls are going for shoulder length these days. Most have to use curlers every night to get the waves you have, though."

"You were right about the fringe. I like the way it covers the scar."

"Why don't you dab some of that powder over the bruising?"

Jane grinned. "I have my own powder, Ethel. I'll go get it." She hurried upstairs to her room and collected the compact from her dresser that she'd found at the house. She ran downstairs, smiling at the lightness she felt; now the weight of her hair was gone.

The powder covered the discoloured skin on her temple and around her eye. "Now I look almost normal."

"You look lovely." Ethel touched her chin with a finger and frowned. "Mm, I have a lipstick in that bag, somewhere."

"Oh, Ethel, no!" Jane protested. "We are going to a church, not to a dance."

"All right, no lipstick. I'll warm that porridge; it's grown cold while we were hairdressing."

Jane received a few curious stares in church, but Ethel soon explained her presence to all her friends, and they accepted her with no further fuss. She sang the hymns, knelt to pray and went through the motions of celebrating the Christmas service, but her heart wasn't in it. She wasn't a Christian.

She didn't know what she was. She didn't feel any affinity for her mother's religion either. She sensed she believed in God, but knew her faith had been severely tested. She didn't want to think too deeply about the rift between her and her God. Everyday life was throwing her more challenges than she could handle. She didn't have space in her head to include doubts about her religion.

She had been trying to force her memories to the surface without success. She was desperate to discover the contents of the message from the man called Sebastian. It was important. The information could save lives if only she could get to it.

She'd tried relaxation techniques. Each night she'd gone to bed with the intentions of trying the meditation she'd practised in the past. She hoped the deep relaxation would help her mind focus. The method was one she recalled from her days at the University of Hamburg. She could remember some of those days clearly now.

As the daughter of a Jewish mother, she would have been at the end of the line for admittance to the University, but somehow, with her father's influence, she secured a place.

She studied philosophy and languages. The languages came easily. Her English tutor was from South Yorkshire in England, and although some students complained about his unusual-sounding accent, Jane had loved the flattened vowels and contracted words. She thought his accent gave his students a more natural edge to the language. He became a good friend in the two years she studied with him, but she couldn't remember his name.

The philosophy studies intrigued her. Why are we here? What is the meaning of life? Finding the answers to these impossible questions fascinated her. It was in these classes that she learned how to control her emotions, how to meditate, and discovered how easily she could be hypnotised.

Jane jumped as if she'd been poked in the back.

"What's wrong, love?" Ethel whispered. "That chest wound giving you some pain?"

"No, sorry, I think I drifted off for a while."

"Can't blame you, love," Ethel spoke with her hand covering her mouth.

The service was continuing with the vicar reading a sermon.

Ethel giggled softly. "This vicar isn't a patch on the last one. You'd think he'd put a bit more effort in. It's Christmas Day after all."

Jane wasn't listening. Her mind was drifting back in time to a lecture theatre full of sleepy students. The hot afternoon of a Hamburg summer was accompanied by the buzzing of insects from the open window and the drone of a soft, soporific voice. "You're on a beach. Feel the pebbles under your bare feet... Wiggle your toes over the smooth, cool stones. Take a step… Take another step. Feel the pebbles rolling gently beneath your feet as you move along. Approach the lapping water. Listen to the gulls above. Smell the scent of the sea in the air, feel the soft breeze caressing your face…"

Jane shuddered. She'd been sitting in a hot lecture theatre but had believed she was on a beach. She could see and hear the ocean and taste salt on her lips. A cool breeze blew on her warm cheeks. She felt cool pebbles under her bare feet. She could feel them crunching as she walked, even though she had sandals on and hadn't moved an inch from her place in the lecture theatre.

She had been hypnotised without being aware it was happening. The tutor had fooled them into a false sense of reality to prove a point. He'd explained that he was going to show them a relaxation technique, and she had gone along with his instructions with the rest of the class. When he brought them back to reality, through a series of consciousness levels, she began to understand what had been done. The more aware of her surroundings she became, the more foolish she felt.

"See how easy it is to create a believable illusion of reality?" He had seemed pleased with the results of his test as many students were shaking their heads and gazing around the room in dismay. "How many of you went under?"

The experiment had been interesting and had given the students much to discuss and laugh about, but now the memory held new meaning.

Hypnosis was the key to unlocking her memories.

Chapter Sixteen – Coming Clean

Jane had an appointment with Doctor Fisher for the third of January. It was a few days away, but it couldn't come soon enough for her. She was sitting with Ethel, taking the time to relax with her after the trauma of the previous day at the cemetery. The glaziers had been while they were out, and the windows were now secure and weather proof. The house was warm and cosy for the first time since the bombing.

"I could have told you it was no use trying to see the doctor over Christmas, love. You could see how busy they were. He'd not have thanked you for turning up early. He didn't have time to see you, did he? That's why appointments are made."

"I don't see why he couldn't make an exception." Jane was annoyed that her plans to see the doctor earlier couldn't be implemented but understood she would have to wait until Friday. She wished she could tell Ethel why it was so important, but the poor woman had enough to contend with without taking on Jane's complicated problems.

She suddenly realised that Friday would be Sasha's birthday. Would her daughter's carers celebrate her birthday? Would they even know it *was* her birthday? Her little girl would be four-years-old and wouldn't remember her real mother. Jane swallowed her emotion. It wouldn't do for her to dwell on the misery. She couldn't change anything. Not yet, anyway.

Perhaps Gottfried would find their daughter. Had he tried to travel to Bavaria? Was he already on his way there now? She wished she knew where he was. If only, she could let him know she was still alive. She couldn't picture his face, and that was irritating her. She loved the man. She loved the essence of him, but couldn't remember his face. She could pass him in the street and not know him.

At various times, many unconnected things came flashing into her head, but stringing a coherent memory together from the disjointed splinters was impossible. Some fragments did eventually unite into a seamless whole, and when that happened, she was always amazed. The good memories filled her with happiness, but the traumatic ones sometimes left her breathless with terror.

The journey from Hamburg had been terrifying. Danger lurked in every railway station or crossroad they came to. Each time their papers were inspected, her heart had hammered so hard she feared it would escape her chest. The time they'd been chased through the forest near Osnabrück by soldiers with dogs had been the most harrowing. They escaped by hiding in a lake, breathing through reeds as they froze in the cold water until the soldiers gave up and left.

What was Gottfried doing? What was he thinking to put himself through that again? Would he be in danger now? Would he find their daughter? Did he know where she was? Would Sasha's carers welcome him? She had so many questions and so few answers. Did she know where her daughter was being kept in hiding? Was that information hiding in her head along with the message from Sebastian, and so many other important snippets from her past?

Lives depended on the information she had in her head, but she realised that Ethel didn't know the importance of her appointment, and she didn't want to take out her frustrations on her friend. The funeral of her family had taken place the previous day, and poor Ethel was still feeling delicate and raw.

The grave had already been covered before the friends and relatives of the dead gathered for the service. Jane had held tightly to Ethel's hand as they walked with the other mourners to the long patch of newly turned earth. The service didn't last long, and Jane was thankful. Poor Ethel stood in the cold, weeping for her lost child and grandchildren while the minister talked about loss and sadness, of rebirth and a life everlasting in eternity.

Jane didn't like the formality of the occasion. She heard no personal references to the people who had died. The grieving crowd were informed there'd be a memorial service arranged at a later date, where they could attend and have the opportunity to add their own contributions. Jane thought the sentiment was right, but the timing was wrong. Ethel didn't want a memorial. She wanted her daughter and grandchildren at her side.

The day had been long and painful for Ethel, but Jane didn't leave her side. She walked her home and made her tea. Talked with her until after midnight, and tucked her into bed when she was half asleep from exhaustion.

Today was the beginning of healing for her friend. With the funeral over, she could begin to rebuild her life. Ethel had talked of applying for a job where her daughter had worked. She wanted to fill her life with something meaningful now she no longer had the grandchildren to care for. Jane promised to go with her. "I need to find paid work too. We can't live on hand outs," she'd said.

"After the New Year we'll both find our feet, you'll see." Ethel had promised. "We'll get by."

The New Year celebrations would be held all over the city tonight. Tomorrow, the world would go on. Nineteen-forty-one would be no different from the previous year for many, but for Ethel, it would be a lonely time of adjustment. Jane wanted to stay with her, to see her through the worst of her grief but was beginning to understand that she had other responsibilities.

She had to find her husband, and she had to get the information in her head to Susan's family and friends. So many people depended on her. Would she be strong enough to face the challenges ahead? She was beginning to think she should try to get to Bavaria to find her family but had no idea how she would do that. She would need documents and travel passes. She knew Susan's father could help her get what she needed, but would he want to?

Could she allow the doctor to hypnotise her? He would discover her true identity. Could she trust him? Would he trust her? Would he think she might be a spy and report her? Would the authorities believe her story?

She was glad to have Tom Gosney on her side. He had already offered to accompany her to the appointment and vouch for her. She realised she would probably need him to be with her. She'd arranged to see him on New Year's Day. The church was holding special services of remembrance and Jane had agreed she would attend his church. She planned to take Ethel with her. The older woman needed something to occupy her mind, and introducing her to the Gosney family seemed a good place to start.

She realised that Ethel would need to know more about her past if she were to introduce her to Reverend Gosney and his group. She didn't want to burden her friend with all the details but knew her story would distract the older woman for a while. Jane decided that now was as good a time as any to tell her what she needed to know.

"Ethel, can I tell you something?"

"What's that, love?" Ethel roused from her thoughts. "Did you say something?"

"I've remembered some things over the last few days, and I think it's only fair that I tell you the truth about me. You need to know who I am and why I'm here."

"That sounds mysterious. Fire away, lass. I'm all ears."

"I don't come from Holland. I'm from Germany."

"Oh, my goodness!" Ethel jumped from her chair.

Jane hastened to explain, "I'm no threat to you. My mother was a Jew."

"You're a Jew!" Ethel clutched the back of her chair for support. She seemed even more shocked.

"My mother was. My father was a Gentile, but he hated what the Nazis did to my mother and her family. He detested Hitler."

"Go on." Ethel seemed wary. "I don't know what to make of knowing you're a German, and everyone knows Jews can't be trusted, but I'll give you the benefit of the doubt, for now. I'm still listening."

Jane thought she was ready to deal with Ethel's responses to learning her true nationality; but had not been prepared for her anti-Semitic response.

"What do you have against Jews?" Jane couldn't help being protective of her mother's religion. "Do you even know any Jews?"

"Well, I know what I read in the newspapers." Ethel sounded defensive.

"You shouldn't put your trust in things that are written about Jews, Ethel. That's how Hitler came to power. By stirring up a storm of propaganda against my people."

"Well, I hope you're not suggesting that I'm like Hitler!"

"I'm not saying that, Ethel." Jane realised she would have to placate her friend before telling her story. The older woman was only displaying the ingrained mistrust that half of Europe had for Jews. "I'm sorry. I never meant to offend you. I'm your friend, Ethel, and I thought you were mine."

"I am! I've nothing against you, love. I know you're a good lass. You're not greedy or mean like they'd have us believe of your sort."

"Oh, Ethel." Jane couldn't help a wry smile. "When you say that, you mean Jews, don't you?"

Ethel lifted her chin defiantly.

"I don't blame you for the opinion you have. I blame the ones in authority who should know better than to spout the damaging propaganda to the proletariat that led us to where we are now."

"I don't pretend to understand all those big words you're saying, love, but folks around here know that Jews can't be trusted." Ethel's face softened. "Look, love, I feel sorry for what's happening to your lot in Germany, and I was glad to hear it when our government opened the doors to the children. Britain took its fair share of those poor little refugees. We're not heartless."

"Sit down, Ethel. I think I should tell you my story." Jane watched Ethel take her seat and decided that the truth would be the only way to persuade her friend to revise her opinion. "You see, I was in a unique position. My mother was from a Jewish family, but my father was a

Gentile. He was a Christian. I saw some differences between the families, but I saw more similarities. We are all the same under the skin." She was generalising because of her lack of substantiating memories, but Ethel was listening with interest.

"Jews have been persecuted for hundreds of years, simply because they worship God in a different way, and perhaps have customs that some people don't understand or agree with. I can't remember much of my childhood, but I know it wasn't easy to be the daughter of both sides of the religious barrier."

"I didn't think Jews allowed marriage to outsiders."

"It doesn't happen often, but it's not unheard of. My father loved my mother very much." Jane knew that was true, and she sighed, remembering how it must have devastated her father to choose between them. He could have tried to save his wife but he stayed to protect his daughter on the horrific day her mother was murdered.

She began her story by outlining the parts of her life that she *could* remember while living in Hamburg. She explained the harsh treatment of her family, the slow but unstoppable exclusion from all areas of life. She explained the death of her mother as simply as she could, but couldn't help weeping.

"Oh, dear girl. Did those boys really beat her to death?" Ethel had a fist clenched to her mouth. "I didn't realise it was that bad for the Jews. I mean, I read the newspapers, but like you just said, you can't believe everything they print. Some of it is too awful to think about."

Jane continued her story, telling of her days at the University until the time when she was excluded. "My Jewish heritage caused them to kick me out. My English tutor tried to stand up for me, but they kicked him out too. That's when my father decided we should make our plans to leave, but I think I must have met Gottfried by then."

"Gottfried?"

"Godfrey. We changed our names when we came to England. It made life easier."

"Godfrey is your husband."

"Yes. I think he's a Gentile too. I have a feeling he's not a Jew. I think we fell in love and married, but I don't know when. We had a child four years ago."

"You're a mother?" Ethel gasped. "Where's the child?"

"She's in hiding in Bavaria. She has her father's colouring. She's blonde." Jane paused. "Gottfried has blonde hair." She saw the outline of her husband, tall and fair. Her chest filled with emotion. She loved the man with all her heart but his face remained fogged.

"Why does she have to hide? Who's looking for her?"

"She is part Jew, and Hitler wants to eliminate all Jews from his idea of a perfect world."

"But that's ridiculous! She's a child!"

Jane shrugged and tried to keep calm. "Why do you think Jewish families sent their children out of Germany? They didn't give them up easily. The families were in real danger, Ethel." Jane stopped short of giving her friend another lecture. The poor woman knew little about Hitler's dehumanising regime, and Jane realised that what she had read, she refused to believe because it was too horrific to digest. She went on, "All Jews in the occupied territories are living in terror, Ethel."

"I didn't realise." The older woman shook her head.

"I've been told that German soldiers now have orders to shoot any Jew who runs away from them. They also have orders to take any Jew sympathisers caught with Jews hiding on their property and send them to the labour camps."

"How could anyone know such a thing? I don't believe it. They must be spies. Who told you that?" Ethel's voice trembled with a trace of fear and she looked at Jane with suspicion in her eyes.

"The people I'm taking you to meet tomorrow."

Ethel gasped. "I won't go. You're not taking me to meet a bunch of spies."

"They're not spies, Ethel. They are a group of English citizens trying to help people like me get to safety. They save lives. They saved mine!"

"How can I believe you?"

"Mr Gosney is their leader. He's a vicar. He's my friend."

"Reverend Gosney?" Ethel looked shocked.

"Yes, do you know him?"

"Does he have a daughter called Susan?"

"Yes, she's my best friend, or so she tells me." Jane smiled. "Do you know them?"

"I know his wife, Millie. We went to school together. I haven't seen her in years, but I hear about her."

"Well, you'll be seeing her tomorrow. I'm sure you two will have a lot to talk about."

"Is she one of these people?"

Jane nodded. "I told you they weren't spies."

"Oh, lass. If all that you told me is true, no wonder we're fighting so hard to get rid of Hitler. I know he's a bad man, but what those men did to your mother! Well! I never heard the like in my life."

"It's all true, Ethel."

"You poor thing. You must miss your little one. What's her name?"

"Sasha, she'll be four in three days' time."

Ethel and Millie couldn't be separated. The two women had nodded greetings before the service began, but by the time tea and cakes were served at the rear of the church, they were chatting like old friends.

"It's a small world." Susan brought a plate to Jane. "Who'd have thought it? Your friend and my mum, eh?"

"Ethel said they went to the same school."

Jane watched the two older women laughing together. "This is just what Ethel needs."

"So I hear, poor woman." Tom came to join them. "Terrible story. She must be devastated."

"Not that you'd know from her brightness today." Susan smiled as she watched her mother guiding Ethel to a seat.

"She's brave. I've never known a stronger woman." Jane remembered her own mother and added, "Well, perhaps I knew one who was tougher, but she was stubborn too."

"Your mother?" Tom asked.

Jane nodded.

"She had principles." The older man patted Jane's shoulder. "She might have chosen the wrong time and place to fight for them, but you can't blame her for that."

"I don't blame her," Jane admitted. "I miss her."

"Nice hairstyle, by the way." Susan flicked a finger through Jane's curls. "Suits you."

"Thank you. Ethel cut it for me. I was finding it too painful to work the tangles out with this." She lifted her fringe.

"Ouch." Susan grimaced. "That looks sore."

"It's better than it was. I'll be seeing the doctor on Friday. I'm sure he'll tell me everything is healing as it should."

"What time do we need to be there?" Tom asked.

"One, I think." Jane smiled at the older man. "Thanks for offering to come with me."

"Well, from what you've told me, I think you'll need someone there to explain a few things. Hypnosis sounds scary to me."

"I'm sure I'll be fine, Tom. Have you heard any news from across the channel?"

Tom pressed his lips together and frowned.

"But you got word from Dungeness. Tell her, dad. She needs to know."

Jane's heart skipped. "What have you heard? Have those people arrived that you were expecting?"

Tom shook his head. "It seems Godfrey has gone over to Belgium. Our contact in Dungeness has a small boat. He risks his life to bring our consignments over from the Belgian or French coast. It seems Godfrey persuaded him to take him back on the return journey."

Jane closed her eyes. "He's a fool! What does he hope to gain? Sasha is safe where she is. If he tried to bring her back to England, they could both be killed. Isn't that why we left her there? She has no papers!"

"Well, that's not strictly true, Grace." Tom took Jane's arm. "Come sit down."

Jane allowed him to steer her to the nearest pews at the back of the church. Ethel glanced at her and smiled uncertainly. She tried to return her friend's smile to reassure the older woman but was too nervous to make it appear genuine. "Why do I get the feeling I'm not going to like what you have to say?"

"Don't be cross, Jane." Susan sat next to her on the long wooden bench. "You agreed to wait until our contacts said it was safer for her."

"Are you saying you have papers for Sasha? Does this mean we could get her out? How long have you had them?"

"We had them made soon after you arrived, but we all agreed that she was safer where she was, and it would be better to wait for the right time. Our resources are not infinite, and others were in greater need of rescue."

"I understand." Jane could feel the emotion of the decision to delay her daughter's rescue. Every fibre of her body was crying out to hold her child in her arms again, but her needs were secondary to the welfare of Sasha. "Where are these papers?"

"They're gone. I think Godfrey took them."

"But it isn't safe! You said yourself that you couldn't risk anyone travelling the routes until you know what Sebastian had to tell us."

"Godfrey knew that, Grace." Tom sighed. "Sorry, but I can't get used to thinking of you as Jane."

"Never mind my name. It's not important."

"He's sensible, Jane." Susan put a comforting arm around her shoulders. "He won't use the known routes. He'll be careful. You know he will."

Jane closed her eyes and tried to concentrate. "I have to know what that message contained. It's the only thing I need to remember. Why won't it come?"

"Don't get upset, love." Susan squeezed her shoulder. "Hopefully, the doctor will be able to help free your memories on Friday."

"But that could be too late. Gottfried has been gone more than two weeks already. He could be in Bavaria by now. He could be risking his life and Sasha's. What if he's on his way back with her and they get caught?"

"Don't do this to yourself, Gra... Jane." The portly man knelt on the floor by her feet and took her hands in his. "I'm praying for them. We can't do more for now. It's in the hands of God."

"God be damned!" Jane quickly bit her lip, realising where she was and just as hastily apologised. "I'm sorry, Tom. I know your faith is important to you, and I don't mean to be disrespectful, it's just..."

"I understand, love. You're upset."

"I'm not upset! I'm angry. I'm angry with God and with myself, and I don't know whether to be angry or pleased that Gottfried has taken the initiative. I want my Sasha with me, but not by taking such risks." She noticed Ethel hurrying over and closed her mouth. "Enough. I can't talk about this now."

"Everything all right?" Ethel asked as she came closer. "What's all the shouting about?"

"I'm frustrated that I can't remember the things I should." She gave Tom and Susan a warning look.

"Well, you only have a couple of days to wait, love. That doctor was convinced he could help you, wasn't he?"

Jane nodded and forced a smile to her lips. She knew she had probably already run out of time. She needed to get to that information now. The lives of her family could depend on her remembering what was in that message.

She could see only one thing for it. It wasn't the most sensible thing to do, but she had no choice. "I think I'd like to go home. I have a headache."

Ethel agreed to leave with her and arrangements were made to meet at the hospital on Friday. Millie fussed around Ethel, making her own arrangements for the old school friends to meet soon.

"Are you sure you're strong enough to walk all the way?" Ethel asked as she threaded her arm through Jane's. "We can take the bus to the end of Bramall Lane if you like."

"I'm fine, Ethel. It's not my physical strength that's letting me down. My head aches, that's all."

She let Ethel chatter for most of the way. The older woman had obviously enjoyed meeting her former school pal, and she'd been impressed by the aims of the organisation.

"I never realised all this kind of thing was going on in my own city. Fancy! All this cloak and dagger stuff, and not more than a few streets away from where we are!"

"It's hardly cloak and dagger, Ethel." Jane smiled. "We don't hide what we do. The local officials and social services know about us and help us settle the families."

"I wonder whether Miss Humphrey has anything to do with your friends in the organisation."

"I don't think she's involved. She would have known me when she saw me at the hospital, wouldn't she?"

"I don't know. You didn't look anything like yourself in the hospital. Now the swelling has gone down; you look different."

"But she would have recognised my voice, surely?"

"You're right there, my love. Your voice is certainly one of a kind, isn't it?"

Jane smiled. She knew why her voice was so distinct. She had her English tutor to thank for that. She could almost picture him. He was tall and had strikingly blue eyes. She felt a jolt of unexpected emotion as she realised the strength of her deep affection for the man. She'd been in love with him! They'd had an affair!

Jane stumbled, and Ethel caught her arm more tightly to stop her from falling.

"I knew we should have waited for the bus. Are you all right?"

"I need to sit down." Jane saw a pile of rubble by the roadside and went to sit on the mound of broken bricks. "I had another flash from my past. I don't understand it."

"You're getting more, and more of those aren't you, love?"

Jane nodded absently and then began to shake her head. "Not like this one."

"What did you remember?"

"I think I was…" she realised that nothing would be gained by admitting her affair. How could she have been unfaithful to Gottfried?

141

Chapter Seventeen – Desperate Measures

Jane excused herself soon after arriving home. Her headache was a good enough reason for an afternoon nap.

"You get some rest, love. I'll make us something nice to eat for when you wake up."

"Thanks, Ethel. I just need a couple of hours." Jane climbed the stairs and went to lie on the bed.

She kicked off her shoes and shuffled until she got comfortable. What she had in mind had nothing to do with sleep, but she needed to be completely relaxed if her idea was to work. She began by taking some deep, slow breaths while concentrating on a smudge on the ceiling. Thoughts drifted into her head, and she examined them before letting them go.

The image of Sasha as a toddler stayed in her mind and was soon overlaid by the photograph of her parents. The essence of her English tutor floated to the forefront, and she felt the overwhelming emotion of intense longing. She had thought that emotion was attached to her husband until she remembered her lover. Gottfried jumped into her head. He was still unfocused and hazy but the emotion she felt for him was quieter, and less powerful than she'd felt for her tutor. What had happened in her past to make her turn to another man?

She realised she was being distracted from her goal and let the thoughts and feelings go. She had to do this properly to have any degree of success. Unlocking her memories would not be easy. This procedure required extreme concentration balanced with complete relaxation to force the tiny octopuses in her head to link their tentacles. Jane smiled at the silly image her mind was creating.

"Now, try to be serious," she whispered aloud to help focus her thoughts. "This is important."

She hadn't done this before, but she'd written an essay about it for her philosophy course. The mechanics of self-hypnosis were widely covered in a variety of publications. She had studied various methods to induce the state, but she thought the one using a visualisation of stairs and water might be the easiest for her to imagine.

With luck, it would work for her. She had two good reasons to try the technique. Her husband and her daughter. Gottfried and Sasha might be in danger right now, and her mind could hold the key to keeping them safe. A third justification for putting herself through this was her recent revelation. She had to know why she felt as she did about her English tutor. What role had he played in her past?

Relaxing, she tried another method of meditation to prepare her mind before entering the state of hypnosis. She started at her feet and consciously released the tension in her toes. Working up her body, she flexed and released her calf muscles, then her thighs, her buttocks, and then her tummy. With each release of tension, she relaxed more and continued until her whole body felt completely light and free.

Imagining a flight of stairs leading downward into water, she began to descend. One, she counted in her head. Feeling each tread of the wooden steps beneath her feet, she continued to count. She imagined the sound of gently lapping water and moved closer. Her feet continued down the stairs until she felt the cool water around her ankles. She counted five and took another step into the coolness.

By the time she reached ten, she was totally submerged, completely relaxed and floating freely in the water. She took a few seconds to experience the cool water on her skin, and sense the freshness of the clean, clear liquid she floated in.

She visualised three chests in the water with her. They were illusions created by her mind to help her with the task in hand, but her state of trance was so deep that they appeared and felt real. She reached to open one and was blinded by a bright, white light.

"I can see the paper." She peered into the chest. "I can see the words on the paper. I can see the words on the paper," she chanted the same phrase continually for what seemed like hours.

Eventually, she was stirred to reach into the chest. Her hand grasped and lifted out a piece of paper. The writing was clear, but she couldn't read it. The language was not one she recognised. She stared at the text, memorising the marks.

When she thought she had committed the words to her memory, she moved to the second chest. When it opened, the light was not as bright, or perhaps her subconscious eyes had grown accustomed to the glare. "I can see Sasha. She is safe in her hiding place. I know where this is. I know her hiding place." Jane stayed near the chest, chanting the words, "I know her hiding place. I know her hiding place." Over and over, she repeated the words. She reached her hand inside the box but her fingers found only space. Nothing happened. She had no flash of inspiration and no idea how to get more from the empty chest.

After a while, she left the chest, feeling despondent. The empty box had given her nothing. She moved to the third chest. It took all her strength to open this one, but the light that came from inside it was soft and warm. She found it difficult to form the questions in her mind. This chest should contain what she wanted to know, but she didn't know how to ask. Her English tutor was important to her, but so was Gottfried. Her heart was torn, and confusion made her tense.

The water began to churn around her. She couldn't be anxious. Relaxation was the key to unlocking the memories.

"Relax, relax, relax," she chanted, but the churning water didn't calm down.

Jane moved to the stairs and quickly began to climb out of the water. She knew her ascent was too fast, but she had no choice. She had to wake up gradually. Her fragile mind could be damaged even more if she hurried this part of the hypnosis.

"I'm getting lighter. Ten!"

Taking two more steps upward, she counted down. "Nine. Eight. My body is becoming lighter."

At five, her heart began to beat more rapidly and a heavy weight pressed on her chest. She paused, taking a few seconds to compose herself before stepping up and counting, four.

At number one, she knew she was conscious again. She kept her eyes closed, concentrating on her body, and mentally checking her hands, her feet and her head to ground herself in the here and now.

When she opened her eyes, she felt elated. She'd done it. She'd seen the words on the paper. They hadn't meant anything to her, but she knew they were important. They were etched in her mind. Scrambling to her feet, she ran down the stairs, ignoring all the advice she'd written about in her essay to stay relaxed and quiet for a time after being hypnotised.

"Ethel, I need a pencil and paper."

"What's the emergency?" Ethel turned from the table where she was peeling potatoes.

"Do you have some?" Jane insisted. "It's important."

Ethel went to the small dresser and opened a drawer. "Here you are."

Jane wasted no time. Sitting at the table, she began to write the letters and symbols she had seen. Ethel watched over her shoulder while she wrote. When she'd finished, she had three rows of unintelligible text.

"What does that mean?" Ethel peered at the writing. "Looks Double-Dutch to me."

"I'm not sure." Jane was grinning. "But I think it's Russian."

"Where did you come up with that?"

"I found it in my mind, Ethel. I remembered a very important message. Now I need to find someone to translate it for me."

"Well, good luck with that. We don't have many Russians living around here."

Jane couldn't help smiling. She knew of one, and she had already arranged to meet her the following evening.

Hannah's colourful scarf made heads turn in the drably dressed crowd at the Crown Inn. Her hair would have made her stand out, but the scarf helped to emphasise her uniqueness. Most customers seemed to know her and greeted her with nods and smiles as she made her way to Jane's table.

"I'm glad you came. I thought I might have scared you away the last time we met."

"Far from it!" Jane pushed a glass of ale over the table. "I bought you a beer."

"Thank you." Hannah took a seat. "Did you think about what I said?"

"You're very direct. Aren't you going to ask me how I am, first?"

"No need to ask. You look fine. I can see your face is much improved. Nice hairstyle, too. It makes you look modern and very English."

"While you still look every inch a Jew or a Russian, I'm not sure which."

"I'll take either. I don't care where you pigeonhole me. I'm happy in my own skin."

"Good for you. I wish I felt as confident."

"Are you still having problems with your memory?"

"Things are starting to come back to me. Actually, as you like directness, I'd like your help with something."

"Oh? What can I do for you?"

Jane fished the paper from her coat pocket. "Can you read this?"

Hannah took the paper and frowned. "This is a crude representation of Russian Cyrillic, but I think I can make it out."

"I thought you might be able to."

"You thought this because I was born in Russia, yes?"

Jane nodded.

"Silly girl, never take anything for granted. I was born there, but I left before I was of age to attend a Russian school. Fortunately for you, my love of languages included my mother tongue."

Jane was getting impatient. "What does it say?"

"Let me see." Hannah took her spectacles and a pencil from her bag. Placing the spectacles on her nose, she peered at the paper. "This part is simple. It's a name. Heinrich Schneider." She wrote the name beneath the script. "Then this part could refer to the man's occupation."

"Who is he? What does he do?"

"Give me a minute. My Russian is a little rusty." She chewed the end of her pencil. "This part translates to the key gamer. But that doesn't make sense." She shook her head. "No, that can't be right."

"The key gamer?" Jane didn't understand the phrase.

"It's difficult to understand the text with all the extra flourishes you gave the letters. I have a feeling these words are only part of the whole message. The sentences are jumbled and disjointed with many missing pieces."

"Perhaps we could fill the gaps." Jane was desperate to know what the message contained. "We have the word 'key'. Could he be a locksmith?"

"It's possible, but where does the word 'game' fit with that?" Hannah sighed. "What other occupation would use keys?"

"A jailor?" Jane shuddered.

"We need to think outside the obvious."

"He could be a pianist," Jane suggested. You'll find keys on a piano."

Hannah grinned at Jane. "Brilliant work!"

"Isn't that what they call the secret wireless operators?"

"That sounds right. Well done, Jane."

"What about him? Why is he important?"

"The message goes on to say the link is broken, no, wait, there is a weak link. The link is not broken, but there is a danger it might break."

"Does it say where the weak link is?"

"Saarbrücken. Someone or something in that town is the weak link."

Jane quickly realised that Saarbrücken would be central to many escape routes from Germany. The town was close to the border with France, and not far from Belgium, Luxembourg or Switzerland. She remembered discussing some routes with her father, but that seemed so long ago. Her memories were dim. "What else does it tell you?"

"It's unclear. Parts of the letters are missing, and it looks like you added a few embellishments of your own. It's difficult to work out, and as I said, my Russian could use some revision."

"Perhaps I didn't remember the message as well as I should have." Jane felt disappointed that her efforts hadn't worked as she'd hoped they might.

"You *remembered* this?" Hannah looked impressed.

Jane nodded. "I managed to drag it from my mind."

"From what I can see, this message could be important to someone in an influential position." The girl leant back in her chair and took a sip from her glass. "Who are you, Jane Smith?" She narrowed her eyes, but her lips held a teasing smile. "And how come you have something like this in your head?" She tapped the paper.

"You told me you work for an organisation that helps Jews escape from Germany."

"Yes," Hannah set her glass down, and her face grew serious.

"It seems I work for a similar group. You might have heard of them."

"There are many groups and organisations working for the oppressed people in Europe. I know of one other with a branch in Sheffield. The Coalition for Liberation."

"Do you know them?"

Hannah nodded. "I keep telling my people we should be working together but they are against joining forces. They say having too many people involved would slow things down and could compromise the safety of our people on the ground."

"Your people need to know this information, Hannah. It came in on the twelfth, the day I was injured." She touched her temple. "I took the message from a man called Sebastian, and I don't remember much of anything after that."

"Sebastian?" Hannah's face paled. "Sebastian Novik?"

"I don't know his surname."

"Was he tall, dark hair with a moustache, brown eyes, athletic build, early thirties?"

"I can't help you, Hannah. I know his name because I was told it. I don't remember the man."

"Did he come to England?"

"Apparently, I met him in the Marples that night." Jane realised Hannah knew the man, judging from her response to his name. She would have to tread carefully. "What is he, to you?"

"He was my lover until he dedicated his life to scurrying around Europe hiding from the Gestapo and helping to bring Hitler down."

"Your lover?" Jane gasped. Hannah was about the same age as she was and she was openly admitting that she had a lover.

"Oh, don't get your knickers knotted. Marriage is for keeps but who can keep anything in the world we came from? It seemed easier not to have ties."

"Do you love this man?" Jane was dreading the answer. She didn't want to give Hannah the news of Sebastian's death.

"If it's the same man, perhaps I did, once." She shrugged. "But I haven't seen him in two years. Long-distance love affairs don't work." She sipped her drink. "It might have been nice to see him, though. I'm surprised he didn't stop by while he was here."

"Perhaps he intended to, Hannah, but he was prevented from doing so."

"By whom?"

Jane took a breath before whispering, "By the bomb that flattened the Marples."

"No!" The glass crashed from Hannah's hand to the table, bounced and landed on the floor without breaking. The beer splashed over the table and soaked into her coat.

"Hannah, don't get upset." Jane hurried to try to tone down the implication of her words. "He might not be the same man. It could be anyone. There must be more than one Sebastian in the world."

Hannah took a handkerchief from her bag and began to dab aggressively at the wet stain on her coat. "There won't be many Sebastians in our line of work who can write in Russian." She sniffed and dragged her coat sleeve over her face to dry the tears on her cheeks. "It's him." She raised her glossy eyes to Jane, but her voice was firm when she asked, "Was he identified?"

"I think they found his wallet. That's what Reverend Gosney told me."

"Why don't I know this?" Hannah cried. "I work at the Central Library, for goodness' sake, and I don't know this!" The girl was getting more agitated.

"Calm yourself, Hannah." Jane reached out to the girl. "People are looking at us."

"Let them look. I have nothing to hide."

"Perhaps not, but don't give them cause to pity you. I know you don't want that."

Hannah took a deep breath. "You're right. I wouldn't like that. How astute of you, to know that about me."

"We are alike, you and I," Jane told her. "I knew it from the first moment I met you."

She had felt they were kindred spirits from the start, and the more she spoke with the girl, the more she was convinced of it. Hannah's revelation about having a lover had shocked her, but she realised that she too had taken a lover. Her English tutor still meant more to her than her husband. Her heart and her emotions told her as much. How could she condemn Hannah when her own morals were no better?

Hannah smiled bravely. "I felt it too. You've grown in confidence since we last met. I hoped you would."

"Why?"

"Because I couldn't ask to take a frightened lamb to the slaughter. The elders would never allow it."

"Is that what I looked like to you?" Jane smiled. "I have to admit I was out of my depth. With no memory and no clear idea who I was, I couldn't trust anyone, and was afraid to open my mouth."

"Not now, though, eh?" Hannah dabbed her eyes with the beer-soaked handkerchief. "Now you are magically conjuring secret Russian messages from your head and demanding to know what they mean." She gave Jane a tremulous smile and whispered, "In some parts that would be enough to have you arrested as a spy."

"But you know I'm no spy, and I'm no longer afraid that you'll have me arrested."

"Do you know what this means?" Hannah picked the wet paper from the table and shook it.

"I think so." Jane didn't understand the full implications of the message but knew this man had to be dealt with.

"We have to tell our people that the escape routes are not safe." Hannah was already gathering her bag and gloves, getting ready to leave. "We have to find this Heinrich Schneider and silence him." She got to her feet.

Jane began to fasten her coat. "Well, *we* can't do that personally, but I'm sure the organisation will know people who can do it for us."

"You're wrong, Jane. We *could* do this. If that really was my Sebastian who died that night, then they will be a man short over there. He would have known what to do. He wouldn't have failed us, and I won't fail him. I'll volunteer to finish the job."

"Are you saying your lover was an assassin?"

Hannah shrugged. "He was in the Secret Service. I think it was part of his job description."

"Then why didn't he just do it?" Jane felt they were missing something. "Why didn't he kill the man and be done with it? Why did he come all this way, at great risk, to deliver a message?"

"You have a point." Hannah resumed her seat. "Sebastian would have dealt with this man. There has to be a reason, why he didn't. We can't see the full picture. There has to be more to this message."

"Take another look. Maybe you'll see something else."

Hannah spread the wet paper on the table and stared intently at the blurred writing. "Heinrich Schneider is definitely a pianist, and it looks as if this man knows something. No, wait a minute."

"What do you see?" Jane leant closer.

"I'm not sure, but if I read this without the flourish you put on those letters, it changes the meaning. I think this man is a key player, not a key gamer. There is something here that could mean 'taken' or 'stolen', I'm not sure, but this last word is clear. It says, 'Gestapo'."

"Then Heinrich Schneider *is* on our side, and he's been captured!" Jane understood immediately. "If he's a key player, he will know about the safe houses and the routes over there. If he talks, the whole organisation could be in jeopardy."

Chapter Eighteen – Clearing the Fog

Jane arrived at the hospital early, eager to see Tom Gosney. She had news for him and hoped he could make use of it. Pacing impatiently outside the entrance, she waited for him to arrive. When a portly man in a trilby and large overcoat walked through the gates, she looked twice and then breathed a sigh of relief. She'd expected to see Tom in his vicar's robes, and the ordinary clothing had confused her for a second.

"Tom!" She waved and ran to greet him. "I know what the message said," she blurted. "I don't need to go in there." She pointed to the hospital. "I remembered the message from Sebastian."

Tom hugged her gently, being careful not to hurt her back. "Tell me."

"A man called Heinrich Schneider has been captured by the Gestapo. Do you know of him?"

Tom frowned. "He's our man on the ground in Saarbrücken. He oils the wheels and crosses the odd palm with silver to bribe people into silence."

"Do you think he'll talk?"

"If the Gestapo has him, I know he will. Poor man won't be able to help himself."

"They won't use torture, will they?"

"Don't be naïve, love. They'll use whatever it takes to get the information from him." Tom pressed his lips together. "We need to act fast. I have to go."

She grabbed his coat sleeve. "What can I do?"

"You can keep your appointment with the doctor."

"No, I want to come with you. I want to help."

"There's nothing you can do for now, but you have to see that doctor. We need you fit and well, Grace. I mean, Jane."

"I am fit enough. I don't need doctors."

"Do you remember where your daughter is?"

Jane shook her head, admitting that she didn't. "But that's not important. I know she's safe, and it will come back to me in time. I know it will."

"She might not be safe for long if Heinrich talks."

His words shocked her. "Does that man know about Sasha?"

"Probably. He knows about all our people in hiding." Tom grabbed her by the shoulders. "Look, Jane, If Sasha is in a safe house in Bavaria, you can bet Heinrich will know about it. He knows everything. He's the king-pin of our operation in Germany. His mind is razor sharp.

He has the rare gift of photographic recall and never has to write anything down. That's why he's so valuable to us. He never leaves evidence of plans or conversations. He doesn't need to. He's our man on the inside, and he has his finger on the very pulse of our operations."

Jane immediately understood the man's importance. "So, that's also why he's such a danger to your organisation now!"

"I'm afraid so, love." Tom's brow creased. "If the Gestapo has him, it means someone has already talked, and perhaps the safe places will already be discovered."

"What about Gottfried? He'll be in danger too, won't he?"

"Even more than before, I'm afraid."

"What about my little girl? I have to get to Sasha."

"But you don't know where she is. You need to remember her address. We can arrange for people to check on her when we know where she is."

Jane knew he was right. She had no choice. "Then I'll have to let that man loose inside my head, won't I?" Jane glanced to the entrance of the hospital. She didn't want to put herself in the hands of the Doctor Fisher but knew she would have to.

"Be careful, Jane. Explain yourself before he tries to hypnotise you. Give him my name. Tell him I was planning to be with you, but couldn't make it."

"Don't worry about me, Tom. I'll go to see him and take my chances. You have to go and do what you can."

Tom embraced her again. "Come to the church when you're done and hopefully, by then, I might know more."

"How will you get to know news from Germany?"

"I have my sources. I don't use them often, but this situation calls for drastic measures. The less you know, the better."

"Then you take care too, Tom."

Jane watched him hurry away and turned to the entrance of the hospital. She had hoped it wouldn't come to this, but now knew she needed expert help to access her hidden memories. Her daughter's and her husband's life might depend on knowing what was concealed in her mind.

The hospital was a busy place with people hurrying to and fro. She read some signs and soon found her way to the outpatients' department. Giving her name at a desk, she was asked to wait. She took a seat on a row of chairs lining the wide corridor.

Not many minutes passed before her name was called and she was directed to the doctor's office.

"Ah, Miss Smith." Doctor Fisher smiled. "Take a seat and tell me how you are."

"I'm much better than the last time I saw you, Doctor Fisher, thank you."

"Glad to hear it." He rose from the chair behind his desk. "Can I take a look at the wound?"

She obligingly lifted her hair.

"Very nice. That scar will soon fade, and I like what you did with your hair. Good camouflage."

Jane smiled, unsure how to broach the subject of hypnosis.

"How much have you managed to remember? Nurse Wallace said you were still having problems."

She decided to get straight to the point. "I need you to hypnotise me. I tried to do it myself, but the results weren't satisfactory."

"You tried self-hypnosis!" The doctor looked surprised.

"I once did an essay about it. I was desperate, and after you couldn't see me the last time I was here, I had no choice."

"Why the rush?"

"I need to tell you something, Doctor Fisher. I hope you'll understand when I tell you that I have some things hidden in my memories that could mean the difference between life and death for some of my family and many others that may also be in danger."

"My goodness, that sounds serious." The doctor took a seat behind his desk.

"I'm putting my trust in you completely," Jane explained quickly. "My friend, Reverend Thomas Gosney can vouch for me, if you have any doubts about what I'm about to tell you."

"Sounds intriguing. Fire away. I love a good mystery."

"Well, to begin with, I'm German, and I'm a Jew. At least, I'm half Jewish. My mother was murdered by Hitler's youth army, and my father brought us to England to escape persecution. He was a Gentile, but I was still treated as a Jew because of my mother."

"You have my sympathy, Jane." The doctor put his elbows on the desk. "How long have you been in England? Your English is excellent."

"I arrived two years ago, but I had a good language tutor. He came from Sheffield."

"That would explain your local accent."

"Yes." She paused, unsure how to continue.

"So what is it that you need to remember?"

"I have a daughter, and she's in hiding." Jane couldn't help pouring out her fears. "I don't know where she is and I have to find her.

My husband thinks I'm dead and he's gone to get her, but he's in terrible danger because the safe routes could be exposed by now, and I have to warn him."

"Slow down, Jane. Where is your daughter hiding? What do you mean by *safe routes*?"

"Sasha is somewhere in Bavaria." She knew her story sounded far-fetched. She decided to back-track a little to try to make him understand. "Have you heard of the kinder transports?"

"You mean the trainloads of Jewish children that were brought to England?"

Jane nodded.

"Go on."

"Well, after war was declared, the routes they used were closed to us, and after May this year, no more children could be brought out safely that way."

"Are you saying that children are *still* being brought out of Germany?"

She nodded. "Children and families are still in danger, but the routes have been compromised, and I might know something about that."

"What makes you think you would you know something like that?"

"Because, err…" Jane realised she would be leaving herself open to accusations of espionage, but she had no choice. If she allowed this man to delve into her mind, he would know soon anyway. "I was given some information on the night of the bombing by a man who worked on the safe routes in Germany. He was in the Secret Service. The message is very important, but I only remembered parts of it when I attempted the self-hypnosis."

"Secret Service! My, this *is* getting interesting. Why didn't the man tell someone else the information after you were injured?"

"Because he died in the bombing."

"I see."

"Do you believe me?"

"I see no reason to doubt you, Jane. It's all very cloak and dagger, and we're at war with your home country, so I can see why you're nervous about telling me all this."

"Reverend Gosney can vouch for me. He's the vicar at St Mary's in Sharrow. He helped to bring me to England."

"And you say that was two years ago?"

"Yes."

"So why is your child in hiding? Why didn't you bring her with you?"

"There was a problem with her papers. I had to leave her behind." Jane's voice broke, and she stifled a sob. "I'm sorry." She struggled but managed to control her emotions and continued. "Can you help me remember where Sasha might be?"

"I can try, Jane. There are no guarantees."

"I know."

"All right, let me get this clear. You want me to help you remember where your daughter is, and the contents of a message that was given to you by a man from the Secret Service."

"Yes."

"Anything else?"

"My husband. I remember his name, and I can feel the emotion I have for him, but I can't remember his face."

"What's his name?"

"Gottfried Rubinstein."

The doctor looked at his watch. "We'd better get started. I have another appointment at two."

"How will you do this?" Jane began to worry. She didn't like handing over control of her mind.

"Just relax, Jane. I'm going to talk to you, and while I'm talking, you'll begin to hear a clock ticking. Can you hear it now?"

He stopped talking, and Jane became aware of the clock on the wall. It was ticking rhythmically, as it counted the seconds away.

"Time is moving slowly. I want you to close your eyes and begin to count the seconds with me. With each number counted, you'll feel heavier and heavier."

Jane closed her eyes and listened to the doctor begin to count down from ten. When he reached number one, she thought his method hadn't worked and tried to open her eyes, but found she couldn't.

"You are completely safe, Jane, and everything in your world is calm and tranquil. Your mind is calm, and your body is relaxed."

Jane felt she was floating. It was a pleasant sensation.

"Open your mind and set it free. Imagine all those little octopuses reaching out their tiny tentacles. They are touching in millions of combinations. They are connecting and allowing your memories to flow easily. Can you see them?"

Jane nodded and smiled. The odd image was etched in her mind.

"Good. Now relax and breathe slowly. Nice, easy breaths. In through your nose and out through your mouth."

Jane did as he asked, taking long slow breaths. She felt herself drifting deeper.

"I'm going to take you on a journey, Jane, but you have nothing to worry about. You'll be quite safe. We'll never leave this office. We are travelling through air and time and space, but we are doing so, only in your head. You are in no danger at all. Do you understand?"

Jane nodded. She was fully aware that she was hypnotised but felt calm and relaxed.

"We are going to visit a time when you met a man from the Secret Service."

"Sebastian," her voice was slurred, but she remembered the name.

"Can you picture Sebastian? Bring his face to your mind. Look at his eyes. What colour are they?"

"I can't see. There's a fog."

"I want you to clear the fog, Jane. You can do it. Push it away. Can you see it drifting from your vision? Soon you'll have a clear view. Can you see now?"

"Blue. His eyes are blue."

"Good girl. What about his hair? Can you see his hair?"

She nodded. "It's brown."

"He is talking to you. Listen to his voice. What is he saying?"

"He's speaking in German. I can't hear him. He's whispering." She strained to hear the whispered words. "Wait! He's giving me something. It's a piece of paper."

"Look at the paper and tell me what is written there."

Jane looked at the paper. This time the Russian Cyrillic text was clear. She recognised each distinct letter. "I can't read it. The words are in Russian."

She heard the doctor sigh. "Perhaps you could copy it and write it down."

"Yes."

She felt a pencil being placed in her hand.

"Open your eyes, Jane. You can see the paper, can't you?"

She saw a sheet of blank paper on the desk.

"Copy the writing in your head onto the paper."

She did as she was instructed, closing her eyes to focus on the message in her mind, and then writing the symbols on the paper. She heard aircraft overhead and the distant rumble of bombs exploding. She was becoming disconnected from her mind. The message was fading as her anxiety and consciousness levels rose.

"Relax, Jane. Listen to the clock. Let the rhythm take you down."

Jane heard the clock ticking, as the sounds of bombers drifted away. The doctor began to talk again. "You are safe and warm. You are still in the office. Nothing can hurt you here. Five, and your legs are heavy. Six, and your arms are completely relaxed. Don't be concerned. You are safe. Let it go. Let the paper float away. Concentrate on the man's words. He talked to you. What did he say?"

"He talked about his girlfriend. He was looking forward to seeing Hannah."

"Who is Hannah?"

"She's his girlfriend."

"Do you know Hannah?"

"Yes. She's my friend. She's Russian."

"Good girl, Jane. That's very good. Now we're going to move on. We're going to find Sasha. Take me back to the last time you saw her."

Jane could easily remember that picture. Her two-year-old daughter was in the arms of her father. He was waving. "No!" Jane called out. "Gottfried!"

"What do you see, Jane?"

"He's leaving me."

"Who is leaving?"

"Gottfried. He has Sasha." Jane could see his tall figure walking away, and Sasha was looking over his shoulder, waving and smiling.

"Where are they going?"

"To his friend's house."

"Where is that?"

"At the city outskirts. She'll be safer there."

"What street? What number?"

"I don't know." Jane didn't know the friend's address in Hamburg. "Gottfried said it was safer for Sasha if I didn't know."

"Do you know where she is now?"

Jane could see the hills and forests of Bavaria but had never been there. She knew the images in her head were from her imagination. "Bavaria."

"Where in Bavaria? I need an address, Jane. Give me the address."

Jane could see a farm cottage, and the address became clear in her mind. Her body felt weighed down by the effort of remembering. "She's at a farm near Rosenheim." She gave him the address.

"All right, Jane, we're almost finished. Now I want you to tell me about your husband. Who is Gottfried? What does he look like?"

"He's my husband," Jane answered automatically. "I know he's in danger! I have to warn him!"

The sound of an explosion overshadowed everything in her mind. A cloud billowed into her head. The fog was thick with dust. She couldn't breathe.

"Jane? Can you hear me?"

She began to struggle. She couldn't get her breath. The fog was choking her.

"I can see you're getting agitated, so I'm going to bring you back. Do you understand?"

Jane nodded, she wanted to run, but her legs were heavy. She began to panic.

Eventually, she heard the doctor's voice again. "I'm going to count now, Jane, and I want you to count with me. Can you do that?"

Jane tried to concentrate and nodded.

"Listen to the clock and count the seconds with me. You'll feel your body getting lighter with each number we count. Ready?"

Jane nodded, struggling to push the dust-filled cloud from her mind. She knew it wasn't real, even though she could taste the cloying soot on her tongue.

"One."

Jane counted and felt herself moving beyond the dust with each number. At five she was above the choking cloud. When she reached ten, she was clear of the fog.

"Now open your eyes, Jane."

She opened her eyes to see the doctor leaning over her with concern in his eyes.

"I want you to stay still for a few minutes. You need to gather your senses."

Jane felt apprehensive. "What happened?"

"Your fear got the better of us. I had to bring you out."

"I remember." Jane could recall the whole experience. "I think I was back in the Marples when the bomb exploded."

"I'm sorry you had to go through that again. It wasn't what I had in mind, but your mind is strong, and I suppose that memory is a dominant one."

"I knew I was safe. I knew it wasn't real, but I could taste the dust. I was struggling to breathe and that scared me."

"That's the power of hypnosis, and the reason I don't offer this treatment to many of my patients."

"I'm glad you offered it to me. We got the information, didn't we?"

"We did!" He grinned. "Here's the message." He handed her the paper she'd written on. "Doesn't mean much to me, but I'm sure you'll have some friends to help you work this out."

"Hannah?"

The doctor smiled. "It does look like Russian, doesn't it?"

"She's on our side." Jane was quick to point out her friend was not an enemy. "She helped with the kinder transports too."

"I believe you." The doctor's smile told her that he meant his words.

Jane looked at the writing. She saw more lines of text than her first attempt to write out the message. "I'm sure Hannah will be able to read this."

"I hope you find your daughter and husband, Jane."

"Thank you, Doctor Fisher."

"I'm glad I could help. If I can do more, please let me know."

Chapter Nineteen – Snap Decision

Jane went directly to the Central Library after leaving the doctor. Hannah was the only person she knew who could decipher the message she'd copied from her mind.

The large hall of the library was quieter than the last time she'd been there, and she saw Hannah immediately. Her bright hair and flamboyant clothing made her stand out in the gloomy place.

"Hannah!" she called as she walked over the cracked marble floor. "Do you have a minute?"

"Of course, Miss Robinson." Hannah greeted her formally and ushered her to the desk where they'd met the first time. She waited until they were sitting across from each other at the desk and bent forward to whisper, "What can I do for you, Jane?"

"I have the message again. This time it is clear, I think." She took the folded paper from her pocket and handed it to her friend.

Hannah unfolded it and placed her spectacles on her nose to scrutinise the text. "This is better, but it still isn't perfect."

Jane felt her hopes beginning to fade.

Hannah smiled and nodded. "But it does give us more to go on."

Jane felt a flush of excitement. "What does it say?"

"The Gestapo headquarters are situated in the castle in Saarbrücken. The message says there is a fortified prison cell in the basement. That's where they are keeping our man."

"I need to get this to Tom. He said he could pass the information to his contacts. These details will help." She got to her feet.

"Wait, Jane." Hannah took off her spectacles. "There's more." She concentrated on the writing. "Apparently, Saarbrücken is not the hub of the operation. The town is one branch line on a few safe routes out of Germany."

"What does that mean?"

"Perhaps it means our people over there have more options."

"They'll have options if this man doesn't talk. He knows everything about the operation. What if they make him talk?"

"Wait, there's a woman's name here. She's the one who gave Sebastian the information. It says here that she's the primary contact."

"What's her name?" Jane perched on the edge of the desk.

"Ursula Meyer. She's the owner of the café, Traum Kuchen."

"Dream Cakes." Jane smiled. "That's original."

"Sebastian says she can be trusted."

"Then I need to tell Tom. He'll be able to pass that to his contacts."

"My friends are working with your vicar already. I passed on the first message to them, and my people arranged a meeting with your people, yada, yada, yada." Hannah faked a yawn. "We've been here before. Many times."

"What are you saying?" Jane resumed her seat on the chair, puzzled by Hannah's lack of enthusiasm for the two organisations working together.

"My friends are working with your vicar and his contacts. They will ask the British intelligence people to send some agents to Germany to free this man before he talks, or to help clean up the mess if they arrive too late."

"Then they'll need to know this information before they go." Jane was eager to leave and find Tom.

"You can be so naïve, Jane." Hannah shook her head. "The British intelligence won't help us. They have limited resources and even less inclination to waste time on the rescue of one man who just happens to be a German and so is of little consequence to the British."

"But there are lives at risk." Jane didn't share the girl's pessimistic opinion. "They won't refuse when they know what's at stake."

"I've been in this game for years, Jane. Don't make the mistake of thinking anti-Semitism is rife only in Germany. Hatred of Jews is worldwide, and most people are blind to what is happening, or are still sitting on the fence while our people are suffering."

"But the British people aren't like that. Tom was convinced he could get his contacts to help." Jane fleetingly remembered Ethel's initial response to learning she was a Jew and began to understand Hannah might have a point.

"Tom is simply another well-meaning man with good intentions. The road to hell is paved with them, remember? He's all talk. Nothing will happen."

"I don't believe you." Even as she said the words, she realised her friend was right.

"Then go ask him!" Hannah hissed through clenched teeth. "Ask your friend what is actually being done by his contacts."

"I will!" Jane rose to leave, but Hannah caught her arm.

"I pleaded to be allowed to help, but they brushed me aside again, as usual." Hannah let out a sigh of frustration. "I know I can make a difference over there. At least I will be taking action, and not sitting around hoping for a miracle."

"What do you think you could accomplish?" Jane was becoming annoyed with the young woman. "You'd be an inexperienced girl in a man's world. You're mad."

"You're the same as they are. *They* think a girl can't do the same job as a man, but they are wrong. *You* are wrong! Men have the brawn and the bravado, but we have the advantage, Jane. We have intelligence, charm and wit on our side."

"Are you *still* suggesting that you should be allowed go to Germany?" Jane couldn't believe Hannah was still determined to risk her life.

"I'm suggesting that we *both* go. Our wireless communications are being monitored. That's why Sebastian had to deliver that message in person." She pointed to the paper in Jane's hand. "Any response to that message will have to be taken back in person. It will have to be delivered and implemented on German soil. They won't risk a wireless message."

"That's why Tom is working with his contacts. They'll send the right people." Jane insisted. "I can't go to Germany." Her legs began to tremble. "We are Jews, Hannah. They'll kill us or send us to the labour camps."

"The British won't send any agents to act on our behalf. We've asked in the past, and the answer is always the same. They say they'll do what they can, but nothing is done, and people die. That's not good enough, Jane! Don't you see?"

"You're wrong. Tom said—."

"Never mind what Tom said. His contacts won't get the results that we could get. That's if they even bother to try, which I suspect they won't. We *can* do this, Jane," Hannah was adamant. "We can help people in hiding. We can rescue your daughter. Perhaps save your husband if he is not already captured or killed."

Jane gasped. "No! He can't be dead."

"He is more likely to be dead than alive by now. Think about it!" Hannah grabbed her hand. "He was not prepared. He was acting from a deep sense of grief and anger. He was not mindful of his own safety. He would be a sitting duck for the Gestapo."

"That's very harsh." Jane hated her friend for pointing out the flaws in her husband's plans, but somewhere deep inside; she knew the girl was right.

"We can liaise with the resistance workers in France and Germany to free our man from the Gestapo. Between us, we have the language skills and the wit to hide in plain sight. All we need are the right papers."

"Listen to yourself!" Jane was getting angry, but she was also afraid for her friend. "You talk of liaising with the French resistance but would you know how to recognise one of them? How would you make contact? How would you find those people you want to help? They are in hiding. You think you'll be able to walk into villages and towns and lead them out like the pied piper did? You are deluded, Hannah."

"No, Jane. I am a realist. I will prepare and plan, and I will not be afraid to ask for help when I need it. That's why I'm asking you to join me. We would make a formidable team."

"I need to see Tom." Jane jumped to her feet again, determined not to waste another minute. "His contacts will need this information before they leave."

Hannah shook her head. "You weren't listening to me!"

"I heard every word, Hannah, but what you say scares the hell out of me. I have to trust Tom. He's my only hope to save my family."

"Ask your vicar friend what is being done. Press him for details, and then pray for a miracle."

Jane marched away from the zealous girl, with her heart racing. Was Hannah right? Would the British refuse to help? Was her husband already dead? Would it be too late to rescue her daughter? She had to find Tom.

The church was silent and dark. It soon became clear there was nobody inside, but Jane didn't know where else to look for the vicar. She didn't have his address. She hadn't thought to ask for it. Despondently she turned her steps to home. Ethel would be wondering where she'd got to. As she walked, a bus pulled up at the other side of the road. She glanced over and saw Susan stepping from the bus onto the pavement. Jane couldn't believe her luck.

"Susan!" she yelled. "Wait!"

Her friend turned to smile. "Jane! What are you doing here?"

"I need to see your father. It's urgent, but I don't know where you live. I came to the church, thinking I could find someone there who could tell me, but it's empty."

"Slow down. You sound breathless."

"Sorry, but this is important. I have the full message."

"Oh, yes, of course! You went to be hypnotised today, didn't you? How did it go?"

"Can we go to your father? I'll tell you on the way. I don't want to waste another minute."

"I'll take you home with me. I'm sure he'll be there."

Jane told Susan about the hypnosis. Giving details about how she'd seen the message more clearly and went on to explain her disappointment at not being able to picture her husband's face.

"I might be able to help you with that. I'm sure we have a photograph of the two of you somewhere."

"You do?" Jane felt foolish. She should have asked about a photograph earlier.

Susan took her to a large house tucked away behind the church, hidden by a line of trees. "Have you eaten? I'm sure Mum will have made enough for an army, though I can't promise it will be edible."

Jane smiled. "Her cooking can't be that bad."

"I'll let you make up your own mind." Susan pushed the door open. "Come in." She took their coats and put them on the coat-stand by the door. "Mum! We have a visitor."

Millie hurried into the hall. "Oh, Grace. How wonderful to see you. Will you be staying for dinner?"

"If you have enough to spare, that would be lovely, thank you." Jane realised she hadn't eaten anything since that morning and she was hungry.

Susan leant close to whisper, "You'll be sorry!"

"I'll take my chances. I'm hungry!"

They followed Susan's mother through to a large, warm kitchen and were met by a strange smell.

"It's boiled cod and onions with mash. I'll have it ready in half an hour."

Susan groaned. "Where's dad?"

"Your dad's on the phone in the office. Don't go pestering him, girls. He's like a bull with a sore head. He's been on the phone all afternoon, and every time he puts the phone down, he comes out to growl at me before racing back in to make another call."

"I need to see him, Millie." Jane didn't like the sound of what Tom was going through. "It's rather urgent. That's why I'm here."

"Oh, well. Be it on your own head, and don't say I didn't warn you when he bites your head off for interrupting him. Show her where the office is, will you, Susan?"

"This way." Susan took her hand. "And take no notice of my mum. Dad's bark is worse than his bite."

Susan took her to a door at the back of the house and knocked. "I'll go search for those photographs while you talk with dad. I'll be in the lounge, over there." She pointed to another door at the end of the hall.

"What is it?" A red-faced Tom opened the office door. "Oh, Grace, it's you." He looked flustered and ran a hand over his bald head. "What can I do for you?"

"I got some more information. The hypnosis worked. At least, it did as far as Sebastian's message is concerned."

"You'd better come in." He held the door wide.

"I'll leave you to it." Susan turned away, and Jane followed Tom into his office.

The room was bright with electric lights, and the furnishings were more feminine than she'd expected. Colourful floral curtains were draped at the windows, reminding her of Hannah's shawls. She shuddered, thinking of the young woman's warnings.

"Take a seat, Gra..., I mean Jane." He indicated a large couch that stood along one wall. What do you have for me?"

"Have they left yet?"

"Has who left yet?"

"The intelligence agents or whoever is going to Germany to deal with this."

Tom sat next to her on the overstuffed couch and ran his hand over his bald pate again. "Things don't happen that quickly, my dear. It takes time, and a good deal of persuasion, to organise what needs to be done."

"But we don't have time." Hannah's words began to echo in her head. "Lives are depending on our timely response to this message. Sebastian faced great danger in coming here to deliver it. Gottfried might be using the known routes to travel to Sasha, and they'll both be at risk if he gets caught."

"Your husband's papers should give him sufficient cover to explain his journey. He still has his Dutch documents. I presume he'll be using them."

"I wish I could be sure of his safety."

"What's the information you have for me?"

"I know where they're holding Heinrich Schneider. The Gestapo headquarters are in the castle at Saarbrücken. There's a prison cell in the dungeons there."

"We already guessed as much. My contacts warned me that extracting our man from that fortress will be well-nigh impossible."

"There's more. Sebastian said that Saarbrücken is not important. It's only a small branch on one of the safe routes. Other options are there for our people to use if Heinrich can hold his tongue and keep them safe."

"I always said it was too risky to trust one man with so much information, but his special talent for keeping everything in his head gave us an advantage. With nothing written down, there was no paper-trail. The Germans are sticklers for evidence and documents. Heinrich gave us a way to avoid detection."

"This man was given a lot of power, Tom. If he talks…"

"Let's hope he doesn't."

"But you said they would torture him!"

Tom swallowed audibly and stared at the floor.

Jane gathered her thoughts. "There is something else. Sebastian said you could trust a local café owner to help. Her name is Ursula Meyer, and she owns a place called Traum Kuchen in the town. That means Dream Cakes."

"How can she help?"

Jane shrugged. "I don't think that was explained in the message."

"Ursula Meyer, eh? I'd better write that down." He went to his desk and scribbled something on a notepad. "What was the name of her café?"

"Traum Kuchen."

"Do you have an address?"

Jane shook her head. "Just that it's in Saarbrücken."

"Well, that's better than nothing."

"What can you tell me, Tom?" Jane was eager to know what arrangements had been made. "What are your contacts planning to do?"

Tom shrugged. "They have agents in France and will try to divert one or two to the area."

"But won't it take more than a couple of men to—?"

"To what, Jane?" Tom's voice shook as the volume of his words increased. "To rescue a man who will probably be dead already? Or to secure the escape routes and bribe every last Jack-booted soldier to look the other way while we bring our people out?"

"Tom!" Jane was shocked by his loud outburst.

"I'm sorry, love." Tom's hands shook, and he clasped them firmly together in his lap. "It's been a long day."

"Are there any plans in place yet?"

Tom shook his head. "Nothing I can be happy with."

Jane realised that Hannah was right. Unless something was done soon, the whole German side of the operation could collapse in ruins.

"But Tom! People need to be warned so they can have a chance to escape their hiding places before the Gestapo goes looking for them." She looked at Tom's unhappy face and realised he felt the same so she went on, "If Heinrich has already talked, and there is every chance he has by now, the soldiers could already be hunting the refugees down."

Jane had firsthand experience of being hunted by the German soldiers and their dogs. She had an image of Sasha being carried through forests, being chased through the trees by an army of bloodthirsty troops. She knew what she had to do.

"If your friends aren't willing to give us the men we need to do the job, then let me go!" she blurted.

"What!" Tom's head snapped up. "Don't be stupid!"

"I am not stupid, Tom." Jane tried not to be offended. "My intelligence has never been in doubt. I'm deadly serious." She realised that she was. Her fear of what might happen to her was eclipsed by the danger to her daughter. "I can be trained. Your contacts couldn't refuse us. If I volunteered to do their work, surely they would agree to help me. I might not be capable of rescuing poor Heinrich, but I can help our people in hiding."

"I don't know, Jane. What you ask is not conventional."

"To hell with convention!" she yelled. "We can't afford to wait, Tom!"

"You can't go. They wouldn't allow it. A lone girl left to defend herself in enemy territory. No! I'm not sure they'd agree to help you anyway."

"I know a girl who would volunteer to come with me. Hannah and I could help to warn our people. We could organise more safe places for them until we can be sure the other routes are operational."

"Hannah Rosenberg?"

"You know her?"

"She's a rather unsuitable companion if you don't mind me saying. Miss Rosenberg is too gaudy and intense for my liking."

"She's a passionate woman. I'll give you that. She cares, Tom, and she's eager to help. She's desperate to go to Germany to help our people."

"The two of you are determined to do this, aren't you?" Tom scratched his head.

"Yes. Will you help us? Will you talk with your contacts? Ask them to give us some training, or at least prepare us and tell us what we might expect to encounter over there. Anything they could give us would be helpful. We'll need papers, identities and cover stories."

"I don't know. This is too sudden. Are you sure you've thought this through, Jane?"

"We can do this, Tom."

"No!" Tom jumped to his feet and marched to the window. "You are out of your mind. Your proposal is preposterous!"

"Why is it so difficult for you to understand?" Jane began. "If the British can't spare agents to help us, what choice do we have? We can do this, Tom. Please give us a chance."

"What makes you so sure two young women could organise the safe extraction of our people in a place you've never even seen before?"

Jane sighed. She wasn't sure how to answer him. What did she know of railway links and roads in the South of Germany? She travelled to England across Northern Germany and Holland but knew that experience wouldn't help her cause now. She had to make Tom understand why she thought she should be trusted with the task.

"I've been hunted, Tom. I've hidden in the reeds at the edges of freezing lakes while German soldiers and their dogs searched the bank a few feet away from me. I witnessed the murder of my own mother by the monsters that Hitler has created by his warped ideology. Don't I deserve the chance to fight back?"

"I know your story, Gra.., Jane. I can understand your need for revenge, but this is bigger than you realise. Those people who put their trust in our organisations deserve more than two inexperienced girls to help them."

"But they won't get anything if we leave it to the British, will they? We two girls will be their best chance. Surely you can see that."

"But you have no qualifications for a job such as this. You have no experience of working in the field."

"Oh, Tom. Listen to me!" Jane pleaded. "Hannah is an intelligent woman, no matter what you think of her. We speak five languages fluently between us. I was considered a star student before they kicked me out of the University. With the right preparation and documents, we could slip right in under the noses of the Gestapo and get to work immediately. We have the café owner's name as a start. You have to let us try, Tom!"

The older man rubbed his head with a trembling hand and seemed to be considering what she'd said. Jane waited with her heart hammering in her chest.

"All right. I'm not happy about it, but I'll try. Let me make some telephone calls."

"Thank you, Tom." Jane went to hug him.

"Don't thank me yet. I don't know whether they'll agree to your idea."

"Do your best to persuade them, Tom. Please! You know it's our only chance to help those people."

She left him to make his calls and walked away on shaking legs. What had she done? Was she ready to travel to Germany? Could she do the things she said she could?

Susan was in the lounge with a tin box open on a small table and a pile of photographs on her lap. She looked up when Jane entered. "What was all the yelling about?"

"I had to convince your father to take action."

"What kind of action?"

"You'll know soon enough." Jane didn't want to get into a prolonged discussion of her plans. They might not come to anything. Instead, she looked at the pile of photographs on Susan's lap. "Did you find what you were looking for?"

"Yes, here is one of you and Godfrey after you arrived in England." Susan passed her the small photograph.

Jane took the image and stared at the couple. She recognised herself. The sad-faced young woman was clinging to the arm of a dark-haired young man. He was a little taller than she was, and he was smiling into the camera.

"But this can't be my husband! This man has dark hair!" Jane was confused. She didn't recognise the young man at all. She felt no emotional attachment to the image in the photograph, and that worried her more. Where were her feelings? Where was the rush of love she should have expected at the sight of her husband's face? Where was her concern for this man's welfare? She didn't know this man!

"Mum always said you are like two peas in a pod, except Godfrey's hair is straight."

"But I thought he was blond." Jane didn't understand.

Were her mixed-up memories fooling her? Who was the tall blond man she held so dear to her heart? She had known the answer before the thought clarified in her head. Her English tutor. She was in love with a man who was not her husband. How long had she been living a lie? Did Gottfried know? How could he know of her betrayal? Her husband loved her. He'd been so grief-stricken after her death that he'd cried like a baby in the bathroom at work. His first thoughts after losing her were to risk his life to rescue their daughter.

What had she done? How could she have had an affair? She wasn't the type, surely? Women like Hannah Rosenberg had affairs, not sensible girls like her.

Where was the English tutor? What happened to him? He was from Sheffield. Did he come back here? Was he here in his home town, grieving for her as Gottfried was doing? Would he be missing her; searching for her? How could she find him when she didn't know his name?

Tom hurried into the room. "Can you be at the railway station by ten in the morning, Jane? I think most trains are running again."

"Why? Where am I going?" Jane asked, feeling the hair on the back of her neck beginning to prickle.

"Hannah needs to go with you, and you must each take the bare minimum of clothes and toiletries to last you two weeks." Tom looked agitated and spoke quickly. "Do you know her address?"

Jane shook her head. "Where will I find her?"

"Here, I'll write it down for you." Tom went to get some paper from a dresser at the back of the room. "If she's not at home, try the Crown Inn on Chesterfield Road."

"Where are we going?" Jane's heart began to pound.

"The New Forest. That's all I know. You are to buy tickets to Brockenhurst, and you'll change trains in London. I can give you some money to help with your expenses." He reached into the drawer again. "Take this, love." He pressed some paper money and coins into her hand. "Put this somewhere safe."

"Where are you going, Jane?" Susan asked.

"Don't ask questions, Susan," Tom warned and turned to Jane. "All I can tell you is that you'll be met at the station in Brockenhurst by my contact and he will tell you what you need to know."

"I'd better get a move on." Jane jumped to her feet. "Thank you, Tom." She went to hug the older man.

"Don't thank me, Jane. I'm not happy about this at all."

"What's going on?" Susan asked.

"Dinner is ready." Millie came into the room wiping her hands on a tea-cloth.

"Sorry, Millie, I can't stay for dinner, after all," Jane explained as she squeezed passed the older woman in the doorway.

"Why the rush?" Susan followed Jane into the hall and helped her with her coat. "What are you and dad planning?"

"I'm going to get Sasha," Jane whispered.

"What? But you can't! It's dangerous!" Susan's face flushed pink. "How can you do this?"

"How can I not?"

"Oh, Jane." Susan hugged her fiercely. "Take care. I don't want to lose you again."

"I'll be careful."

Susan pulled back but held tightly to Jane's sleeve. "If you were worried about eating Mum's boiled cod and onions, you could have used a less dramatic excuse, you know." Susan tried a wobbly smile.

Jane's smile was equally shaky. "My appetite has gone anyway." Jane knew she couldn't have eaten a thing. Her insides were churning. "Wish me luck."

"Take care, Gerda."

Jane heard her true name and tears sprang to her eyes. "Thanks, Susan. I will."

Chapter Twenty – The First Step

"I can't believe you did it!" Hannah was like an excited child setting out on vacation. "I've been asking for months, but all my pleas went unheard. How did you persuade them?"

Jane smiled patiently at her enthusiastic friend. "I didn't. It was Tom. I told him what we wanted to do and asked whether his contacts would agree to help prepare us for the task."

"Yes, but they *did* agree!" Hannah clapped her hands gleefully. "I still have to keep pinching myself. We're going, Jane. We're really going!"

"We don't know that for sure, yet," Jane pointed out. "I'm sure they'll want us to jump through hoops and pass all kinds of tests before they allow us to go anywhere." She glanced at the other passengers in the train compartment. They were talking quietly and didn't seem to be taking notice of Hannah's eagerness for the journey.

"We're taking the first steps, at last!" Hannah's elation couldn't be contained.

"Try to get some sleep," Jane suggested. "We could be in for a long haul. Tom said to expect disruption all along the line to London."

"I'm too excited to sleep."

"Read your book, then. I'm going to try to get some shut-eye. I didn't get much last night, and I'm tired." Jane wanted time to think and feigning sleep would be a good way to avoid Hannah's distracting chatter.

"Spoilsport." Hannah didn't sulk for long. She opened her book and was soon absorbed in the fictional romance.

Jane took advantage of the peace to try to collect her thoughts. Things had happened too quickly. Yesterday she was only concerned about remembering enough to help Tom and his friends, and today she was on her way to becoming a…, what would she be? She'd be working undercover with another false identity. Would she be a spy? Would the Germans consider her a spy?

She shuddered. She was no such thing. Saving her fellow human beings was work that she'd been involved with for the last two years. She remembered the children from the kinder transport that she'd found foster homes for. She remembered the language lessons she'd held at the house on Priory Road to help them learn English so they could settle into their temporary homes more easily.

She now remembered many more things since the session of hypnosis the previous day. Somehow, the doctor had allowed her to access much more of her memory than she'd expected to, but still had some empty spaces that frustrated her.

She couldn't fully picture her home in Hamburg. She didn't remember anything about her childhood or meeting Gottfried. She couldn't bring the English tutor's face or name to mind, but she knew she loved him. The emotion was raw and strong. She knew she would have died for the man; her feelings for him were so deep and powerful. She felt guilty because the feelings she had for her husband were nothing in comparison. Poor Gottfried. How she must have deceived him. How could she have been so heartless?

She carried so much guilt. She felt guilt for not intervening to stop her mother's murder. She had guilt about her father dying prematurely after enduring the harrowing journey to England to keep her safe. Her guilt about having an affair weighed heavily on her heart. She also felt guilty to leave Ethel so abruptly. The older woman was still vulnerable and fragile.

"Don't you worry about me, love," she'd said. "I have my friends, and now I've found Millie, thanks to you." Ethel always saw the brighter picture. "You go off and have your adventures. I don't need to know what you're up to." She'd tapped the side of her nose knowingly. "Loose talk cost lives, and all that."

"Oh, Ethel. What will I do without you?"

"You'll do just fine, love. Just you remember, there'll always be a roof here for you."

Jane could not tell Ethel where she was going, or why she was leaving her so suddenly, but her friend didn't ask questions. Jane embraced the brave, older woman before leaving her that morning. She was leaving behind a safe haven and stepping into unknown territory. She was afraid, but tempering her fear was a determination that was growing stronger inside her.

People were dying for no reason other than their religion, or their race. Germany was turning on anyone that didn't fit Hitler's ideal of the perfect Aryan. Her daughter was on that list because her grandmother was born a Jew. Jane wouldn't allow her daughter to be thought of as less than perfect by anyone. Sasha was the most important person in her life. The love she felt for the English tutor was wrong, and she decided it couldn't be allowed to flourish. She would save her child and hopefully find Gottfried as well. Together, they would make a future for their family away from the oppressive rule of inhumane dictators.

Hours later, Jane woke from another nightmare with a startled jump.

"Welcome back, sleepyhead." Hannah was putting her book away. "We're stuck in Leicester until they clear the line ahead."

"How long have we been travelling?"

"Well, that depends on what you call travelling, love." One of their fellow passengers tipped his hat to her. "We spent two hours moving slowly and another two standing here."

"Are you hungry?" Hannah asked. "There's a café on the platform. We could be here another hour or two, and I'm famished."

Jane was hungry. She'd not eaten much since the previous morning. Her tummy was still in knots, but she knew she would have to eat something. She pulled a small purse from her bag and handed over some of the money Tom had given her.

"What would you like me to get you?"

"Anything. I don't mind."

When Hannah came back some twenty minutes later with some newspaper-wrapped fish and chips, she was amazed.

"The café had nothing to offer but stale cheese and chutney sandwiches. I asked the guard, and he said I would have enough time to go to the chip shop a few streets away."

"They smell divine!" Jane's mouth began to water. "Thanks, Hannah."

"No problem, Jane. I had a feeling you hadn't eaten. We have to look after ourselves, now, eh? We can't afford to be fainting from hunger in our new roles, can we?"

"Are you two joining our armed forces, by any chance?" The gentleman passenger asked.

Jane smiled. "You could say so." She felt a fizz of apprehension in her tummy. She and Hannah could be getting into something much more dangerous than any girl in England could imagine. More young women were enlisting in the services daily, but very few would be preparing to do what Jane was considering. She shuddered and began to eat the meal.

Hannah giggled. "We're heading to a basic training camp in The New Forest."

"Good luck, girls. It makes my heart swell to see what our young folks are doing for Britain."

Jane continued eating; even though fear and anxiety were making the fish and chips taste like their paper wrappings in her mouth. She would need all the strength she could get for the coming ordeals she might face.

They arrived in the early hours of the morning to a dark and desolate railway station where they were the only two people to disembark. Jane watched the train chugging away with an empty feeling in the pit of her stomach. She looked around for signs of their contact but could see nothing. Hannah was staring at a dark building at the end of the platform.

"Can you see anyone?" Jane asked.

"Not a soul," Hannah whispered.

An owl hooted, and both girls jumped and quickly moved closer to each other.

Hannah giggled nervously. "It's only an owl."

"Let's take a look at the building. Whoever is meeting us might be sheltering from the cold in there."

"I doubt anyone will be here at this time of the morning. They will have tired of waiting and gone home. I think we might be in for a long wait, my friend." Hannah threaded her arm through Jane's elbow. "But it might be warmer to wait inside if we can find a way into that ticket office."

Jane allowed Hannah to guide her to the dark building. They saw no signs of life. The girls peered through windows and listened at the door. No lights showed through the blackouts, and no noise came from inside.

"Try the door," Hannah urged Jane. "It's freezing out here."

Jane tried turning the doorknob. "It's locked."

"Of course, it is." Hannah's voice oozed sarcasm, but she tugged eagerly at Jane's sleeve. "Let's try the windows."

"We can't break in!" Jane was shocked by the suggestion.

"We can't spend the rest of the night out here; we'll freeze!"

"But we'll get into trouble," Jane pointed out.

"I think we're way past worrying about that, don't you?" Hannah was already pushing and tugging at a window frame. "I think I can work this one loose. Give me some help here, will you?"

Jane dropped her bag and went to help her friend. Between them, they managed to prise the window open.

"In you go." Hannah cupped her hands. "Climb up."

Jane stepped into Hannah's hands and hoisted her bottom onto the windowsill. "I don't like this, Hannah."

"Don't be a coward, Jane. Where we're going, we'll be expected to do much worse than break into a deserted railway office. Hurry up."

Jane swung her legs inside and reached to take the bags from Hannah before helping her friend over the sill to join her.

"There, that wasn't so bad, was it?"

Jane could hear the amusement in Hannah's voice, even though, she couldn't see her face; she knew her friend was grinning. "You're enjoying this, aren't you?"

"Tremendously!" Hannah moved away from the window. "Let's see if we can find something to eat. I'm hungry."

"When are you not hungry?" Jane smiled and followed her.

They found a back room with a fireplace where the embers were still glowing orange.

"What luck!" Hannah went to stir the fire before throwing some lumps of coal into the grate. "Look around for the kettle. I'm sure there'll be some tea around here somewhere."

Jane knew it would be no use arguing with the girl. She began to open cupboards until she found what she was looking for. The flickering light from the fire helped her to see what she was doing, and soon the girls had the makings of some tea. Hannah found some bread, which they sliced and then toasted at the fire.

"A feast fit for a king." Hannah bit into her toast and sank to the floor to get comfortable in front of the small flames. "Eat up, Jane. Don't feel guilty. Whoever we are stealing from won't mind, I'm sure. We are in need. It's a gift of charity, really."

"Charity is something given freely, not taken as we are doing." Jane could not agree with her friend's opinion. "I'll leave some money to cover the cost of what we've taken."

"Well if that makes you feel better, go right ahead."

"Oh, you're impossible!" Jane snuggled into a fireside chair and wrapped her coat around her legs for extra warmth.

"Listen, Jane." Hannah sounded serious. "We'll probably have to do much worse things than breaking and entering when we get to Germany."

"What makes you think that?"

"We'll be living on our wits over there."

"I know," Jane admitted. She'd had plenty of time to think about her decision on the long journey from Sheffield. She knew she was moving into dangerous territory and she didn't feel ready at all.

"Well," Hannah continued, "There may be times when we have to hide or run or trust our luck to the elements. We have to be prepared to take drastic measures. You do realise that, don't you?"

"I've been on the run before, Hannah. You know how I came to England."

"I know, but you had your husband and your father with you. They would have done the thinking, and they would have made the decisions. I'm right, aren't I?"

Jane remembered her father ordering her into the freezing lake when the dogs were baying in the forest only a hundred yards away. Would she have thought to hide there without his insistence? Would she have known to use the stalk of a reed to breathe through while she stayed below the surface, out of sight?

"I can't do this, Hannah," Jane admitted. "I don't have the first idea how to be a spy."

Hannah laughed in the darkness. "We're not spies, Jane. We'll never be spies."

"The Gestapo will treat us like spies if they catch us."

"They won't catch us."

"How can you be so sure?"

"Because Tom's contacts will prepare us, and we'll be ready for anything by the time we get to Germany."

"I wish I had your confidence."

Hannah sighed. "It's easy to be confident when you have nothing to fear."

"Are you saying you're not afraid?" Jane couldn't believe her friend's bravado.

"Not really. What is the worst thing that could happen? We could get shot. We could get caught, be questioned, *and then* shot. So we die! So what? Death waits for us all. The only uncertainty about death is when and how it will come."

"What about your family? Don't you care what they will think if you die on this venture?"

"I have no family, Jane."

"I thought you told me your father was in Salzburg."

"I haven't heard a word from him in months. I don't know whether he is alive or dead."

"Oh, I'm sorry, Hannah. You must be concerned about him."

"I am, but what can I do?"

"Perhaps we could try to find him when we get over there."

"I don't know. Perhaps it would be a wild goose chase. He took risks in helping to forge documents for our friends. If he is caught... Well, he is old and wouldn't last long in German hands. In my heart, I know he is dead." Hannah shook her head.

"You can't know that for sure."

"Perhaps not, but I'm a realist. I don't believe in false hope. Optimism without foundation is a waste of energy."

"But you are the most optimistic person I know."

"I try to look for the best in each situation. For a man in my father's position, I can see no best-case scenario, can you?"

Jane didn't have an answer and shook her head.

"You see, I now have no reason to be careful with the time I have left."

"What are you saying?"

"My father is probably gone, and he was my only family left alive. The one person I loved as much as my dear papa is also gone." Hannah dropped her head. "My future means nothing without him."

Jane suddenly understood. "Sebastian."

Hannah stayed silent.

"Now he's gone, you think you have no reason to continue living?"

"Perhaps."

"But you're young, Hannah. You could meet someone else. You can make a good life after this war is over."

"I can't share your opinion, Jane. Sebastian was my life. I might not have been the most important thing to him, but he was my heart."

"He was a good man. We spoke for a long time before the bomb dropped." Jane remembered the conversation she'd had with the man.

Hannah shuffled on the floor. "What did he say?"

"After he told me the message, he gave me the Russian note. I had the message in English, straight from the horse's mouth, but I couldn't remember it. Why could pluck out an obscure Russian note, but not remember the words until now?"

"Don't torture yourself. We got there in the end, didn't we?"

"He couldn't wait to see you again." Jane could hear Sebastian's voice. She remembered every detail of the conversation now. "He told me you'd been apart for two years and he was concerned that you might have met someone else."

"I would never do that to him. He knew that." Hannah protested.

"He told me he couldn't imagine a future without you being part of it."

"Why would he tell you that?"

"We were sheltering from the bombs. The cellars were full, and we were crammed into a tiny space under the stairs. We were there for hours with nothing to do but tell our life stories to each other."

"What else did he tell you?"

"He said he loved you and wanted you to be his wife one day if he made it through the war."

"Don't tell me more; I can't bear it." Hannah's voice broke on a sob.

"Then, he told me he didn't think he would survive the war."

"He was right, wasn't he?" Hannah sniffed. "He wouldn't have expected to die in a bombing raid, though, would he? He probably thought a bullet in the back would be a more likely end for him."

"Whatever he thought about himself, you were important to him, Hannah. I didn't know you then, but I remember feeling envious. Sebastian loved you very much."

"Why would you be envious? You have a husband, and he loves you, doesn't he?"

"Yes." Jane suppressed a sigh. She didn't want Hannah to know of her inner turmoil. How could she explain that no matter what Gottfried felt for her, she didn't love him the same way? She loved her English tutor, whoever he was. "But Sebastian's love for you was something special. I could tell."

"What good is his love to me now?" Hannah blew out a long breath. "I'll never see him again. I may as well be dead too."

"Don't talk like that, Hannah." Jane reached to touch her friend's shoulder. "We have everything to live for. We owe it to our families to live the best lives we can. Your parents made sacrifices; just as mine did, to make sure we survived. We now owe it to them to do the best we can to help those people depending on us. After that, well, our future is in God's hands."

Chapter Twenty-One – Taking Instruction

Jane woke to the sound of someone whistling softly. She stayed quiet and listened to footsteps moving closer to the building. She thought she could hear two sets of feet walking on the platform.

"Hannah!" she whispered urgently and shook the sleeping girl awake. She clamped her hand over the girl's mouth. "Shush! Keep quiet. Someone is coming."

Hannah pushed Jane's hand from her face and whispered, "It's probably our welcome party, silly."

"What if it's the man who works here?"

"What if it is? You said you were going to pay him for the things we used. You worry too much!"

Despite Hannah's brave words, both girls flinched when they heard a key at the door. They were on their feet by the time the platform guard entered the room, closely followed by a tall man in a mackintosh and trilby hat.

"What are you two doing in here?" The middle-aged guard stared at the two young women and then looked around the room. "I see you've helped yourselves to my breakfast."

"Sorry, we had nowhere else to go," Jane began. "Our train was late last night, and the people we expected weren't here to meet us."

"So you thought you'd break in here and help yourselves?" The man in the mackintosh looked at the guard. "What should do with them, Sam?" His stern-set mouth twitched with amusement when he turned his attention to Hannah. "How did you get in?"

Hannah glanced at Jane before she pulled her shoulders back and spoke defiantly. "The window frame was loose."

"It was freezing," Jane tried to explain. "We had no choice."

"Yes, I can see." The guard went to inspect the remnants of his loaf of bread. "I suppose it was a matter of life and death. It usually is with your sort."

Hannah and Jane exchanged a puzzled glance.

"I'll pay you for the bread." Jane took some coins from her pocket.

"Keep your money. My wife packed me some breakfast this morning." He smiled and winked. "That bread was stale anyway."

"Oh, err," Jane glanced at the other man uncertainly. "That's very good of you."

The man in the mackintosh took off his hat and smiled. "I'm sorry to tease, girls. I'm Mr Wilcox. I expect you two young ladies are Jane Roberts and Hannah Rosenberg."

"Yes, we are!" Hannah grinned.

"Are you our contact?" Jane asked warily.

"Good luck with these two, lad. One's as brazen as a barrel of monkeys, and the other one is a scared rabbit."

"Oh, I think they'll do all right." He put his hat back on his head. "They already showed initiative by taking advantage of your food and shelter." He began to walk from the room. "Quick as you can, girls. My boss won't wait for dawdlers."

Jane and Hannah reached for their bags and hurried after the man.

Jane glanced over her shoulder. "Thank you," she called to the guard.

"Where are we going?" Hannah asked when they were outside. "We haven't been given any information."

"That's the way we like it here. You'll know what you need to know when you need to know it and not before. Loose talk costs lives."

He took them to a sleek, black car. "In you get, ladies. Chop-chop."

Jane opened the back door of the car and jumped in. Hannah took the front seat, next to the man, who quickly started the car and began to drive it away from the station.

"Can you tell us anything about where we're going?" Hannah asked when they pulled onto a narrow country lane.

"Persistent, aren't you?" He took his eyes off the road for a second to grin at Hannah. "You'll see soon enough."

"Oh, you're infuriating." Hannah folded her arms.

"Let me give you girls some advice." He looked at Hannah and then flicked his eyes to glance at Jane through his rear-view mirror. "You're going to be put through the mill here. We can teach you survival methods to keep you alive on a snowy mountain, and how to find food in the depths of a forest. You'll be instructed on how to conduct yourselves while in enemy territory, and how to hide in plain sight among the local population." He gave Hannah's bright shawl a disdainful glance. "Looking like a stereotypical Jew or Gypsy will make you a target for extra scrutiny. You need to learn to blend. We'll teach you these skills."

Hannah huffed and flipped her shawl over her shoulder but didn't interrupt him.

"You'll be provided with papers and cover stories if you pass muster. What we can't do, is guarantee your safety. No matter how much training we give you, in the end, it's up to you. Your common sense and quick-wits are the only things you can rely on over there."

The man caught Jane's eye again in his rear-view mirror, and he smiled at her. "You don't have much to say for yourself."

Jane smiled nervously. "When I have something to say, you'll hear me."

"Touché."

"You speak French?" Hannah asked.

"Do you?"

"I speak Russian and German too," Hannah boasted.

"That's interesting." He glanced in his mirror to look at Jane. "How about you?"

"French, German, English and Italian."

"Fluently?"

Jane smiled. She was warming to the good-humoured man. "Like a native."

"That's quite an achievement for a girl from South Yorkshire."

"That's where you're wrong, Mr Wilcox." Jane suddenly remembered what he had said earlier about loose talk and decided to keep her origins to herself. She had no idea how much this man had been told about her. She poked Hannah's arm around the side of the seat to warn her to keep quiet.

"Sorry, that was crass of me. I didn't mean to offend you. I'm sure Yorkshire girls are—."

"No offence taken," Jane interrupted him and smiled sweetly.

"What do you know about us?" Hannah asked.

"I know you have volunteered to join our service and have a particular task in mind. It's my job to prepare you for that task, and then advise the boffins who make the final decision whether they can afford to let you loose."

Hannah turned to him. "Will you be training us?"

"Some of the time. I've been given a tight schedule. You'll be worked hard over the next two weeks. Are you fit?"

"As fit as any young woman of our age, but Jane has—."

Jane quickly interrupted again. "Jane has the advantage of enjoying long walks, so is perhaps fitter than most."

"I see. Well, that might help. We usually send our recruits for some specialised fitness training, to begin with, but in your case, that's been waived. I believe there is some sense of urgency to your mission."

Jane nodded. "How much do you know?"

"Well, the first part of your mission is already obsolete."

"Why?" Jane didn't know what Tom had said to his contacts and didn't know what she would be expected to do other than to help people in hiding get to safety.

"The German collaborator, who you intended to rescue, has been taken out by the Gestapo."

Hannah gasped. "Are you saying Heinrich Schneider is dead?"

"Afraid so."

"How do you know?" Jane asked.

"We know a lot of things. We also know that he talked. Activity in the area suggests that he didn't give details, but gave enough to prolong his life. Not that his bravery did him any good in the end."

"What are you saying?" Hannah pushed for more information. "What activity? Have they discovered the locations of the safe houses or the routes our people used?"

"I don't know details. We know that patrols around the town have been increased, and more people are being stopped and searched than usual."

Jane breathed a sigh of relief. Saarbrücken was not the hub of the operation, but merely a branch line on the route to safety. Sasha might still be safe at the farm in Bavaria, which was more than three-hundred miles away.

"You sound relieved." The man caught Jane's eye again in the mirror.

"If they are stopping and searching people in the street, they are not looking for the safe houses. Our people will be safe for now."

"Don't be too sure. We have limited eyes and ears on the ground over there. Germany is a large country. If Herr Schneider had been made to talk about other areas of your operation, we wouldn't necessarily know about it."

Jane felt her mouth go dry. If Sasha was in danger, she couldn't afford to waste another minute.

"Let's hope our man was brave and kept his mouth closed." Hannah stared out of the window.

Jane saw a large house in the distance. "Is that where we're going?"

"That's Beaulieu. It will be your home for the next week."

Hannah turned to look at Jane. "But I thought you said we'd be here for two weeks."

The man chuckled. "I've been given one week to lick you girls into shape, and then you're to go to Manchester for parachute training. After that, you'll have two days with the small-arms people, and then we'll do an assessment."

Hannah and Jane gasped simultaneously.

"Parachute training!" Hannah turned to stare at Jane over the back of her seat.

"Small-arms!" Jane blinked.

"Welcome to the party, girls." Mr Wilcox grinned. "I think Sam was right. We're going to have fun with you two."

Jane fell into bed, aching from head to toe from sitting at a desk until late into the evening. The day had been long and exhausting. Her mind was now crammed with countless pieces of new information, and her headache was so bad she thought her head would burst.

As soon as they'd arrived at the training camp that morning, the two girls had been subjected to a series of physical and mental tests.

Jane had been worried when the doctor has asked about her previous medical history. She'd shaken her head, acknowledged she'd suffered the usual childhood ailments, and then admitted her recent injuries.

"But I'm fully recovered," she quickly pointed out. "My head doesn't hurt, and my chest wound is healed."

The doctor examined her back and the scar on her head. "Any headaches?"

"No," she lied and received a clean bill of health.

After breaking for a hurried lunch, they went on to learn some emergency survival techniques. They were given instruction on how to apply a tourniquet, how to splint a broken bone, how to use camouflage in mountains, forests and urban areas and how to get clean water by digging a deep hole next to a stream.

"Don't drink directly from the stream," the teacher had warned them. "The hole you dig will fill with water that has been filtered by the surrounding mud. The water won't be as clear as you're used to, and ideally, should still be boiled for a few minutes before drinking, but if you can't build a fire, it will keep you alive when you're dying of thirst."

They were shown easy methods to distract the enemy and instructed on how to avoid confrontation and avert unwelcome interest.

"Don't forget that you are attractive young women and most of your enemies will be men," another teacher explained later in the afternoon. "Use your strengths. Flirt if you have to. The aim is to distract interest from your goal. If you need to get to particular building quickly, make your enemy believe it is the last place you are interested in. Using your femininity as diversion and evasion tools are the best assets you girls can make use of."

They had been shocked to learn they would be undergoing a dramatic change to their appearance. They had appointments at six in the morning with a woman who was coming to restyle their hair.

"What is wrong with my hair?" Hannah had protested. "What will you do to it?"

"Your red hair is too conspicuous, Miss Rosenberg. You will attract attention and attention is what we are trying to avoid, is it not?" the camouflage instructor told her. "We'll change the colour and make it darker, and we'll cut it shorter to make it easier to conceal."

"Why would I want to conceal my hair?"

"We'll come to that."

Jane was unsure what they planned for her, but didn't dare ask.

"I can see you're wondering, Miss Robinson. We're going to make you a blonde."

"Why?" Jane was surprised.

"Because you have the classical features of a Jewish woman and where you're going, it is not a good look to have. Being blonde will divert the attention from your sallow complexion and dark eyes. We won't need to cut any from the length."

The instructor went on to explain how to use simple camouflage tricks while avoiding capture.

"You might find yourself compromised at any stage of your mission." He held up his hands and flapped them exaggeratedly in the air. "Don't tell me a thing! I don't need to know what your mission might be. My job is to equip you with the necessary skills, not to know where or how you intend to use them."

Jane and Hannah exchanged a glance of amusement at the man's theatrics.

"Now, let me see…" He went on to explain some simple ways to change a person's appearance. With the aid of photographs, he demonstrated how the addition of a pair of spectacles and a hat could work in the short term. "If you are being followed, do simple things to change your appearance. Remember; always avoid the complicated. We have a saying. Keep it simple, stupid. Remember that, and it might well save your life."

"How?" Jane asked.

The instructor had sighed heavily. "Imagine you are being followed or chased by the enemy. He knows what you look like. He's seen your striking wavy hair and your long red woollen coat." He pointed to the coat hanging over the back of her chair. "You won't have time for lengthy transformations, so you keep it simple." He picked up Jane's coat and put it around his shoulders before running to the door of the room and throwing it wide.

"You dash into a darkened doorway." He hopped through the open door and peered at them from behind the doorjamb. "Or you sneak down an alleyway." He took the coat from his shoulders and tossed it aside. "You discard the coat behind the door, or over a wall." He took out a large handkerchief from his trouser pocket and put it over his head. "Tie a scarf over your head and step confidently back into the street." He stepped back into the room. "You will adopt a different gait. Not exactly a limp, but walk more slowly." He walked with slightly bent knees. "Act twenty years older than you are. Drop your chin, stoop your shoulders. Your pursuer won't recognise you if you're careful."

"That looks too easy. Will it work?" Hannah asked.

Jane was trying to imagine how she might feel in such a situation and didn't think she'd have the presence of mind to do as he suggested while under such stress.

The instructor stood to his normal height and smiled at her as he removed the handkerchief. "I can see what you're thinking, Miss Robinson. You *will* remember this lesson if you should ever need to. That's why we say, keep it simple, stupid. Even when you are stupefied by fear, you will be able to do the simplest of things to stay safe."

Jane remembered the last lesson of the day as she listened to Hannah's soft snores. She hoped she would never have the need to try the instant camouflage techniques. She felt she was being drawn into a dangerous world of subterfuge and even though it was her deepest wish to save her daughter, she was beginning to realise the gravity of what she'd volunteered for.

The following day was almost a repetition of the previous one. The lessons were different, but the gruelling timetable was the same. They endured a visit from the hairstylist first, who frowned at Jane's amateur cut before snipping away at the concealing fringe to give it a more natural line.

"This colour will last about six weeks before your natural hair growth will start to come through," the hairdresser had told them while she worked the pungent smelling lotion into their locks. "I'll give each of you a bottle of colour to touch up your roots when that happens. If you're in the field longer than that, you'll have to take your chances with the local hairdressers."

After breakfast, taken in a long room with a few young men in uniform who kept giving the girls curious stares, they were taken to a low building away from the house.

Mr Wilcox greeted them. "Good morning ladies. Nice hair. I barely recognised you."

Hannah sulked. She was obviously not happy with her new look.

"Don't be so downhearted, Miss Rosenberg. I'm sure your lovely red hair will grow back in a few months. Now let's get down to business." He took them to an array of items laid out on a bench.

He rubbed his hands together and proceeded to demonstrate the equipment.

"You'll be issued with some basic kit like these items here. Keep them safe. You will get lipsticks and powder compacts that double as flashlights and signalling mirrors." He lifted a lipstick and twisted it to show the beam of light. Shining the narrow beam on the mirror inside the compact, he reflected the light onto the wall. "You don't have time to learn Morse, but you can arrange to exchange simple signals with other agents on the ground or with each other."

He reached for a small pencil and notebook. "You'll also have a small diary and a pencil." He held up the small notebook. "This is to be used sparingly. Don't write anything in here unless you know you're not going to remember it. Even then, be careful. Write a sequence of numbers backwards. Or use mirror writing. It's a simple ruse but surprisingly works well. At the very least, it can slow down someone trying to decipher what's been noted down. If you and the recipient know a foreign language, use that." He grinned and added, "As long as it isn't German."

He picked up the tiny pencil. "This holds a blade." He pressed the side of the pencil, and a blade sprang out from where the lead should have been. "You can still use it like a pencil. The other end has a nominal amount of lead in it."

"That blade isn't big enough to harm anyone. You can't expect us to use it as a weapon." Hannah scoffed.

"Well spotted, Miss Rosenberg. You're right." He grinned. "But if you find yourself tied up in a Gestapo cell, this little beauty will cut the rope and free you."

"That's all very well, Mr Wilcox, but how do I get out of the cell?" Hannah asked, smirking.

"Using the same blade, my dear." He brought a lock mechanism, attached to a representation of a tiny door, to the bench. "The secret is not to twist. You'll break the blade. Poke it in and press hard. The idea is to push the locking pins until they move, or break." They heard an audible click, and he opened the mechanism. "Voila!"

"Can I try that?" Hannah asked.

"Of course." He gave her another miniature door with a full-sized lock and handed over the pencil blade.

Hannah worked the lock as her instructor had demonstrated and soon heard a satisfying click.

"Impressive!" Mr Wilcox opened the small door attached to the lock. "It will also work with handcuffs, bank safes and some of the more modern car ignition systems, but don't tell anyone you got that from me."

"What else will we be given?" Jane asked.

The rest of the morning was filled with more explanations and demonstrations of various pieces of equipment. In the afternoon they were tested on the knowledge they'd gained so far, and after the evening meal, they were expected to report to the costume people for a fitting of their new wardrobe.

They learned that every item of clothing they had brought with them would have to be left behind. They would only be taking clothing that could be bought in German shops. No detail had been overlooked. Even the underwear they were issued with bore the labels of Schiesser and Triumph.

The end of the second day saw the girls falling into an exhausted sleep soon after they'd gone to bed in the shared room.

Jane woke to darkness in the early hours and listened to the sounds of the night. An owl hooted in the distance, a fox yipped, but apart from those unfamiliar sounds of nature, the grounds of Beaulieu were quiet. She tried to go back to sleep, but her mind was too full of all the new information she'd been bombarded with. The last two days had been intense, and she knew there was more to come. In three days, she would be travelling to Manchester to learn how to jump from an aircraft. The thought terrified her. She'd envisaged travelling to Germany by boat and train, but it seemed the British Intelligence Agencies had other ideas.

Chapter Twenty-Two – Uncomfortable Wait

At the end of the two weeks, Jane felt like a different person. She'd grown in confidence and strength. From learning how to avoid an enemy agent to handling a small pistol, she had acquired many new skills. From jumping out of a static balloon and then a moving aircraft, at three-hundred feet, she had excelled all expectations. Hannah had not been as enthusiastic at jumping from a great height, but her confidence in the field crafts, and with small weapons, was admirable.

The girls now waited in the room they shared in the accommodation huts in the grounds of Beaulieu, for the final decision from the top brass. Would they be allowed to go to Saarbrücken and begin to help their people in hiding?

They'd been briefed on the mission, according to what the British wanted them to do. They'd been given documents and identities with the cover story of two single cousins from Hamburg visiting family in the South. Ursula Meyer would be their first point of contact, and the girls had been advised to refer to the woman as Aunt Ursula.

They were also given the code names of two agents who would meet them at the drop zone. 'Eagle' and 'Fox,' would take them into the town under cover of darkness. They were to ask the men a question, and the answer would confirm they were the contacts. Any other response would mean the girls had fallen into enemy hands.

Everything was arranged to get the girls started. After that, it was up to them. Initially, they were to follow instructions from Frau Meyer.

"Should we try to report back to you?" Jane had asked.

The British intelligence officer had explained patiently that the woman at the café would be their primary contact and she would get word back to Britain. "Rely on the friends we put you in touch with. Those are the only people you can trust. Take their advice when in doubt and never, I mean, *never*, trust a stranger."

Jane hoped for the best while fearing the worst. The British seemed more interested in gathering information, but she wanted to take action. If the hiding places were intact, she hoped to work with Hannah, and the contacts on the ground, to try to find safe routes to bring the refugees to England.

"Do you think we passed the tests?" Hannah nibbled her fingernail. "They can't refuse to let us go after all we've been through, can they?"

"I can't say." Jane worried that her injuries might let her down. Her chest had been painful during the physical training for the parachute jump, but she'd borne the pain stoically and didn't think anyone had noticed. Her head injury had healed, but she still suffered headaches. Her personal memories were still unreliable, but she had retained all the new information she'd been swamped with during the last two weeks. Her short-term memory was functioning well.

"You're afraid aren't you?" Hannah asked. "You look like you did that day you came to the library."

"I'm petrified." Jane smiled. "But I can't wait to get to work."

"It scares me that so many are depending on us. I don't want to let them down."

"I feel that way too, but you know we might not be able to save them all. Some may already have been captured. It's more than a month since Sebastian came here with that message."

"It would have taken him some time to travel from Germany. The Gestapo will have had weeks to investigate the places that man knew about."

"And our people will have had just as long to hear about what was happening and take some action themselves." Jane had been thinking about what she would have done, had she been one of the people they were hoping to help. "This woman we are hoping to meet. Ursula Meyer. She will know some information. She must, or Sebastian wouldn't have given us her name. She will surely have helped to spread the word to the refugees in hiding."

"Do you think so?" Hannah looked up, hopefully.

"That's what I would have done in her shoes."

"Yes. Me too." Hannah smiled. "Perhaps our job will not be so difficult when we get there. We'll have help, won't we?"

"I hope so." Jane sighed. "What can be taking so long?" She glanced at the door. "Time is ticking. We should be planning our journey."

"Do you think we could sneak off camp and find a pub?"

"Why would you want to do that? We've been told to stay put and wait."

"I'm sick of doing everything I'm told. I've followed every instruction they've given me for the last two weeks, and I'm in danger of losing sight of myself. Don't you feel the same?"

Jane shrugged. She'd never felt better. The training had given her back some degree of control, and after losing her memories, it was a good feeling.

"One of the soldiers told me there's a pub not a hundred yards from the gates. Let's go there, Jane." Hannah jumped to her feet.

"Please and pretty please!" She pleaded, clasping her hands under her chin. "Just for a little while. I want to feel ordinary for a time before they send us into the jaws of hell."

Jane laughed. "Well, since you put it so poetically, how can I refuse?" She reached for the drab coat she'd been given. "I don't know why you're so worried. They might not let us go anyway."

"After everything we've been through, they'd better." Hannah pulled on her brown coat. "I can't go back to Sheffield with this joke of a hairstyle." She dragged her decorated blue-velvet beret over the offending short, dark curls. "I'll be the laughing stock of the library staff. My hair was my crowning glory. Look what they did to me!"

They both whirled at the knock on the door.

"May I come in?" Mr Wilcox called.

Jane quickly took off her coat and threw it on the bed and signalled for Hannah to do the same. When the girls were seated on the beds, Jane called, "Yes. Come in."

Mr Wilcox was smiling when he entered the room. "You did it, ladies. You proved your worth."

"We can go?" Hannah's voice sounded small and wary.

"You leave tonight."

"Tonight!" Jane gasped.

"You are to take these to your contact." He handed a small cardboard folder to Jane. "Don't let this fall into enemy hands. The contents could get you shot."

"What is inside?" Jane asked, holding the folder as if it might bite her.

"Blank identity cards. There is also an official rubber stamp, complete with an ink pad, filled with authentic German ink. Your friends will find these invaluable."

Jane realised she was holding the documents that could enable many people to travel through Germany more safely.

"If you get yourselves in a tight spot over there, ditch these before the Jerries get you."

"Yes, of course." Jane clutched the folder close to her chest. She knew she wouldn't give the false documents up easily. They would be a lifeline to many.

"Now, I'll leave you to pack. You have an hour."

"That's too soon. We're not ready."

"Then you'd better rectify that quickly. I'll have a car waiting for you in an hour at the gate. Don't pack anything other than what we've given you." He grinned at Hannah. "And that includes your ridiculous hat."

Hannah dragged the beret from her head.

Two hours later they were climbing into the back of a light aircraft with a small bag of belongings each. The propellers were already turning, and as soon as the door was closed, they were moving.

A young man in air-force uniform told them where to sit. Another passed them each a dark, canvas bag. "Put your shoes and bags into these sacks, ladies. Anything loose in your pockets can go in there too."

"How long until we have to jump?" Hannah didn't sound happy about the prospect.

"You have hours yet," the first man told her as he moved around the aircraft fastening cables and checking ropes. "Put on your jumpsuits and boots; they'll help to keep you warm. Try to relax and get some shut-eye. I'll wake you when it's time to get ready."

"Sleep!" Jane's voice came out an octave higher than usual. "How can you expect us to sleep?"

"First mission is it, ladies?" The young man sitting next to Jane smiled sympathetically. He was already wearing his flying suit. "Take it from one who's been a few times. It never gets easier. You won't know when you'll be able to sleep peacefully again. Get some shut-eye while you can. I'll ask Private Brown to sing us a lullaby if you think it'll help."

"Are you a spy?" Hannah asked as she climbed into her suit, tucking her skirts down the legs. Her eyes sparkled in the semi-darkness of the aircraft.

"We don't use that word. I'm a British agent. I'll be getting off over France after we drop you."

"What will you be doing?"

"Naughty, naughty. We don't ask personal questions. Didn't they teach you anything at spy school?" His smile was wide and filled with warmth. "I'm Private Jackson, codename Unicorn. What about you two?"

"Hannah Rosenberg, travelling under the name of Hannah Schmidt, and this is Jane Robinson, travelling under the name of Gerda Schmidt."

"Are you supposed to be sisters? You don't look alike."

"Cousins." Jane corrected as she tied the laces on her boots.

"You'll be working together?"

"Now who is asking too many questions?" Jane smiled.

"Sorry, it's difficult to have an ordinary conversation when we're not allowed to discuss our work. Perhaps you could tell me about your life before this mess?"

The situation felt surreal. Jane laughed nervously as the thought occurred to her that she might have slipped into an alternative existence. She'd never been in an aircraft until a few days ago, and this flight was only the second time she'd flown. She was preparing to jump from it while it was still four-hundred feet in the air and then run as fast as she could to get to a place of safety before German guards had the chance to either shoot or capture her on the ground. She shook her head. "Perhaps we should try to get some sleep like the man said."

Shutting her eyes, she closed off any further attempt at conversation. Sleep would be impossible, but she couldn't discuss her past, her present or her future with this man. She was a German Jew who had fled from persecution and was now heading back to the most dangerous place in the world for her kind. The bright-eyed British agent could never understand who she was or why she was sharing this perilous journey with him, nor would she wish him to.

It was cold in the body of the aircraft and Private Brown handed out blankets. "Snuggle down. I'll make sure you're awake in time to disembark."

"Thanks." Jane took the blanket and wrapped it around her legs.

She closed her eyes again and listened to Hannah talking quietly with the British agent. They discussed books they'd read and places they'd been, avoiding any references to personal lives or what might lie ahead. The drone of their voices lulled her into a state of relaxation, and before she knew it, she felt a hand on her shoulder shaking her awake.

"Time to get ready. Your chutes are over there. I'll help you fasten them." He pointed to the line of backpacks hanging among the cables along the side of the aircraft.

Jane fumbled into her parachute. She tied the canvas sack to her waist and checked the small spade in the pocket on her left leg. That would be used to bury the parachute after she landed.

She watched Private Brown help Hannah fasten the parachute to her back before he came to check hers.

"Now you don't have to worry about anything," he tried to reassure them. "Jump when I say, and the parachute will open automatically, just as it did in training. Who's going first?"

Hannah's face was white, and Jane tried to smile to reassure her friend. "See you on the ground." She took her place near the door of the aircraft as the pilot cut the engines.

"Oh, what's happened?" Hannah cried in the silence.

"We're gliding in. Don't worry." Private Jackson touched Hannah's arm. "It's standard procedure. We don't want to alert people on the ground."

"But we'll crash!" Hannah was obviously not reassured by the young man's words.

"No, we won't. The pilot will restart the engine when we're clear of the drop zone, but you'll be on the ground by then." Private Brown yanked the door open, and Jane moved closer to the opening.

"Good luck, girls." Private Jackson called as the wind rushed in through the open door.

Jane felt a hand pat her shoulder, and she launched herself into darkness.

The tug on her back told her the parachute was opening and she counted the seconds, knowing the ground was rushing up to meet her but not knowing what else might be waiting for her when she landed.

Chapter Twenty-Three – Panic and Fear

Jane found it difficult to judge distance in the darkness. She scanned the ground far below her and thought she detected a darker line to her left. Her brain translated the line, to mean a river or a stand of trees. A pale ribbon of something that might be a road was to her right.

The slight wind was making her parachute sway as she descended and she began to feel nauseous. Her previous two jumps had been in daylight, and she'd felt quite euphoric for a while, on the way down, after the chute had opened. Now there was only the starlight to guide her, and it was a completely different experience. She peered at her feet, worrying that she could suffer a broken ankle if she didn't land correctly.

A flash of light caught her attention. Someone was shining a flashlight near the ground, illuminating a patch of grassy meadow. The meadow rushed up to greet her, and she tucked up her legs. Her feet hit the ground, and she rolled, feeling the hard spade bruise her leg as she became tangled in the ropes of her parachute.

She was dragged to her feet and hands reached to tug the ropes from her body. A sharp blade sliced close to her clothing as lines were cut efficiently and quickly.

"Déshabiller!" (*undress*), a man's voice ordered in French from the darkness.

"No!" Jane answered automatically and then realised she was being asked to remove her jumpsuit. "Désolé." (*sorry*).

She began to unfasten the buttons but forgot the canvas bag tied around her waist. Her fingers fumbled, and someone took hold of her hands, moving them roughly out of the way. The knife sliced again, cutting ties and releasing the remaining buttons. She stepped from the suit, and the man began to gather her discarded clothing and parachute into his arms.

She bent to unfasten the laces on her boots. The shoes in her canvas bag would be more in keeping with the stylish woollen suit she wore.

"Gardez vos bottes sur," (*keep your boots on*), he ordered.

She straightened quickly. Her eyes were now adjusting to the darkness, and she could see Hannah a few yards away. A tall man was with her friend and seemed to be subjecting her to the same rough treatment.

Jane began to worry that they were in the hands of the enemy. Surely their contacts would not treat them so harshly. She remembered the password, and realised she should have already asked the question by now, but tried it anyway. "Où est votre fils?" (*where is your son*)?

The man laughed. "Louis est à Paris." (*Louis is in Paris*).

Jane sighed with relief. He'd given the expected answer.

The man took her arm and pulled her over to where Hannah was standing with the other man. "Zese two are still wet be'ind ze ears." He spoke in heavily accented English and laughed again. "Ze British must be desperate to send 'alf-trained, frightened schoolgirls."

"We are not schoolgirls, and we are not British!" Hannah sounded angry.

"Well, at least you 'ave passion. That will 'elp." The other man's voice was not as strongly accented, and he laughed and pushed Hannah's shoulder. "Walk!"

"Where are you taking us?" Jane asked as she stumbled along. "We're supposed to bury our parachutes before we go anywhere."

"What!" The man laughed again. "We do not waste good silk and ropes in these parts."

"But they might be discovered, and then they'll know we are here!" Hannah planted her feet and stood her ground. "Give me my spade!" she demanded.

"No one will know you are 'ere, little sparrow." The taller man spoke softly. "You are quite safe, at least, for now."

"Come, we need to get you to Frau Meyer before sun up." The shorter man tugged Jane's sleeve.

"Is she expecting us?" Jane asked.

"Per'aps, per'aps not, but she will make you welcome."

"Which is more than can be said for you," Hannah hissed through clenched teeth. "Do you know what we went through to get here?"

"Hannah, calm down." Jane took her friend's arm. "These men are here to help us."

"Well, they should be taught some manners!"

"We do not 'ave time for zis! Get down!" The short, stocky man grabbed both girls and pushed them to the ground.

"What are you doing?" Hannah tried to get up, but the other man held her down and clamped his hand over her mouth.

Jane could see lights in the distance and whispered, "What is that?"

"Allemands." (*Germans*). Her companion spoke close to her ear. "Zey must 'ave been alerted by your plane. Zey will be looking for you."

Hannah whimpered.

"What should we do?" Jane asked.

"Come, we must 'urry." The taller man got to his feet but crouched low. He helped Hannah to stand and took her hand. "Keep quiet and stay close."

Jane followed the tall man who was leading Hannah by the hand. The stocky man was close behind as they ran, crouching and stumbling in the darkness. On reaching the line of trees, the men scrambled through thick underbrush, pulling the girls with them, and then helped them down a steep, slippery banking.

Jane could smell wet vegetation and knew they were close to a riverbank. She could make out the outline of a small boat. "You have a boat!"

"Quiet." The taller man helped her to climb aboard the rowing boat. "Get down and stay down."

She crouched in the hollow of the boat with Hannah, and the taller man threw the bundles of parachute and ropes in with them before covering them with a rough and foul-smelling tarpaulin.

Jane was too scared to speak, but Hannah whispered, "Where are we going?"

"I said to keep quiet," one of the men whispered. "Zere is a small island in ze river. We can 'ide over zere and wait it out. Zey will soon get tired of ze search."

"How can you be sure?" Hannah asked, keeping her voice low.

"You talk too much. Be quiet or I'll 'and you over to zem myself!"

They heard the soft sweep of oars through water and the boat began to move. Jane held her breath for a few terrifying seconds. If the German soldiers came to the riverbank, the boat would be a sitting target on the water. The sound of the oars would echo for miles in the silence of the night. The German flashlights would easily find them.

Hannah reached for her, and the two girls clasped hands tightly.

After a few nerve-racking minutes, the boat thudded against something solid.

"Don't move and stay silent," one of the men warned. "We are 'idden from sight but may 'ave to stay 'ere for a time."

Jane felt Hannah squeeze her hand and knew her friend's fear matched her own.

After many minutes had passed, Jane's legs began to cramp, but she dare not move. She suffered the pain and clamped her jaws to keep from crying out. Wriggling her toes, she tried to ease the cramps.

"All right, you can come out now."

The tarpaulin was lifted, and Jane sat up, shaking her legs. "Cramp," she explained.

"What now?" Hannah asked.

"We row into ze town. It is better zan walking, eh?" The shorter man grinned. "And soon we will be surrounded by larger boats. Zey will give good cover."

"What about the German soldiers?" Jane asked, still stretching her calf muscles to ease the kinks in them.

"They did not come this way." The taller man took up the oars. "We are safe, for now."

"Which one of you is Eagle?" Hannah asked.

The tall one grinned. "That will be me."

"Are you in the French resistance?" Jane asked.

"Per'aps," the shorter man, Fox, said as he pulled the oars through the water. "But sometimes we find acting alone gets more done."

"Why?" Hannah looked interested.

"Too many fanatics muddy the water." The taller man shook his head. "Not many want to work on this side of the border anyway."

"Will you be helping us while we're here?" Jane asked.

"We keep in contact with Frau Meyer. If you need us, she will know 'ow to get 'old of us."

"What do you know about Heinrich Schneider?"

"Ee is dead. Ze Gestapo left 'is body in ze street when zey finished wiz 'im." Fox spat into the river. "Pigs!"

"Did he talk?" Jane asked.

Fox shrugged. "Per'aps. It would take a brave man to resist questioning by ze Gestapo."

"Have any of the safe houses been discovered?" Hannah clutched the tall man's arm. "Please! Do you know?"

Eagle nodded. "We 'eard of two families taken away last week from a farm near Halberg."

"Where is that?" Jane asked.

"Two kilometres from Saarbrücken," Fox answered.

"Where did they take them?"

Eagle shrugged. "We 'eard they went to a labour camp near Munich."

Jane sighed heavily. "We are too late."

"Not for the others. Don't lose heart." Hannah gave Jane a tight smile. "We still have work to do."

Jane glanced at a large dark shape looming from around a bend in the river behind them. "Is that a barge?" she whispered.

"It is our cover for ze 'omeward stretch." Fox steered the small rowing boat to the shadowy side of the river, allowing the larger, noisy barge to get closer. "Keep your voices low."

With help from Eagle, Fox manoeuvred the small boat into the side of the larger one as it came near, and quickly tied some ropes to link the two craft together. "We will piggy-back a ride into town from 'ere."

"Is it safe?" Jane whispered, glancing uncertainly at the hull of the huge barge.

"Zese coal barges are manned by four or five men," Fox explained. "And only one of zem will be awake at zis time of night. We will be as a flea on a cat. Ee will not notice we are 'ere."

"Don't worry, little sparrow." Eagle grinned. "Tell me, what do you 'ope to achieve 'ere?"

"You know about our people in hiding." Hannah glanced nervously at the large barge chugging along beside them. "There are hundreds of them, all over Germany and Austria."

"All Jews?" Fox looked wary.

"Mostly Jews," Jane admitted. "Heinrich Schneider was helping to get them out."

"And take zem where?" Fox sounded flippant.

"To safety, of course." Hannah squared her shoulders and lifted her chin defiantly. "Do you think we can't do this?"

"No one could do what you suggest." Eagle's voice was soft. "The best you can 'ope for is to keep them well 'idden until this is over. Especially now Schneider is dead."

"Why do you say that?" Jane asked. "Why would it be worse for them now he is dead?"

"Ze Germans are obsessed wiz records." Fox sneered. "Every word zat man spoke will be written down and catalogued. Just because zere is little action at ze moment, does not mean zey are not planning to block the routes, or swoop on all ze safe 'ouses."

"Then we need to work fast." Hannah was still defensive. "We *will* find a safe route out of Germany. We will get our people to England and from there; our organisation can arrange safe passage to wherever they want to go."

"Fool!" Fox shook his head. "We are at war! You are in ze middle of 'undreds of square kilometres of enemy territory. You will get us all killed wiz your idealistic, fanatic mentality."

"Do not let Frau Meyer hear you talking like that, Fox." Eagle dropped his head. "She is a good woman, but does not like to be called a fanatic."

"We are 'ere." Fox pulled the ropes from the barge and pushed off with one of the oars.

He rowed a few feet, shipped the oars and allowed the small craft to drift to a wooden jetty. They watched the barge chug on farther down the river.

"You are on your own now." Fox wrapped a rope loosely around a mooring post.

"What about the documents we have for you?" Jane began to open her bag.

Eagle grabbed her arm and stopped her from taking the documents from the bag. "Give them to Frau Meyer."

Jane nodded and put the bag on her shoulder. "Where do we go?" she asked, glancing around the small, deserted dock.

"You 'ave the name of the café?"

Jane nodded.

"Go there. Turn left at the top of that ramp. First right and second left will take you to a square. Take the alley beside the clock shop and go left at the end."

Jane tried to memorise the directions and hoped Hannah was also listening.

"Thank you."

The two girls stepped from the boat and watched the men pull away.

"Better change into our shoes. We'll stand out a mile in these army boots and fashionable clothes." Hannah lifted one foot. "Not exactly blending in this combination, are we?"

Jane sat to unfasten the boots. When she had the low-heeled, lace-up shoes on her feet, she turned to Hannah. "What should we do with these?" She picked up the heavy boots.

Hanna lifted her boots and dropped them into the river. "We can't take them with us. They are no use to us now."

Jane lowered hers noiselessly into the water. "Can you remember the directions?"

"Turn right at the top of the ramp. We'll get there, but let's hurry. I don't want to bump into any German patrols."

Lights were on in the back room of the café when the girls knocked on the door. The walk through town had been worrying. They jumped at small noises and kept to the shadows, but were relieved when the short walk proved uneventful, and the painted sign of the café came in sight.

Their knock was answered by a round-faced woman in her late forties wearing a large white apron over her floral dress. "Guten morgan." (*good morning*).

Jane smiled nervously. "Tante Ursula? Es ist Ihnen?" (*Aunt Ursula? Is it you?*)

The woman glanced up and down the empty street, and then held the door wide. "Schnell." (*quickly*).

Hannah squeezed passed the woman with Jane following close behind.

The café was filled with the aroma of baking bread and pastries, reminding Jane how hungry she was.

"Kommen durch." (*come through*). Frau Meyer took them through to the kitchen.

"Oh, that smells divine." Hannah inhaled the delicious aroma.

"Speak German," Frau Meyer warned, in German. "Don't take the risk of speaking English here. I have a waitress who will arrive soon. She knows of my nieces coming to visit, but you are from Hamburg, not London! Speak only German when under my roof, even when you are alone. Do you understand?"

"Of course," Hannah answered in German.

"It is good of you to accommodate us, Frau Meyer," Jane began, but the German woman tutted, sighed and held her hand up to interrupt her.

"Would you call your real aunt by her family name?"

Jane immediately realised her blunder. "No Aunt Ursula. Sorry. I won't make that mistake again."

"Good. Then we'll get along well. Which one are you?"

"Gerda," Jane answered.

The woman nodded and turned to Hannah. "Then you are my dearest niece, Hannah."

Hannah smiled nervously. "Yes, Aunt Ursula."

"Welcome. I know you will have endured a perilous journey of which I have no desire to hear about. The less I know, the better, you understand?"

The girls nodded.

"Perhaps you can take your bags upstairs to the apartment, and I'll bring you some breakfast. We won't have much chance to talk until the café is closed this evening, so I suggest you get some sleep today and stay out of sight."

Hannah stepped toward the woman. "But—."

"No buts. You do as you are told until I know I can trust you to behave like the good German nieces you are meant to be. I'm taking a risk with you two. Don't let me down!"

"No, Aunt Ursula," they chorused.

"Then what are you waiting for? Go!" She clapped her hands and shooed them to a door at the back of the kitchen. "You'll find your bedroom at the top. I'll be up in ten minutes."

Jane began to climb the narrow stairs.

"Oh, and make sure you take a wash, and then air your clothes. You both stink."

Hannah lifted her arm to sniff her armpit. "I can't smell anything terrible."

"I think she can smell that tarpaulin on us." Jane sniffed her sleeve.

"What *was* that smell?" Hannah's giggle was more a release of tension than a genuine sound of amusement.

"Fish guts?" Jane chuckled. "Oh, dear. We'll need to fumigate everything."

They found the room with two single beds at the top of another staircase. The small window looked out over rooftops and Jane could see the sky beginning to lighten in the East. She opened the window, letting the chilly air into the room.

"Brr, we'll freeze in here," Hannah complained.

"But we need to air our things. Two fashionable young women from Hamburg cannot go around town stinking of fish guts. Our cover will be blown in no time."

"Why?" Hannah chuckled. "Do you think the Gestapo will be searching high and low for two girls who stink of fish?"

They both washed, using the soap and water they found on the washstand. When they had changed into looser fitting dresses from their bags, they hung the rest of their belongings around the room to air.

"Gerda!" Frau Meyer called from the bottom of the stairs. "Hannah! Breakfast is ready, my sweet things."

"I could get used to this." Hannah grinned.

Jane picked up the folder containing the documents and followed Hannah down the stairs.

Frau Meyer had placed a tray of bread and coffee on the table by the window in the living room of the apartment. "You will find pots of preserves in that dresser, and cheese and ham in the cold store over there. I brought enough bread for two meals, and I'll return upstairs this evening."

"Thank you, Aunt Ursula. You're very kind." Hannah licked her lips.

"Stay out of sight. I know you are eager to begin your sightseeing, but you need to rest. Today will be a busy day in the café. The Gruppenführer is holding his daughter's birthday party here this afternoon."

"Who is the Gruppenführer?"

Frau Meyer lifted her head but kept her face neutral. "He is the man responsible for killing my dear friend Heinrich."

"You knew Heinrich Schneider?" Hannah gasped.

"He was a friend, but the Gestapo have no idea of our connection. The dear man protected his people to the end." She sniffed and blinked a few times but showed no other sign of emotion. "Do you think Gruppenführer Leitz would be gracing my café with his presence if he knew?"

"You must hate the Gruppenführer." Hannah glanced at Jane.

"I do," her voice was flippant. "But his money keeps me in business, and his friendship gives me the respectability to remain above suspicion." She turned to smile at the girls and said sadly, "This is not the life I would have chosen, but it is the life I must live now."

"You are in a difficult position, Frau, I mean, Aunt Ursula." Jane quickly corrected herself. "How can you bear to encourage the friendship of such a man?"

Frau Meyer smiled. "Because he would crush me like a beetle if I gave him any cause to suspect me. He believes he is a friend, and that's how I like to keep things. His friendship gives me great power, my sweet girl. I know things, and because of this, I am useful to you and your friends in England. Sebastian knew this."

Hannah clasped her hands together. "How well did you know Sebastian?"

"Well enough to know he must be dead. He would have returned by now if he could."

"You're right, Aunt Ursula." Jane went on to explain, "He died in a bombing raid."

"What did he do here?" Hannah was obviously eager hear about her lover. "Did he help our people to escape as we've been told?"

"He helped some braver ones to try to escape, but mostly, he tried to ensure the ones in hiding stayed safe. That task is equally as important as trying to get them out of Germany. Especially now that the

German army occupies most of Europe and travelling is practically impossible for people such as you are talking about." She held up her hand and whispered very quietly, "We do not speak of Jews here. It is far too dangerous."

"We understand." Jane was beginning to appreciate how difficult their work might be. "But we were asked to bring you these documents. Won't these make it easier to get them out?"

Frau Meyer took the folder and opened it. "Blanks, that's good. Did they send the official Saarbrücken stamp? Do you have it?"

"It's in there." Jane pointed to the folder.

Frau Meyer took out the rubber stamp and examined it. "All looks good. I'll have my man check these out."

"Do you have many people working with you?" Jane asked.

"You ask too many questions."

"Sorry."

Hannah smiled. "I think you are very brave."

"Or foolish." Frau Meyer laughed. "Depending on your point of view. Now I must go. Remember to stay out of sight. The Gruppenführer is aware that I will have guests staying, but if he hears those guests are two attractive young women, well, it might cause complications."

"What kind of complications?" Jane asked.

"Let me just say that Gruppenführer Leitz likes young women. He is not above taking what he wants, whether the object of his infatuation agrees or not. I can't take the chance that he will not lust for one or both of you if he sees you."

"But you said he has a daughter!" Hannah sounded shocked. "How old is she? Does he also have a wife?"

"Oh yes, my dear, he does have a wife, but that doesn't stop his roving eye. I'm fortunate that I'm too old for his tastes. His stepdaughter is twelve and too young as yet, but I fear he may have plans for her. She's a pretty little thing."

Hannah gasped again. "You don't think he would..?"

"The man would stop at nothing to get what he wants. He is evil and corrupt, and if I told you half the things I know about him, you would run for the mountains."

Jane didn't want to waste time on gossip. She was impatient to start doing something positive. She wasn't concerned about a lecherous old Gestapo officer. "When can we start work?"

"When I tell you." Frau Meyer's tone turned stern. "We will talk more this evening. For now, eat, and then sleep. I suspect you didn't sleep much in the last few hours, am I right?"

Hannah nodded.

"Well, I'll need you fresh this evening. You have a job to do if I think you can be trusted to do it properly."

"What do you want us to do?" Jane asked. She was eager to make plans.

"You'll find out this evening."

Chapter Twenty-Four – Fishing

Later that night, toward midnight, the girls prepared to leave the café. Ursula had given them men's trousers with warm jackets and knitted woollen hats to wear as camouflage.

"If you are seen, you are simply fishing. Take these." She handed them some nets and rods and a bag with four large trout and a box of bait in the bottom of it. "If you are asked questions, explain that trout bite better at night. Set up your surveillance of the docks on the opposite bank to the railway terminal. It is a good spot for fishing, and for watching the river traffic."

They were tasked with watching the boats coming and going. Ursula had asked them to count how many barges were unloading there and to notice what the busiest times were, throughout the night.

"Why is this important?" Jane asked, wondering what use the information might be to their cause.

"Sebastian was trying to set up some escape routes using the rivers to bring people here. It makes for a long and arduous journey for them, but worth it if we could prove the viability and safety of such an audacious plan."

"So you are still trying to move our people out of Germany?" Hannah asked. "Yesterday, you said it was a foolish idea to try to get them to safety."

"It is, but I can't take away their freedom of choice. Your British friends have offered to continue to drop the documents into the waiting hands of our friends, Eagle and Fox. With their help, we are duty bound to assist where we can. That is what Sebastian would have wished, and I will uphold his wishes to the best of my ability. Heinrich gave his life to keep our plans safe. I owe it to my old friends to continue their work."

Hannah lifted her chin. "We will help all we can."

"You think the river routes will be safe?" Jane asked. "The journey will be slow. It could take weeks to travel the winding routes to here and what about people in the West and the North?" Jane knew Germany was vast, and their small organisation couldn't possibly help them all. "What is being done for them?"

"We can only help people close to us, Gerda." Ursula sighed. "We are three women with limited resources. Whatever we do will be minuscule in comparison to what *needs* to be done, but we can't do *nothing*. It isn't an option, is it?"

"She's right, Gerda." Hannah nodded and asked Ursula, "What makes you think the river routes will be safe?"

"Saarbrücken is an important hub for distributing coal and ore for factories all over this part of Germany. The port is busy with boats from the mines and quarries. They unload their cargo to the railways for the onward journey to factories all over Germany."

"How does that help our mission?" Jane asked.

"With so many barges using the Saar now, a few extra smaller boats will not be noticed so much. The larger barges use rowing boats as tenders while waiting their turn to dock. We can bring people by boat into the town, just as you arrived yesterday. They will not be noticed in the busier periods. When they are safe in my café, we give them the papers and travel documents and prepare to move them by road or rail to the French coastal ports."

"I don't know." Hannah was not convinced. "If they are caught on the water, with no papers, they will be shot."

Ursula had huffed. "We cannot distribute the documents to every safe house from here to Munich without risking exposure to ourselves. This is the best we can offer, and I'm taking a huge risk by allowing them into my café under the noses of the Gestapo."

"Why don't we simply try to get them to neutral Switzerland?" Jane suggested. "That border is closer and not as risky as trying to get them to the Channel ports in France by road or rail."

"You think?" Ursula had huffed. "Try crossing mountains with children at this time of year and tell me it is not treacherous."

"Come, Gerda," Hannah shook her net and rod. "We have some fishing to do."

Jane pulled her dark woollen hat over her hair, tucking the blonde locks under and out of sight.

"Take care, girls." Ursula waved them off. "You have your identity papers. Mention my name if you encounter difficulties. Most of the soldiers know me."

The girls set out to the river, retracing the steps they'd taken the previous day, but then crossed a bridge next to the wooden jetty to get to the other side of the water.

"Walk tall, Hannah," Jane advised. "We have nothing to fear. Don't act suspiciously or you'll draw attention to us."

Hannah giggled nervously. "Can you hear yourself? I suppose that two girls walking through town after midnight, dressed as men, are not at all suspicious!" She flounced along, shaking her net and rod for good measure. "Who would question such a thing?"

"Well," Jane laughed softly, "I suppose you have a point. We do look odd, don't we?"

"I'll be glad when we're settled on the riverbank with our lines dangling in the water. At least we'll be in the shadows and out of sight."

"Down there, look!" Jane pointed to a grassy bank just off the footpath. "I can see the rail wagons waiting on the tracks over there, see?"

"Is that a barge approaching?" Hannah was staring upstream.

"I see two of them. One is behind, can you see?"

"Let's go down there and set up our rods. I wouldn't want anyone to notice us taking interest in barges and trains. No matter how well-connected Aunt Ursula might be, I don't want to risk getting caught."

They sat on the cold banking for hours, watching barges unloading cargo directly into the waiting rail wagons. Ursula had been right about the number of smaller boats on the water. It seemed the bargemen like to visit each other's boats, as well as the shore while waiting for their turns to be unloaded.

"I count seven barges now." Jane peered up the river. "And there's another one approaching. What time is it?"

"Five." Hannah stretched and yawned. "Why don't these people work normal hours?"

"Thank goodness they don't. I'm beginning to see why Sebastian would think this was a good plan. Our people could easily slip into town at this time of day. Look how busy the water is, and no one is taking notice of the little boats."

They both turned quickly at a noise behind them. Silhouetted against the wall of the bridge, two soldiers were pointing rifles at them.

"What have we here?" one of the soldiers called. "What is your business?"

"We are fishing." Hannah got to her feet. "Come see." She beckoned them closer.

"Fishing?" The other soldier sounded amused. "What fish could you catch in the Saar?"

"Trout." Jane reached for the bag with the fish, hoping they still looked fresh. "They bite better at night and will make a good meal. We like trout for breakfast."

The soldiers lowered their guns and moved closer. Jane's heart began to pound. If these soldiers suspected anything, they would be in great danger. She tried to keep her voice light and jovial. "We have been fortunate. We caught four so far. Would you like to take one?"

"You are girls!" One soldier gasped. "Why are you dressed as men?"

Hannah pulled her hat down to cover more of her face. "It's more practical, don't you think? We'd freeze on this riverbank in women's clothing."

Jane hurried to add her voice, "You won't tell anyone, will you? Think of our reputation!" She put her hands to her cheeks and giggled coquettishly. "My poor papa would not be pleased to know he raised a tomboy."

Hannah reinforced the ruse. "Uncle Herman had hopes of a high-class marriage for Gerda, and if this gets out, well, you can see how things are, boys, can't you?"

"We'd better see your papers, girls." The first soldier rested his rifle against his leg and held out a hand. "You do have them on you, don't you?"

"Yes, of course." Hannah reached into her jacket pocket and took out a slim wallet. "Here you are."

The soldier took the wallet and flipped it open. He shone a flashlight over the exposed documents and handed them back.

Jane had hers ready when he'd finished with Hannah's. "Is everything in order?" she asked. "I mean, are we in trouble for fishing here?" She thought she'd embellish the story for effect. "We're new in town, and if we have broken any rules of the river, then, we are very sorry. If we're not allowed to fish here, we'll make sure not to do so in future." She realised she was babbling and closed her mouth.

The soldier handed her papers back. "All is good."

"Did you say you have some fish?" the other soldier asked.

"Yes." Hannah lifted the bag. "In here." She opened it to show the soldiers their supposed catch.

One reached in, to lift out a trout. "These are gutted." He flapped the fish. "Did they jump into your arms ready for the pan?"

Hannah stiffened, but Jane laughed girlishly. "Well, we had to gut them, didn't we? Any fool knows that to leave the guts in after the fish is dead would spoil the flesh, and we want the fish to be at their best for our breakfast."

The soldiers exchanged a glance. The one with the fish replaced it in the bag.

"I see." The first soldier shouldered his rifle. "You might enjoy dressing as men where you come from, but this is not what we expect of our women here in Saarbrücken."

"Oh, we didn't mean to offend," Hannah was quick to respond.

"And it is not usual for young women to be out at such an hour." The other soldier tapped his watch. "Go home, girls. We have more important matters to attend to."

"Oh, of course." Jane couldn't help take an interest but kept her tone flirtatious. "I'm sure two handsome young men such as you have much more important work than checking the business of two foolish girls. We're sorry to have wasted your time."

"Well, perhaps you could make it up to us by agreeing to attend the dance at the castle on the last Friday of this month as our guests." The first soldier clicked his heels and bowed his head. "Private Hans Kessler, at your service, girls, and my friend here is Private Johan Hoff."

Jane and Hannah exchanged a glance, and Jane quickly shook her head and tried to refuse, but Hannah jumped in.

"That is very kind of you, boys. We'd be delighted."

"Would you allow us to escort you home?"

"Don't you have important business to attend to?" Jane asked, worrying how she would explain the escort to Frau Meyer.

Private Kessler picked up the bag of fish. "Gather your things, girls. We'd be happy to see you safely home."

"What were you thinking?" Jane spluttered over her breakfast. They were discussing the encounter with Frau Meyer.

"They seemed like nice boys." Hannah giggled. "I could see from the moment they realised we were girls; they had no intention of reporting us."

"How could you know such a thing?" Jane asked.

"Body language, my friend. Those boys were nervous as schoolboys, but they were intrigued. They wanted to know more about us. The last thing on their minds was to report us and let us slip out of their hands."

"Can you tell so much from looking at them?" Frau Meyer asked.

"She'd good, isn't she?" Jane knew how good her friend was at reading body language.

"Anyway, we don't have to meet them, do we? That's why we left them in the square." Hannah shrugged. "They don't know where to find us."

"Come!" Frau Meyer got to her feet. "Help me tidy this kitchen, girls, and tell me what happened on the river."

Ursula had insisted on making them a breakfast of trout and fried potatoes when the girls eventually arrived back at the café, and now she looked curious. "I hope those two young men didn't distract you from your purpose." She grinned. "Have you been making friends instead of doing your job?"

Jane followed the older woman and took a drying cloth from the peg near the sink. "No, we did the surveillance as instructed and you're right about the boats, but thanks to my enthusiastic cousin, we now have to attend a dance in three weeks. Those two soldiers questioned us and then invited us to a dance at the castle."

"Did they?" Ursula looked thoughtful.

"But how can we go? We don't have suitable clothing, and besides that, we would be exposing ourselves to the kind of attention that we could really do without!"

"What did that man at the training camp say to us?" Hannah asked. "Hiding in plain sight is often the best place to be. The enemy won't suspect us if we act like one of them. If we hide away; or if we'd refused the invitation, they would have been more suspicious."

"She is right, Gerda." Ursula shook her head and handed Jane a plate to dry. "I can't say I like it, but perhaps it's not so bad. I could think of worse things that could have happened, and we can turn this to our advantage."

"What do you mean?" Jane asked. "How can a dance invitation be taken advantage of?"

"A dance at the castle, don't forget." Ursula raised her eyebrows. "The castle holds the headquarters of the Gestapo. You will be on the inside of that fortress, and I know some people who would kill their own grandmothers for access to that place."

"We'll be attending a dance and probably won't be going anywhere near the headquarters." Jane pointed out. "What could *we* do?"

"Leave it with me. I'm sure we'll find this turn of events useful." Ursula frowned. "You *can* dance, I presume?"

"I can waltz and foxtrot." Jane nodded. "And I can do the dances we were taught in school."

"What about you?" Ursula asked Hannah.

"I have two left feet and no sense of rhythm." She put her head in her hands. "What was I thinking?"

"It is of no consequence." Ursula grinned mischievously. "Those boys probably don't have dancing in mind anyway."

"Oh, my goodness!" Jane gasped. "What have you got us into, Hannah?"

"You don't need to worry, Gerda. They sound like nice German boys. They will treat you with respect."

"But I'm a married woman!" Jane protested.

"Not here!" Ursula snapped. "And not now! You are single while under my roof. Do you understand!"

Jane nodded contritely.

"We'd better take this upstairs. My waitress will be arriving shortly. Come!" She opened the door to the flight of stairs, and Jane and Hannah followed her from the kitchen, up to the apartment.

"I know this is difficult, Gerda." Ursula began. "You are playing a part just as surely as an actress on stage, and I understand it can't be easy, but your lives depend on this."

"I know. I'm sorry." Jane felt bad at pointing out her marital status. Especially as she knew, deep down, that her marriage vows had meant nothing to her. She had an affair with her English tutor. She certainly knew how to act a part. She'd been acting the part of a faithful wife, and poor Gottfried knew nothing of her infidelity.

"Here in Saarbrücken, those boys have no idea who you are. They think you are two young girls who are available for their attentions. You will flirt and show those two boys a good time. You will encourage them to drink lots of beer, and if you get the chance, you will take advantage of the situation."

"What can we do?" Hannah asked.

"I'll contact Eagle. I'm sure he will have some ideas."

"But I wanted to go to Rosenheim as soon as our work here is done." Jane protested. "I can't waste time going to dances! I have personal business there."

"Your personal business will take a backseat, for now, Gerda. What we are doing is for the greater good. You do understand this, don't you?"

Jane nodded and sighed.

"What business do you have in Rosenheim?" Ursula asked.

"My daughter is in hiding there. I want to take her back to England. I have papers for her."

"What!" Hannah was obviously shocked. "Why didn't you say?"

"We had enough to contend with." She turned to Ursula. "Sasha is secondary to the mission. I understand that, but I had to take a risk. I took advantage of our situation and got Mr Wilcox to secure documents for her while he was organising ones for us. If I get the chance, I *will* save my child."

"Very commendable, Gerda, and exactly what I would do in your place, but your child is safe where she is, isn't she?" Ursula asked.

Jane shook her head. "As far as I know, her father will have arrived there by now, and goodness knows what story he is telling the locals. Gottfried has papers for our child, but is unprepared and is still deep in his grief. I don't know what is happening in Rosenheim."

"Her husband thinks Gerda is dead," Hannah explained. "She was in the same building with Sebastian when it was hit by a bomb. She lost her memory and was not included in the list of casualties. She was presumed to be among the unidentifiable dead, with Sebastian."

"Were you with him?" Ursula asked.

"My mind is unclear. I know I was sheltering in a cupboard with him at one point. He wasn't with me when I was rescued, which is odd, don't you think?" Jane had thought about that night often but still didn't understand why Sebastian's body was not found next to her. "The cupboard was very small. There was nowhere else he could have been."

"Bombs are destructive," Ursula said. "Perhaps your hiding place was blown to pieces, and you were blown some distance from it."

"Anything is possible. His wallet was discovered in the cellars, so perhaps he left me before the bomb dropped."

"If that's the case," Hannah looked puzzled, "Why didn't you go with him?"

Jane shrugged.

"We are getting nowhere, and interesting as this story is, Sebastian is dead, and you are alive. It changes nothing to mull it over. We have work to do. You've been up all night, and I'm sure you have lots of information for me. What did you see?"

Chapter Twenty-Five – Change of Plan

The girls spent every night, concealed by the shadows on the banks of the Saar, watching the river traffic and noting the number of barges while pretending to be fishing. Ursula provided fresh fish every evening to give them a reasonable cover story, but they didn't need it. No other soldiers stopped or questioned them. They slept in the daytime and stayed up all night talking softly in the shadows and watching the barges come and go.

"What good is all this, Hannah?" Jane asked one night. "I feel we are wasting our time sitting freezing on this riverbank."

"This is the job we've been given, Gerda. Our information will be a small piece of a larger jigsaw, but I'm sure it will be important."

"I think Mr Wilcox was fobbing us off by agreeing to send us here. Think about it!" Jane huffed angrily. "Two inexperienced girls insist on being sent to help the cause. They would see us as a liability, wouldn't they?"

"What are you getting at?"

"How better to keep us out of the way of the important work than to have us sitting around in the cold taking notes?"

"To be fair, Gerda, Mr Wilcox and his team have invested a lot of time and money in our rapid preparation for this mission, and as far as I understand it, he didn't know what we'd be doing when we got here, did he?"

"No, I suppose he didn't," Jane admitted. "And I'm grateful he agreed to my request to have documents made for Sasha. When I think about it, he must have known we'd want to use our initiative and do our own thing."

"I can't believe you didn't tell me about your daughter. How could you keep that to yourself?"

"You didn't need to know, Hannah. You have your own heartache, and I couldn't burden you with more of mine. I was planning to travel on to Rosenheim alone when we've finished our work here."

"You think I'd let you go alone and have all the fun?" Hannah grinned. "Besides, you need me."

"What makes you think I need you?" Jane smiled at her friend. "Am I not skilled enough to operate as a spy on my own?"

"Two heads are always better than one," Hannah quipped.

"How long do you think Ursula will expect us to do this surveillance? I'm impatient to move on and do some real work."

"Me too, but Mr Wilcox said we were to do whatever Frau Meyer asked of us."

"I still think we're wasting our time here."

"Look, that's three barges at the dock now. What time is it?" Hannah turned their attention back to the task they'd been given.

The last Friday of the month came around too soon, and Jane was dreading the evening. Ursula had communicated with the men in the resistance and received word that they would, indeed, like to see the inside of the castle.

"Are you clear about your part in this?" Ursula asked the girls as they changed into the evening wear she had procured for them.

"I'm not happy about it." Jane struggled with the buttons at the back of her silky dress. "How do we know the soldiers will do as we ask and drink themselves to oblivion for our benefit?"

"We don't, and for that, I have prepared these for you." Ursula took out two small bottles from her pocket. "These contain vodka laced with a sleeping draft. You should find an opportunity to pour this into their drink while no one is looking and then escort the poor boys to somewhere more secluded to wait until they fall asleep."

"How long will that take?" Hannah presented her lace covered back to Jane. "Do me up, will you?"

"Each of these holds enough to knock a man out for a few hours, but hopefully, you'll only need a few minutes to complete your task."

"Won't anyone think it odd that two respectable girls are sneaking off in the middle of the dance?" Jane stood at Hannah's back to fasten the buttons on her black lace dress.

"It's clear you have never had the pleasure of going to a ball at the castle under Gruppenführer Leitz's command." Ursula went to fasten Jane's dress. "I'm afraid they have the reputation of being bawdy and not altogether what a good girl would choose to attend."

"Oh, now she tells us!" Jane whirled on Ursula. "What are you sending us into?"

"Nothing two intelligent girls can't handle." The older woman's tone grew stern. "You signed up for this. You can't expect everything to be on your terms. We give-and-take in this business. We help the resistance, and they'll help you with your people. They may even help you get your daughter if you play your part well tonight."

Jane closed her eyes and nodded. She had known this mission wouldn't be easy, but she hadn't fully appreciated what might be expected of her.

"I think it might be fun." Hannah wrapped a lace-knit black shawl around her exposed shoulders.

"Fun!" Jane was shocked.

"Oh, come now, Gerda. We'll have the privilege of seeing the inside of that great fortress, and we might get to make fools of the Gestapo while we're there. What better way to spend our time, eh? You've been complaining that our work here so far is not as rewarding as you'd hoped."

Ursula handed the girls a small, beaded handbag each. "I put the sleeping drafts in there, along with your identity papers, and the lipsticks, compacts and pencils you showed me. You have everything you need." She stepped back, appraising the girls. "You both look enchanting, but your faces give you away! Relax and smile! Listen to your friend, Gerda. If you have your mind focused on fun, your nerves won't show. You can do this. We're counting on you." She touched Jane's shoulder. "Put on your wrap; it's cold outside. Come. I think you should get moving."

Private Kessler and Private Hoff were waiting in the square as arranged. Both men looked to have taken extra care with their appearance. They were clean shaven with freshly pressed uniforms. Hans held his arm for Jane to link and Hannah and Johan fell in behind as they walked the few streets to the castle.

"I didn't recognise you, Miss Schmidt, without your fisherman's outfit." Hans grinned at her. "I had no idea I would be escorting the most beautiful woman in Saarbrücken this evening."

"You flatter me." Jane was beginning to feel guilty. Her date was an ordinary German boy and didn't deserve what she had planned for him. If he survived the night, his army career would probably be in ruins.

Hannah giggled, and Jane knew Johan was probably using similar smooth talk on her friend. To anyone watching, they were two young couples embarking on a night of enjoyment.

Jane glanced at the shadowy doorways. She knew they were being watched. Fox and Eagle would be making sure the girls were admitted into the castle without problems. She had promised to play her part, and that meant not arousing suspicion. She tightened her grip on the young soldier's arm and looked up into his face.

"I see you've taken care with your appearance too, Hans. You're so handsome in that uniform."

The young man smiled down at her. "We make a fine-looking couple. I'll be the envy of every man there."

Jane lowered her head demurely. "I'm quite excited about this evening. I haven't danced in months."

As they neared the castle, Jane noticed guards were checking only the papers of guests and not the escorting soldiers. She opened her bag and took out her identity card. She smiled, trying to look relaxed while her heart thumped loudly, but the guard only gave her a cursory glance before waving her inside. She looked back to see Hannah was right behind her. They'd passed the first hurdle. Their papers were in order.

The soldiers took them to a room where people were crowded around a bar and ordered drinks for the girls.

Jane took the ornate glass and sniffed the liquid. She wrinkled her nose. "Champagne cocktails are a little ostentatious, don't you think?" She took a sip from her glass and winced. "These must be expensive."

Hannah made a show of sipping from her glass, but Jane could see she hadn't drunk any. They needed to keep a clear head.

"The drinks are free for the first hour," Hans explained. "Don't feel sorry for us poor soldiers. We are taken care of here. Let's enjoy the Gruppenführer's hospitality. Another one, ladies before the free bar runs dry?"

Jane smiled and nodded. When the young men went back to the bar, she took Hannah's arm. "I see a useful plant pot behind you."

"Good idea. Give me your glass."

Hannah quickly tipped the drinks away and returned Jane's empty glass to her hand. "Pretend to drink the dregs."

Jane tipped the empty glass to her lips.

"That's what I like to see." A tall man in the dark uniform of the Gestapo joined them and put his hand on the back of Jane's waist. "Two beautiful women, enjoying themselves at my expense. Allow me to introduce myself." He clicked his heels. "Gruppenführer Franz Leitz, at your service, ladies."

Jane struggled to keep a smile on her face. Her fear of this man had frozen her vocal cords.

Hannah was obviously not as afraid. She reached a hand out to the man. "So pleased to meet you, Gruppenführer. We have heard so much about you."

"Who has been singing my praises?" The man looked impressed.

"Your reputation is widely known, sir." Hannah gave Jane a quick glance and made it clear in that second that she was not going to mention Ursula. "We heard you are firm but fair, and that is commendable in a man of your position, is it not?"

"Then I am doubly pleased to make your acquaintance. Please tell me your names."

Hannah touched her chest. "I am Hannah, and this is Gerda."

"Beautiful names for such entrancing young ladies."

Jane caught sight of their escorts hovering uncertainly near the bar and managed to find her voice. "Excuse me, sir, but your distinguished presence seems to be intimidating our young men, and they are waiting patiently with our cocktails."

The Gruppenführer lifted his head and smiled at the two nervous-looking soldiers. "Come, boys. Don't show an ounce of trepidation in the presence of these delightful young ladies. They will respond more to boldness than to cowardice." He turned to Hannah. "Am I right?"

Hannah smiled and held out her hand to receive the cocktail from Private Hoff.

The young soldiers seemed awkward with their superior officer present.

Hans gave Jane her glass and stood to attention. "May we get you a drink, sir?"

"Thank you, Private. I'll have a beer. Cocktails don't agree with me."

"I'll get it." Johan hurried away looking relieved to escape.

Jane made an attempt at conversation, "So generous of you, sir, to provide your guests with a free bar."

"I find a few cocktails helps to oil the wheels of romance, don't you agree?" The man leered at Jane's chest.

Hans frowned. "Would you like to dance, Miss Schmidt?"

Jane was grateful for the young man's tact in rescuing her from the Gruppenführer's unwelcome attention. "Thank you. I'd love to." She turned to the lecherous man. "Will you excuse us, sir?"

"Only if you agree to dance the next one with me." He grabbed her hand and raised it to his lips.

"I'd be delighted, sir." Jane didn't falter. Her heart was sinking to her feet, but she managed to keep the smile on her face while allowing the young soldier to escort her to the dance floor.

"Be careful, Miss Schmidt." Hans took her into his arms and began to lead her around the floor of the domed room. "My Gruppenführer is not as gallant with the ladies as he likes to think."

"What do you mean?" Jane asked.

"He is not above taking what he wants, without consent, if you understand what I mean."

"Oh!" Jane pretended she was shocked. She already knew of the man's reputation. "I hope Hannah will be safe in his company. Will your friend protect her?"

"I think my superior officer has his sights on you. He likes blondes, so I hear."

"But I'm with you, Hans." Jane snuggled closer as she danced. She knew she had to fool this young man into believing she was interested in him. "Surely your officer will not break the rules of etiquette and try to steal me away from your strong arms."

"He wouldn't think twice. You must leave, Gerda."

"Why would I leave? The dance is just beginning?"

"For your safety."

"But surely, I'm not in any actual danger." Jane continued to play her part as a naïve young woman. "He is an officer. He wouldn't harm me."

"I'm sorry to be blunt, Gerda, but he would take you without a thought, and he would be convinced that it was what you wanted all along."

Jane gasped for effect and whispered, "Are you saying he would rape me?"

"I would not use such an indelicate phrase, but yes. That's what he has in mind, I fear."

"Then you must protect me." Jane's mind was working quickly. She'd been given a job of work and completing it was her priority. If she could help the resistance fighters, they would help her save her daughter. "Where can we go? We must hide from him."

"But you promised to dance with him. He'll be furious if you break your promise. He'll lose face, and believe me; you would not want to raise his anger."

"Then I'll dance with the man, and excuse myself immediately the dance is over. You will be waiting for me, and we will escape the castle." Jane smiled her most seductive smile. "Or perhaps we could go to somewhere more private and safe nearby."

"I don't know." The young soldier glanced at the glowering officer. "He would be angry and if he sees that I…"

"Then we must ensure that he does not see your involvement." Jane realised that things would happen much faster than they'd planned and hoped the resistance men would be prepared. "Listen, while I am dancing with the Gruppenführer, you can tell Hannah and Johan they must assist us. Show my cousin a place, a room perhaps, where we can be safe, and you boys wait there, out of sight. She can come to get me, perhaps with the excuse that she is unwell and we have to visit the ladies powder room."

"But he might suspect…"

"What if he does? He can't stop us going to powder our noses."

Hans nodded. "I won't let you down, Gerda. I know of such a place."

"Good. Then I'll meet you there after the next dance."

Jane couldn't believe she'd manoeuvred the situation to fit the plan. She knew she could rely on Hannah to do her part.

Jane suffered the unseemly pawing of the Gruppenführer throughout the slow and intimate dance. She tried to smile while removing his hand from her bottom numerous times and avoiding the closeness of his cheek against hers. She was aware they were the centre of attention, and all eyes were on them as the officer waltzed her slowly and seductively around the room.

He whispered in her ear the whole time, leaving her in no doubt of his intentions, and it took a supreme effort of will, on her part, to stay in the circle of his arms.

"Your body is perfection, Gerda. I feel fate has put us together this evening. We were meant to meet. I will teach you how to appreciate a man."

"Sir, you go too far!" Jane tried to giggle coquettishly, but could only manage a throaty croak.

"Your laughter is very sexy." He pulled her closer. "You can feel how aroused I am, can't you?"

"Sir!" Jane tried to pull away, but he held her tightly against his obvious erection. "You are scaring me."

"You don't need to fear me, little one. I will treat you as gently as a virgin deserves."

"Please, I admire you, sir, but I have no wish to lose my virginity this evening." She tried to stay polite to the obnoxious man while fearing for her safety.

The small orchestra ended the music with a flourish, and the Gruppenführer spun her around. When he caught her, he pulled her close to whisper, "Follow me. No games, now."

Jane began to panic until she saw Hannah hurrying across the dance floor. Her friend grabbed her arm. "Gerda! I don't like to interrupt, but those cocktails have made me feel unwell. Please come with me to the ladies room."

Jane looked at the glowering Gruppenführer. "I'm so sorry, sir. You can see I have to…"

"I will not allow it!" The officer glowered at Hannah. "Find somebody else to pander to your weak liver!"

Jane gasped but clutched the Gruppenführer's arm and looked into his face beseechingly. "Please, sir. Allow me to take care of my friend and I'll hurry straight back to your side, I promise."

"Go if you must!" the officer snarled. "I'll wait here. Don't be long!"

Hannah took Jane's hand, and they hurried from the room. "I saw what he was doing. How could you stand it?"

"What choice did I have?" Jane hissed and hurried up a flight of stairs. She followed Hannah along a corridor. "Where are we going?"

"Hush, we're almost there." Hannah halted at a door and listened for a few seconds before opening it. "In here."

Jane looked back down the empty corridor and breathed a small sigh of relief. She'd escaped the Gruppenführer for now, but would he come looking for her? How long would he wait before losing his patience?

The room was in darkness, but Jane could make out the bodies of the two soldiers asleep on sofas.

"Thank goodness. That didn't take long." Hannah pushed a chair to the door and wedged it under the handle. "Get to work; we won't have much time. I had to share my sleeping draft between their drinks. Perhaps it won't last as long as we'd hoped."

Jane went to her escort and began to remove his jacket.

"Hurry, I'll signal from the window and hope our men are looking in this direction. We're early, but that can't be helped."

By the time Jane had both soldiers undressed, Hannah was opening the window.

"Thank the stars! They signalled back. They'll be here soon. Are you ready?"

Jane was folding the uniforms into a manageable bundle, tying the pieces together with the two, brown leather belts she'd removed from the trousers.

"How will we get out of here?" Jane asked.

"We wait until all is chaos in the castle, and then we can make our escape in the ensuing panic."

"I hope you're right." Jane took her bundle to the window. "Are they here yet?"

"I think I see them. Wait." She held the curtain back. "Yes, it's them. Drop the uniforms now."

Jane pushed her bundle through the open window and heard the soft thud as it landed in the street below. "Now we wait." She closed the window.

"Do you think they'll get in?" Hannah nibbled a fingernail as both girls watched the two men below scurrying away with the uniforms.

"The guards were only checking guest's documents." Jane pointed out. "Dressed as soldiers, Fox and Eagle should have no trouble."

"I hope you're right." Hannah stared out of the window. "We could be here all night, if they don't manage to create a diversion for us."

Jane didn't want to think about enduring a night in the castle. If the Gruppenführer came looking for her, she didn't know what she'd do. She shivered and pulled her light wrap around her shoulders. "We need to get out of here."

"Perhaps we could climb down the wall. It's not so high."

Jane peered out at the road two floors below. "Are you mad?"

"We can't stay here much longer. They could wake at any moment. How will we explain their state of undress?"

"Perhaps we should take our chances and simply walk out now." Jane looked at the door.

"What about Gruppenführer Leitz?"

"You just said we couldn't stay here." Jane glanced at the snoring soldiers.

"All right, but let's give it five more minutes. Fox and Eagle should be in position by then."

Jane paced the floor impatiently, waiting for the minutes to tick by. "Do you think we should tie them up?"

"Why?"

"To give us more time. If they come to their senses and raise the alarm before we get out of here…"

"The idea was to let them think they'd had their wicked way with us. They won't think they had enjoyed an evening of sexual frivolity if they are trussed up like a roast goose when they wake."

"Oh, we forgot! We need to write the note." Jane remembered the plan and quickly found the pencil and notebook in her bag. She ripped a page from the book and hastily scribbled the note they'd agreed on. "There, that should keep them quiet for a while."

"What did you write?"

"Thank you for a lovely time. We can't wait for a repeat performance, boys. You were wonderful."

"Oh, my! Do you think they'll believe they actually seduced us?"

"They might question where their uniforms have gone." Jane worried about the small detail they hadn't covered. "They'll come searching for us, won't they? If they ask questions in town, they might work out who we are supposed to be. If they discover we are posing as Ursula's nieces, she will be in terrible trouble. She'll be implicated in all this, won't she?"

"We've been careful not to mention our connection with her. She should be safe, but she knew the risks." Hannah nibbled her bottom lip. "I'm sure she'll have excuses and explanations ready if she's questioned about us."

"I wish we'd thought about this more carefully, Hannah. We are leaving too many loose ends."

"We can't worry about that now." Hannah looked at the two sleeping soldiers. One of them sniffed, and his eyes flickered open for a second. "I think it's time we left."

Jane was already at the door, removing the chair. She opened it a crack and peered out. "All clear." She reached for Hannah's hand, and the two girls hurried down the corridor.

"Ah, there you are!" The Gruppenführer was standing at the bottom of the stairs, his hands behind his back. "I was beginning to worry you wouldn't return."

Jane realised she was trapped. The officer would never let her leave. She was expecting a diversion, but Eagle and Fox would need time to get into position and set up the explosives.

"I'm afraid I will have to take Hannah home. She's quite unwell." Jane tried to brazen it out.

"I'll have one of my men take her." The officer stepped closer and put an arm around Jane's shoulder. "You are coming with me, my sweet thing."

Jane tried not to shudder but she was repulsed by the overbearing man. "Will you be all right, Hannah?" she asked Hannah, feeling her courage melting away.

"No!" Hannah grabbed Jane's arm. "I don't want to be taken home by a stranger." She turned to the officer. "Please, sir. I am quite unable to make my way home alone."

"What became of your escorts?" Gruppenführer Leitz asked. "I'll have to chastise those two privates. It is very remiss of them to leave you ladies to fend for yourselves." He attracted the attention of a passing soldier who was trying to avoid eye contact.

"Private!"

"Yes, sir!" The young soldier stood to attention.

"Escort this young lady home."

The soldier looked relieved to hear the request. "It will be an honour, sir."

"You, my dear, are now free of obligations and can come with me." The Gruppenführer linked Jane's arm through his and began to lead her away.

She looked over her shoulder and caught her friend's eye. She gently patted the beaded bag under her arm. Hannah nodded her understanding and allowed the young soldier to guide her back to the entrance hall.

Jane walked on shaky legs as Gruppenführer Leitz took her up a flight of stairs and on, to the back of the castle.

"These are my private rooms." Leitz opened a door onto a suite of rooms. "We won't be disturbed here."

Jane had to think fast. She already had something in mind and hoped it might work. The hastily hatched plan would be her only chance of escape. "Do you have something to drink, sir?"

"Please call me Franz. We are alone and can be more friendly here."

"Franz." Jane smiled and tried to keep her lips from trembling.

"What would you like? I have champagne, red wine, cognac…"

"Do you have a beer? I'm feeling thirsty." She remembered that was the Gruppenführer's drink of choice.

"I do." He went to a small cabinet and took out a large bottle of ale.

"Oh, that's far too much for me." Jane tried a coquettish giggle. "Would you share it with me?"

"I'll get two glasses. The bottle opener is here." He handed her the opener.

When the Gruppenführer went to look for the glasses, she opened the bottle and poured some beer into the nearest potted plant. She quickly topped up the bottle with the sleeping draft and sat in the chair nearest the plant to wait. She would need to dispose of her share of the beer quickly.

"Here we are my sweetness. Will you pour, or shall I?"

"I will." She took a glass and filled it to the brim.

They swapped glasses, and she half-filled the second one. "Bottoms up." She tipped the glass to her lips but didn't drink.

The Gruppenführer drank half his glass and burped. "Now, let's not waste more time. Come here."

"You promised not to hurt me, Franz." Jane tried to play for time.

"I did, but you will learn that pleasure and pain are close bedfellows." He made a grab for her and roughly pulled her into his arms.

She steeled herself against his advances and tried not to struggle. She went into his arms reluctantly but allowed him to fondle her buttocks while he kissed her throat. She was repulsed by his hot breath on her face and his groping hands on her body, but if she'd tried to put up a fight, she knew it would only make her situation worse. She tried to think.

"Excuse me, sir, but would you mind if used your smallest room?"

"What?" He pulled back, looking puzzled.

"I need to use your facilities."

"But you just came from there!"

"I didn't go," Jane insisted, trying to think quickly. "I was concerned for my friend." She crossed her legs and squirmed around. "I'm sure I'll feel more comfortable if you let me..." She shrugged and jiggled some more.

"Oh, if you must!" He sounded impatient.

"I won't be long, I promise." She kissed his cheek, to placate him.

"Good girl." He reached for his glass of beer and lifted hers too. "You didn't drink your beer."

"It's not to my taste," she quickly explained. "I'll take some water."

He showed her to a bathroom leading from the bedroom, and Jane escaped the obnoxious man. She stood in the small room with her back to the door, breathing deeply. How would she get away from him? Would the sleeping draft work in time? How long would she be able to hold him off?

After using the crude facilities, she waited as long as she dared before going back to the Gruppenführer. He was sitting in a chair with his eyes half closed. Two empty glasses were on the table next to him. Jane's heart leapt. The sleeping draught was working. He had taken the whole dose. She crossed the room and knelt at his side.

"Franz? I'm back my dear. Here I am." She peered into his face.

He surprised her by lunging from the chair. His arms grabbed her in a vice like grip. He planted his wet lips over hers, fell on top of her and knocked the wind from her chest. Jane panicked but didn't have the breath to scream. She dragged her face to the side, and his wet lips dropped to her throat but didn't move farther.

He quickly became a dead weight, and she eased herself from beneath his sleeping body.

She sighed with relief and couldn't believe how easy it had been to put the tough and arrogant man out of action. He was on the floor, comatose and vulnerable. The Gruppenführer was at her mercy, and she had every reason to inflict revenge on the evil man, but she was not the sort who could hurt another human being. She couldn't lower herself to his level. Instead, she smiled and turned him on his back.

She quickly unfastened his trousers and pulled them down. Exposing his genitals, she giggled. "You'll think you had a wonderful time, Franz Leitz."

The explosion rocked the floor beneath her. One of the glasses crashed to the floor and plaster dust fell from the ceiling. She glanced uncertainly at the officer, but the Gruppenführer slept on.

Jane sprang to her feet and ran to the door. The corridor was empty, but she could hear screaming and shouting from the floor below. This was the distraction she'd been waiting for. She hurried to the stairs and joined a stream of panicking people hurrying to leave the castle. Smoke drifted down the corridor toward the entrance hall and a few women screamed. She hurried on with her head down. She was certain that Fox and Eagle had done their job as planned. The acrid smoke told her that the records office would be in flames, and any trace of written evidence extracted from Heinrich Schneider's mind under torture would be destroyed.

Chapter Twenty-Six – Escape

Hannah was packing when Jane arrived back at the café. Ursula was pacing the small bedroom, wringing her hands.

"What happened?" Ursula quickly took Jane into a bear hug, and then held her at arm's length to inspect her from head to toe. "Dear girl, did he hurt you?"

Jane shook her head and smiled. "No. I managed to play for time and left him sleeping like a baby with his genitals on display."

"You didn't!" Hannah giggled. "I'd like to be a fly on the wall when he wakes."

"You should make sure you are as far away from here as you can be when that man wakes." Ursula resumed her pacing. "We heard the explosion. He is not a stupid man. He'll soon put everything together and know you two had a hand in what happened at the castle tonight."

"What about you, Aunt Ursula?" Jane was concerned for the woman's safety. "What if those soldiers can trace us back to you?"

"They won't. We were careful." Hannah threw some things into Jane's bag.

"What about the soldier who walked you home?" Jane remembered the poor man's face. He'd not been happy.

"I didn't allow him to bring me all the way. I told him to go back to the party and assured him I was fine. He didn't take much persuading to leave me once he understood I was not interested in him."

Ursula took Jane's wrap and began to unfasten the buttons on her dress. "Hurry, you need to get out of those clothes. You don't have much time."

"Where are we going?"

"Eagle and Fox are taking you undercover. I don't know where, and it is better I know nothing about where you'll be going." Ursula handed Jane the men's clothing she'd worn every night while she'd been there. "Saarbrücken won't be safe for you after tonight. Gruppenführer Leitz will scour the town looking for you if he suspects you had anything to do with that explosion. I would imagine he will want you both for questioning at the very least."

"Why would he think we had anything to do with it?" Jane asked, stepping into the mud-stained trousers.

"The missing uniforms, Gerda!" Hannah knew instantly. "Poor Hans and Johan will have some explaining to do and when the Gestapo put two and two together. We both know where they'll point the fingers."

"Are you sure you didn't mention, to anyone, that you are my nieces?" Ursula stoked the fire and threw the silk and lace dresses and wraps into the flames.

"What a shame to destroy those lovely clothes." Jane fastened the buttons of her rough shirt.

"I can't take the risk of keeping them. If I am suspected, and my place is searched, they must find no evidence of you here. You must take the beaded bags with you. The beads won't burn." She tucked the bags into the girls' canvas holdalls.

"We've been careful, Aunt Ursula." Jane tried to reassure the woman as she hurried to put on the dirty trousers. "You have nothing to fear."

"I think I see our friends by the alley." Ursula stood on tiptoe to peer down into the street below. "Yes, they are here. You have to go."

"How will you explain our hasty departure?" Jane asked. "Your friends know we were here. I don't like to leave you to face the consequences of our actions."

"I'll tell them Saarbrücken was not as lively as you'd expected and you moved on to relatives in Munich."

"Not lively!" Hannah laughed wryly and picked up her canvas bag. "That's not how I'd describe our time here."

"Hurry, girls." Ursula ushered them down the stairs. "Don't come back here. It would be too dangerous." She hovered by the door with her fingers touching the handle. "Good luck, Gerda. I hope you find your little girl."

Jane was surprised when the older woman pulled her into another close embrace. Ursula then thrust open the door, pushed her outside and quickly turned to Hannah.

"Take care, Hannah. You are a rare breed of woman. I can see what Sebastian saw in you."

"Oh, Ursula." Hannah hugged the older woman. "Thank you for everything."

"Go." Ursula pushed Hannah into the street. "They are waiting for you in the darkness near the alley. Go quickly. God go with you."

The girls kept to the shadows close to the buildings and hurried to the alley where Fox and Eagle were waiting. The two men were still dressed in the uniforms Jane had thrown to them from the castle window.

"We 'av a truck waiting. 'Urry." Eagle reached to take their bags, and the girls followed Fox down the alley.

"Why a truck and not a boat?" Hannah asked.

"The river is too quiet tonight. We would be noticed."

"Where are we going?" Jane asked as she ran.

"You don't need to know until we get zere." Fox grabbed her arm. "Down."

They tumbled into the shadowed doorway of a shop and froze. A group of soldiers hurried along the other side of the road, quick-marching and heading in the opposite direction. Jane held her breath until they were out of sight.

"Zat was close." Fox stepped into the road. "Come."

On the next street, the two men ushered the girls down another alley where a German army truck was parked close to a wall.

"Get in." Eagle helped them climb into the back of the vehicle. "Get down, put this over you and stay still. They will have checkpoints all over the town."

"Oh, dear God!" Hannah scrambled under the tarpaulin.

"Don't worry." Eagle tucked the oiled sheet around them. "We are dressed as German soldiers, and we are in one of their trucks. We won't be stopped."

"And if you *are* stopped?" Jane asked. "Can you speak German?"

Fox shrugged. "Enough to get past zese fools."

Eagle shook his rifle. "And if that doesn't work, we 'av plan 'B'"

"Make sure your 'eads are under ze cover," Fox warned.

Jane and Hannah slipped deeper under the smelly tarpaulin.

"Do you think they will really shoot the soldiers at the checkpoints?" Jane whispered to Hannah.

"They may have to."

"Oh, my God, we'll all be killed." Jane's heart jumped erratically in her chest.

"Hush, Gerda. We have a good chance to get out of this alive. Keep quiet."

The engine started, and the girls clung together as the vehicle began to move. They slid from side to side as the truck took corners at speed.

"If they are not careful, our two friends will crash and kill us before the Germans get a chance to do the same." Jane tried to brace her feet against the sides of the truck.

They heard and felt the change of gear as the truck slowed. Jane's chest flooded with adrenaline when she heard a German voice ask their friends what they were doing and where they were headed.

"Wir haben aufträge von Gruppenführer Leitz." (*We have orders from Gruppenführer Leitz*).

The answer from the checkpoint guards was muffled, but Jane realised they'd been allowed through when the truck began to pick up speed. She let out the breath she'd been holding but waited until they were clear of the checkpoint before she spoke. "That was close."

"Eagle's accent was terrible!" Hannah spoke just loud enough to be heard over the noise of the engine. "But close enough to an Austrian one, to fool a man from Dusseldorf."

"Can you really tell the difference?" Jane asked.

"What can I say?" Hannah sounded smug. "It is a gift I have."

Jane's heart began to slow to a steadier rhythm as the truck continued on with a smother motion. She was bone tired but her fears prevented her from drifting into sleep. Hannah had no such problems. Her regular breathing told Jane she was already asleep.

After what seemed hours, the truck eventually slowed and stopped. Jane didn't need to shake Hannah awake. The girl stiffened and grabbed Jane's hand. They stayed still and quiet. Listening for any sound, they waited impatiently under the tarpaulin. They heard no voices and knew they would be some distance from the town by now, but stayed still anyway. They were both too afraid to move.

When they heard someone climb into the back of the truck, they froze.

Eagle pulled back the tarpaulin. "We are safe. You can get up and stretch your legs."

They both let out the breath they'd been holding and allowed Eagle to help them to their feet.

Jane jumped down from the truck to find herself in the middle of a forest.

"Watch out for ze wild pigs," Fox warned. "Zey are more dangerous zan ze Gestapo in zese parts."

"Where are we?" Hannah asked, climbing down to the forest floor.

"On the outskirts of Karlsruhe. We have to dump this truck now and get rid of these uniforms. Then we can make our way to the harbour." Eagle began to unbutton his jacket. "Sebastian already made allies of some barge captains before 'e left. They will provide you with safe passage to the Dutch coast."

"Where will we go from there?" Jane asked.

"It is dangerous for you to stay longer in Germany." Fox lit a cigarette. "You will go 'ome."

"We can get you on to the barge," Eagle explained. "It operates on the Rhine all the way to the Dutch coast. Your people will be informed and will get you across the channel. You will be 'ome in time to enjoy springtime in London."

"No!" Jane protested. "I have to go to Rosenheim before I leave."

"What is in Rosenheim?" Fox asked.

"My family."

"Merdre!" (*shit*) Fox shook his head. "Why do zey only tell us 'alf ze story?"

"And we haven't done anything yet?" Hannah protested. "We are meant to be helping our people in hiding. All we've done is to report on some river traffic and attend a dance. What good is that! We have a mission to complete!"

"You 'av done important work. Do not underestimate your worth." Fox dropped his cigarette and stamped out the ember. "We needed to log ze busier times on ze rivers. Zey are ze safest times to move people by boat. You girls did zat wizout arousing suspicion. You did well."

Eagle put his hand on Jane's shoulder. "What you did tonight was incredible. We destroyed all written trace of Schneider's confessions. Most of your friends in 'iding will be safer now, because of what you 'elped us to do."

"We could not 'av done it wizout your 'elp," Fox agreed.

"Perhaps he is right, Jane." Hannah sighed and looked at Eagle. "But we wanted to do so much more."

"I can't go back yet. I have to go to Rosenheim," Jane insisted.

Eagle sighed. "All right. Tell us what is so important about that town."

Days later, Jane and Hannah cowered in another forest with the two French men. "You do it our way, or you go back to England," Eagle insisted. "We watch first before we go near that place."

"Why?" Jane couldn't see the point in wasting more time. She was so close. She knew her child was in the house beyond the forest. She hadn't seen her in two years, and she was desperate to know that her little girl was still safe and well.

After discussing her intentions with the French men, they had decided to keep the truck and the uniforms a little longer. Driving through the night, hiding by day, they eventually arrived at the address two days later. They turned into the dense forest near the small farm some hours before dawn with no incidents. Fox then insisted on scouting the whole area to make sure German soldiers were not watching the house.

"But, Fox!" Jane was impatient to make a move. "We've done everything you said. Why are you making me wait longer?"

"Because zis is a safe 'ouse, and we 'av no idea if ze Germans 'av been tipped off."

Jane stared at the small house in a clearing some distance from the edge of the forest. She was crouched low in the frosty underbrush with Hannah and the two men.

"We watch, and we wait." Fox took a loaf of bread from a bag on his shoulder. He'd taken the cooling loaf from the windowsill of a house in the last village they'd passed through. "We eat now, and no one goes near ze 'ouse until we are sure it is safe to do so."

Hannah shuffled closer to Jane. "I know you're disappointed, Gerda, but they are right. If we show ourselves too soon, and the Germans are watching from inside the house, we could all be sent to the labour camps."

"But we've been here for hours already." Jane argued. "We've covered all the ground around the house and found nothing. The Germans are nowhere near this place," she insisted.

"We do zis my way, or I take you back to Karlsruhe and put you on zat barge," Fox threatened.

"How much longer will you make me wait?" Jane asked, trying to keep control of her patience.

"Until we feel it is safe." Eagle jerked his head to the house. "Look!"

Jane turned to stare at the house. A small child skipped from the door, closely followed by a tall man. They were both swaddled in thick coats and hats. The child reached to take the man's hand, and they walked to a small animal enclosure some distance from the house.

Jane watched their progress and felt a lump in her throat. "That must be Sasha." Her baby was no longer a toddler, but a little girl who skipped and ran and laughed with the strange man who held her hand. "My baby is so big." Jane felt desolate to realise how much her daughter had changed. "She won't know me."

"Who is that man with her?" Hannah asked. "Is that Gottfried?"

Jane shook her head. "I don't think so. It's difficult to tell from here, and he has a big coat on." She peered into the distance, concentrating on the distant figures. She felt there was something familiar about the man. Something in the way he moved was striking a chord with her, but she knew it wasn't her husband. "I can't see his hair. Gottfried is dark and muscular. I don't think he's as tall as that man. I can't be sure, but I don't think that's my husband."

"But you're sure it is your child?" Eagle asked.

Jane shrugged. "How *can* I be sure? I haven't seen her in two years. She fits the description I would expect. That little girl looks to be about four, doesn't she?"

"We are on a wild goose chase." Fox lit a cigarette, keeping the match flame hidden behind his cupped hands. "You don't know anything about zat 'ouse or who lives zere, do you?"

Jane shrugged. "I already told you that I know very little, apart from the address. We decided it would be safer that way." She couldn't take her eyes off the figures in the distance. The little girl was throwing something from a bucket into the animal pen, and the tall man was helping her. "You know why I wasn't told anything about the family who took her. It was for Sasha's protection."

While they continued to watch, another man came out of the house and began to walk to the animal enclosure.

"That's Gottfried!" Jane put a trembling hand to her mouth. "That's my husband. I recognise his build and the way he walks." She turned to Fox. Her heart was doing somersaults.

"Are you absolutely sure?" he asked.

"I'm positive." She was desperate to make a move. "Surely you have enough proof now. Gottfried wouldn't be here if German soldiers were around. They would have packed him off to a labour camp if they were suspicious about him. Can we go now?" Jane started to get to her feet, but Eagle took her arm and held her down.

"We go slowly. Edge around the ploughed field, keeping to the cover of the trees. Don't let them see you. We'll be right be'ind you."

Jane wanted to run from the forest and cross the muddy field straight into Gottfried's arms. She couldn't wait to let him see she was still alive. Her daughter was right there, but she quickly understood she couldn't walk into the little girl's life without giving her some preparation and explanation. The French men were right to urge caution, but their reasons were quite different from hers.

By the time she'd reached the edge of the tree cover, the two men and the child had returned to the house. All was quiet in the farmyard, and in the surrounding countryside. Jane saw no good reason to delay her approach.

"Please let me go to the house now!" she implored the surly French man. "We are wasting time!"

Fox huffed and turned to Eagle. "What do you say?"

"All right, but you go alone," Eagle whispered. "We wait 'ere,"

"Why?" Hannah asked. "It's cold out here."

"We will give you twenty minutes." Fox looked at his watch. "If you don't come out to tell us it is safe, we leave."

"Signal like this." Eagle waved his left arm twice over his head. "Left arm. If you use the right, or wave more than twice, we leave."

"Why?" Hannah looked amused and chuckled softly. "You men are so dramatic!"

"Being dramatic saves our lives." Fox sneered at her laughter. "You wouldn't laugh if zat 'ouse is full of German soldiers."

Jane felt her heart skip a beat. "It won't be." Her husband had seemed relaxed. He wouldn't have been walking around freely if the house were harbouring soldiers. She felt a fizz of excitement in her tummy as she got ready to step into the open. "You worry too much."

Pulling her collar up and her woollen hat lower to shield her face from the cold, she stepped from the cover of the trees and made her way around the edge of the ploughed field until she came to a gravel path leading to the house.

Her footsteps crunched on the sharp stones, and she knew the occupants of the house would hear her approach, but she didn't care. She ran the last few yards and tapped on the door. As she waited, she couldn't keep still and twisted her hands together while staring at the door. She willed it to open.

When it was drawn back, she expected to see Gottfried, but a young woman was standing there, and she frowned at Jane.

"Yes? Can I help you?"

Jane was thrown for a second but soon recovered. "May I see Gottfried?"

"Who are you?"

"His wife."

The woman looked puzzled. "Gottfried has no wife." She looked over Jane's shoulder. "Are you alone?"

Jane nodded. "He thinks I'm dead, but I'm not. I have to see him."

"Gerda?" Gottfried came to stand behind the young woman, his face wary and unsure until he saw Jane's face. "Is it really you?" His eyes widened. "It can't be, but it is! It *is* you! How? How can you be here?"

"Yes, I'm here." Jane's eyes filled with tears at Gottfried's response to seeing her. "It really is me. I didn't die."

She lifted her hand to reach for him, but another man rushed to the door and pushed Gottfried out of the way.

"Gerda!" The tall, blond man threw his arms around Jane and pulled her close. "Oh, my darling, it really is you!" He drew back and looked down into her face. "When Gottfried told me you were dead, I thought my life was over. But you're not dead. Oh, my God! You're not dead!" His arms pulled her close again. "What happened? How did you get here?"

Jane's mind fizzed and buzzed with confusion. This man's closeness was causing her body to fill with a familiar warmth and love. She knew she loved this man with all her heart and soul but why was he here? Why was her lover here in the safe house with her daughter? Why was he here with Gottfried? She pulled away from the close embrace. Feeling guilty, she glanced at her husband. Gottfried was smiling with tears running down his cheeks. He'd watched her lover embrace her and yet he was smiling. He seemed happy about the lover's reunion. What was happening?

She remembered her friends in the forest and asked, "Is it safe here?"

Her blond lover grinned and pulled her close again. "Safe and sound, my love. Come inside."

"Wait." She gave the signal and watched the three friends step from the cover of the trees. "I have company. They helped me get here. Don't let the German uniforms scare you. Those men are with the French Resistance."

Her lover looked at the approaching group. "What are you doing with the French Resistance?"

"It's a long story." She glanced at Gottfried and wanted him to understand why she was there. Her lover was still holding her close in his arms, and she felt guilt washing through her in waves. How could Gottfried be so relaxed about this man's display of affection? "I wanted to find my husband."

Chapter Twenty-Seven – Explanations

"I still don't understand." Jane couldn't take her eyes off the tall blond man. Her emotions were in turmoil from having him close, and he appeared to feel the same way. His eyes held hers, and he seemed to be looking directly into her soul. She tore her eyes away and turned to Gottfried. "Why did we pretend we were a married couple while living in England?" Jane asked the man who claimed to be her cousin.

"It was Jacob's idea. He felt you'd be safer if we travelled as a couple," Gottfried explained. "He said the papers he acquired for us would be for a married couple."

Jacob squeezed her hand reassuringly. "We'd heard that single females who travelled alone were easy prey to some German soldiers. Being married would offer you some protection, especially if your husband was travelling with you."

"I understand that," Jane was finding it difficult to understand the lengthy explanations. She turned to Gottfried. "But why continue the lie after we reached safety?"

"When we arrived in England, it seemed a good idea to continue the deception." He sighed sadly. "We didn't receive a warm welcome, Gerda. Most people are wary of Jews. We have a bad reputation all over Europe. People believe the propaganda being spread about us. I wanted to protect you. Your father agreed it would be for the best."

Jane remembered some small incidents of anti-Semitic attitudes and nodded. "But that doesn't explain why we pretended to be married."

"Jacob wanted me to keep you safe." Gottfried glanced at the blond man. "Your father suggested we continue the charade. We were less conspicuous as a couple. You drew less attention because you were a married woman."

Hannah was sitting at Jane's feet playing with little Sasha, and she sighed. "Oh, this is so romantic."

"It's confusing." Eagle scratched his chin and looked at Gottfried. "So you are not the husband she thought you were. You are Gerda's cousin."

"That's right." The dark haired man confirmed. "My parents were sent to the camps early in thirty-seven. Uncle Herman, Gerda's father, protected me and saved me from the deportation."

"Dinner is almost ready," Rosa announced.

"Sausages, Mamma Rosa?" Sasha asked with a note of hope in her voice.

Jane smiled at the little girl. Her heart was breaking to see her daughter treat the young woman as a mother figure, but she understood that it would take some effort to rebuild a relationship with her estranged child. Jacob explained that Sasha knew Rosa was not her mamma. She had been given a photograph of Gerda and Jacob with Sasha in her mother's arms to remind the child who her real parents were. He had brought it from the bedroom to show her, and Jane realised it was the one she remembered her father taking.

The young woman in the photograph had dark hair. The baby was as blonde as her father. Sasha was obviously suspicious of the blonde woman who now claimed to be the dark haired woman in the photograph. Jane realised she would have to earn the little girl's love and the task seemed daunting.

"No, my sweet." Rosa bent to stroke Sasha's blonde locks. "We have potatoes and ham for our guests."

"Sounds delicious." Fox rubbed his stomach.

"We've been living on stolen bread and squirrels for the last two days," Eagle told Sasha and grinned.

"You can't eat squirrels." The little girl sounded surprised and turned her large, round eyes to Jacob. "Can you eat squirrels, Papa?"

"Well, you can't find much meat on them, Sasha." Jacob smiled at his daughter. "But I hear they are tasty."

Hannah licked her lips to tease the child. "Yum, yum," she said, patting her tummy.

"Ugh, you're disgusting!" Sasha picked up her doll and whispered to the toy, "Don't listen to her."

Jane couldn't take her eyes off Sasha. Jacob had explained to the little girl that the strange blonde woman was her mother, but it didn't seem to mean much to the four-year-old. Sasha had known Rosa as her mother figure for the last two years. Jane was beginning to understand it could take months to rebuild the bonds between mother and daughter. She worried there might not be enough time to earn the child's trust before she planned to take Sasha back to England.

"I lived with you and your father for a year, after my parents were taken," Gottfried was still telling his story. "I didn't leave the apartment once; not even for a second, until we fled to England."

"I don't remember any of this." Jane shook her head.

"How odd for you, darling." Jacob squeezed her hand again. "I can't imagine how all this must seem to you." He stroked her hair. "I'm finding it quite bizarre to see you with blonde hair. You look so different."

"The intelligence service said I looked too Jewish. Colouring my hair is a disguise." She flicked her fair locks over her shoulder. "Though, in this weather, wearing a hat is just as good."

"Your poor head." Jacob touched the small scar on her temple. "How much can you remember?"

"More than I could after I first regained consciousness. Things are coming back to me slowly."

"You remember me, don't you?"

"Yes." Jane was beginning to realise how mixed her memories were. "But you are not who I thought you were. I thought we were having an affair." Jane tried to smile but still felt too bewildered to feel happy about the revelations that were now muddling her mind. "I was so sure Gottfried was my husband, and everyone in England believed he was too, so all this is enormously confusing for me." Jane stared at the little girl sitting by the fire playing with Hannah and the doll.

"I can explain that, Gerda." Gottfried smiled softly. "When we left Hamburg with Uncle Herman, the British had given us papers for a married couple, just as Jacob instructed." He grinned at Jane's husband. "As he is a British subject, your husband could have travelled on his original documents. But because Sasha's papers didn't arrive, Jacob decided to stay behind with her. As a Gentile, he was in no immediate danger. Unlike your father and the two of us. We'd been summonsed for deportation. Time was fast running out for us."

"There was no time to lose, my darling." Jacob went on to explain, "Our daughter's papers were mislaid or damaged in transit," Jacob explained. "Whatever happened to them, we didn't get them. Our little owl could not travel without them."

"So you stayed in Germany to keep her safe. Why didn't I stay with you?" Jane asked still feeling very disoriented.

"As Gottfried just said, you'd been called to the park, don't you remember?" Jacob asked. "They were going to send you all to the labour camps, including Sasha."

Jane nodded. "It isn't clear, but some details are beginning to come back to me." She did remember parts of the story. She remembered someone taking Sasha away to keep her safe. Jane knew she wouldn't see her daughter for some time, but hadn't realised two years would pass. She had hoped Jacob would find a way to bring her to England at some point in the next few months but it never happened. She glanced again at Sasha, playing quietly on the floor with Hannah. She was so close to her daughter but still felt a thousand miles away from her.

She turned to Gottfried. "When did you arrive here in Rosenheim?"

"I've been here a month."

"What about you, Jacob? Why are you here?" Jane couldn't understand why her husband would hide out in Bavaria for all this time.

"My current work is in this region." Jacob shrugged and took her hand. "You know what I do here, Gerda. We discussed this many times."

Jane shook her head. "I'm afraid my memory of you is fragmented. To be totally honest, I'm still coming to terms with the fact that you are my husband and not my lover." Her heart was rejoicing at the news, but her head was still struggling to assimilate the new information. "I don't know what you are doing here in Germany. All the memories of my past, before the bombing, are pitted with holes, and it's so frustrating." She lifted her face to look into his eyes. "I still can't understand how you could be my husband. I've spent the last few weeks convincing myself I deserve to be whipped because of our affair. I couldn't bear the thought that I'd cheated on Gottfried."

"Oh, Gerda." Gottfried laughed. "We are close. Perhaps we are closer than cousins would normally be, because of our shared experiences. I can't tell you how happy I am that you are alive, but you are definitely married to Jacob." His face softened as he smiled at her. "I can assure you that you *have* been faithful to him."

Jane remembered hearing how upset Gottfried had been when he thought she was dead. Apparently he had been inconsolable. She had a feeling that his emotions were not a continuation of the charade he'd been playing. She knew her cousin loved her. Perhaps he loved her more than a cousin should, but after his declaration, she was sure he would never step over the boundary of their special relationship.

Her cousin went on, "When you were reported as missing, presumed dead, I searched for you. I tried every hospital and homeless shelter." He closed his eyes and dropped his chin. "I posted your name on lists and searched the lists that were already put up in the town hall and other places."

"Oh, Gottfried!" Jane could see the young man was becoming emotional.

"When it became clear that I wouldn't find you, I had to let Jacob know." Gottfried looked at Jane's husband. "I couldn't write you a letter, Jacob. I had to find you and tell you in person." He turned to Jane. "I owed him that much."

"You don't owe me anything, but I'm glad you came in person. I could not have accepted the news of Gerda's death from a letter." Jacob dropped his head.

He looked upset, and Jane leant into his side and gently touched his cheek. "I'm here, my darling. I didn't die. You have no reason to be sad any longer."

"Dinner is ready. Will you eat from your laps?" Rosa began to hand out some steaming dishes. "I have no room at the table for so many guests, and I am sorry the food is not plentiful."

"It's good of you to feed us, Rosa." Jane took the dish the young woman proffered. "I know we are imposing on your good nature."

Rosa glanced at Sasha. "No, I am happy to do my part."

Jane realised the young woman had a genuine affection for Sasha. Rosa would be upset to have the little girl torn away from her. She felt she should say something. "I'm very grateful for everything you have done for my family."

Rosa held up her hand. "No need for thanks. It has been a pleasure. Sasha is a delight. You'll find she is resilient and will soon adjust to her new situation."

Jane realised the woman understood that Sasha would be leaving her care soon.

Rosa smiled. "Eat your dinner while it's hot. You don't need to be concerned. I have always known this day would come."

"Sasha will soon be replaced, Rosa." Jacob spooned some potatoes from his dish. "You know there is a waiting list, and that grows shorter by the week as the Germans send more to the camps."

"What can ze Germans want with children at labour camps?" Fox asked. "Zey can't work, and zey would be a drain on resources."

Jacob rested his spoon in his dish. "You haven't heard?"

"What?" Fox lifted his head.

"Some labour camps are not what they seem."

"What are you saying?" Eagle asked.

"Not here." Jacob looked at his daughter. "Perhaps after this little one is in bed. It is not a subject for discussion in front of a child."

"Dachau is on the other side of Munich. Until September last year, Jews, political prisoners and Gypsies were arriving by the trainload and were being starved to death or worked until they dropped. We managed to rescue a few prisoners before they turned the place into a training camp. We still do what we can to disrupt the camp, but it will never be enough." Jacob sighed heavily.

"It sounds dangerous work." Fox took a pull on his cigarette. "Zat camp would be heavily guarded."

"That's the strange thing about all this. It isn't!" Jacob shook his head. "The guards are lazy until a superior officer shows up. Half-starved prisoners don't have the energy for plotting escapes, and if they do, they can't run fast. The guards have an easy time of it."

"You say this place is now a training camp. So where are all the prisoners?" Hannah asked. "What did they do with them?"

"I believe they sent them by train to Mauthausen in Austria," Jacob answered.

"Do they receive better treatment there?" Jane wanted to know.

Jacob shook his head again. "My contacts tell me they are forced to work in the quarries. Men, women and older children are made to labour until they drop from exhaustion, starvation, or both."

"What they are doing is inhumane." Hannah pressed her lips together and lifted her chin. "What can we do to help?"

"How do you propose to help those prisoners?" Jane asked her friend.

"Could we try to get some of them out?" Hannah asked.

"You want to try to rescue the prisoners from Mauthausen?" Jacob asked the young Russian girl.

"You are insane!" Jane could understand Hannah's enthusiasm but knew that any rescue attempt would be extremely hazardous. "The guards will notice when some are missing and send out soldiers to search for them, won't they?" She turned to her husband for confirmation.

Jacob lifted his head. "When I managed to rescue the last group of people from Dachau, the Germans sent out a troop of SS men. They didn't waste time searching for half-starved prisoners. Instead, they went to the nearest village. They believed local people were responsible for helping the prisoners break out. The SS shot all the men in that village in retaliation, to teach the locals a lesson." He dropped his chin. "After that, how could I risk rescuing more?"

"And you say these atrocities are happening all over Germany?" Hannah's eyes were wide with shock.

"They say these places are labour camps, but most people arriving at them don't live long enough to do much work." Jacob ran his hand through his hair. "They are starved to death, or worse. Some stories I've heard would shock you."

"Tell us!" Fox demanded.

"They intend to murder anyone who doesn't fit their ideal. In Poland, they are already gassing Jews using the exhaust gasses piped into the back of trucks. They load the trucks with people and drive around until the screaming stops."

"No!" Hannah covered her mouth with her hand. "That's barbaric!"

"We are working on ways to get people out of the camps, but it's not easy. These camps are usually in the middle of nowhere, and the prisoners we are trying to rescue are so weak from malnutrition and overwork that they can't walk far. We need more trucks for transportation, and we could always use more men."

"We can 'elp," Eagle offered. "Stealing trucks and saving lives is our new occupation." He glanced at Jane and smiled.

She gave Eagle a trembling smile in return and turned to Jacob. "We have to take Sasha away from this horror. We can't risk her being found here."

"She is safe with me, Gerda." Rosa went on, "My husband is serving with the Luftwaffe, and I am left alone to run this small farm. Nobody bothers me here. My neighbours know I have a little girl staying with me, though I keep her out of sight. They think Sasha is my sister's child and I am keeping her safe from her home in the city, which is being bombed by the British."

"How do you explain the frequent visits from her father?" Jane asked, glancing at her husband.

"My German papers describe me as a mechanic. My story is simple. I travel the country working wherever I am needed. On my travels, I can call to see our little owl occasionally without suspicion. I repair tractors and small farm machinery as well as cars and trucks. Rosa has a small tractor that needs regular servicing." He smiled at the young German woman.

"Have you ever been stopped and questioned?" Hannah asked.

"Frequently," Jacob admitted. "But they always seem satisfied with my answers and explanations. My papers are good forgeries."

Jane's heart skipped a beat. "I can't believe how much danger you live with. Did I know this?" Jane asked. "Was I aware of what you are doing here?"

"Perhaps not completely, my love, but we are part of the same organisation. We always said we wanted to help free your people. I work here to set them free and put them on the journey to Britain. You work in England to help them settle and stay free after they reach safety."

"I remember." Jane did remember the conversations she'd had with her husband before she'd left Hamburg with her father and Gottfried. "But Sasha was never meant to be a part of this." She waved her arm around the room.

"She isn't, Gerda," Rosa tried to explain. "I am not involved at all. Sasha is not involved in Jacob's dangerous occupation."

"How can you be sure you won't be discovered?" Jane asked.

Rosa sighed heavily. "Listen to me. My part is to shelter the children. I only take one child each time. Always a small girl. I keep them hidden here. I never expose them to prying eyes. My cover for them is good. They are not in danger. Sasha is safe here. *She* is not involved. She is safe. We are safe!"

"But if her father is caught, they will ask questions. They will investigate Jacob's contacts. Sasha could be traced and found," Jane insisted. "It can't be safe for her to stay in Germany while Jacob is risking his life here. It can't be safe for you, Rosa. What would the authorities do to you if they discovered you were harbouring a Jewish child?"

Rosa nibbled her lower lip nervously but said nothing.

"What do you propose?" Jacob asked.

"I have new papers for Sasha. She can travel with me as my daughter to the Dutch border. We can cross into Holland and be home in England in a matter of weeks."

"I 'ave a better suggestion." Fox threw the stub of his cigarette into the fire grate.

"I'm listening." Jacob turned to the French man.

"An aircraft is bringing transmitting equipment and a new operator next week. We can't risk ze wireless on a parachute. We lost two previously. Zey broke apart on landing."

Jane's hopes began to rise. "Are you saying the aircraft will land?" She hastily added, "Where?"

"Close to where you landed last month," Eagle explained. "But if you plan to hitch a lift home, it will be risky."

"What do you think, Jacob?" Jane took her husband's hand. "Will we take the risk?"

Jacob shook his head. "I don't know, Gerda. What if the plane is heard or seen? You could be shot from the sky."

"But think about it, my love," she pleaded. "If we travel by boat or train, we will be exposed for days while making our way to England. I've done that journey and believe me; I wouldn't want anything to go wrong like it did the last time. Poor Sasha is too young to suffer an ordeal like that."

"What happened?"

"Of course, you wouldn't know, would you?" Gottfried quickly explained about the train breaking down and the German guards being suspicious of their documents.

"They took our papers for further examination." Jane remembered the heart-stopping moment when their documents were taken from them. "Father said we should make a run for it while the guards were busy inspecting our papers in the railway office."

"What happened?" Rosa's face paled.

"We escaped." Jane looked at Gottfried and willed him to keep quiet about the details. She didn't want to frighten Rosa. The young woman might refuse to allow Sasha to leave if she knew the kind of danger the little girl would be exposed to. "It wasn't easy." She simplified the arduous and perilous journey in those three words. "But we made it." She gave her cousin a brief glance and hoped he would keep quiet about the frightening details. When he nodded to show her he understood, she let out a quiet sigh of relief and Gottfried continued the story.

"We managed to get away and made our way to Amsterdam. People were waiting for us and had boats ready to take us to England."

"How far did you have to walk to get to the Dutch coast?" Rosa was obviously asking out of concern for Sasha.

"Three days." Jane shortened the trek by half. "I know what you're thinking, Rosa. I wouldn't put Sasha through anything like that if I had any other choice." She looked at Fox. "Would it really be possible for us to get on that plane?"

"I don't see why not?" He shrugged. "If you are zere when it lands, zey won't refuse to take you. I can explain to zem."

"Then we must prepare." She turned to her husband. "Jacob, will you agree to this?" She didn't wait for an answer but looked to Fox. "When do you expect this new operative to arrive?"

Fox shrugged. "Soon. Details are not yet confirmed."

Jacob asked, "How long will it take to get to the landing site? Where is it?"

"We plan to use a high meadow near Saarbrücken. It will take us two nights to get there, if we use ze truck. We'll 'ave to stay on the back roads and forest tracks."

"I know Saarbrücken well." Jacob nodded.

"You can't take Sasha on such a dangerous journey," Rosa exclaimed. "She is a child. What if you are discovered?"

"I understand your concern, Rosa." Jane knew she had to make a stand. "But she is *my* child, and I'll be the judge on what danger she can be exposed to."

"Gerda," Jacob's tone was gentle, but Jane heard the note of warning. "Perhaps we should sleep on this. You've walked into our lives so suddenly after we all thought you were dead. We need time to get used to you being here. We all need to make some adjustments. This isn't easy for Rosa."

"Jacob?" Jane felt uneasy. She couldn't believe her husband wasn't immediately supporting her decision.

"I think we should all try to get some sleep. It's been an eventful day," Gottfried suggested.

"Good idea." Jacob looked at Rosa. "Where can they bed down?"

"The men can sleep in here perhaps, with you. I have some spare blankets in the bedroom. Gerda and Hannah can have the floor in my bedroom."

"Where do you usually sleep when you visit our daughter?" Jane was beginning to be suspicious. Rosa was an attractive young woman, and Jacob had seen more of her in the last two years, than he had his wife. The pang of jealousy felt uncomfortable as it rippled through her belly.

"On that sofa, Gerda." Jacob laughed. "Rosa sleeps with Sasha in the bedroom."

Jane felt foolish to have asked. Jacob's warm smile was enough to reassure her. She could see his feelings for her were strong.

When the sleeping arrangements were made, Jane went to her husband. "I wish we could be together tonight. It has been such a long time since I slept in your arms," she whispered.

"I feel the same, Gerda, but as much as I would love to have you in my bed, you know we can't."

"We'll soon be back in England, and then we can be together at last. Our family will soon be safe, Jacob. After all this time, we now have hopes that it will all turn out well for us."

"Perhaps, my love." Jacob touched his lips to hers.

The gentle kiss stirred something deep inside Jane, and it was all she could do to keep her sudden flush of passion under control. She became aware of the other three men watching her and bowed her head. Reluctantly she drew away from Jacob and moved to the bedroom door. "Goodnight, gentlemen."

Chapter Twenty-Eight – Facing Reality

The week was dragging while they waited for confirmation of the aircraft arrival. Jacob went out with Gottfried and the two French men each evening to meet fellow resistance workers in the area and borrow the use of their radio. Fox and Eagle were soon made aware of the local situation and offered their help.

"We can supply the transportation. Stealing wagons is child's play, but getting fuel is a major problem. We'll need to get more for the truck we have, before making the journey back to the landing strip," Eagle pointed out one evening before the men left.

"Let me take care of that," Jacob offered. "I have money and contacts."

"How do you manage to have money, my love?" Jane was surprised how well her husband was surviving while supposedly working undercover.

"There is more to me than a simple language tutor, darling. I am actually a pretty good mechanic. My papers wouldn't get me very far if I couldn't substantiate the occupation written on those documents, now would they?"

Jane had a small flare of recognition in her mind. "I remember!" She could see Jacob kneeling next to a motorcycle with a tool in his hand. "You fixed a neighbour's motorbike."

He nodded. "I know about engines. The mechanics of how they work is fascinating. Tinkering with them has always been a hobby of mine."

"I can see you would be very useful to your organisation." Fox grinned. "What do you know about wireless transmitters?"

"Not much, I'll admit," Jacob answered. "But I'll have a go at most things. Why do you ask?"

"We 'av two broken ones. Per'aps you could make one good one from ze two?"

"You can't bring them here," Rosa was quick to voice her objections. "They have detector vans monitoring the wireless communications. Don't you know this?"

"We wouldn't bring anything here, Rosa," Jacob reassured her. "I'll go with them to wherever it is they have these machines."

"They are in France," Eagle explained. "Per'aps after we put your wife and child on the plane, we could take you with us?"

"No!" Jane looked at her husband with fear in her eyes. "I thought you'd be coming with us."

"But I thought you understood, darling. I can't leave Germany. I have to continue my work here."

"But you can't!" Jane felt panic rising and tried to control her emotions. "You have to come home with us."

"I'm staying too, Gerda," Gottfried announced. "Jacob is right. We can't go back to the safety of Britain while Germany is slaughtering our people. Someone has to stand up to them."

"No! You can't stay!" Jane wailed. "What can you do, Gottfried?" she argued. "What difference can you make, Jacob? The German army is so big and so brutal, and you are two men with no training in espionage or subterfuge or anything."

"I've done all right for the last two years, Gerda." Jacob stood to put his coat on. "Your friends here are still trying to create havoc where they can." He nodded to Eagle and Fox. "Every disruption and inconvenience we cause the enemy *has* to be worth it, don't you think?"

"But you'll be in danger, and I want you to be safe at home with me." Jane knew she was being unreasonable but couldn't help the way she felt. "I feel you've been missing from my life for far too long. Now that I've found you again, I want our family to be together and safe." She couldn't stop her tears from flowing. "I'm sorry if that sounds selfish, but I can't let you go again, Jacob. I can't!" She dashed her tears away with the back of her hand.

Jacob went to take her into his arms. "Calm down, my love. I know. I know. But we have to make the same sacrifices that many other families have made. Thousands of husbands and sons are fighting this war. Do you think their wives and mothers are happy about it?"

"That's different. Those men have had training." Jane wanted to make him see things from her point of view. She had to make her husband see sense. "Those men undergo weeks of training and they are prepared for the job they are expected to do. What training have you had? Hannah and I are better prepared than you to survive in enemy territory."

Jacob looked at Hannah. "Really? Is this true?"

Hannah nodded. "We had an intensive course of training before being dropped into position."

"Dropped into position?" Jacob frowned. "What do you mean?"

"We parachuted into the arms of these two friends, who then guided us to our contact," Jane boasted.

"Parachuted!" Jacob's face paled. "You jumped from an aircraft?"

Jane nodded. "It was exhilarating!"

"Well, that is not the word I would use to describe the feeling of your stomach coming up to meet your brain while your heart somersaults in your chest." Hannah lifted her brows and rolled her eyes while Jane chuckled.

"So, you had other reasons for coming to Germany?" Jacob asked. "Aside from wanting to find Gottfried."

Jane nodded. She knew Jacob wouldn't know much about what she'd been attempting to do in Saarbrücken and wondered how much to tell him.

"These good men helped us to find our contact in the town." She smiled at Fox and Eagle. "We worked for Ursula for some weeks."

"Ursula?" Jacob looked interested. "Are you talking about Ursula Meyer?"

Jane nodded. "Do you know of her?"

"I worked with her. She helps the Jews in the Saarbrücken area."

"Did you know about Schneider?" Eagle asked Jacob.

"I knew Heinrich worked for us, but I never met him."

"Did you know the Gestapo killed him?" Hannah said quietly, glancing at the little girl in Rosa's lap.

Jacob nodded and lowered his voice. "He will be missed. The Jews of Saarbrücken will suffer more now he has gone. I'm sure he would have talked. The Gestapo would have tortured him."

"Per'aps zey did. But any record of zat man's words are destroyed, and we 'av zese girls to praise for zat." Fox looked to Jane and Hannah. "Zese girls also 'elped to find anozer safe route for ze Jews to leave by."

"Really?" Jacob grinned at Jane. "What did you do?"

Jane shrugged and tried to make light of what she and Hannah had accomplished. She kept her voice low so as not to disturb her sleepy child. "After doing some boring surveillance on the river, we attended a party, where we assisted these men to blow up part of the Gestapo headquarters in Saarbrücken. Then I narrowly avoided being sexually assaulted by a German officer before escaping to come here to find Sasha."

Jacob looked stunned. "You really did all that?"

"We couldn't have done as much as we did without training, Jacob." Hannah glanced at Jane with a smile. "The British agencies were generous when we told them what we wanted to do. They trained us and made sure we were ready for anything before they sent us over here."

"Come back with me, please!" Jane began to realise that her husband would never agree to give up his work in Germany but hoped she could persuade him to spend some time with her before resuming his mission. "If only for a little while." She looked at their daughter. The child was almost asleep on Rosa's lap. "You could help Sasha to settle with me in England, and I could ask our contacts to give you some training. You'll have a much better chance of staying alive if you are better prepared."

"Pah!" Fox huffed. "We 'ad no such training. Our wits keep us alive."

Hannah turned a worried face to Jane. "Fox might be right. Jacob is experienced."

Jane was not about to give up her argument. She could see Jacob was wavering. "Tell me, Fox," she began. "Would you have agreed to help us, if we had no preparation for working in the field?"

Fox shrugged. "Per'aps not, but wiz you it is different."

"Why?" Jane asked.

"You are women!" Fox gave a nonchalant shrug as if that explained everything.

"I see!" Jane pressed her lips together and turned to her husband. "Come back with me, Jacob. A few weeks are all I ask. Take a break from the pressure and stress of this life and be with me. Just for a few weeks, my love. Don't we deserve to spend some time together?"

"I'll think about it." Jacob reached for his hat. "We need to go. The local resistance men won't wait all night."

"Who are you meeting?" Jane asked.

"It's better you don't know." Jacob kissed her cheek.

"Some locals want to discuss plans for taking prisoners from Mauthausen." Fox grinned and shrugged as he looked at Jacob. "What?" he challenged him. "She knows no details, but is now 'appy to let us go."

Jane watched the men leave but felt a desperate longing for them to stay. The work they were doing was necessary but extremely dangerous. The Germans would not ask questions if the men were caught in one of their army vehicles. They would shoot them on the spot for theft if they discovered they were not genuine soldiers.

"Come, Gerda." Rosa poured some steaming water into a mug. "This will help to calm you."

"What is it?"

"I don't have tea, but this is a pleasant drink. I make it from lemon balm leaves. It is good for calming stress."

"Thank you." Jane took a sip. "It's good."

"I'm glad you like it." She turned to Hannah. "Would you like some?"

Hannah shook her head. "I'm not stressed. I'm furious!"

"Why?" Rosa and Jane asked the question at the same time.

"I wanted to go with them, but they didn't think to include me. They don't want me along because I'm a woman. Did you hear Fox? I can't believe he said that about us. Women are as good as men in this business. We are better in some ways!" Hannah hissed through a clenched jaw. "Could they have got into that castle without our help? Could they have used their ingenuity and quick thinking when plans changed suddenly as we had to? They make my blood boil!"

"Oh, Hannah, calm yourself." Jane refrained from chuckling at her friend's anger, knowing her mirth would be like adding coals to a fire. "I'm sure Fox didn't mean to imply we were inferior."

"Oh yes he did! Well, I'll show him. I'll stay here too and I'll make them take notice of how women can be as good as men in the field."

"Oh, Hannah." Jane chuckled. "Don't you think you've done enough?"

"Not nearly enough!" She huffed angrily. "I'm not ready to go home, Gerda."

"But you can't stay, Hannah." Jane began to worry about her friend.

"Why not?"

Rosa lifted the sleeping child into her arms. "Time to get ready for bed, little one."

"But I want to play with Hannah," Sasha protested sleepily.

"She'll be here in the morning when you wake. You can play again tomorrow."

Sasha's eyes flickered open. "Will you, Hannah?" she asked. "Will you still be here?"

"We'll both be here, Sasha. Your mamma will play with you too."

Jane smiled at her sleepy daughter and knew she should be making more of an effort to get to know her, but she was still feeling out of her depth with her husband. "Perhaps you could show me how to feed the goats and pigs after breakfast tomorrow."

"Anyone can feed goats." Sasha's tone was decidedly unfriendly.

"Don't be rude, Sasha," Rosa chastised the little girl. "Your mamma is trying to be friendly. Perhaps she can read your bedtime story this evening."

"I want *you* to read it, Mamma Rosa."

"I'm tired, darling. Why don't we allow your real mamma to read to you and tuck you in?"

Sasha sulked but when she was changed into her nightdress and settled into bed, she grudgingly allowed Jane to read the story. Jane was nervous at first, but opened the book and climbed on the bed. Sasha shuffled close to her so she could look at the pictures while Jane read the words.

Jane could feel the warmth of her child's little body and couldn't resist putting her arm around her. When her embrace met with no resistance, she gently pulled Sasha closer and was relieved when the little girl didn't complain.

She read the story quietly, animating the various characters and was delighted when Sasha giggled approvingly.

"You are good at storytelling," Sasha whispered.

The story ended too quickly but Sasha was almost asleep in her arms. She settled the little girl against the pillow and pulled the blankets over her to keep her warm. She bent to kiss her daughter's soft cheek. "Goodnight, sweet child."

"Will you ask Mamma Rosa to come kiss me?" Sasha sighed sleepily.

"Of course, my love." Jane felt she'd won a small battle, but knew the war of winning her child's heart was going to be a long one.

"How did that go?" Hannah asked when Rosa went into the bedroom.

"Better than I expected," Jane admitted. "She is so adorable. My heart melts when she is in my arms."

"You are fortunate to have found her."

"I know." Jane also knew that she would never give her up again. She watched Rosa come back into the room. The young woman looked troubled.

"What is it, Rosa?" Jane asked.

"I will miss her."

"I'll take great care of her, and she'll be much safer in England."

"Do you live in the countryside?" Rosa asked.

"No, my home is in Sheffield."

"And you recently almost died in a bombing raid in that city, is that true?" Rosa's face was tense with suppressed anger. "How can you promise to keep her safe when your hometown is being repeatedly bombed?"

"I can't," Jane admitted reluctantly. "But she will be safer there than here. In Germany, she is in danger of being taken to the labour camps. They would shoot you for hiding her, Rosa. You'll be safer without her here."

"Jacob knows of another girl about Sasha's age waiting for a safe refuge. I'll take her after you've gone. Perhaps another needy child will help to soothe my pain after losing your little one."

"I'm so sorry, Rosa. I know how much you love my little girl." Jane didn't want to hurt the woman who had cared for her child for the last two years. "I have to take her. You do understand, don't you?"

"Of course, I do, but I won't rest until I know you are safely in England. I keep imagining countless terrible things that could happen to her."

"Don't, Rosa." Hannah got to her feet and crossed to the window. She peered out of the crack in the curtains before closing them tightly against the darkness outside. "Danger is everywhere. We can't protect Sasha from everything that might happen. A bomb or a bullet or a plane crash, they all lead to death, and as I said to my friend some weeks ago, death waits for us all."

"How can you be so insensitive?" Rosa was obviously not placated. "She is a child!"

"We are all children of God, and He chooses when to take or leave us." Hannah snapped. "Sometimes I think the ones He takes are more fortunate than the ones He leaves here to suffer."

"Hannah?" Jane grew concerned about her friend. "Where is this coming from?"

"Oh, don't mind my miserable notions. Rosa mentioned the bombing in Sheffield. I'm feeling sad because my Sebastian was killed by the same bomb that almost took your life." Hannah slumped on a stool near the fire. "He was the only man who ever loved me, and he was taken from me right when he could have become more than a lover. He might have become my husband!" She turned from Jane and Rosa who both looked at her with a mixture of pity and compassion. "Oh, I'm being silly and sentimental, but I can't help thinking that your situation seems petty compared to what I lost. Both of you love Sasha. She's a lucky girl to have two mothers fighting over her welfare. The only person to ever care about *my* welfare is gone. Think of that!"

"Don't you have a family?" Rosa asked.

"All taken by God, as far as I know. Though Hitler might be responsible for taking my father!" Hannah slumped onto a chair.

"Then you have my sympathy." Rosa glanced at Jane. "She's right; we shouldn't be squabbling over who cares most for Sasha. She will be leaving with you. I accept that, but it doesn't make it easier for me."

"I will protect her with my life, Rosa." Jane wanted the young woman to feel better about what would happen but knew that if the tables were turned, she would feel as bad as Rosa did. "Perhaps when all this horror is over, we can meet again. I know you will always hold a special place in my daughter's heart and I won't let her forget you."

"That is more than I could have hoped for." Rosa smiled. "Thank you."

Chapter Twenty-Nine – Truth and Hope

Rosa had tears in her eyes as she waved good-bye to little Sasha, but Jane could see determination in the young woman's face. She knew Rosa would not let her tears fall until the little girl was out of sight.

Jane held Sasha in her arms and leant to embrace Rosa. "Thank you for everything you have done for my family," she whispered in Rosa's ear, "I know how difficult this parting is for you."

"Please take her quickly." Rosa kissed Sasha's cheek and forced her face to smile. "I can't bear a prolonged farewell."

Jane turned from the sad woman and climbed into the back of the waiting truck. "Come my sweet thing, we will get comfortable over here."

"I want Mamma Rosa!" the little girl protested.

"You will see her again, I promise." Jane tried to console her child.

"Where is your doll, Sasha?" Hannah came to sit beside them and was obviously trying to distract Sasha. "Perhaps dolly would like to wave good-bye before your daddy closes the doors."

Jane smiled at Hannah and took the doll from her bag. "Here you are my sweet thing."

Sasha took the doll's hand and wiggled it at the young woman standing by the cottage door. "Bye, Mamma Rosa."

Rosa clutched her jacket tightly with one hand while she lifted the other to wave. Her face wore a frozen smile and Jane could see it was an enormous effort for the young woman to keep her tears inside.

Jane felt a wave of sorrow for Rosa and called out, "We will see you after the war, God willing."

"Keep her safe!" Rosa called as Jacob climbed aboard.

"I will see you soon, Rosa." Jacob closed the doors and banged on the sidewall of the truck.

The engine started and their journey began.

"Thank you for agreeing to come back with us," Jane said as Jacob sank to the floor of the truck next to her. "I know you won't regret it."

"Mr Wilson will organise your training and give you lots of helpful advice," Hannah added. "Our heads were spinning after the first week, weren't they, Gerda?"

"Yes, I remember." Jane smiled. "But each of those lessons was valuable. His advice and the training kept us alive."

"What did you learn?" Jacob asked, lifting the child into his lap. "I can't imagine your contacts could teach me anything I don't already know. After all, I've survived so far and I've managed to save many lives."

"Where do we start?" Hannah giggled. "Oh, I know! Remember that time we were shown how to break into a locked building?"

They talked and reminisced for hours as the truck drove on through the night, carrying them through Bavaria. Jane snuggled into Jacob's side and relished being close to him. Sasha was cuddled into her father's arms and it was pure bliss to have her family together.

As the miles rolled by, Sasha fell asleep and conversation turned to more serious topics.

"Are you sure Fox was speaking the truth when he said the aircraft will take us?" Jane asked her husband. "After all, the crew will not know who we are."

"Those boys know to expect last minute changes of plan. I sometimes sent families back this way in the past."

Hannah lifted her head. "You should have said you've done this before! We've been worried."

Jane saw a flash of Jacob's teeth as he smiled in the darkness.

"How many people did you send back to England?" Jane asked.

"Not enough," he said sadly. "The journey is dangerous, no matter how meticulously we organise the routes. Aircraft are shot down, trains are always stopped and searched, the roads are patrolled..."

"We know," Hannah said quietly. "But we worked on plans to get people out by using the rivers."

"I heard about that idea." Jacob shifted his position. "Will it work?"

Jane realised Jacob was becoming uncomfortable. "Would you like me to take our little owl?"

"I'll put her down on the floor. She'll sleep more soundly on a nest of blankets, I think."

The truck slewed sideways and the sudden movement threw Jane against Hannah. Sasha woke and cried out in alarm. "Daddy!"

"What is happening?" Jane asked, clutching Jacob's sleeve as she struggled to stay upright.

The truck was rumbling over uneven ground, bouncing the passengers into each other. Sasha was sobbing in her father's arms as Jacob held her tightly.

"Be quiet," Jacob warned. "Eagle and Fox will have everything under control."

"How can you be sure of that?" Hannah asked. "We can't see what is happening!"

"No, but I hear no gunshots." Jacob's voice was calm and hushed. "We are obviously taking evasive action. Perhaps they saw something on the road ahead."

"Daddy!" Sasha cried. "I'm scared."

"Shush, baby. We are safe."

"I hope you are right, my love." Jane couldn't help thinking about what Eagle and Fox might have seen.

Eventually, the truck stopped. The engine switched off and the only sound to be heard was Sasha's quiet sobbing.

"Hush, my sweet thing." Jane reached a hand to comfort her daughter.

They listened to Eagle and Fox leaving the cab and walking through rustling vegetation. The doors opened to show a dense dark forest.

"Where are we?" Jacob asked.

"Not close enough to where we intended to stop." Eagle answered. "We 'ad to take a detour."

"What happened?" Hannah asked.

Eagle held out his hand to help Hannah jump down from the truck. "We saw a convoy of army wagons crest the 'ill about mile in front of us," he explained. "We 'ad to move fast to get off the road. Sorry about the bumpy ride." He reached to help Jane climb down.

Jacob passed Sasha to Eagle's waiting arms. "Did we scare you, little one?" he asked her. "Dry your tears. We are safe 'ere."

They had planned to stop in the depths of a forest close to Ulm for the first day, but now they were forced to remain here, some miles away from the preferred destination.

"Will we still make it to the landing strip in time?" Jane asked.

"All being well." Fox took out a cigarette and put it to his lips. "If we set out as soon as ze sun goes down zis evening, we should get zere in time."

"If we don't run into more problems," Eagle handed the little girl back to her father. "Want some breakfast, Sasha?"

The girl nodded. 'Do you have sausages?"

"I do, but we will 'ave to eat them cold."

"Why?" Sasha sounded suspicious.

"We don't 'ave an oven."

"Do they have ovens in England?" Sasha asked her father.

Jane laughed. "Oh, my darling, of course we do. We have sausages too."

"All right." Sasha said, sleepily and closed her eyes.

They stayed in the forest through the daylight hours. Hannah found mushrooms and wild greens to make a salad, but none of them had much of an appetite for the meagre meal.

"My stomach is in knots," Jane admitted. "What will happen if we don't make it in time and the aircraft leaves without us?"

"Then we will approach Ursula in Saarbrücken," Jacob suggested. "We can hope she might help to get us out on the river routes."

As the darkness of the forest closed in, they set out once again, bouncing over the uneven ground.

"I don't like this, Daddy." Sasha complained as she was jiggled around in his lap.

"I've got you. My little owl is safe."

Jane clutched Jacob's arm for support until the truck steadied. "What a relief to be on a smooth road, at last."

"Sorry for the pun, but we are not out of the woods yet." Jacob warned. "Eagle will have to drive at top speed if we want to make it to the high meadow in time. We might attract unwelcome attention."

"Now he tells us!" Hannah moaned. "We will be sitting ducks on these open roads. Patrols will no doubt be swarming everywhere—."

"Hannah!" Jane interrupted her friend. "Keep your voice down. What has got into you?" She looked to her daughter in Jacob's lap. "It's not like you to be so pessimistic."

"If we don't make it in time, we may have to return to Saarbrücken." Hannah shuddered as she spoke. "And that prospect fills me with dread."

"What happened there?" Jacob asked. "You didn't explain the details."

"Perhaps I'll tell you when Sasha sleeps." Jane looked to her child. "Some details are indelicate and not for the ears of children."

"We can't risk going back to Ursula, Gerda." Hannah warned. "We can't put her in danger."

"Then you girls will stay with Eagle and Fox and I will go into the town. I wouldn't want to put anyone in danger."

"Let's hope it doesn't come to that." Jane knew the onward journey would be fraught with danger, no matter which route they took. They were wanted women in the Saarbrücken area. Patrols would be on the lookout for two young women, one blonde, and one brunette. She shivered. "We have to get on that aircraft." She clutched Jacob's arm more tightly. "We simply have to."

They waited in the dark field behind a stand of bushes. Sasha was wrapped in a blanket and Jacob held her close. They had made it to the landing strip in good time with no further incidents on the road.

"Not long now, my sweet angel," Jacob told his daughter. "Listen well and tell us when you can hear the plane."

"I'm so happy you decided to come back with us, darling." Jane gripped her husband's hand tightly. "You scared me when you said you wanted to stay and continue the fight."

"I will return, Gerda. You do understand, don't you?" Jacob squeezed her hand. "I have a responsibility, and I can't abandon our cause."

"I know," Jane sighed. She did understand. Jacob would be useful to the cause, but she didn't want him to leave her. "Well, at least you'll have the advantage of specialised training. I know Mr Wilcox will agree to take you under his wing, and you'll certainly benefit from the instruction he can give you."

"As you and Hannah did?" Jacob glanced at the young girl crouching with Fox and Eagle a few feet away from them. "When I first met her, she seemed full of life and bravado, but beneath that front, she is a troubled young woman, isn't she?"

"Her lover was killed in the same bombing raid that almost destroyed me. She pretends to be fatalistic about it, but really, she's heartbroken."

"As I was, when I thought you were gone." Jacob hugged her close.

"Ouch, Papa," Sasha complained. "You squeeze too tightly."

"Sorry, my angel, I was cuddling your mamma."

Sasha lifted her face. "Are you really my mamma?"

"I am, my sweet." Jane touched her daughter's face. "And you mean the world to me."

"Mamma Rosa was my mamma before. She'll be sad now."

Jane looked at her husband. His eyes glittered in the starlight. "She will soon have another little girl to love, Sasha. You were only meant to be with Rosa for a short time." She turned to Jacob. "Why didn't you try to bring her back to me sooner?" she asked.

"Because she was safe where she was, and there was so much work for me to do. You know the reasons, Jane."

"I know." Jane found it difficult, but she did understand. "You have been so brave."

"Gottfried is braver. I'm British and would be treated harshly if captured but your cousin is a Jew, and yet still decided to stay behind. If he is caught…"

"He must not be caught." Jane knew her cousin felt a desperate need to help his fellow Jews after Jacob explained what was happening to them in the camps. "His new false documents should be in order if he does get taken for questioning. They proclaim him to be of good Aryan stock."

"As long as he doesn't get caught in the act of rebellion, he should be fine, but there are no guarantees in this game, as well you know, my love."

"I know." Jane rested her brow against Jacob's. "We have been lucky so far."

"Papa, I hear the plane."

Jane lifted her head to listen. "I think you're right, my darling. Hush now. We have to stay very quiet."

"Like a little owl?" Sasha whispered.

"Yes, my sweetness. Just like a little owl." Jane smiled at the child in her husband's arms.

Jacob stared into the dark sky. "I see it." He pointed to a dark silhouette approaching the grassy meadow. "Get ready."

Jane looked at Hannah, standing with the French men. She was hugging them and saying her good-byes. The boarding of the plane would be done swiftly, with no time for sentimental farewells.

Jane's heart was hammering rapidly. As she watched, the plane bounced down and travelled to the end of the meadow where they waited.

"We go!" Fox began to sprint to the plane, his arm around Hannah, urging her to run faster.

Eagle followed at a slower pace, rifle in hand, scouting the surroundings for signs of movement.

Jacob lifted Sasha to his shoulder and took Jane's hand. "Come, my love. We have to hurry."

The plane door opened as they ran over the meadow and a tall man jumped down. Jane watched him turn back to the aircraft to catch a bundle that was thrown to him.

Fox jumped on board, but the aircraft continued to trundle over the grass, turning in a circle until it faced the way it had come. The tall man hurried to Hannah's group and stopped abruptly. As Jane got closer, with Jacob at her side, she realised Hannah was embracing the man.

"Quickly, zey 'av agreed to take you. Get on board now." Fox jumped from the plane and urged Jane forward.

"Hannah?" Jane quickly understood what was happening. The man was Sebastian. "What? How?"

"No time for explanations, get on the plane, now." Sebastian urged Hannah to board the plane. "You have to get out of here quickly."

"No, I'm staying," Hannah was shouting above the noise of the engine. "I'm trained! I can help you."

Jacob took Jane's hand and pulled her closer to the open door. Hands reached down to help her climb aboard the small aircraft. She turned to help her child and heard Hannah arguing with her lover.

"I thought I'd lost you! I won't leave you now!"

"You must! I want to know you are safe, Hannah!"

"I am staying with you, and nothing you can say will change my mind."

Jacob climbed into the aircraft and turned, waiting to help Hannah.

Jane touched his arm and shook her head, immediately understanding what was in Hannah's heart. "I don't think she'll be joining us."

"We have to go, sir." The young flight crew member took hold of the door. "We weren't expecting return passengers."

"Sorry, but we had to get this little one to safety." Jacob touched his daughter's head.

"Last call for boarding," the young man yelled to the group on the ground.

"I'm staying!" Hannah called back and waved. "Good luck, Gerda."

Jane choked back her tears and waved. The cabin door was closed, and the small aircraft bumped along, gaining speed. They felt the change in motion as the wheels left the ground.

"Are we flying, Mamma?" Sasha asked. Her large, dark eyes reflected the red cabin lights.

"Yes, my love." Jane held her tears in check. Her daughter had called her, Mamma, and the sound was sweetness to her ears.

Everything had happened so quickly she'd had no time to say good-bye to her friend. She had only known the girl a few months, but she knew she would miss Hannah enormously.

Her friend had made a hasty decision, but she was a big girl and knew what she was doing. Sebastian had survived, just as Jane had. Seeing him must have been an incredible shock. If she'd been in

Hannah's shoes, she wouldn't have left her lover's side, either, no matter what the dangers might be.

She took her husband's hand. The future was still uncertain. Jacob was planning to come back to Germany to do what he could for the Jews in the camps and the ones still in hiding, but for now, they could enjoy a short reprieve, if they made it back to England safely.

She raised her voice above the background drone of the engine to speak. "I'm so glad you are my husband, Jacob."

"I'm happy too, Gerda," Jacob spoke loudly, close to her ear. "But if I'd known what you've been doing these past weeks, I would have forbidden it."

"But my darling, I would have had to disobey you." Jane drew back and smiled into his eyes. "I had a responsibility. When I thought Gottfried was my husband, I knew I didn't love him the same way I loved you, but I couldn't let him continue to think I was dead."

Jacob shook his head. "I can't believe you thought you were married to Gottfried, and I was your lover."

"It seems unlikely now I have most of my memories back, but I was very confused. My memory was mixed up. I convinced myself that I would be faithful to my husband, even though my lover meant so much more to me." Jane clasped Jacob's hand and looked at her daughter. "You and Sasha were, and will always be, the centre of my world." Jane smiled as she watched her daughter's eyes close. "She'll soon be asleep."

"Best thing for her. She won't experience the fear of travelling over occupied territory in a tiny plane that could be shot down at any minute."

"Are you afraid, my love?" Jane smiled and realised she didn't share the fear. She was with her husband and child, and nothing the Germans could do to her would spoil the happiness she felt at that moment. "I don't fear anything now you are with me."

"I can't keep you safe in the skies. Only God can do that."

"Then I'll put my trust in Him, though I'm still confused about my religion. Am I a Jew?"

"You didn't observe your religion. We married in a Christian church. It seemed the wise thing to do at the time."

"I don't remember getting married. If I close my eyes, I can see you waiting for me at the end of the aisle, but I don't recall the ceremony. It's so frustrating and confusing."

"Well, you have nothing to be confused about now, my love. Everything is as it should be. We are together."

Jane rested her head on his chest and savoured the moment. She knew she wouldn't have him close for long, but she was determined to make the most of every minute. She touched his face and watched her fingers tracing the line of his firm jaw.

"My ring!" She noticed her naked ring finger. "I wore my mother's wedding ring, and now it is lost. I have no idea where it might be. I wish I could remember those details."

"I can help you with that memory." Jacob smiled. "We used your mother's ring as your wedding band when we married, darling. You wore it on your left hand because I am British and that's where I wanted you to wear it. It isn't lost."

He pulled back the neckline of Sasha's sweater, careful not to disturb the sleeping child. He revealed the ornately engraved ring on a slim gold chain.

"We gave it to our little owl to keep safe for us. We knew that we could identify her from this ring if ever we lost touch with her or Rosa."

"I don't remember." Jane tried to force the memory, but it wouldn't come.

"You don't need to remember, darling. All you need to know is that we love each other."

"I do love you, Jacob." Jane grinned in the darkness. "Even when I thought you were my lover and not my husband, you were the one I loved with all my heart."

"That's good to know, because you are all I ever wanted, Gerda. From the moment I saw you I was determined you would be mine."

"Gerda." Jane smiled. "Say my name again."

"Gerda." Jacob obliged.

"I'll never be Jane again." Her smile grew wide. "My name is Gerda."

Dear Reader

I really appreciate that you took the time to read this work of fiction. I hope you enjoyed it.

I would be grateful if you could leave a review of the book on Amazon, Goodreads or your favourite review site.

If you have not enjoyed this book, or found faults with the work, please feel free to contact me to let me know how I may be able to improve your reading experience of this novel.

With very best wishes from the author,

Pearl A. Gardner

<u>Get your FREE eBook here</u>
http://www.pearlagardner.co.uk/html/free_book.html

Exclusive to new subscribers.
Be the first to hear about my new releases,
offers and occasional
FREE GIFTS.

About the Author

Pearl writes for the love of words and often compares herself to a ballerina performing to an empty theatre. Reader reviews are the sound of the distant audience and each one is greatly appreciated.

Flitting between genres ensures Pearl's stories are always fresh and exciting. She has a wide ranging and eclectic author list from chick lit, historical romance, to science fiction and the paranormal.

Pearl has enjoyed success, in the past, with short story fiction, winning some national competitions. Her articles and stories have been published in popular magazines, both fiction and non-fiction, but in recent years she has concentrated on full length works.

Published Work

Fiction and non-fiction novels by Pearl A. Gardner

More Novels set in WW2

WW2 Women of Courage – Series set in the Second World War, showing how women broke stereotypes to make a difference. – each book can be read as a stand alone novel, but can be better enjoyed in sequence.

Your Name is Jane, WW2 Women of Courage, Book One
http://amzn.eu/6avvPJ2

A World War Two moving mystery drama - After a devastating air-raid, a young woman finds herself trapped in the ruins of a building. She has no idea where she is or how she got there. The only fact she is certain of is adding to her confusion. Her thoughts are in German, but her rescuers are speaking English.

When asked what her name is, she is disturbed to realise she doesn't know the answer.

As parts of her memory slowly return, she begins to understand her life has not been easy but is afraid to tell anyone about the incriminating and confusing fragments she can recall.

Not knowing who to trust, she sets out to uncover the mystery of who she is, and why she is in Sheffield when her home country is at war with England.

Hannah's Conflict, WW2 Women of Courage, Book Two (Coming soon)

A World War Two moving espionage drama - After escaping Europe before the outbreak of WW2, Hannah's passionate response to the oppression of her fellow Jews leads her back to Germany.

Working undercover, she helps to free prisoners of the labour camps and rescue them from certain death.

Women of Wakefield - A two book series set in the Second World War, telling the stories of how women lived and loved in those testing times. – each book can be read as a stand alone novel, but can be better enjoyed in sequence.

Evelyn's Fight, Women of Wakefield, Book One
http://www.amazon.co.uk/dp/B01H745L9G

A World War Two moving saga - World War Two interrupts Evelyn's life when her husband decides to enlist.

After a tragedy in the street, her mother, Nora, confesses secrets that rock the foundations of Evelyn's world.

When a telegram informs her that Dennis suffered wounds in action, she has no idea what to expect.

His injury changes everything. More secrets are revealed and Evelyn finds she's been living in a web of lies for years. Determined to fight to keep her family together, she faces an uphill struggle.

Will she win the fight? Can life ever be the same again?

Peace for Gladys, Women of Wakefield, Book Two
https://www.amazon.co.uk/dp/B01N05FP97

World War Two story of secrets and inner turmoil - Gladys hides a secret past that could ruin her marriage, but fortunately for her, John is still away, fighting. With the war in its fifth year, she believes the gossips may have forgotten her past mistakes, but still worries what might happen if her husband should ever learn what she'd done.

When she comes into an inheritance, she uncovers more family secrets that are just as troubling as her own. Should she tell what she knows, or let the past stay hidden?

Will she be forced to live her life looking over her shoulder, or will she ever know peace?

More WW2 Sagas

The Scent of Bluebells
http://www.amazon.co.uk/dp/B00FYZX7QU

A World War Two, poignant romantic saga - In spring of 1939, Amy falls in love with Jimmy and life seems full of promise for the young girl from a northern mill town. War was brewing in Europe, and it would change her life forever.

Through the following five years of turmoil, Amy endures heartache and loss. Her husband returns briefly and leaves her pregnant with his child. She writes to him of the news but shortly before the baby is born, Jimmy is reported missing in action and presumed dead.

After more than a year with no further news of her missing husband, she slowly begins to enjoy freedom and independence like she'd never known before.

The war continues with no news of Jimmy and she dares to love again.

Will this love survive the war?

Will Jimmy be found?

A Snowdrop's Promise
http://www.amazon.co.uk/dp/B00LWBD5U

A World War Two, moving romance - At twenty-four-years old, Agnes felt she was headed for a spinster's life. Being taller than most lads was a disadvantage, but she didn't mind being the wallflower while her petite and pretty cousin drew men like a moth to a flame.

When Agnes fell for a tall Irishman's charm, she thought she had found the love of her life. When Andrew asks Agnes to marry him, she has no idea where his proposal will lead them. Her Catholic father would not permit a Protestant son-in-law and he refused to listen to their pleading.

The young couple continued to meet in secret, and when Andrew decided to talk to Agnes's father and try and win him around, none of them could have anticipated the outcome, or the repercussions of that fateful meeting.

War breaks out, giving a frightening and eventful backdrop to Agnes's life of secrets and lies. She lives in fear of the truth emerging, to ruin the lives of her children, but eventually begins to feel that the truth may perhaps lead to her salvation.

Can she face up to her fears and disclose the secrets of her past?

Lost in the Memories
http://www.amazon.co.uk/dp/B00P6LDJO2
World War Two mystery romance - Pam treasures the notes, letters, cards, and photographs that her mother and grandparents left her. When

her uncle asks for information about a secret sister, she uses the file of memories to help him embark on a search for the lost baby.

Cross-checking dates with the written accounts of war time events they are drawn into the past to discover a web of family secrets.

Can they find the love child? Will their questions be answered?

Weaving between past and present, using the written words as guides, they see between the lines and discover a love story full of passion, loss and sacrifice.

Women of Verdun – A Three Book series telling the story of three generations of courageous women from Verdun- This trilogy will cross two centuries, three generations and two World Wars.

Women of Verdun, Book One, Belle
http://www.amazon.co.uk/dp/B00YQ4CTY6

A Pre WW1 story of love and loss - Belle is nineteen in the late nineteenth century. The world is changing rapidly, but in France, in the district of Verdun, life flows at a slower pace.

Belle is in love with her childhood friend and hopes he feels the same way. While visiting the Exposition Universelle in Paris, in the most romantic place in the world, Julien proposes but to her disappointment he does not speak of love.

Belle settles for a marriage of convenience, but realises her mistake when she discovers the husband she adores has a terrible secret that could ruin both their families. Can she find the courage to confront him? How can she love him after such a betrayal? How will she protect her family?

Women of Verdun, Book Two, Belle's Girls
http://www.amazon.co.uk/dp/B013GVCFLQ

WW1 story of love and jealousy - In the middle of the First World War, Collette is afraid for her fiancé, Antoine, who is fighting to save the town of Verdun. They should have been married by now, but the war puts a halt to their plans.

Her sister Felicity is secretly in love with Antoine but hides her feelings. Only their mother knows of her pain, but Belle is too involved with helping to feed the stricken soldiers to offer support to her youngest.

Felicity helps in the casualty station in the grounds of the chateau, assisting the Australian nurses to care for the injured and dying. Collette helps her mother and finds herself drawn to the dangerous work of taking food to the front line.

The turmoil of war changes the lives of the two French girls who are both in love with the same man.

Who will Antoine choose and what will the consequences of that choice mean to the family?

Women of Verdun, Book Three, Nicolette
http://www.amazon.co.uk/dp/B016UMCRLG

WW2 story of intrigue and love - Nicolette was raised in England but her French roots go deep. She is determined to follow in the footsteps of her grandmother to try to make a difference in the war that is changing her life. Her fiancé is less than enthusiastic about enlisting which causes her to rethink her relationship.

Instead of getting married on her twenty-second birthday, she embarks on a dangerous course that will lead her back to Verdun, the home of her grandmother. She works undercover to defend her country of birth and the homeland of her family. Blending seamlessly into the local population she discovers secrets of the past and moves towards a future that she had never considered.

Novels in other Genres written by this author

Ella's Destiny
http://www.amazon.co.uk/dp/B00N0U5RMI

A romantic saga with a hint of sci-fi and a touch of time travel - War is imminent when Ella Stevens applies to join the Eden Venture in the hope of saving her teenage children and salvaging her failing marriage. Amid riots and unrest the family travel to their designated camp where they prepare for a future beyond anything they could have imagined.

During a perilous journey through space and time, Ella realises her marriage can not be saved, but is determined to fulfil her dream of finding a better future for her children. Arriving at the fresh new world, filled with hope and endless opportunity, Ella begins to build a life without her husband. However, the settlers soon discover that Eden is not the paradise they hoped it would be.

With no escape from the hostile and dangerous environment, survival becomes a priority. Ella embraces the challenges of her life with a new-found courage and moves into a future that no one could have predicted.

For the Missing Girls, A Kerry Malone, Psychic Novel
http://www.amazon.co.uk/dp/B01BFJ9YNI

A paranormal crime investigation - Kerry is almost thirty. She can see and hear dead people. She grew to understand them as naturally as other children learned to speak. She also sees auras and can sense the emotions and moods of people around her.

Her family struggled to understand her powers but now see Kerry's colourful and unusual view of the world as a gift. However, Kerry prefers not to witness some things from the other side. Most spirits are benign but some scare the hell out of her.

When she is asked to use her gift in the investigation of some abducted girls, she is eager to help. With guidance from the spirit of a child, she uncovers a series of atrocities and is drawn into the ages-old battle of good versus evil. Will Kerry be strong enough to face the demons? Can she save the missing girls?

It's Penguin Shooting Day
http://www.amazon.co.uk/dp/B00FRIO2ZO

A true diary account of the first weeks following brain injury. - From my son-in-law, Simon's, point of view, he awakes in a bizarre place full of strangers and doesn't know why he is there. His yesterday is ten years ago and the only memories he has between then and now, appears to be no more than hazy fragments. However, his first words to his wife, Natalie, when he wakes from the coma are, 'I love you, honey.' Even though he doesn't remember who she is, he knows that he loves her.

Amazingly, his emotions are still intact even though his memories don't support them. He has no recollection of his wedding day, or of his daughter's birth but the love he feels for his wife and child are overwhelming in their intensity.

So we use Simon's emotional strength and Natalie's inspirational positivity to form the foundations of a future we can only begin to imagine.

Pushed on the Shelf
http://www.amazon.co.uk/dp/B00FW5U32I

A romantic comedy. - Forty-something Trisha is reeling from the shock of being dumped by her husband, Alan, aka DISCWIFF (Dick in Sports Car With Foot Fetish.) Trisha now has to support her two children financially, as DISCWIFF has set up home with TITSNOBB (Tits no Brain Bimbo) and left her in a house that is about to be repossessed.

With no qualifications or experience, the job market looks bleak but she is determined not to go under.

As Trisha struggles to hold together all the threads of her unravelling life, her emotions get in a tangle when the owner of the local flower shop takes a keen interest in her and she agrees to go out on a date with him.

Trisha feels like her life is being lived inside a pressure cooker that's ready to blow a gasket. Something has to give, but what?

Science Fiction
Pearl's science fiction novels are set in the real world, with true to life characters living through extraordinary circumstances. Based on scientific facts and extensive research, her science fiction works are believable, page turning stories that raise questions about the world we live in.

They Take our Children, Book One, The Truth Revealed– Soft science fiction / family saga about alien abduction.
http://www.amazon.co.uk/dp/B00GF3M4RI
Courtney is an astonishingly beautiful teenager. She is also a brighter than average young woman but is otherwise as ordinary, happy and well adjusted as any other girl her age.

On her sixteenth birthday, Courtney's neurotic mother, Helen, calls her a monster in a fit of rage. The teenager runs off, causing panic in the family. Courtney's father, Gavin, has long suspected something sinister hiding in his wife's history, but nothing could have prepared him for the truth. Helen's father, George, tries to reveal what he knows about the mystery but the family find it hard to accept his far fetched version of events as realistic.

Weaving between past and present the facts about Courtney's shocking alien origin are exposed and the search for the whole truth begins.

They Take our Children, Book Two, Taking Control– Second book in the two book series about alien abduction.
http://www.amazon.co.uk/dp/B00HWWPR16

Courtney's family is drawn into the murky world of ufology experts. Subterfuge and concealment become a part of their lives as they search, for the secret, to open the gateway to the second dimension where they hope to meet face to face with the aliens who abducted Courtney's cousins.

Talk of government agencies and 'above top secret' organisations make them fearful but when they discover how much information has been covered up about the alien abductions, they become even more determined to take control and find the missing children.

Discover more

Discover more about Pearl A Gardner on the web site
www.pearlagardner.co.uk

Connect with Pearl A Gardner
Email: pearl@pearlagardner.co.uk

On Goodreads
https://www.goodreads.com/author/show/7350328.Pearl_A_Gardner

On Facebook
https://www.facebook.com/pearlagardner

On Twitter
https://twitter.com/PearlAGardner

Printed in Dunstable, United Kingdom